PLOTS AND ERRORS

By the same author

Record of Sin
An Evil Hour
The Stalking Horse
Murder Movie

The Lloyd and Hill Mysteries

A Perfect Match
Murder at the Old Vicarage
Gone to Her Death
The Murders of Mrs. Austin and Mrs. Beale
The Other Woman
Murder . . . Now and Then
A Shred of Evidence
Verdict Unsafe
Picture of Innocence .

Jill McGown

PLOTS AND ERRORS

Ballantine Books
New York

A Ballantine Book
Published by The Ballantine Publishing Group

www.randomhouse.com/BB/

Library of Congress Cataloging-in-Publication Data
McGown, Jill.
    Plots and errors / Jill McGown.—1st American ed.
        p.   cm.
    ISBN 0-345-43313-0 (alk. paper)
    I. Title.
    PR6063.C477P58   1999
823'.914—dc21   99-14226

Manufactured in the United States of America

First American Edition: August 1999
10   9   8   7   6   5   4   3   2   1

Dramatis Personae

Lloyd, *a Detective Chief Inspector*
Joe Miller, *a Detective Inspector*
Judy Hill, *a Detective Inspector, Colleague and Lover to* Lloyd

Tom Finch, *a Detective Sergeant*
Len Case, *a Detective Superintendent*

Angela Esterbrook, *Widow to the late Paul Esterbrook Sr.*
Paul, *Son to* Angela *and the late Paul Sr., and Half brother to* Josh
Elizabeth, *Daughter-in-law to* Angela *and Wife to* Paul
Josh, *Son to the late Paul Sr., Stepson to* Angela *and Half brother to* Paul
Sandie, *Wife to* Josh

Kathy Cope
Ian Foster
Arthur Henderson
} *Private Enquiry Agents*

Debbie Miller, *Wife to* Joe
Andy Cope, *Husband to* Kathy
Lucy Stephenson, *Daughter to* Andy *and* Kathy Cope
Freddie, *a Pathologist*
Mary Alexander, *a Police Sergeant*
Brian Vickers, *a Detective Chief Inspector*
Comstock, *a Detective Sergeant*
Billy Rampton, *an Acquaintance of* Josh *and* Paul
Howard, *a Sub Aqua Instructor*
Letitia Markham, *a Professor*
James Harper, *a Barrister*

A Forensic Medical Examiner, a Forensic Scientist, Sundry Officers and Servants

Scene: Bartonshire, Cornwall, Devon, and Other Counties

PLOTS AND ERRORS

Prologue
The Police

All is not well;
I doubt some foul play.
Hamlet, Act 1, Scene 2

S CENE I—BARTONSHIRE
Saturday, September 27th, 11:00 A.M.
The garage and various rooms of a semi-detached house in Stansfield

Detective Chief Inspector Lloyd looked at the two bodies in the elderly Ford Fiesta and sighed.

The man, he had never met. He was about Lloyd's own age—late forties, early fifties; difficult to say at the best of times, and this was not the best of times. He had more hair than Lloyd, but most people did. He had the same dark colouring, but he was much bigger, taller. The car had been specially adapted for a disabled driver; he was in the driving seat.

The woman he *had* met, and had worked with, but that was a long time ago now. She had been twenty-four when he'd seen her last; she had left the job to marry the man whose hand she had been holding while their car had filled up with lethal fumes, pumped through a vacuum-cleaner hose from the exhaust pipe.

"Their daughter found them this morning, sir," said the constable. "She walked along the passage between the house and the garage, to the back door of the house, and heard the engine. She pulled the hose from the exhaust, but she couldn't get into the car to turn off the engine."

The garage, its overhead door closed and firmly locked, still held the heavy odour of exhaust gases; the small door at the rear stood wide open to admit as much fresh air as possible, but even diluted and dispersed, the pollution in the atmosphere was unhealthy. Undiluted, confined in the small car, it would have been lethal in about ten minutes.

"It wouldn't have made any difference if she had. They'd been dead for hours by the time she got here," said the Forensic Medical Examiner, straightening up from the car. "Life pronounced extinct at . . . " She looked at her watch. "Eleven-seventeen A.M.," she said, and smiled at Lloyd. "I'm a bit puzzled about why you're here, Chief Inspector. How come you got called out? Am I missing something?"

"No," Lloyd said. "You're not missing anything. I'm not here on duty—the officers dealing thought I'd want to know, that's all."

He could hear his own Welshness when he spoke; usually his accent was very carefully controlled, ranging from barely discernible to impenetrable, depending on the impression he was choosing to give. It was when he got what Detective Sergeant Finch called a gut-feeling that it popped out all by itself. From his soul, he liked to think, rather than his gut.

"I knew Kathy—twenty years ago, admittedly, but I knew her." He smiled at the slightly wary look on the FME's face. "I wouldn't rush round to see all my friends' dead bodies," he said. "But I want to be sure that this is really a suicide pact, because I don't think Kathy was a quitter."

"Oh, I'm sorry," she said. "I didn't realize you knew her. But there's nothing to suggest she didn't go through with it of her own accord."

"No," sighed Lloyd. "But it doesn't add up," he said, almost to himself, then smiled apologetically at the doctor. "Kathy always had a tendency to wade in first and think second," he said. "She never thought ahead. She survived by finding a way out of whatever problem she found herself with. She was famous for it."

"Well," said the doctor doubtfully, "this *is* a way out."

"True," Lloyd conceded. "And I don't know what her problems were yet—this may have seemed the *only* way out." He took the notes that she had made. "Thank you, Doctor," he said, lifting a hand as she left. "Where's the daughter now?" he asked the constable.

"She's with Sergeant Alexander in the house, sir."

Mary Alexander had joined Bartonshire Constabulary on the same day as Kathy White, as she then was, and Lloyd, and there was a bond between raw recruits all learning the ropes together that never quite went away; she had known that Lloyd would want to be sure of this one.

Lloyd walked past the young man and stood in the open door at the rear of the garage. "Odd, about this door being unlocked," he said. "Don't you think?" He didn't wait for a reply. It was just a little puzzle. "Don't stay in there," he said. "You can keep an eye on things in the fresh air." He went along the pathway to the back door, knocked, and let himself in.

"The electric's off, sir," said Mary, coming into the kitchen and closing the door behind her. "They came to cut it off just before we got here—about an hour ago, I suppose. Lucy—that's Kathy's daughter—said they might as well go ahead and do it."

"Money," said Lloyd, like an oath. "Was that the problem? I can't believe that."

"Big money. The house was about to be repossessed. But—it seems that Kathy was running some sort of detective agency, and the front room's been turned into an office. It's absolutely full of brand-new office equipment. I can't work that out. Why would she buy all that stuff when they were broke? The agency wasn't getting a lot of business, according to her daughter, so she couldn't have had much hope of paying for it."

Another little puzzle, like the unlocked door. Judy was who he needed on this, but he was going to have to get used to doing without her soon. Still, he'd try them out on her when he got home; it would help take her mind off all the things that were worrying her. Her late, unplanned pregnancy had been confirmed at virtually the same time as she had been offered a year's secondment to HQ and the promotion that went with it; Judy found change of any kind unsettling, never mind wholesale change. That was why she and Lloyd still lived in separate flats, a situation he hoped the baby would remedy. But she was at his flat now, as she usually was at the weekend, and he would see what she made of all this.

"How's Kathy's daughter?" he asked. "Is she all right?"

"Yes, sir. Well, as all right as you can be in these circumstances. She's in the living room with the Coroner's officer—he's explained about the need for a postmortem and an inquest. She's not taken it too badly, considering. But—" She wrinkled her nose, shook her head. "No," she said. "Forget it."

Lloyd smiled. "You know no one can, once someone's said that," he said.

"Well, it's probably nothing. But I was going to make her a cup of tea, before Lucy remembered about the electricity being off, and she told me the tea bags were in that tin. It was empty, and she said there would be a new packet in this cupboard." Mary opened the cupboard, which had various tins and packets in it. "But it wasn't. It was up here." She pointed to the shelf on the unit. "So she started checking, and lots of things weren't where she expected them to be."

Lloyd lived on his own, hopefully not for too much longer now that he and Judy were to be blessed with issue, but he lived on his own, and had for several years. He had decided the day he moved into the flat where he kept everything in the kitchen, and that was where it had stayed. But perhaps having a change-round helped cheer Kathy up, or something. That hardly counted as a puzzle.

"And some things are in two different places," Mary went on. "Beans, for instance. There was one tin in this cupboard and two in this one down here. That just seemed a bit strange."

"I agree. You keep tins of beans wherever you keep tins of beans," said Lloyd. That *was* another puzzle.

"Lucy says her mum and dad always went shopping on a Friday

night," Mary said. "And there's some cold ham in the fridge still in its supermarket deli bag. That's another thing she was surprised about, because her mum always put stuff like that in clingfilm before she put it in the fridge. And the eggs are in the fridge—she says her mum usually kept them in the larder. Of course, its been very hot—"

"Right," Lloyd said, making his mind up. "I want the duty inspector informed, and I want the SOCOs down here, and the pathologist."

"Scene of crime people? To a suicide?"

Lloyd sighed. "There are too many little puzzles for my liking," he said. "And yours—that's why you rang me, isn't it? You weren't happy."

"Well . . . that was before I found out about the electricity," said Mary. "Kathy seems to have had it very hard this last couple of years. Her husband had that accident, and from what I've heard, he was always a bit—you know—overbearing. What he said went. Well, you know yourself he made her leave the job when she married him." She smiled a little sadly. "I reckon that's how he got her in the first place, because she just let him talk her into doing what he wanted, and poor Joe came home to find her in bed with his flatmate."

Oh, yes, of course. Lloyd had forgotten that little scandal. She had been engaged to Joe Miller, and his best friend Andy Cope was going to be his best man until he seduced the bride-to-be. Lots of canteen jokes about may the best man win, that sort of thing.

"So if Andy said—" Mary began.

"If Andy said, 'Go and get the vacuum-cleaner hose, Kathy, I think we'll kill ourselves,' you're saying she would just *do* it?" interrupted Lloyd, his voice rising with irritation. "She might go to bed with him on that principle, but she'd hardly—"

"Ssh," said Mary.

Lloyd put a hand to his mouth. "Sorry," he said, with a quick glance at the closed door. "I hope she didn't hear me. But honestly, Mary! Kathy was a fighter—she would have a contingency plan if she was in money trouble. If *he* was suicidal, fine—but she wouldn't go along with it. I don't like this thing about the shopping. Sounds as though maybe he put it away instead of her."

"It looks like a suicide pact," she said immovably. "They're holding hands."

"I *know* what it looks like," Lloyd said. "Are you thinking of getting the SOCOs and the pathologist before the bodies putrefy, by any chance?"

"And what am I going to say when the inspector asks why I want them? *I'm* here officially, Lloyd," she said in a fierce stage whisper. "You're not. I wouldn't have called out CID, never mind the whole circus!"

"I'm here officially now," said Lloyd. "And I'm treating this as a suspicious death." He left Mary summoning reinforcements, knocked and went through the living room, where a young woman, tear-stained, pale, trembling slightly, but reasonably composed, sat on the sofa with the Coroner's officer.

"Just finished," he said, getting up. "Thank you, Mrs. Stephenson. We'll be in touch."

Lloyd introduced himself and sat down beside her. "This must have been a terrible shock," he said.

"Well—finding them and everything. But I think I saw it coming, in a way."

"Oh?" He had hoped for an ally in the Copes' daughter.

"Well, my dad's been getting worse and worse, and—"

"His disability, you mean?"

"No, not the actual problem. Just dealing with it. He got very bitter."

"How did it happen?"

"It was so silly—he was clearing the guttering, and the ladder went from under him. He hurt his spine. He didn't get any compensation or anything, of course—he wasn't insured for that sort of thing, and there was nothing wrong with the ladder. It was all right to start with, because my mum had a job, but he said he couldn't manage without her, so she had to leave. That's why she thought of the detective agency, because she wouldn't be out all day every day—it would just be now and then. But he just went on at her about it, saying she was poking her nose into other people's business and all that—it was really getting her down."

"What brought you here this morning?"

"I always come on a Saturday morning. Just to see how Mum's do-ing. He wasn't just giving her a hard time about the agency—he gave her a hard time about everything these days. I just liked—you know—giving her a bit of moral support."

"Mary says your mum seems to have been rearranging the kitchen cupboards," he said.

Lucy shook her head. "I don't understand that," she said.

"Oh?"

"Well—she's got all the usual things where my dad can reach them from the chair. I don't know why she would put the tea bags up there."

Lloyd was more than ever convinced that something very strange had been going on here, and he moved on to another of his puzzles. "Do you know where she got all the new office equipment from?" he asked.

"No. I know my dad was angry with her for getting it." She looked worried. "She never used to do things like that," she said. "She never dared."

"Was she afraid of him?" Lloyd asked, as gently as he could.

Lucy shook her head, and wiped her nose. "No," she said. "He shouted a lot—but he would never have hit her or anything like that, if that's what you mean. He just liked things done his way, and he made such a fuss if they weren't, that she always did what he wanted. Anything for a quiet life. Until now." She shrugged. "Maybe she did change the kitchen cupboards round."

"To annoy him, you mean?"

"Oh, I don't know! I shouldn't be saying things like this." She wiped away tears. "It's probably just my imagination, anyway. I just . . . " She began to cry. "They couldn't keep up with the bills, and he went on and on at her like it was all her fault, making her cry, and—and then—well, she sort of changed. She started getting all that stuff that they couldn't afford. He was furious with her, but it made no difference. I asked her why she was doing it, and she just said she needed them, but she didn't! It was like she was doing it on purpose to get back at him or something."

Her husband arrived then, and Lloyd decided to give the questions a rest. He didn't want to put her through all this for nothing. But it didn't feel right to Mary despite what she had said, it didn't feel right to him, and, if he was any judge, it didn't feel right to their daughter either.

"Thank you," he said, and went out to the garage, where the tent that would shield the activities of the scene-of-crime officers from the curiosity of the neighbours was being erected. He asked the young constable to have a word with the said neighbours and find out if they had seen or heard anything last night, and detailed Mary to look for receipts, hire-purchase agreements, credit-card vouchers, anything to account for the new office equipment, as Freddie roared up in his sports car and jumped out over the door, the easiest way for someone as tall as he was to get out.

"One day you'll be too old to do that," Lloyd said.

Freddie grinned, his professionally sombre features suddenly transformed, and followed Lloyd into the garage. The big door stood open now, and scene-of-crime officers milled round in the pale blue light created by the canopy, taking samples, dusting for prints, carrying away the equipment used to effect the Copes' death.

"Stand back and let the pathologist see the corpses," said Freddie cheerfully, moving Lloyd out of the way. He bent down, looked into the car, then straightened up, his face puzzled, and a shade disappointed. "Why am I here?" he asked.

"I wanted you to see the bodies as they are now, not lying on a slab. I want to know if they're really holding hands, or if he's got hold of her to stop her getting out, or anything. I want to know if—" Lloyd floundered, and sighed. "Help me, Freddie," he said. "I just don't think this is what it looks like."

Freddie was probably his oldest friend; it was an odd friendship, having been forged over suspiciously dead bodies, but Lloyd knew where he stood with Freddie. If there was anything to be found, his old friend would find it.

Freddie looked thoughtful, nodded, and then began his examination of the bodies with as much care as he always took, touching nothing until his eyes had told him everything they could, making notes into a memo-recorder.

Lloyd took a walk round the car; the boot was open to reveal the usual stuff to be found in car boots, and a folding wheelchair. He hadn't seen a wheelchair in the house. He left Freddie to it, and met Lucy and her husband on their way home.

"Lucy—did your dad have more than one wheelchair?"

"No," she said. "Just the folding one."

That suggested that Andy Cope had never left the car. Lloyd frowned as the young couple left and the probationer came back. "Anything?" he asked.

"They said they'd noticed that there wasn't any yelling on Friday night, sir. The Copes had had very loud rows all the time for the past few weeks, apparently. It was his voice they heard, mainly."

"Did they happen to hear what he was yelling at her about?"

"Money. And possibly another man, they thought. I asked if they'd heard any names mentioned, sir, but they couldn't remember."

Another man was interesting, and much more in keeping with what Lloyd remembered of Kathy Cope than suicide was. He went through to the front room, where Mary was searching through Andy and Kathy's financial papers, most of which were in an old cardboard box, rather than the gleaming new filing cabinet. Mary had found nothing at all to account for the office equipment, and nothing else of any note.

Lloyd looked round the makeshift office, at the desk, the filing cabinet, the computer with all the multimedia bits and pieces, the photocopier, all brand-new. Why would she buy all that stuff? And why was there no paperwork of any sort to account for them?

Lucy said that her father had been very angry about it; he might have lost his temper, accidentally killed his wife, then tried to make it look like a suicide pact, but how, if he had never got out of the car? Kathy would have had to go and get the hose and the sticky tape and all the rest of it. He could hardly have forced her to do that. So, perhaps she had been a willing participant. And, if she had been contemplating suicide, she might not have noticed where she was putting the shopping.

But that still left his other puzzle. Why had they locked the main garage door, and all four of the car doors, but left that little door unlocked?

He opened the filing cabinet and took out a couple of files. Small jobs, for small money. The most recent was six weeks ago, and the file was fairly cryptic: *Mrs. A. Esterbrook, Little Elmley, Barton,* was the heading. There were no reports or copy letters, but there were copies of receipts. She'd done a job for Mrs. Esterbrook in Plymouth in August; no details, but a stay at a very expensive hotel had been thrown in, for Kathy and Andy Cope. The actual fees weren't any better than the others, though, certainly not enough to account for all the office equipment.

Esterbrook—he knew that name. Oh, yes, of course. The Esterbrooks owned IMG Limited. In the late fifties, their choice of Stansfield for their head office had been the jewel in the then very new town's crown, and the family-owned firm had just got bigger and bigger since then, with plants in every major town in the UK. They were far and away the richest family in the county, and one of the richest in the country.

Now, thought Lloyd, why would someone with that sort of money to spend employ an untried, underfunded, two-man operation run from a semidetached in Stansfield to carry out an investigation in Plymouth for her? Another little puzzle.

Freddie appeared at the door. "I've arranged for the bodies to go to the mortuary," he said. "I can't see anything suspicious, Lloyd. It looks like a suicide pact."

"I know what it looks like," Lloyd said wearily as he walked with Freddie back to his car. "Call it a hunch."

Freddie looked back at the garage, and the people going in and out. "You're spending an awful lot of money on a hunch," he said.

SCENE II—BARTONSHIRE
Saturday, September 27th, 4:00 P.M.
A semidetached house in Barton

Detective Inspector Joe Miller had just spent an awful lot of money on a hunch of his own, and then had watched it limp past the post sixth out of a field of seven. The bookie had cleaned him out again, and he drove home in disconsolate mood, letting himself into the empty house with a sigh.

He should have been beginning his early retirement this weekend, but instead he was at a loose end, because he was working on the Assistant Chief Constable's pet project in Barton, ahead of the rest of the team. He'd been there six weeks; he was enjoying setting everything up, but sooner or later the others would be joining him, and he was not looking forward to that at all.

For one thing, he was going to have to share an office with his boss; it was bad enough having to do the job at all without that. He was, in part, the technical support, and he didn't mind that bit; he had embraced the computer age with zeal, surprising everyone, not least himself, with the expertise that he had very quickly acquired. But two months ago the job was to have been a part-time advisory civilian post purely concerned with the technical aspects, and he put himself forward for it the moment he'd heard about it. It was perfect—a couple of days a week playing with computers to supplement the pension he'd receive when he got early retirement, which he was convinced he was going to get. Gambled on getting, you might say; no one had told him officially.

A week after that he'd been told that the post would be full-time, involve some administrative work, and would be a police appointment, starting immediately. That he would not be getting early retirement after all, but would be seconded to the project, if he still wanted the job. It was either that or a uniformed appointment out in the sticks, and he had decided to go to HQ, as the lesser of two evils. But it was nine to five, Monday to Friday, no travelling expenses, no perks, no nothing.

And he would be working for Judy Hill. She'd been a detective sergeant when she had come to Bartonshire Constabulary eight years ago. He'd found that quite hard to take, since she was five years younger than he was, and female into the bargain, and he had been struggling to pass the sergeant's exam. It seemed he had no sooner caught up than he was passed again, rather like his hunch in the three-forty.

Judy was all right, he supposed. They had worked together for years before his transfer as sergeant to Force Drug Squad, and again when he had returned to Stansfield, having at last got promotion to inspector, working on computer fraud, thanks to his knowledge of information technology. But he hadn't even been considered for the so-called supremo job; no one had. She had just been given it. And no prizes for guessing why, in Joe's opinion. Judy Hill was very fanciable, and Joe didn't suppose he was the ACC's type.

Not that Joe had fancied her himself; she was too brisk and efficient for him. Too cool and collected, with her short dark hair always looking as though she had just washed it, and her clothes never looking as though she had spent all night in them even when she had. Too worldly-wise; there was a look in her brown eyes that always made Joe feel as if she knew something he didn't. Too capable, always appearing to have everything under control, which she usually had. His preference was for someone a little less astute, a little less independent, a little less superior. Like Kathy.

But taking up with Kathy again after all these years had been a costly mistake he still wasn't sure how to put right. He had thought she could light dark corners, fill empty spaces, but she couldn't. It wasn't her fault; it was his. He had hoped, perhaps, for more weekends like the one he'd had with her, but with her it was all or nothing, so nothing it had to be. And the weekends were the worst part of this job. Once he'd made his Saturday donation to the bookie, he had too much time to think, to reflect on the mistakes he had made in his life, to give in to regrets.

He was glad when the telephone interrupted his morose self-examination, and answered it to Mary Alexander. He listened in shocked, uncomprehending silence as she told him what had happened.

"I just thought you ought to know," she said.

"Yes. Thanks, Mary." Joe hung up, still trying to make himself believe what he had just been told.

A suicide pact? That was ridiculous. That was nonsense. Wasn't it? Money worries, Mary had said. Yes, sure they had had money worries. But Kathy hadn't been suicidal. Andy Cope might have given up on life, but Kathy certainly hadn't, and if he had made her do that, then it wasn't suicide, not as far as Kathy was concerned; it was murder. There would be a postmortem, of course, but force of will didn't show up in postmortem examinations, and that was almost certainly the weapon Andy Cope had used.

He wondered, guiltily, if his actions had contributed to that final breaking of Kathy's own will, which had reasserted itself briefly when he had taken up with her again, and might have deserted her altogether when he had finished it. He took out the whisky and a glass and spent the evening drinking steadily and earnestly, reviewing his own actions, wishing that he had done some things differently and others not at all. Wishing that his conscience had begun to bother him about what he had done a little sooner than it had.

Maybe then, just maybe, Kathy would still be alive.

SCENE III—BARTONSHIRE
Saturday, September 27th, 11:05 P.M.
A second-storey flat in Stansfield

Judy was wondering if it would be possible for her to retire without offending Lloyd. There was no point in trying to entice him to bed with her womanly wiles; he was much too wrapped up in this suicide to be interested in that sort of thing. She had spent the entire evening with the Copes, and was horribly aware that Lloyd was quite capable of continuing to discuss it until three in the morning.

He had told her his little puzzles, and while she knew that it was foolish to dismiss the things that struck Lloyd as odd, in this case they did seem a little nebulous. But it wasn't the misplaced groceries, or the unlocked door, or any of the other little niggles that had made him so certain that it wasn't suicide. It was that he wouldn't accept that Kathy Cope would do that, however much under her husband's thumb she had been, and Judy began to wonder if she had meant more to Lloyd than she had realized.

"Did . . . ?" She hesitated. She had always made it very clear to Lloyd that any relationships that she might have had in the past, other than her ill-considered and ill-fated marriage, were not open to discussion, and she ought to accord him the same privacy. But it might help her understand. "Did you know her very well?" she asked.

Lloyd smiled, obviously hearing the mixture of sympathy and suspicion in her voice. "Not like that," he said. "In fact, I didn't really like her all that much."

Judy frowned. "Why the crusade?" she asked gently.

"Is that what it is?" He nodded. "I suppose it is," he conceded. "But you get to know someone very well, don't you, walking a beat with them, manning a car? And yes, she was easily led. Yes, she could be bullied, because she always felt that someone else—anyone else— was in charge, especially a male person. That was why she got herself into situations that she had never meant to get into, because people could intimidate her, sway her." He gave a short sigh. "But she was . . . I don't know . . . she was *used* to being in trouble. She always looked for an escape route. And I can't believe she would kill herself because she owed people money, Judy. People don't change fundamentally, not even in twenty years."

Judy smiled. "I should save that speech for Case," she said. "Do you realize how much money you've spent trying to prove that she didn't commit suicide?"

"That's what Freddie said. And I know it's just a hunch. But I don't care how much of a doormat you are, you don't just sit there and die because someone's told you to. Self-preservation would take over as soon as the stuff started coming into the car."

"Maybe he gave her something to knock her out," Judy said. "The postmortem should show it, if he did."

He shook his head. "That doesn't explain the door or the groceries," he said. "Besides, it looks as though he didn't get out of the car."

Judy frowned. "But if he didn't get out of the car," she said, "Kathy must have been a willing participant, surely?"

"Perhaps," Lloyd said slowly. "Or . . . perhaps the shopping was put away by someone who simply didn't know where things were kept. Perhaps the door had *had* to be left unlocked, because whoever did it had to leave the keys in the ignition, and then make good his exit. Perhaps neither of them was a willing participant."

"You think they were *murdered?*" She sat back. "Lloyd, you don't have any evidence to support—"

"I know." He smiled again. "But what about this job that she had in Plymouth?" he said. "How do you explain someone like Mrs. Esterbrook employing someone like Kathy?"

Judy's mobile phone rang; it had to be work, at this time of night; she was on call. She picked it up, listened to what her caller had to say, said that she and Lloyd would be there in thirty minutes, then put down the phone and looked at Lloyd.

"What?" he said. "What is it?"

He was always claiming a sixth sense, second sight, Welsh wizardry, that sort of thing. She had often had reason to believe him. But this was his finest hour. "There's been a fatal shooting," Judy said. "At Little Elmley. A Mrs. Angela Esterbrook."

She had thought she had seen him look smug before when he was proved right, as he was with irritating regularity, but she hadn't seen anything, she realized. This was Lloyd at his very, very smuggest.

SCENE IV—BARTONSHIRE
Saturday, September 27th, 11:30 P.M.
Little Elmley, a private estate near Barton

Little Elmley was entered through massive wrought-iron gates, and the house itself was reached by driving along a tree-lined road; it was the sort of building in which Judy found it hard to believe that people really lived. How *did* you live in a place like that? What did you do with all the other rooms?

The uniforms were already searching the house, and the duty

inspector filled them in with as much as he knew. Angela Esterbrook had lived there with her stepson Josh, but he was at the Little Elmley diving club; officers had been dispatched to fetch him. Her daughter-in-law Elizabeth had found her when she arrived for dinner; she was married to Paul Esterbrook, Angela Esterbrook's own son and Josh's half brother. He was on his way over from Barton, where he and his wife lived.

"There's no sign of the gun in the house. If it's out there somewhere, we aren't likely to find it until we can search in daylight," the inspector said. "But I doubt it's here at all. The body's in the kitchen—the daughter-in-law says that the back door was open when she found the body, but that Mrs. Esterbrook kept the door open in warm weather like this when she was working in there. The FME's here, and the pathologist is on his way."

He led the way round the outside of the house to the open back door. Angela Esterbrook lay across the doorway on the tiled kitchen floor, in the pool of gore that had seeped from several wounds in her head. Judy was not fond of dead bodies, even unmutilated ones, and one of the more interesting aspects of her interesting condition was her readiness to throw up at the best of times. She retreated to a safer distance, out on the terrace.

"She's not been dead long," said the FME. "A couple of hours, I'd say." She looked up. "You're keeping me busy today."

"I don't actually kill them myself," said Lloyd, as Tom Finch arrived.

"Guv," he said to Judy, with a nod of his blond curls by way of greeting, and glanced into the kitchen. "Nasty, isn't it?"

"Ah, Tom," said Lloyd, coming out of the kitchen. "I want you to look through Mrs. Esterbrook's personal papers for a report from the Cope Detective Agency."

"Right, guv," said Tom. "I'll check out the study. The daughter-in-law's in the dining room, and her husband's just arrived."

"I think you should have a word with her now that she's had a chance to recover," said Lloyd, and Judy reluctantly made to go into the kitchen, where the FME was making notes for the pathologist.

"You don't have to cross the crime scene, guv," said Tom. "All the rooms at this side of the house have patio doors onto the terrace."

Tom was protecting her, as Lloyd often did; under the guise of keeping the crime scene uncontaminated, he was making sure she didn't have to look at the body again. Her belief in equality ought to make that offensive, she supposed, but her squeamishness made it very welcome. She smiled. "Good," she said as Tom went off to the study. "Thanks, Tom."

The sound of a high-performance engine on the road up to the house heralded Freddie's arrival; he would like the body, whatever condition it was in. His sports car screeched to a halt on the road and he jumped out. "Are you going for some sort of record?" he asked Lloyd. "Good evening, Judy, how nice to see you again. Lovely as ever."

She happily left Lloyd and Freddie to it, following the paved terrace round to find a lawn area fringed with trees, garden tables and chairs, and a large window standing open in the warm night, leading into what she would have called a dining hall, rather than room.

The end of a long, heavy, deeply polished table was set for two, and an opened bottle of red wine sat between the two settings, beside a small vase of early autumn flowers. Elizabeth Esterbrook, mid-thirties, blond, designer-labelled and good-looking, sat on one of the dining chairs, pulled slightly away from the table, so that she didn't look as though she was expecting dinner. A man of roughly the same age, perhaps a couple of years older, dark, well-built, handsome, his casual weekend clothes equally expensive—her husband, presumably—sat a few seats down from her. The scene looked to Judy like one in a glossy hotel brochure; they looked like models playing a couple.

The introductions were barely over when another man came in from the terrace, flanked by two uniformed constables; there was a distinct family resemblance, and he did indeed turn out to be Josh Esterbrook. He sat at one of the many chairs round the table, barely acknowledging the other two.

Elizabeth Esterbrook looked pale and shaken, her husband looked suitably and, Judy felt, studiedly shocked, but Josh Esterbrook sat back with a would-be air of indifference. His fingers tapped lightly on the table, though, so perhaps he wasn't as relaxed as he wanted to appear.

"Ma'am?" said one of the constables, and drew Judy back out on to the terrace, speaking to her in a low voice. "Mr. Esterbrook was in the middle of giving a group of people diving training when we got there," he said. "And his wife was with him. But someone's been knocking her about—the injuries aren't too severe, but she looked a bit unsteady, so we sent her to Barton General for a checkup, to be on the safe side. She reckons she was mugged earlier in the day, but she didn't report it to the police."

Judy thought that as unlikely as the constable obviously did. She sneaked another look at Josh Esterbrook. Women were usually covering up for their partners when they lied to the police about injuries. But then again, there could have been a violent argument with her mother-in-law which had ended in tragedy. "I take it someone's with her?"

"Yes, ma'am. She'll be brought back here if the hospital don't keep her in."

Judy went back into the room, sat down and opened her notebook. It wasn't her official notebook; she made entries in that one from the copious notes she took in the much larger one she carried round with her. Unlike Lloyd, she couldn't rely on her memory; she liked having her observations down in black and white. She decided to begin with Josh Esterbrook, who might have been giving his wife some sort of alibi by going diving in the reservoir, and taking her with him. "I understand you live here with your stepmother," she said. "Is that right?"

"Yes," he said. "But I have my own set of rooms in another part of the house."

First person singular. No specific mention of his wife. Judy decided to leave it like that, just for the moment, until she had the lie of the land. "Can you tell me anything about what might have gone on here tonight?" she said.

He shook his head. "I was out," he said. "All day. I left just before ten o'clock this morning, came back at about four o'clock for an hour or so, and this is the first time I've been back again since."

"Was your stepmother here when you came back this afternoon?"

"No. It was her day for the beautician. She goes to Barton and gets herself pampered once a month."

They could check up on Mrs. Esterbrook's movements in Barton, presumably. Judy took a note of the name of the beautician, and Mrs. Esterbrook's preferred restaurant, supplied by Elizabeth Esterbrook.

"Can you tell me where you were this evening?" she asked Josh Esterbrook.

"Where I was most of the day—at the sub aqua club beside the reservoir. And then later in the evening I was with a group of divers in the reservoir, doing a night dive—I'm an instructor at the club. Your officers were waiting for me when we got back to the diving platform."

"The club is in the grounds of this estate?"

"Well, technically. But it's open to the public. It's about three miles from the house." He smiled at her as she looked up from her notes. "That isn't an exaggeration," he said. "All the land here is in Esterbrook ownership. We only keep some of it private." He shrugged. "Some people buy Scottish islands. My father bought Little Elmley."

"And when did the night dive get under way?"

"At around half past eight."

She turned to Elizabeth Esterbrook then. "I understand you found Mrs. Esterbrook," she said. "Do you know what time that would have been?"

The other woman shuddered, and put a hand to her mouth, a muscle working in the side of her face as she fought nausea; Judy felt almost as bad, but there was something about being in charge of a situation that helped you cope with that sort of thing much better than when you were just a witness to it.

"Nine-thirty," said Mrs. Esterbrook, when she felt able to speak. "Maybe a few minutes before that."

"You were coming for dinner, I think the Inspector said. At

nine-thirty?" Judy didn't know why that should surprise her; Lloyd frequently ate as late as that, and, as a result, so did she.

"Yes. I was in London all day, and she knew I might be late back, so she made it a late dinner. She quite often had dinner very late. I rang the bell, and when Angela didn't come to the door, I let myself in."

"You have a key?"

"Everyone does. The family, that is. The house belongs to the Esterbrook Family Trust, so everyone was given a key. Angela and Josh are the only ones who live here, though."

Ah. If Josh and his wife were estranged, that might well account for bruises that she didn't want to explain to the police. She might have turned up here, and caused some sort of scene that had finally and fatally got out of hand. Judy turned to Josh Esterbrook. "Your wife doesn't live here with you?"

"Yes, she does," he said.

Paul and Elizabeth Esterbrook were looking totally baffled. "Wife?" Paul Esterbrook said. "What wife?"

Judy looked up quickly. *What* wife? What sort of family was this?

"Sandie," Josh told them. "We got married two months ago." To gasps from the other two Esterbrooks, he turned back to Judy with a smile. "We didn't make it public, as you can see."

To the extent of not even telling his own brother? "Might I ask why?" said Judy.

"A clause in my father's will could have made things difficult for Paul—he's chairman and managing director of IMG, and Sandie works for him. Her marriage to me might have contravened the conditions under which Paul operates. It's a bit complicated, but it could have meant his removal from the board, since under the terms of my father's will he isn't supposed to employ any member of my family."

Judy decided that the reason for this ban was not one into which she could legitimately probe at the moment.

"Sandie and I got married on an impulse," he said. "It was only as we were being pronounced man and wife that I realized, and Sandie didn't want to give up her job before she'd found another, so . . ." He smiled, shrugged. "Angela's precept was always least said, soonest mended, and we all thought it best to say nothing to Paul and Elizabeth until Sandie found another job." He glanced at his half brother as he spoke, and the smile vanished. "But she won't be working for you anymore," he said, his voice suddenly cold and hard. "So you've no need to be concerned."

Judy made notes as he spoke, and wondered about all of this. Had Sandie been having an affair with her boss? Was that what the Copes had found out, at her mother-in-law's request? Was that why her husband had assaulted her? Did that explain Mrs. Esterbrook's murder?

She made a note, and moved on to Paul Esterbrook. "Perhaps you wouldn't mind telling us where you've been this evening?" she asked.

He took a little time to compose himself before he started speaking. "Josh has a boat berthed at Penhallin in Cornwall," he said. "We usually go diving at the weekends, but—"

"Who do you mean by 'we'?" asked Judy.

"Josh, Sandie, and myself. But the boat's been out of commission for a few weeks. I thought it was back in business this weekend, and I went to Penhallin early this morning."

"When did you leave?"

"About half past seven. It takes the best part of six hours to get there. I made an early start."

"So you arrived in Penhallin at about lunchtime?"

"I stopped in Plymouth for an hour or so. I got to Penhallin at about three, I think, and discovered that Josh wasn't there. But the boat had been broken into, and that worried me, in case something had happened to him."

"Did you know about that, Mr. Esterbrook?" asked Judy, turning to Josh.

"First I've heard of it," he said. "I just forgot to tell Paul I wasn't taking the boat out after all. I know nothing about a break-in."

"Anyway, I drove straight back, and came here," Paul Esterbrook went on. "Mother—" He took a deep breath, and released it. "Mother said that she thought Josh was in Penhallin, and that got me worried, but I didn't say anything to her about the boat. I knew Sandie was doing a night dive here, so I went to see if she knew where Josh was, but the dive had started. I could see them both out on the reservoir, though, so I stopped worrying and went home."

There, he had taken a nap, and had been awakened by the phone. It had been his wife, ringing to tell him what had happened to his mother. His voice had broken as he got to the last bit, but Judy felt, as she had throughout his account, that she was watching someone playing the part of the shocked and bereaved son. His reaction to his brother's marriage had been real; this was manufactured.

No one seemed too touched by the tragedy, and yet she didn't get the impression that Mrs. Esterbrook had been disliked; it was more as though they were all sitting round discussing someone they didn't know.

"So your mother was alive at . . . what time would you say it was when you arrived, Mr. Esterbrook?"

"About ten or five minutes to nine, I think."

Lloyd had come in during Paul Esterbrook's account of his evening, and was introducing himself to the group when a young woman in her twenties, with short dark hair, a black eye, a bruised face, a split lip and a police escort arrived. Judy needed even fewer of her detective powers to work out who this particular Esterbrook was. Her husband jumped up, helped her to a seat, and sat beside her, his arm round her.

Sandie Esterbrook was deathly pale, and under other circumstances Judy would have had to ascertain if she was fit to be questioned, but she wasn't a suspect, she wasn't under arrest, and the hospital had released her. Judy glanced at Lloyd, who gave a slight shake of his head. He wanted to let things ride, see what happened.

Both the other Esterbrooks looked horrified, but once again Judy felt that Paul Esterbrook's horror was a touch theatrical. She was used to Lloyd, who was a natural actor; Paul Esterbrook wasn't. They asked what had happened, and Judy made notes, not just of what the girl was saying, but of the reactions of the others as Sandie told them that she had been mugged in the multi-storey car park in Stansfield when returning to her car. She had refused to let go of her bag, and they had run away.

Stansfield's multi-storey didn't have security cameras, so there was no way of checking her story. It also didn't have many muggings, despite that. It did have a lot of custom; it was hard to think of any time on a Saturday when the incident wouldn't have been seen. Elizabeth Esterbrook glanced at her husband, often, while the girl spoke, and Josh Esterbrook never took his eyes off him. Judy was glad he wasn't looking at her like that.

"Can I ask when this happened?" she asked when the girl had finished.

"I'd been shopping—well, window shopping. I couldn't see anything I wanted. About half past six, I think."

"And after it had happened, what did you do?"

"I got into the car and sat there for a long time. When I felt better, I came straight to the club, because I would have been late for the dive if I'd come home first. Josh and Howard didn't want me to do it, but I felt I had to. It was probably silly."

She had actually done the dive? In that condition? Judy didn't know much about the sport, but she didn't imagine it had been a good idea. "Was it that important that you do it?" she asked.

Sandie Esterbrook shrugged a little. "It seemed to be," she said. "It was all I could think of, that I'd be late for the dive. I don't know why—it just seemed important to do it. Not to let what had happened stop me doing what I wanted to do."

Judy nodded. "I can understand that," she said. She *could* understand it; she just didn't really believe it. Or that Sandie Esterbrook had received those injuries less than six hours ago.

Lloyd sat down and took them all in with a slow look round the room. "I really am very sorry to be so blunt, but can any of you think of any reason why someone would want to kill Mrs. Esterbrook?"

"I presume a burglar or something must have got in, and my mother surprised him," said Paul Esterbrook. "The house is usually empty at weekends."

He was offering a plausible explanation, unlike the others. That quite often indicated a desire to shift blame. And there was something going on between him and his half brother that they would have to investigate.

Tom knocked, and appeared in the door from the hallway, speaking to Josh Esterbrook. "There's an answering machine in your mother's—"

"Stepmother."

"Sorry. In your stepmother's study. It's flashing, which I presume means there are messages, but I can't get them to play. I wondered if—"

"It's done that before," Elizabeth Esterbrook said. "It must be a faulty tape or something. Because it's quite new—I put it in not long ago. But it wouldn't play once before—remember, Josh? You fixed it."

"Oh, yes," he said, and turned back to Tom. "You have to rewind it manually and record a new message before it'll work again." He smiled. "But I expect you want to know what's on it, don't you?"

"Can I ask what you do when you come here at weekends?" Judy asked Elizabeth Esterbrook.

"I'm helping—" She took a breath, and corrected the tense. "I *was* helping Angela with her autobiography."

"Ah, yes," said Lloyd. "She was a novelist, wasn't she?"

"Yes. She couldn't use the word processor anymore, though, because of her arthritis, so I was helping her out." She looked at Tom. "You won't be able to play the tape, I'm afraid," she said.

"Oh, that's all right. It'll keep."

Tom went back out, and Lloyd smiled apologetically. "Might I be very familiar and call you all by your first names, should the need arise? Otherwise, this is going to get rather confusing."

There was a general nod of assent.

"Perhaps you could help me, Paul. It would be foolish of me to pretend that I don't know just how wealthy your family is—can you save me some time by telling me if anyone stands to benefit financially from your mother's death?"

"I'll come into a bit of money," said Paul.

"And—forgive me again, but I don't imagine you and I put quite the same construction on the phrase 'a bit of money.' Perhaps you could give me what the Americans call, I believe, a ballpark figure?"

What he *believed* they called a ballpark figure? Judy wasn't sure who Lloyd was playing, but he was playing someone. Someone frightfully British and solid and dependable. Not someone happily at home with Americanisms, and entirely unpredictable in his approach to problems.

It was Josh, not Paul, who gave him the ballpark figure he had requested. "Oh, let's say twenty million pounds as a nice round figure," he said with a smile.

Lloyd gave a low whistle, which just might have been his first genuine reaction that evening, Judy thought. But even she, after twenty years, rarely knew what was genuine and what wasn't. That was one of the reasons she had never moved in with him. She never knew what he truly felt about anything, not even the baby. He just produced whatever reaction he felt appropriate. Or amusing. He could always fool her.

"Quite," said Josh. "It sounds like a hell of a lot of money to me, too. But to Paul . . ." He shrugged, and glanced coldly at his half brother again. "No. Paul has much, much greater expectations, don't you, Paul?"

"Oh?" Lloyd looked at Paul.

"In a few years I'll come into the major shareholding in IMG currently held by the Esterbrook Family Trust," Paul said stiffly. "I imagine that's what Josh is referring to."

"I see," said Lloyd.

"I doubt that you do," said Josh. "Paul stands to acquire seventy-five percent of a business worth three-quarters of a billion or so. He wouldn't murder his own mother for a few measly millions."

"I don't think I suggested that he would," said Lloyd, looking positively hurt; Judy knew that look, and saw through it. So did Josh Esterbrook.

"No," he said, looking as contrite as Lloyd had looked injured. "Of course you didn't."

"It's all right, Josh," said Paul. "I can fight my own battles."

"Oh, it's not a battle," said Lloyd, apparently even more shocked at that suggestion. "Just questions. We have to ask them, I'm afraid, even at times like these. And you yourself, Josh? Do you benefit at all?"

"No," said Josh. "Paul gets this place, which is what I would have got if Angela hadn't died." He smiled. "I'll tell you what, Chief Inspector—I'll give you a copy of the will, so you can sort out for yourself exactly who gets what now that Angela's dead. But it's quite simple where I'm concerned. I get nothing."

Lloyd gave a little nod of thanks as Freddie appeared in the patio door, smiling at Judy behind the backs of the other people in the room, the broad, beaming smile that he never allowed his customers' nearest and dearest to see, and winked at her. "I'll be on my way," he said.

"Oh—hang on a minute," said Lloyd, getting up, and going out on to the terrace with him. After a brief conversation, Freddie left and Lloyd came back into the room, sitting down at the table as he thought for a moment. "I take it you have domestic staff here?" he asked Josh Esterbrook.

"During the week. They don't live in, and they don't work at weekends."

"Is that generally known?" Lloyd asked.

Josh shrugged. "It isn't a secret," he said. "We're usually all in Penhallin at the weekend."

"Your mother went diving too?"

"No, she hated it," said Josh. "But she had a weekend cottage in Penhallin."

"Where exactly is Penhallin?" Lloyd asked.

"Just across the Sound from Plymouth."

Judy and Lloyd mentally glanced at one another.

"But once a month Angela gave herself a treat in Barton, as I told Inspector Hill. Elizabeth's usually here during the day on Saturday and Sunday, but she was away all day today too, of course."

Sandie Esterbrook had fallen asleep, her head resting on her husband's shoulder, and Judy was certain that Josh was quite unaware of that, unaware, almost, of her presence, and yet entirely aware of it, as though she were a part of his own body. She tried to think what it reminded her of; a mother with a baby, perhaps. She was just part of him: safe now, and sleeping, and he was behaving as though she wasn't there at all.

Lloyd asked Elizabeth where she had been, and Judy watched him look politely baffled when she told him she had been queuing up for tickets to the one-off reunion concert of a seventies supergroup. He asked her to repeat the name as though he had never heard of them. Judy knew that he had given quite long consideration to lining up for tickets himself, before deciding he wasn't quite that keen. Last night the news had shown the people camping out on the pavement, laughing and joking, and he had looked wistful.

"So Mrs. Esterbrook would have been here entirely on her own?" said Lloyd.

"Yes," said Josh. "That was how she liked it, really."

"Didn't she find it difficult being here on her own if she suffered from arthritis?"

Josh shook his head. "The arthritis only stopped her doing fiddly jobs like—well, changing the tape in the answering machine, as Elizabeth mentioned. Chopping vegetables, that sort of thing—she couldn't hold a knife. But she was all right most of the time, and she never did get used to having servants floating about. She preferred having the family help her out. And she really liked having the place to herself once in a while."

"That's why a burglar seems the most likely answer," said Paul.

"A burglar who thought the house would be empty?" said Lloyd. "I can't see why he would be carrying a firearm, in that event." He stood up. "I think that's probably all for now, really, but if you would excuse us for a moment?"

They left the Esterbrooks to their own devices as they went down the hallway to the study, a few doors along from the dining room and looking out onto a large, glass-sided building, which Tom told them was a swimming pool.

"Any luck with the Copes' report?" asked Lloyd.

"No, guv. It isn't in any of the obvious places."

"Right. I want everything in this room searched," said Lloyd, looking round. "I want to find that report, or know for a fact that it's missing. Meanwhile, I borrowed Freddie's little memo-recorder thing." He took it out of his pocket. "Let's see what we've got on the answering machine."

Tom took the tape from the answering machine, put it into the player, and they all listened to the only message on it, delivered in an urgent, angry voice. "*What the fuck are you doing? Are you trying to get me fucking disinherited?*" There was a pause, then he spoke again. "*Jesus!*" There was a moment before he spoke again, the words being forced out between clenched teeth. "*I'm at the cottage, I've got your letter, and I'm on my way back right now.*" The last word was almost growled, and the call was terminated.

"That's Paul Esterbrook's voice," said Lloyd.

"The last call made to this number was at 2:47 this afternoon," said Tom. "It's the dialling code for Penhallin in Cornwall. I rang it back, but got no reply."

"Mrs. Esterbrook's cottage, if I don't miss my guess," said Lloyd. "But check it out, Tom."

Tom checked it out, and five minutes later he was leading Paul Esterbrook out to the waiting car.

SCENE V—BARTONSHIRE
Sunday, September 28th, 12:35 A.M.
On the road from Little Elmley to Stansfield

Judy frowned as Lloyd pulled off the main carriageway down a B-road, and the car transporting Paul Esterbrook to Stansfield police station went off into the distance. "Where are we going?" she asked.

"Little detour," Lloyd said. "I want to see what cars are in the car park of the Little Elmley diving club."

Judy smiled. "Because Sandie's car ought to be there if that story she told us was true," she said.

"Did you think it was true?"

"No," said Judy. "I don't believe that someone mugged by two total strangers wouldn't tell the police. And I don't believe that she just happened to get mugged the day her mother-in-law just happened to get shot dead."

There were no cars in the Little Elmley diving club car park, and Lloyd looked almost as smug as he had when they had got the call about the shooting at Little Elmley. "So what do you think did happen to her?" he asked as they headed back to Stansfield.

"Husband?" she suggested.

"Did you get that impression?"

Judy thought about that. The relationship between Josh and his wife seemed quite intense, which sometimes led to violence, but the truth was that she hadn't got that impression at all. All she had seen had been protectiveness and closeness. She shook her head. "But I noticed a lot of animosity between Josh and Paul," she said. "If anything, I got the impression that—"

"—that Paul beat her up, and Josh is very angry about that," said Lloyd. "So did I. So where does that fit into this little scenario?"

"An affair?"

"It seems likely," said Lloyd. "Especially in view of his mother having employed private investigators. Whatever she said to him in that letter, he thought it threatened his seventy-five percent of IMG. We might understand more once I've looked at the will."

"Why would she put private investigators on to her own son?"

"Who knows? It's just another little puzzle, isn't it?"

Judy already had a lot of little puzzles to work on, and she had a feeling that there would be a lot more before they had sorted out exactly what had gone on at Little Elmley that night, and in what way it had involved Josh's wife being beaten up and the Copes' deaths. Because one impression that she had definitely got was that the Esterbrook family was closing ranks, and she would swear that not one of them had told the truth.

SCENE VI—BARTONSHIRE
Sunday, September 28th, 12:50 A.M.
Stansfield police station

Tom Finch took Paul Esterbrook to an interview room. He was sitting in on the interview rather than DCI Lloyd because Lloyd had got a copy of the will from Josh Esterbrook, and he wanted to get to grips with it.

They knew now that the call made at 2:47 that afternoon had been made from Mrs. Esterbrook's cottage; Paul Esterbrook said that he had not been to his mother's cottage, nor, therefore, had he made a phone call from there.

He went over his story again, expanding on it in reply to their questions. He had stopped in Plymouth for lunch, had arrived in Penhallin at about three o'clock, had gone straight to Josh's boat, and then come straight back to Little Elmley. His mother, he said, had come to the door just as he had inserted his key; their conversation had taken place on the doorstep. He hadn't gone into the house, so he had no way of knowing if she was alone. His mother had not seemed ill at ease; she had asked if he wanted to join her and Elizabeth for dinner, but he had said that he was too tired after his long drive.

Judy reached down and picked up the tape from the answering machine, now enclosed in a plastic bag. "I am showing Mr. Esterbrook an evidence bag marked TF1," she said. "This tape was recovered from your mother's answering machine this evening, Mr. Esterbrook. A copy has been made of that tape. I am now going to play it to you."

Paul Esterbrook's face grew red as he listened to his own voice, and he avoided eye-contact with Judy, Tom noticed, looking instead at him, and then down at the table. The message terminated, and the ends of other, earlier messages played until Judy switched off the machine.

"Did you leave that message for your mother, Mr. Esterbrook?" she asked.

"Yes," he said. Then looked up. "But I didn't make it today."

The additional information seemed to Tom to have come a little belatedly. "When did you make it?" he asked.

"A month or so ago. The last time we all went to Josh's boat."

"Unfortunately," Judy said, "these old answering machines don't give a date and time. But a month is a very long time for a message to remain on a tape without being recorded over. Did your mother receive very few calls?"

Esterbrook sighed. "No, she received a lot of calls," he said, and jerked his head at Tom. "But he said the machine wasn't working. She must have changed the tape, like Elizabeth said. Put in an old one."

"We didn't find a discarded tape," said Tom.

"And according to your brother," said Judy, "your mother's arthritis would have made changing the tape difficult, if not impossible."

"Then I don't know how it got there!" Esterbrook shouted.

"Did you go to your mother's cottage today?" Judy asked again, just as though she hadn't asked before.

"No. And I didn't make that call today. I made it a month ago."

"Well, we can perhaps check if a call was made from the cottage to your mother's number—a month ago . . . that would be what?" She did an admirably quick mental calculation; Tom was still mentally counting fingers. "Saturday the thirtieth of August?"

"Oh, no. It was the Bank Holiday. The weekend before that. It was Sunday that I made the call. And I didn't use the cottage phone. I used a mobile."

"Oh, that's all right," said Judy. "Just let us have the details of your mobile phone and we can—"

"It wasn't mine. I didn't have mine with me."

"Whose was it?" asked Judy.

"I can't remember."

"You can't *remember*?" said Tom in an involuntary reaction. He glanced at Judy quickly; she was sometimes less than pleased with his interviewing technique, especially when he just said whatever came to mind. But she didn't seem to have objected to his intervention.

"No," said Esterbrook. "I can't remember. I'd borrowed one. Everyone I know has a mobile phone."

Tom saw the suspicion of a smile, heard the note of triumph in Esterbrook's voice as he managed to come up with a logical reason for being unable to remember whose phone he'd used. He seemed to be less broken up by what had just happened to his mother than he had been, Tom thought, and Judy must have felt the same.

"Well," she said sweetly. "Don't worry about that just now, Mr. Esterbrook. You might remember when you've had a chance to get over the shock of your mother's death."

Esterbrook's eyes fell away from hers, and Tom grinned at her. He always liked it when she injected some acid into her interviews.

She gave him a tiny wink, and looked at Esterbrook's bowed head. "Were you at your mother's cottage today?" she asked again.

She could only get away with her favourite trick when lawyers weren't present; they were always quick to point out that their client had already given an unequivocal answer. But Tom had discovered that by asking the same question over and over again, in exactly the same tone of voice as the first time, Judy Hill very often got an answer where none had been forthcoming, and sometimes even got a truthful answer instead of whatever lie she had been getting. No one else could do it like she did; everyone *sounded* as though it was the third time they'd asked. She didn't.

Esterbrook looked up. "No. And I made that call five weeks ago."

"It's a strange call, Mr. Esterbrook," Judy said. "A little threatening, I would have thought. Would you like to explain it?"

"I didn't make it this afternoon."

"So you've said, but that doesn't make it any less strange, does it? What did you mean about your inheritance?"

"It's none of your business what I meant."

"What was in this letter that it got you so worked up?" asked Tom.

"Nothing! I didn't even read it. It was a letter from her solicitors that my mother had left there. She wanted me to pick it up and take it back to her."

"It was a letter *to* your mother?" said Judy. "We got the impression that it was one *from* your mother, to you."

"Well, it wasn't. Why would she be writing me letters at her cottage?"

"I don't know," said Judy. "But I think we can be forgiven for thinking that, because if you had no personal stake in this letter, your reaction to being asked to take it to her seems to have been a bit extreme." She glanced down at her pad, and quoted from the transcript of the tape. " 'What the fuck are you doing? Are you trying to get me fucking disinherited?' That seems an odd way to talk to your mother."

Esterbrook coloured up again. "I . . . I was talking to someone else when I said that" was all he could come up with this time, and Tom jumped on it immediately.

"Who?"

"The person whose phone I'd borrowed."

"Oh, you can remember swearing at this person, and being with them in your mother's cottage, but you can't remember who it was?"

"It was just someone who'd dropped in."

"We have established that a call *was* made from the cottage phone to your mother's phone this afternoon at 2:47," Judy said.

Esterbrook's mouth opened slightly. Judy obviously believed that he was genuinely surprised, either that a call had been made, or he was genuinely surprised that a subsequent call hadn't removed it from the stored memory. Tom wasn't sure which, but he did know that was what she thought, because he could read the note she was making. *Gen. surp.* it read. He had got quite good at what Lloyd called Judyscript.

"And that time fits with your message that you were leaving straight away," Judy went on. "The trip does take about six hours, doesn't it? And you say you were at Little Elmley at about eight-fifty or eight fifty-five." She smiled. "Were you at your mother's cottage today?" she asked again.

"No."

Esterbrook was almost as good as she was; his answer was just as patient as her question, just as unemphatic. You couldn't tell from the way he gave it that she had asked him several times before, and that he had answered her each time. That meant he was working just as hard at it as she was, and that, in Tom's opinion, meant that he was lying.

"Someone was there," Judy said. "Someone who rang your mother's number. Do you know who else might have been there?"

"No," he said. "But everyone's got keys."

"Does the cottage belong to the Trust too?"

"No. No, it was my mother's. But she thought we all ought to be able to use it."

"All?"

"Josh and me and my wife." He paused. "I don't know about Sandie. Look—this is just a coincidence," he said. "My mother obviously put in an old tape when the machine went on the blink, whether she has arthritis or not, whether you've found a discarded one or not. I don't know who made the call today, but it wasn't me. I made that call the last time I was in Penhallin."

"But you can't remember whose phone you used?" said Tom. "Did *all* these people you know who own mobile phones just happen to drop in? Or can't you remember who it was because you didn't borrow anyone's mobile phone, but used the phone in the cottage? Because you made the call on that tape today, not five weeks ago? And did you make that call because your mother had put private investigators on to you and had left a letter for you at the cottage telling you she knew what you were up to? Did that threaten your inheritance in some way?"

Paul Esterbrook had gone very red indeed during Tom's bout of rapid questioning, but he hadn't answered. He didn't, as Tom had hoped, give himself away by betraying any knowledge of a private investigator's report.

"If your mother asked you to bring the letter to her," Judy said, "then presumably she telephoned you at the cottage? We could perhaps check that with the telephone company. That would go some way towards clearing this up."

"No. That is, she didn't phone *me*. She phoned Josh. *He* phoned me."

"Well, presumably he can confirm that much, at least."

Esterbrook closed his eyes and shook his head. "I think if you intend to continue questioning me, I would like my solicitor to be present after all," he said.

Now it was Tom's turn to feel triumphant. Esterbrook obviously didn't think that Josh would confirm his story, and had given up thinking that he could tough this out. His method had won, and he couldn't help feeling pleased about that.

"I don't think we have any further questions for the moment," Judy said. "You're free to go, Mr. Esterbrook. Interview terminated . . ."

Tom couldn't believe what he was hearing, and watched with dismay as Paul Esterbrook walked away. "We had him, guv!" he said as soon as Esterbrook was out of earshot. "It has to have been him! All that stuff about borrowing a mobile phone off someone he can't remember! He must have nicked the Copes' report from his mother's study, and murdered the Copes to make sure they couldn't tell anyone what was in it!"

"If he murdered the Copes, why didn't he remove their file on the case while he was at it?" she asked reasonably. "Then we wouldn't have known anything at all about a report."

"Oh," said Tom. Demolishing Lloyd's instant theories was Judy's stock-in-trade; Tom knew he still had a tendency to take them at face value. Lloyd had told him that they were advanced purely as working hypotheses; they weren't to be acted upon. But they always seemed so *right*. Until Judy Hill got her hands on them.

"Besides," said Judy. "How could we hang on to him? All we've got is a phone call, which even if he *did* make it today could be construed as abusive, but isn't overtly threatening. His solicitor would have pointed that out soon enough."

Lloyd nodded when they gave him the results of their labours, such as they were. "OK," he said. "We'll see what Josh Esterbrook has to say tomorrow. I think Tom and I should tackle him, and I think you should have another go at Sandie Esterbrook to find out how she really came by her injuries. And I'm going to take a trip to the seaside. I want to have a look at Josh Esterbrook's boat, since it's been broken into, and I don't believe this crime wave that has hit the

Esterbrooks is all pure coincidence. I'll arrange for the local SOCOs to take a look at Mrs. Esterbrook's cottage too, see if we can get hard evidence that Paul Esterbrook was there this afternoon." He looked at his watch. "Yesterday afternoon," he amended. "I'll need to get the key from Josh Esterbrook, so we're all going to have an early start. I suggest we all go home and get some sleep."

SCENE VII—BARTONSHIRE
Sunday, September 28th, 7:30 AM.
Little Elmley

Judy felt as though they were mounting a dawn raid on poor Josh and Sandie Esterbrook as she drove up to the big house. It wasn't exactly dawn, but it was very early. That hadn't stopped Lloyd sitting up half the night reading the Esterbrook will; he had said, however, that he was only halfway through and no wiser for the experience.

There was no reply when Tom rang the old-fashioned bell-pull. Judy got back in the car after he had rung a second time. "He said he lived in a different part of the house from his stepmother," she said. "Let's drive round and see if we can find another likely door."

Tom and Lloyd got back in, Judy drove along the road which curved round the building, and they at last found a wing at the rear of the house with its windows curtained, and another door, this time with a modern doorbell. After a few moments the door was answered by an unshaven, tousled Josh, wearing only a pair of jeans.

"Sorry to call so early," Lloyd said, "but we would like another word with you and Mrs. Esterbrook, and I wondered if I might have a key to your mother's cottage in Penhallin?"

"What for?"

"A phone call was made from there to your stepmother yesterday afternoon," said Lloyd. "I want to see if I can find out who might have made it. I'd also like to have a look at this break-in which your brother says he found when he went to your boat, Mr. Esterbrook. You're welcome to accompany me."

"Half brother." Josh Esterbrook stepped back, shivering slightly as a breeze got up. "Come in," he said. "Sandie's still sleeping. I was just going to take her some coffee. I'll come with you to Penhallin if you can wait until I've had some too. I'm not human until then."

"Certainly," said Lloyd. "You can even eat. The car's not due for about an hour or so."

"No, coffee'll do. Does anyone else want any?"

Tom and Lloyd did; they sat at the kitchen table while Josh Esterbrook put the kettle on and got the mugs. Judy declined the offer; she wanted to get the girl alone, in case she and Lloyd were wrong, and it *had* been Josh Esterbrook who beat her up. If Sandie was still in bed, that might present the perfect opportunity.

"We would like to ask you some questions about your last visit to Penhallin, if we may," said Lloyd.

"Fire away," said Esterbrook, back to being as relaxed as he had been last night, now that he had got over his mild irritation at being woken up at this ungodly hour for a Sunday.

"Paul was with you?" said Tom.

"Yes, but not for long." Esterbrook told them that on the Saturday there had been an accident to the boat, and they had had to cancel the weekend. He had returned home, but Paul had stayed until the Sunday. He was spooning coffee into the mugs as he spoke.

"Where did he stay?"

"The Excalibur Hotel in Plymouth, I suppose. He usually stayed there."

"Why? It's a long way from where the boat was berthed."

"You'll have to ask him that," said Esterbrook.

"Did he go to his mother's cottage that weekend at all?" asked Judy.

"Yes," said Esterbrook. "She wanted him to pick up a letter for her. That's why he had to come back on the Sunday, rather than staying until Monday."

"Did you ring him at the cottage?" asked Tom.

"Yes." Josh poured boiling water into the mugs and turned to face them. "What's this about? Why should what Paul did in Penhallin weeks ago be of any interest to you?" He produced sugar, and milk from the fridge, and put three of the mugs on the table.

No one answered him, but Tom had a question.

"If you thought he was staying at the Excalibur, why did you ring him at the cottage?"

Josh smiled. "Help yourselves to milk and sugar—I'll just take this to Sandie."

"Could you ask her if she feels well enough to have another word with me about the assault on her?" Judy asked. "She doesn't have to get up—I'd be happy to talk to her where she is."

"Sure." He set off down the hall, then came back and popped his head round the door again. "Was that you ringing the front door-bell?" he asked.

"Yes," said Judy.

"Did you see my brother's car by any chance? His wife says he didn't go home last night."

"There was an Audi there."

He shook his head. "That's Angela's car," he said. "Paul's got a Range Rover. Thanks, anyway." He disappeared again.

"There's a Range Rover parked in the wood by the road up to the house," Tom called after him. "I thought it might be an estate worker or something."

Esterbrook didn't answer. He was gone for a few minutes, and Judy kept a weather-eye out for his return as they discussed the situation.

"I reckon his brother's been here," Tom said, "wherever he is now. Told him what to tell us."

"I don't think they're likely to be that friendly," Judy said.

"Who knows?" said Lloyd. "Families are funny things."

"But they're not really a family, are they?" said Judy. "He always in-sists on saying stepmother and half brother."

"He could be doing that to put us off—" began Tom.

Josh emerged from the bedroom, carrying a T-shirt, and came into the kitchen pulling it on as he spoke. "The groundsmen don't work on Sundays," he said to Tom. "And they don't have Range Rovers. It must be Paul's car. And I want a word with my half brother," he added grimly.

Judy didn't think it advisable to allow that; Josh Esterbrook was very angry indeed, and she imagined that was because of what had happened to his wife. Tom and Lloyd seemed to be of the same opinion, she discovered.

"I don't think *he's* there," said Tom. "The car looked empty."

"Well, he won't have gone far without it," said Esterbrook, opening the door.

"Why don't we give you a lift down there?" said Lloyd. "I would rather like to have a word with him too."

"Fine," said Esterbrook after a moment. "Let's all go and have a word with Paul."

Three minutes later all four of them got out of Judy's car and walked to the Range Rover. It looked empty, as Tom had said, but Judy could see from Tom's reaction that it evidently wasn't. His macho image—cultivated to offset his blond curly hair—would have been compromised by any show of revulsion, but he stood quite still, then blew out his cheeks, and that was eloquent enough. Judy steeled herself, and once again found herself looking at the result of a bullet in the brain.

Paul Esterbrook lay slumped across the front seats, a revolver lying on the floor beside his gloved hand.

SCENE VIII—BARTONSHIRE
Sunday, September 28th, 7:50 A.M.
The wood at Little Elmley

Josh Esterbrook had melted away after the discovery of Paul's body; Judy, anxious for something to do, walked in the direction he had taken, into the wood, finding him idly kicking up the first few fallen leaves. If he had had a reaction to what he had seen in the car, it was gone; he was back to looking nonchalant, and she actually found herself thinking that he looked as though this sort of thing happened every day, until she realized that it apparently did. His stepmother yesterday, his half brother today, and Josh was behaving as though none of it touched him at all. But she ought to make sure before she started demanding answers to questions.

"Are you all right?" she asked.

"For the moment," said Esterbrook. "But the family ranks are being depleted fairly rapidly. I might be next, so make the most of it while you've got me."

Judy decided to take his line. "I take it that condolences aren't in order?" she said.

"I'd rather he'd done it on his own doorstep."

"But this was his own doorstep, wasn't it? Since last night?"

"Very good, Inspector Hill," he said. "You were paying attention. I expect it's Elizabeth's now."

"His death doesn't alter your position?"

"No. The entire Esterbrook Family Trust will form part of Paul's estate now that he's dead too. And the bulk of that goes to Elizabeth—he was very conventional." He smiled. "He even took the traditional military way out," he said. "Paul was in the army, you know, where they know how to do these things."

"You've no doubt that he killed himself?"

Esterbrook shook his head. "I think his life had got out of control," he said. "Paul needed to be in control, like my father."

Judy nodded. "Do you think he murdered your stepmother?"

Esterbrook looked through the trees to where the Range Rover stood, and back at her. "Either that, or he felt responsible in some way," he said.

"Did you see him again after he left Little Elmley last night?"

"No." Esterbrook smiled again. "I think the police were the last people to see him alive, Inspector," he said. "Shouldn't you be interviewing one another?"

She might well find herself on the receiving end of an interview if she had caused Paul Esterbrook to become suicidal and had just let him leave. "You didn't hear the shot?" she asked.

"No. But this is a very long way away from my part of the house."

It was. They walked back towards the others, and Judy joined Lloyd and Tom, relaying the conversation, jotting down the salient points, then reproaching herself. Why hadn't she hung on to Paul Esterbrook when she had the chance?

"You couldn't," Tom said. "His brief would have got him out anyway, like you said."

"But maybe if he'd seen his solicitor, he wouldn't have blown his brains out," she said. "We didn't really have anything on him. I just made him believe we had."

"Maybe he didn't blow his brains out," said Lloyd as backup began to arrive. "Can I leave you to take care of this?" he asked, before she had time to ask him what he meant, then rounded up Josh Esterbrook, inviting him to lead the way back up to the house.

Judy thought it would be best if Tom went to see Elizabeth Esterbrook while she tried to get the truth about the assault from Sandie. "Oh, and Tom?" she added, as he got into her car. "Find out if she knows where her husband could have got hold of a revolver."

"Will do, guv," said Tom cheerfully.

She wished she could feel as cheerful. Lloyd was treating it as a suspicious death, naturally, but it did look like suicide. Still—Lloyd had an almost uncanny habit of being right, and she hoped very much that he was right this time.

SCENE IX—BARTONSHIRE
Sunday, September 28th, 10:00 A.M.
The morning room of a Georgian terraced house in Barton

"I'm very sorry," Tom had said when he told Elizabeth Esterbrook what had happened.

She hadn't broken down, or fainted, or cried. She accepted what he said with a little nod, and invited him to sit down. But then that was the way the whole family had reacted to Mrs. Esterbrook's death, he thought, so it might not be significant. Perhaps they just had stiff upper lips. Despite what Lloyd had said, Tom thought that Paul

Esterbrook had topped himself. They couldn't all be going round bumping one another off. Could they?

"Can you think of any reason why your husband would have taken his own life?"

She shook her head, then frowned. "Only if he truly believed he was going to lose his inheritance," she said. "I can imagine that he might kill himself then."

"And how could he have lost his inheritance?"

"If I could prove he'd been unfaithful to me. His father was . . . well . . . eccentric, to put a kind construction on it. He believed almost ferociously in the sanctity of marriage, and Paul doesn't, to put it bluntly." She frowned a little. "Didn't," she said. "Anyway, he was going to get his inheritance on his silver wedding anniversary, but only if he managed to get there."

It turned out that Paul Esterbrook had been unfaithful to Elizabeth all their married life. Not, she added, that they had had what you would call a married life for ten years, and very little before then, because Paul had been in the army, and had been away from home for long periods.

"And would you have taken him to court?" Tom asked. "If you had been able to prove adultery?"

"Yes," she said. "I had a considerable financial incentive, because I would have got fifteen percent of the major shareholding. The other sixty percent would have gone to benefit some pet project of his father's, and Paul would have got nothing at all. Whereas if he'd made it to the silver wedding, he would have got the lot, and he would have tied everything up in a way that meant I couldn't get any more of it than he was prepared to give me, you can be sure of that."

"And did you have evidence of his adultery?" asked Tom.

"No. But even if I had, it would all have to go through the courts, and Paul would have fought it to the last gasp before he gave up."

"Would what happened to his mother have affected him like that?"

"No," she said.

Tom wasn't used to being diplomatic, but he was having to tread very warily. You could never be sure of these people, what would offend them, what would injure them. Give him good honest villains any day. "Do you think he could have had anything to do with what happened to his mother?" he asked.

"No." She shook her head this time, to reinforce her answer.

"If she was in some way threatening his chances of inheriting the business?"

Her head was still shaking. "No," she said again. "Paul had a very nasty temper. He could be violent. But he would never have hurt his own mother." She looked slightly embarrassed. "I . . . I might even be able to prove it."

"How?"

"I'm not proud of it," she said, "but I finally resorted to a private detective. I had him watched when he went on the diving weekends."

Tom's eyebrows rose. *She* had employed a private detective? Kathy Cope? He frowned. The Copes' file had had the Little Elmley address on it. Had her mother-in-law let her use her address? But no— the initial was wrong. The Copes' file was for Mrs A. Esterbrook. There couldn't be two lots of private detectives involved, could there? No. She must have employed the Copes.

"I know what you must think of me," Mrs. Esterbrook said, misinterpreting his puzzlement. "But you don't know what it was like." She looked down at her hands. "He taunted me with it. Practically told me what he was doing, knowing I couldn't prove it." She looked up again, her face defiant. "And I know you'll think I'm mad," she said, "but I believe he even used Sandie as some sort of red herring. Made me think it was her, when it was someone else all the time."

There was a pause before she spoke again. "And I think he beat her up," she said. "I think he must have found out she'd married Josh and he couldn't use her as a decoy anymore. Lost his temper with her, and—" She gave herself up to the tears.

Tom didn't think it was as complicated as that. Sandie had been

Paul's personal assistant, and had had an affair with him, then fell for his brother, if you asked him. That was why Paul had lost his temper with her. He didn't speak; he would wait until Mrs. Esterbrook felt able to continue with the interview.

He presumed that Judy was trying to smooth some of his rough edges by sending him here; he had failed his inspector's exam, and she thought if she took him in hand she could get him through it, but he wasn't sure he was cut out for this sort of thing. Elizabeth Esterbrook had, after all, just lost her husband, and even if she had been humiliated by him, reduced to having him followed, she had been married to him for over eighteen years, and now she was having to face the possibility that he had killed his own mother and then himself. And even if it was self-pity, it was the first real emotion he had seen from an Esterbrook; Judy would be better at dealing with it than he was.

"I haven't been able to get hold of the private investigator," Mrs. Esterbrook said, her voice still shaking.

No, thought Tom. You wouldn't have been, on account of she and her husband are both dead.

"But his name's Foster. His office is in Barton—I can give you the address. Perhaps you can get him at home, or something, because his report will clear Paul, I know it will."

Not the Copes. Tom had to start rethinking his stance once more. Did everyone in this family reach for a private eye when things got sticky? Angela Esterbrook must have had some investigation of her own going on. Also into Paul? Maybe. But that could wait. Right now, Tom wanted to talk to this Foster person. Paul Esterbrook had said that he hadn't gone into the house, that he had spoken to his mother on the doorstep. If he left her alive, then presumably Foster, whoever he was, would indeed be able to confirm that. On the other hand, if Esterbrook *did* go into the house, then they would know Paul had been lying. And he had a feeling, as he took Foster's address, that this report would show just that. He was pretty sure Esterbrook had topped himself, whatever Lloyd thought, and he probably did that because he had killed his mother.

"Did your husband own a revolver, Mrs. Esterbrook?" he asked, almost answering the question himself. A souvenir of his army days, just kept for sentimental reasons, didn't even know it still worked . . .

"No," she said. "But Josh keeps one on his boat."

Tom's eyes widened. He thought he'd better make sure Lloyd had that piece of information before he got to Penhallin. This was getting a lot more complicated than he'd thought. "Why does he keep a revolver on his boat?" he asked.

"He thinks that some man who went to prison with him might come after him," she said.

This time Tom's eyebrows shot up.

"Didn't you know Josh had been in prison? He shot a man dead during a raid on a petrol station. Fifteen years ago. Josh pulled the trigger, but the other man got life, and he's due out about now."

Josh Esterbrook had already shot someone dead? My God, that put a different construction on the bodies at Little Elmley, if Esterbrook was a convicted killer. Fifteen years ago, thought Tom. That would be when Lloyd was in the Met, so he wouldn't have known anything about it. And he still didn't know. He abandoned the other questions he had been going to put to Mrs. Esterbrook in favour of making sure Lloyd didn't end up like Angela and Paul Esterbrook.

SCENE X—BARTONSHIRE
Sunday, September 28th, 10:30 A.M.
On the road from Little Elmley to Penhallin

Lloyd was glad Josh had accepted his offer to accompany him to Penhallin; he thought it best that the Mr. and Mrs. Josh Esterbrooks be questioned separately, and that might have been difficult, since they had no reason to suspect either of them of Mrs. Esterbrook's murder. But Lloyd was certain this was not as straightforward as it seemed, and this way they might get to the truth.

When the car had arrived, Josh Esterbrook had taken his leave of his wife, and there had been nothing lovey-dovey about it, no extravagant shows of affection. But there had been an obvious, open belief in one another that had convinced Lloyd that Josh had not beaten up his wife. And if his brother had, and his brother was dead, then Josh Esterbrook had to be a suspect for that death, however apparently extreme that action would have been. There were so many crosscurrents and undercurrents in this family that the beating could merely have been the culmination of all manner of resentments and betrayals.

The powerful car had left Little Elmley, its blue lights flashing, going as fast as the traffic conditions allowed, in an effort to cut down the journey time, and they had spoken a little about Josh's relationship with his half brother; it had not been good, and had been getting worse. He was entirely open about it, or at least seemed to be.

Lloyd's mobile phone rang; he answered it, and listened with interest to what Tom had to say. "Do you have one of these?" he asked, waving his mobile at Josh as he put it away again.

"Sure," said Esterbrook, pulling his from his jacket pocket. "Doesn't everyone?"

Lloyd smiled. "We got issued with ours a couple of months ago," he said. "I don't know how we managed without them. For instance, that was my sergeant, telling me that you keep a revolver on your boat. Is he right?"

"He is."

"And did you get a look at the revolver beside your brother's body?"

"Half brother. I did, and yes, it certainly looked like mine. A Smith and Wesson .38, blue steel, walnut grips."

"Who else knew about it?"

"Paul, Elizabeth, and Sandie. I showed it to them. Paul's been giving Sandie lessons—she's a very good shot."

SCENE XI—CORNWALL
Sunday, September 28th, 2:00 P.M.
A small cottage in Penhallin

They had been to the boat, and Lloyd had got the SOCOs to go over it very carefully indeed; he hadn't expected to find anything; he just wanted as much evidence as he could get about who exactly had been on *Lazy Sunday* since it had come back from the boatyard.

Then it was on to Mrs. Esterbrook's cottage, sitting alone on the headland, the sea round it dark green and slightly threatening today as the autumn weather began to take hold. Josh Esterbrook let them in, and they looked round downstairs. Lloyd wandered into the kitchen. The larder held dry goods, the kitchen cupboard the usual sort of stuff. A torch and candles for when the weather on this exposed coast cut off the power, cleaning materials.

"Chief Inspector?" Detective Sergeant Comstock said, and Lloyd went back through to the living-room-cum-office.

Comstock was the local man who had been assigned to him on his arrival in Penhallin. One of the scene-of-crime men came over to the desk, closely followed by Esterbrook, and they all looked at where Comstock was pointing. In the wastepaper basket were the incinerated remains of a sheet of paper. The letter? It seemed likely.

"Beyond resurrection, I imagine," said Lloyd.

"Don't be too sure," said the scene-of-crime man. "I'll get the specialists to bag it up. Daren't do it myself, not when it's in that state. But you never know with lab technicians these days—they can perform miracles. They might get it so some of the writing can be read."

Lloyd looked at the unlined pad on the desk, and glanced at Comstock. "Do you suppose she used that?" he asked.

Comstock bent down, looking at the pad from the tabletop level. "There are imprints," he said. "It's probably her shopping list, but it's worth a try." He took out an evidence bag and sealed the pad inside it.

"What's upstairs?" asked Lloyd.

"The bathroom and my stepmother's bedroom," said Esterbrook.

And the latter was where, upon opening the door, Lloyd saw his third corpse.

SCENE XII—CORNWALL
Sunday, September 28th, 2:30 P.M.
The bedroom of the cottage

Lloyd asked permission from the evidence gatherers before he went in, then stood for a moment looking round the room. The bed was made, spread with a duvet that matched the curtains and cushion covers on the window seat; the bedside cabinet had a table lamp, a radio-alarm-telephone, and two paperback books, neatly arranged; the dressing-table had toiletries and cosmetics, a comb and brush, laid out ready for use; the window seat's cushions were plumped up and placed just so; the old fashioned wardrobe doors were closed, a small key in the lock.

And the only thing out of place was the body, lying on its side on the carpet, the yellow hair matted with the blood that had seeped from a gaping wound in the back of his head. It was the body of a youth; no more than a boy, really, his unbuttoned shirt half tucked into jeans with the fly undone, as though he had been killed in the act of dressing or undressing.

Lloyd crouched down, feeling the skin. The boy's shirt had pulled away from his neck as he had fallen; the bared shoulder revealed what looked like a spider tattoo. A mobile phone, which, as Josh Esterbrook had said, everybody had these days, was tucked into the shirt pocket. Lloyd looked up and saw Esterbrook's face, much more shocked than when they had found his brother.

"Do you know him, Mr. Esterbrook?" he asked.

The other man nodded. "His name's Rampton," he said. "Billy

Rampton. He's one of the people who came diving with me on the boat."

"How old is he?"

"Fifteen, I believe."

"What else can you tell us about him?"

"Not much. He's a rent-boy, basically. Is that what you wanted to know?"

Ah. Private investigators, rent-boys, threatened inheritances . . . it was money, not sex, that was at the root of these killings, but it was sex, illicit sex, that had been the catalyst. Was Billy the companion that Paul Esterbrook had been unable to recall? And if so, had he really made that call five weeks ago, using Billy's phone? And if he had made the call five weeks ago, what had gone on here this weekend? Nothing, if you looked at this room. Something quite dreadful, if you looked at the boy.

"How well did you know him?"

"Well enough to know he was a waste of space."

Lloyd shook his head slightly. "That's a very harsh judgement on a very young man," he said, straightening up, joining Esterbrook on the landing.

"Maybe."

Lloyd regarded Esterbrook, his eyebrows slightly raised. "It looks as though your revolver may have been the instrument of all these people's deaths, Mr. Esterbrook. How do you feel about that?"

Esterbrook shrugged.

Lloyd looked again at Billy Rampton, and wondered about Paul's inheritance, and the threat to it that his mother might or might not have posed. Tom said that if Paul Esterbrook had been proved guilty of adultery, he would have been disinherited. So now they had a motive to go with the apparent scenario at Little Elmley. That was very handy, very neat. Almost as though it had been produced to give them all the information they needed to wrap the whole thing up.

"It's beginning to look," Lloyd said slowly, "as though your brother shot this boy and your stepmother in a desperate attempt to hang on to his inheritance." He turned to Esterbrook. "Does your position under your father's will alter if that is the conclusion at which we arrive?"

Josh Esterbrook looked back at him, his eyes thoughtful. Then he smiled. "What's my situation under the will got to do with it?" he asked. "Are you accusing me? Are you going to arrest me for murdering them all just because it was my gun?"

Lloyd smiled back. "You seem somewhat lacking in the opportunity department, if the boy's been dead as long as I think he has. But of course it isn't necessary actually to pull the trigger to be guilty of murder, as you, of all people, must know. *Would* it alter your situation? If Paul *had* murdered his mother?"

There was a moment of silence before Esterbrook answered, during which he looked at the boy's body. "I don't know," he said. "It wouldn't affect the IMG shares—they go to the Esterbrook Marine Research Fund if Paul has in any way disqualified himself from inheriting. But the Trust could be up for grabs, I suppose." He shrugged philosophically, and smiled at Lloyd. "I expect there would be a lot of legal wrangling. I doubt it, to be honest. You've got a copy of the will—maybe you can work out exactly who gets what now that this has happened, because I'm damn sure I can't. This is a situation my father failed to foresee."

"Then you seem to be a little lacking in the motive department, too," said Lloyd. "If that *is* the case. I don't think we're going to arrest you, Mr. Esterbrook, at least, not for the moment. But the Penhallin police will want to talk to you about Billy, since you and he went diving together. And they will be interested in your revolver, whether or not it was used to kill Billy or anyone else."

Comstock had checked the last number called from the phone in the bedroom, and had found himself talking to the scene-of-crime people who were searching Angela Esterbrook's study in Little Elmley. "So that call you found on the answering machine was the last one made from here," he said to Lloyd as they went back downstairs.

"Perhaps," said Lloyd. "I'll just check the hall phone."

Comstock frowned. "Won't that be the same?" he asked.

"No," said Lloyd. "It's the phone itself that records the last number dialled from it, not the line."

"Is it?" said Comstock, startled. "I never knew that."

Lloyd checked the hall phone, and it was answered by George Farmer, First Class Butcher, who thought it must have been at least two weeks ago that Mrs. Esterbrook had rung him. Wanted to know if he had any pheasant. Partial to a pheasant, was—"

"Thank you," said Lloyd hurriedly, before he was taken on a gastronomic tour of Mrs. Esterbrook, and hung up, hoping that somewhere in Penhallin there was a George Butcher, First Class Farmer. Then he left the local SOCOs to it and accompanied Josh Esterbrook to Penhallin police station, to which reinforcements had been called in the shape of Chief Inspector Brian Vickers, who knew all about Billy Rampton, apparently.

Lloyd sighed. Comstock might not be privy to the arcane workings of modern telecommunications, but he had been right; the call to Angela Esterbrook's answering machine was the last one that had been made from the cottage. And it looked as though it must have been made by whoever shot Billy.

SCENE XIII—CORNWALL
Sunday, September 28th, 3:30 P.M.
The police station in Penhallin

Vickers was of much the same low opinion of Billy as Esterbrook, Lloyd discovered when they retired to an empty office.

"He was what is called 'gay for pay,'" Vickers said. "I think, to be more accurate, he was anything at all for pay. He was a nasty piece of work, who worked out of Plymouth mostly."

Where Paul Esterbrook had chosen to stay when he went on his diving weekends, Lloyd thought. More evidence for the prosecution.

"Good riddance, if you ask me," said Vickers.

Lloyd sighed. "He was a fifteen-year-old boy," he said.

Vickers shook his head. "He was very attractive to look at," he said.

"People who didn't know him trusted him, but people who did know him were scared of him. He was a sort of turn-of-the-century Pinkie, if you know what I mean. A vicious little crook—not your average fifteen-year-old boy."

Lloyd was pleased to hear a reference to literature from a fellow police officer, a rare and unexpected occurrence, but he couldn't agree with Vickers that Billy's life could be dismissed like that. It was still murder.

It turned out that Billy had been alive and kicking on Saturday morning in Plymouth, and the medical examiner said that he had been dead for between twenty-four and thirty-six hours, so Josh Esterbrook was in the clear, having been taking a highly visible part in the affairs of the Little Elmley Sub Aqua Club at the time of Rampton's shooting.

He was not, however, in the clear about the revolver, which was the weighty matter that had really taken up the time of Penhallin's finest. In the end they decided to send details of the firearms offence to the CPS to see if charges should be brought, which puzzled Lloyd a little. It was, after all, a reasonably straightforward offence.

At last they were on their way back, and Lloyd settled back in the car, trying to catch up on his sleep. He had a lot of thinking to do, and he'd do it better when he wasn't tired, because the more straightforward this business seemed to be, the more complex it got.

For one thing, there were too many clues in that cottage. For another, Elizabeth Esterbrook had accused her husband of the assault on Sandie Esterbrook. Also, after talking to Judy on the mobile phone, Lloyd ascertained that this time round she got a different, equally unlikely story from Sandie to account for her injuries. And attempts to get hold of Foster, Elizabeth Esterbrook's private detective, had failed; he wasn't at home, and his house was up for sale. But he still seemed to be working for Mrs. Esterbrook, so presumably he would be in his office tomorrow.

And tonight Lloyd was going to have a word with young Mrs.

Esterbrook, and she was going to tell him the truth, if he was there until tomorrow morning.

SCENE XIV—BARTONSHIRE
Sunday, September 28th, 4:00 P.M.
A small terraced house in Stansfield

"It's just that . . . well, I used to work with your mum."

Lucy Stephenson was putting Joe Miller's flowers in water as he spoke. He had picked them from his own garden; they had come up all by themselves, because he hadn't so much as looked at the flower beds. He had mowed the grass when it had started to grow in the summer; that was all. He didn't even know what sort of flowers they were; Debbie had done all that until she'd upped and left, taking the kids with her. He didn't blame her, not really.

"How did you know where I lived?" Lucy asked.

"Oh, you know. Policemen have their methods." Kathy had told him where she lived. But his name had obviously meant nothing to Lucy, so she presumably didn't know that he'd once been engaged to her mother, and she certainly wouldn't want to know about their more recent relationship.

"It's very kind of you," she said, taking the vase through to the front room, putting it on the table.

It wasn't, not really. He had wanted an excuse to see her, to tell her that he really did need to get all the equipment back that he had bought for Kathy, because he couldn't afford not to have it back. But he couldn't make himself ask her about it. "I always think it's a shame giving flowers to—" He didn't know what to say. The deceased? Cop-speak got in the way of normal communication. "—you know" was the masterly substitute he came up with. "It's the people who are left that need cheering up."

"It was nice of you to come round. Can I get you something?"

"Oh, no, thanks. I won't stop. I just . . . well, if you can let me know when the funeral is. I was a friend of your dad's, really, even though I worked with your mum."

She looked surprised; that hurt him. Andy had obviously never mentioned him either.

SCENE XV—BARTONSHIRE
Sunday, September 28th, 6.30 P.M.
Joe Miller's house in Barton

He got home, poured himself a drink, put a ready-made meal in the oven—having never been entirely sure of the microwave—and switched on the television. The short Sunday news bulletin was full of the usual depressing things, and then the longer Aquarius TV regional news came on.

"Bartonshire police have today confirmed the rumours that a second fatal shooting has occurred at the Little Elmley estate outside Barton owned by the wealthy Esterbrook family. They are not at present releasing the name of either victim. In a joint statement with the Devon and Cornwall police, they also confirm that they have not ruled out a possible connection between the Little Elmley shootings and the death from gunshot wounds of a fifteen-year-old Plymouth youth whose body was discovered this afternoon in Penhallin, Cornwall. Mrs. Angela Esterbrook, widow of Paul Esterbrook, founder of Industrial and Medical Gases, is known to have a holiday cottage in the area, but a police spokesman would neither confirm nor deny that this was where the youth's body was found."

The news would have been startling to anyone who had been too wrapped up in his own affairs to have heard about the original shooting, never mind the others, but Joe was staring at the screen, his mouth open.

The pictures of the Little Elmley estate turned into pictures of a rather different kind of estate in Stansfield, of scene-of-crime officers coming in and out of the masked garage of a semidetached house.

"And in Stansfield, Bartonshire, police say that the investigation is
continuing into the mystery of a couple found dead in the garage of
their home, and that they have not yet ruled out foul play."

Joe sat down with a bump, his hand at his mouth, his eyes
wide, his brain barely functioning. Oh, dear God, dear God. What
the hell had he got himself mixed up in? What in God's name had
happened?

Why were all these people dead?

And let me speak to the yet unknowing world
How these things came about: so shall you hear
Of carnal, bloody and unnatural acts,
Of accidental judgments, casual slaughters,
Of deaths put on by cunning and forced cause,
And, in this upshot, purposes mistook
Fall'n on the inventors' heads: all this can I
Truly deliver.

Hamlet, Act 5, Scene 2

Eleven weeks previously . . .

Act I
The Esterbrooks

A little more than kin, and less than kind.
Hamlet, Act 1, Scene 2

S CENE I—BARTONSHIRE
Saturday, July 12th, 6:20 A.M.
The en suite bathroom of Paul and Elizabeth's
house in Barton

"You could come too," Paul said, picking up his weekend bag and his dive bag, standing in the bedroom doorway as though half expecting her to change her mind and join him.

Elizabeth looked at his reflection in the mirror, shook her head and carried on applying careful, subtle makeup to her fair skin. Paul liked to imagine that issuing a certain-to-be-declined invitation to join him on his weekend jaunts would allay the deep suspicions she harboured as to their true purpose, and that calculated risk, that deliberate, taunting challenge, made her angrier than even his constant infidelities.

"Why not?" he persisted. "It's a glorious day—it's even better in Cornwall, according to the weather forecast. It'll be like a mill pond—I guarantee you won't be seasick."

He smiled, the smile that had captured her heart almost the moment she was introduced to him, but had captured too many others since. Now he was possibly even more handsome than then, and three years ago, when his father had died, he had become chairman of Industrial and Medical Gases Limited, with a salary to match. Women were queuing up, and the only one he had no time for was her.

Anyone listening to this early morning conversation would find that difficult to believe, but everything was in a code that had evolved over the last eighteen years, a code that only she and Paul truly understood. This little charade was simply a slight variation on the big one that they called their marriage.

"Spending all weekend watching people jump off a boat into the sea isn't my idea of fun," she said.

Paul went to considerable and, these days, literal lengths to conceal his infidelities; his brother Josh had acquired a boat in the spring, berthed at Penhallin in Cornwall, a six-hour drive away, and Paul's diving weekends by the sea entailed rising at five-thirty on Saturday mornings. These preparations invariably woke her too, which was why she was up and dressed at this ungodly hour. She found it hard to believe that her husband rose at that time on a Saturday morning just to go diving.

"We don't jump off the boat all the time. We eat and drink and enjoy ourselves, and stay in nice places. Maybe when you saw how much fun everyone was having, you'd want to take it up." He put the bags down and went to the phone, going momentarily out of her view. "I can give Sandie a ring, say I'll be a bit late, if you want to come. You could throw some things in a bag—we'd still be there in plenty of time for lunch."

Sandie? Elizabeth thought. He was taking her with him, was he? "Isn't a mobile P.A. just a little over the top?" she asked. "Most people settle for a mobile phone." He, of course, always left that at home, ostensibly so that he could get away from it all, but in reality to stop her ringing him up and interfering with his pleasure.

He laughed, reappearing in the mirror as he walked to the door again and picked up his bags. "I give her a lift down, that's all. No point in taking two cars—Stansfield's on the way. Are you sure you don't fancy a weekend in Cornwall?"

"And it just so happens that Sandie's a diver too, does it?" she said. "That's quite a coincidence."

"No coincidence. That's how I met her." He looked puzzled. "I thought I'd told you all this. She's Josh's girlfriend."

"*Josh's* girlfriend?"

"Well," Paul amended, clearly realizing that he had overplayed his hand. "She's a friend of Josh's who happens to be a girl. I don't know if there's any romance there. Anyway, she needed a job, and she seemed bright, and keen, so when the P.A. job came up, I advised her to apply for it."

Oh, sure. If Josh had a girlfriend of any sort, Elizabeth thought, she would have heard all about it from her mother-in-law, because Josh seemed to have forsworn women since his marriage had broken up. Nothing would please his stepmother more than to think he might settle down again with someone else, because she was worried that he might return to his old ways without some female influence to keep him steady.

The possibility of nailing this lie at least was too tempting for her to ignore, because for the story to hang together, Sandie Townsend had to be a diver, and that seemed very unlikely indeed. "I think I will go with you after all," she said, reaching over for her toilet bag and flashing a brittle smile at him. "No need to ring Sandie—I'll be five minutes."

It was worth the prospect of a long, embarrassing journey just to see the look on his face as she spoke the words.

SCENE II—BARTONSHIRE
Saturday, July 12th, 6:25 A.M.
The master bedroom of the house

Eighteen years. Eighteen years he had been married to the bitch, since she had been a blond, blue-eyed seventeen-year-old, and she had never shown the slightest interest in diving. That was why he had believed it was safe to invite her along to Josh's weekends, as he had done religiously since they began. But it wouldn't surprise him in the least if Elizabeth had put a private detective on to him, and now that he had decided to take Sandie along on his weekend in Cornwall, he had thought it wise to tell Elizabeth about her before anyone else did.

But he had misjudged the situation, because for some reason the mention of Sandie's name had lit some sort of touch-paper. Now he just had to hope that Sandie could carry off the deception with no pre-knowledge. She probably could. She *was* bright. And keen, he thought, with a smile, which vanished when he realized that there would be none of that this weekend, as Elizabeth literally threw some clothes into a weekend bag. And Josh would enjoy his predicament hugely.

"Ready," she said.

And there were other problems. The hotel room, for a start. "I've only got a single room at the hotel," he said.

"Do you think it might be too crowded with the three of us?"

He sighed. He could barely remember the last time he and Elizabeth had shared a bed, never mind a single bed. His eyes widened a little as she picked up the phone and asked him for the hotel's number. Reluctantly, he found the reservation and told her the number. She had a brief conversation, then hung up, turning back to him.

"They can't switch us to a twin room," she said. "But they can put another bed in your room, so I've asked them to do that."

Five minutes later he was pulling away from the elegant Georgian terrace in Barton and heading towards Stansfield.

SCENE III—BARTONSHIRE
Saturday, July 12th, 6:35 A.M.
On the road from Barton to Stansfield

Paul's eyes were on the road, but he could feel Elizabeth smiling. She had called his bluff, the cow, and she was convinced she was going to catch him out. But she wouldn't. This was just another inconvenience to add to the long list of inconveniences he had had to suffer since he was twenty years old and standing at the altar under duress. Sandie would come through for him.

He had known that things were bound to get worse once Elizabeth was given a huge financial incentive; the wonder was that it had taken her this long to think of some new way of embarrassing him. She was wasting her time, though. He wasn't going to get caught. If the army had taught him nothing else, it had taught him the value of forward planning. And if his father had hedged his financial legacy with conditions, he had inherited one thing from him that was his to use whenever he chose: the ability to anticipate and cover every contingency. Including this one. He just hadn't anticipated the need for Sandie to extemporize, that was all.

There was virtually no conversation until they were into Stansfield. Only he and Elizabeth could manage a thirty-mile journey without speaking, but finding yourself welded to the wrong person for half your life made communication an unnecessary luxury unless it had some wounding purpose. And it suited him that it should be so, because he was having to work out several conversational gambits that would give Sandie clues as to what he'd told Elizabeth.

He pulled up outside the flats and hooted, mentally crossing his fingers that Sandie was as quick on the uptake as he believed her to be. A moment later she came out, her step faltering just a little when she saw him open the rear passenger door, and realized why.

"Sandie," he said, as she got in. "This is Elizabeth, my wife. Elizabeth, this is Sandie, Josh's girlfriend, to whom I very wisely offered a job."

Sandie shook Elizabeth's hand awkwardly over the headrest. "It's nice to meet you at last," she said. "I've heard a lot about you."

"Well, I've heard practically nothing about you," Elizabeth said. "It's not like Josh to be secretive. Have you known him long?"

"No, not long," Sandie said.

"How did you meet?"

"Oh, I was with some friends in a pub, and he came over to say hello to someone. We got talking."

"And they discovered they had something in common," Paul said. "Hasn't the insurance company come up with the readies yet?" he asked, glancing over his shoulder. "I notice a distinct absence of diving gear." He turned back to Elizabeth. "Sandie's kit was stolen," he said as he drove off, mentally ticking off what he had managed to communicate so far.

"But I thought I'd go and keep Josh company anyway," said Sandie. "I'll sun myself on the deck."

Paul relaxed a little. Sandie was a natural, unlike him. He had to plan his deceptions ahead.

"And have you been doing this all your life, like Paul and Josh?"

"No. I'm just a beginner compared to them."

"And how long have you been going to Penhallin at the weekends? It's quite a trek, isn't it?"

"Oh—since I've known Josh, really."

Brilliant. Now, Paul really relaxed, because thankfully, Elizabeth knew as little about the subject as Sandie did; had she been a diver herself, she could have tripped Sandie up, but she had run out of things to pump her about, and the first round in this heavyweight contest had undoubtedly gone to him.

SCENE IV—CORNWALL
Saturday, July 12th, 12:45 P.M.
On the road to Penhallin

They had stopped at a service area just once, and just for long enough to use the toilet facilities and change drivers; Paul had had no chance to speak to Sandie alone. And as they crossed the Tamar into Cornwall, he didn't know whether to be glad or sorry: on the one hand, it meant that this particular odyssey was almost over, but on the other, it meant that now Josh would be put through his paces. Josh could think just as quickly as Sandie, but he had a wicked, wicked streak.

Oh, Jesus, Paul thought as Penhallin at last welcomed his careful driving and he remembered—he was supposed to be picking up lunch, but lunch on board would be impossible since Josh had no way of knowing the fictitious background he and Sandie had concocted. He'd have to get Elizabeth away, so Sandie had time to brief Josh.

"Josh'll be expecting you to get something for lunch, won't he, Sandie?" Paul said, driving through the busy little town to the supermarket. Sandie agreed that he would.

"Will you be joining us?" she asked as she put various things in a basket.

"No," said Paul. "We'll have lunch at the hotel." He smiled at Elizabeth. "I think you'd rather eat on dry land, wouldn't you?" He turned back to Sandie. "I only managed to persuade her to come because there isn't a breath of wind."

"I'm glad you did," said Sandie, and smiled at Elizabeth. "You'll be company for me."

There was something almost unsettling about the ease with which Sandie could do this, Paul thought as they piled back into the car, but he was grateful for it. He pulled on his driving gloves and was just setting off again when he glimpsed a familiar car coming into the car park.

"I think that's your mother," said Elizabeth.

"Is it?" he said, and drove off.

SCENE V—CORNWALL
Saturday, July 12th, 1:00 P.M.
The deck of *Lazy Sunday* in Penhallin harbour

Josh Esterbrook watched as his weekend group left the boat and went off to have lunch at various places.

Divers. It was an appropriate name for them, given the range of occupations, or lack of them. They came from every conceivable kind of background, and in amongst the holiday-makers, he had a group of semiregular locals who turned up every time he took the boat out. They included a peer of the realm who had never worked a day in his life, and a hard-living, if not exactly hardworking, rent-boy, a retired stockbroker, and a property dealer's wife. And, of course, his half brother, who had his own reasons for spending the weekend in Cornwall, which didn't often include diving, and whose car was pulling into the car park even now. Josh's eyes widened as he saw the two women emerge. One was Elizabeth. The other, slim, dark, mid-twenties, floppy sunhat, was presumably Sandie Townsend.

"Hello, Elizabeth," he said, helping them on board. "This is a nice surprise. What do you think of *Lazy Sunday*?"

"Nice," said Elizabeth.

"Lunch," Sandie said, emptying a supermarket bag out onto the deck as she spoke. "Sandwiches, sausage rolls, coleslaw, Coke, and fresh orange juice. And some biscuits and Brie, and a couple of apples. But I've still got no kit, I'm afraid, so I'll just have to be decorative."

Josh realized he was being drawn into some subterfuge of Paul's, but he was pretty sure he didn't know enough about it to comment, so he changed the subject altogether. "I'm surprised to see you here," he said to Elizabeth. "Angela said you'd got a letter telling you you could pick up your ticket for the concert. I thought she said something about Saturday."

"She probably did," Elizabeth replied. "But it's the last Saturday in September."

Josh grinned. "You mean they've given you nearly three months' notice of when you can get a *ticket*? When's the concert?"

"Not until the end of the year."

"Can you believe it?" Paul said. "A grown woman prepared to queue all day for a ticket to a geriatric rock concert?"

"It's a onetime reunion," Elizabeth said defensively.

"Oh," said Sandie. "*That* concert. They say people are going to be queuing all night."

"I'm not quite that keen," said Elizabeth. "But I really would like to see them live, whatever Paul thinks."

"Good for you," said Sandie. "I hope you manage to get a ticket."

"Well, I think we should leave Sandie and Josh to have their lunch and go and check in at the hotel," said Paul. "I'm sure they don't want us playing gooseberry."

Playing gooseberry? Josh smiled. So that was the story, was it? He could have fun with this. "Which hotel are you in?" he asked.

"The Excalibur," said Paul. "I like to stay there, if I can," he said to Elizabeth.

"Then I presume it's the biggest and the best," she said.

"It's certainly the biggest," said Josh. "But it's on the outskirts of Plymouth, so you'll have to put your foot down if you want lunch."

"It has a brasserie that serves food all day," said Paul.

"We could have stopped there on the way," Elizabeth said, looking puzzled. "Why didn't you?"

"I couldn't let Josh starve while we all had lunch," said Paul.

"Why on earth do you stay in Plymouth, anyway?"

"I prefer big hotels, and there aren't any round here."

Elizabeth looked unimpressed, but dropped her interrogation. "Where do you usually stay, Josh?" she asked.

"I rough it on the boat," he said. "One of the cabins is habitable. The other one's used to stow the divers' gear."

"Do you stay on the boat too?" she asked Sandie.

Josh smiled. "I think you're advancing our relationship a little further than Sandie wants to take it just yet," he said. "But carry on. I welcome your assistance."

"Oh, I'm sorry," Elizabeth said, not sounding in the least sorry. "I just assumed—"

"Oh, ignore him," said Sandie. "No, I'm staying at The Point. It's expensive, but everyone says it's very good."

"You haven't stayed there before?" said Elizabeth.

"No," said Sandie. "I like to stay in different places. Get to know the area."

She was a quick thinker. Josh liked that. He liked it a lot. With that, Paul and Elizabeth went off to have lunch; Sandie stripped off her outer clothes to reveal a yellow bikini, and sat down on the deck, smiling at him.

"Sandie Townsend," she said, her hand outstretched.

"Josh Esterbrook." He shook her hand. "So what's the story?"

"I seem to be your girlfriend. You met me in a pub, and we realized we both did scuba diving. I haven't known you very long, but I have been coming to Penhallin ever since I met you, and Paul gave me a job on the strength of our relationship." She paused. "I think."

Josh grinned. "Did you get notice of any of this?"

"None whatsoever." She lay back on the deck, covering her face with the hat.

Josh had been interested in Sandie from the moment he had been told about her, and now that he had actually met her, he was even more interested.

"Isn't this weather gorgeous?" she said from under the straw hat, and stretched like a drowsy Siamese cat, not an ounce of spare flesh on her body. "We could be in the south of France." She removed the hat and smiled. "Why don't you just head her out, skipper?"

Josh reached out a suntanned arm and patted the deck rail of the compact little boat that had been built in the sixties for the Monte Carlo set, and could outrun some speedboats if you gave her her head. "She'd get us there," he said. "But I'm afraid it would add maritime twocking to my list of criminal activities."

"What's twocking?" She sat up again, putting the hat back on her head, her close-cropped dark hair no defense against the sun.

"It's an acronym. Taking without the owner's consent."

She smiled, as though at the discovery of a new word, but Josh knew her a lot better than she thought he did, knew that she was no stranger to street slang. She was very good, though. You would never guess.

She frowned slightly then. "But I thought Paul told me it was your boat."

"Nope. It belongs to my stepmother. I don't have the money to buy boats. I don't have any money at all. Except what I make doing this, and most of that goes on upkeep."

"How come your mother's rich and your brother's rich, and you've got no money?" She reached down and picked up a packet of sandwiches.

He felt a flash of anger, not at the question, but at the terminology. "My *step*mother's rich, and my *half* brother's rich," he corrected, then the smile returned, to be chased away again by her next question.

"What happened to your own mother?"

"She died."

"Sorry."

She unpeeled the packet, and they ate their sandwiches in silence. Most of the other occupants of the harbour were away having lunch or eating picnic-style on deck, as they were, and the boats themselves seemed to be taking a breather, sitting dozing in the sun, nudging one another occasionally when some more energetic craft's slipstream disturbed the surface of the water. The constant little creaks and groans that boats at rest made could be heard in the quiet little harbour, like the settling of a house at night. Josh helped himself to some biscuits and Brie.

"Have I offended you?" Sandie asked.

"No," said Josh.

She looked at him a little speculatively. "If I'm supposed to be your girlfriend, perhaps I should know a bit about you."

He smiled. "Fire away."

"What list of criminal activities?"

"Too late," said Josh. "If you didn't already know, that would have been your first question."

She smiled again, shielding her eyes as she looked up at him. "Paul said you'd been in trouble with the police since you were thirteen. And that you'd finally gone to prison when you were twenty-one. He didn't say what for."

"I shot someone dead." He watched for her reaction. The wide-eyed surprise was something he was used to, but there was more than just surprise in those dark blue eyes. There was something very like respect, and he had never seen that before in response to his oft-repeated history.

"Honestly?"

"Honestly. They reduced the charge in my case to manslaughter. But the other guy was found guilty of murder. He got life, I got eight years. I served six and a bit, and I got out just over eight years ago."

"What was it like?"

"Prison?"

She shook her head, smiling. "Killing someone," she said.

Josh grew even more interested in her. She had dismissed the victim of his crime as easily as he had; there had been no shock, no desire to see remorse that he didn't feel, but which he had professed with some success at his trial. "It was very easy," he said. "We were robbing a petrol station, I had a gun, and bang. He was dead." He shrugged. "It was like . . . being God, or something. But I didn't mean to kill anyone."

"Maybe neither does God."

More quiet clicks and bumps as the boats stirred in their sleep, and another silence fell, which she broke.

"How old were you when your mother died?"

"Five."

"And when your father remarried?"

"Five. The funeral baked meats did coldly furnish forth the marriage tables, you might say."

She smiled a little. "What's that from?"

"*Hamlet.*"

"How did your stepmother meet your father?"

"He came here to dive. She lived here then—she still has a cottage here." He jerked his thumb in the general direction of his stepmother's weekend retreat, and Sandie twisted round to look, but you couldn't see the cottage properly from the harbour, not now that the town had been built up. Only the sunshine glinting on the red-tiled roof marked out the cottage now, and he directed her gaze towards that.

"Does she rent it, or what?" Sandie asked.

"No. When Paul and I were young, it was used as a holiday cottage. After he retired, she and my father used it as a base in the summer, and went walking on the moors. Now she uses it at the weekends so she can keep an eye on me."

Sandie looked puzzled. "Keep an eye on you?" she repeated.

"My father asked her to keep an eye on me, so that's what she does, even though I'm sure she'd much rather not. She runs me down on Friday evening and takes me back Sunday lunchtime. To be fair to her, I think she might have worked at the cottage anyway, so she's just helping me save on petrol, really. But she did make him a promise on his deathbed, and she's keeping it."

"She did really love your father, then? I mean, you don't think she married him for the money?"

"Worshipped him would be nearer the mark. He was fifteen years older than her, and she thought he was all things wise and wonderful. What he said went, even if she didn't agree with him." He frowned. "What made you think I thought she'd married him for his money?"

"Oh, nothing. What does she work at in her cottage?"

"She writes. She's quite a well-known novelist."

"What name does she write under?"

"Angela Laurence. But now she's writing her autobiography."

"Is her life interesting?"

"She thinks it is."

Sandie picked up an apple, and conversation ceased for a while.

Josh looked round the little harbour, not yet a tourist Mecca, but going that way. The town grew busier every year, and at the weekends its population very nearly doubled, along with its road traffic. One of the old harbour buildings was being renovated, about to turn into a restaurant, so somebody thought that Saturday lunchtimes wouldn't always be as quiet as this one, and he was probably right. Josh would like to have lived here, to be able to offer his diving sessions all summer rather than just at the weekend, but his father had made that impossible, and his stepmother saw to it that the terms of his ludicrous will were adhered to without question, so she wasn't open to deals being done about who lived where.

Sandie threw the apple core over the side and sat in the chair beside him. "Was the holdup the end of your criminal career?"

"I don't know."

She smiled again. He liked Sandie Townsend. He liked her very much indeed.

SCENE VI—CORNWALL
Saturday, July 12th, 3:30 P.M.
The deck of *Lazy Sunday*

The conversation had covered rather more mundane topics after that interesting introduction, as Sandie gathered the sort of information she might be expected to have about a boyfriend, and Josh supplied it. He had no need to ask about her; Paul had told him everything he needed to know.

She picked up her beach-robe, feeling in the pockets, drawing out cigarettes and lighter. "Why didn't you get charged with murder like the other man?" she asked.

"I told the court that I had no idea he'd got a gun until he told me to cover the attendant while he emptied the till, shoved it into my hands and it went off. He said that *I'd* brought the gun with me, and he had been nowhere near it when it went off. They didn't believe him, and they did believe me."

"And which version was true?"

Josh smiled. "Well, I know which one my father believed."

"But he *was* wrong, wasn't he, Josh?" said Paul's voice.

Josh swung lazily round to see his half brother walking noiselessly across the deck in his entirely correct footwear which went with his entirely correct casual wear, and his entirely correct wife.

"No one meant to kill the guy," Josh said. "It was an accident."

"Either way," said Sandie, "it was because you gave evidence against this man that he got done for murder and you didn't?" She threw her cigarette over the side and picked up another apple. "You can't be his favourite person."

"I'm sure I'm not. And, as you may have worked out, his sentence is almost up, which is why I recently took out insurance."

"Insurance?" said Sandie.

Josh nodded towards the wheelhouse. "See that little cabinet in there? Open the top drawer."

Sandie made to get up; Paul sighed loudly, and Elizabeth glanced over at him. "What's wrong?" she asked.

"Josh, I don't honestly think the girls should be involved in—"

"The girls?" said Elizabeth. "Sometimes you're very like your father, Paul. We got the vote some time ago, and if either of us objects to whatever it is, I expect we'll say so. Go on, Sandie. Let's see Josh's insurance."

Sandie put down her apple and went into the wheelhouse. Pulling open the drawer of the cabinet, she turned to Josh, her eyes wide.

"Take it out," he said. "But make sure no one on any of the other boats sees it."

She hesitated for just a moment before drawing out the Smith & Wesson .38, holding the butt between her fingers and thumb, and looked over at Josh, her face slightly flushed. "I've never even seen a handgun before," she said. "Is it real?"

"Not much use if it wasn't."

"Is it loaded?"

"Yes."

Paul jumped up, taking it from her. Pushing out the cylinder, he emptied the cartridges into his hand, dropped them into the drawer, and glared at Josh. "Idiot," he said. "She could have killed someone." He handed the gun back to her. "OK," he said. "You can look at it now."

She pointed it towards the deck and pulled the trigger. "I can't make it work," she said.

"Pull the hammer back."

She pulled back the hammer, and this time the cylinder turned and the hammer clicked. She looked at Josh, her eyes shining. "Can I fire it for real sometime?" she asked.

Josh held her eyes and smiled. "Why not?" he said, almost to himself.

SCENE VII—CORNWALL
Saturday, July 12th, 3:40 P.M.
The wheelhouse of *Lazy Sunday*

Sandie wasn't sure if he meant it. She ran her fingers along the blue-grey barrel, then closed her hand round the shiny wooden grip. It was beautiful, she thought, excited at the thought of making it shoot. But he might not have meant it.

Josh smiled at her. "Paul will show you how to use it properly," he said, a glint of wickedness in his eyes as he deliberately forced Paul to acknowledge her presence. "Won't you, Paul?" he added, still looking at her.

Paul had little option but to agree that he would show her how to handle the revolver, but Sandie doubted that he really wanted to.

"Paul was an officer in the SAS," Josh went on. "He learned how to shoot properly."

"Unlike you," said Paul. "And it wasn't the SAS, as you very well know."

"Well, it was some super-secret outfit," Josh said, still addressing all his remarks to Sandie. "We'll need a target for you to shoot at," he said. "We'll fix something up for tomorrow morning, before the first diving session."

"You can't go letting a gun off round here," said Paul.

Josh smiled. "Show him what else is in the drawer, Sandie. Not the boxes of ammunition—the other thing."

Sandie pulled the drawer open a little further and drew out a metal tube. "This?" she asked.

"A silencer?" Paul said. "You told me it was for self-defence. Where does a silencer fit in to that?"

"If that bastard comes after me, I will defend myself quickly and quietly, take him out to sea and tip him over the side well weighed down."

Paul sighed. "Silencers don't work as well with revolvers as they do with pistols," he said. "It might not be as quiet as you think."

"Doesn't having an illegal revolver count as inappropriate behaviour?" asked Elizabeth.

"Sorry, Elizabeth," said Josh. "The inappropriate behaviour clause only applies to the family home. I don't keep it at the family home. I keep it here."

Sandie hadn't the faintest idea what they were talking about; she hoped she wasn't going to get drawn into the conversation, in case a girlfriend of Josh's would be expected to know. She was bemused at the matter-of-fact way they all spoke about Josh's crime and its aftermath, but then, they had had a long time to get used to it, she supposed, and Josh clearly encouraged discussion of it. She liked that. And he didn't give a damn about it. She liked that too.

Elizabeth was watching her, her eyes resting as frankly on hers as Josh's had done a moment ago, and Sandie had no way of knowing what was going on in her head, because she knew nothing about Elizabeth at all. She had lied even when she had said she had heard a lot about her, because Paul mentioned her name only when he was trying to impress on her the need for secrecy, and his choice of language in describing her was less than flattering, which had given Sandie the wrong impression.

Elizabeth was about ten years older than Sandie, she was attractive, slim, and, Sandie thought, probably a natural blond. She did look a little battle-hardened, but that was hardly surprising. Sandie hadn't known Paul long, but she could imagine that his wife had not had an easy time of it.

The two brothers—half brothers, she reminded herself, though Paul never used the qualification—were very alike; Paul was more classically handsome, but they were both dark and well-built, both attractive. That was where the resemblance ended. Josh seemed to be much more honest, in an odd sort of way, than Paul, even if he had robbed a petrol station. He had only known her for a couple of hours, but he had answered her questions directly in a way that Paul never had, and never would.

Josh took the gun from her and carefully reloaded it before putting it back in the drawer, his eyes still holding the question that they had had when she had first said she would like to fire it. She looked back at him, smiling, feeling as though she had known him all her life.

"The customers are coming back," he said. "Wouldn't do to let them see it."

She looked over his shoulder at the small group of people making their way down the harbour. Josh had told her about some of them; she amused herself by trying to pick out the bank manager, the stockbroker, the two Australian tourists. She got most of them wrong.

One, she had no problem with. Billy the rent-boy looked every inch what he was, though not quite what she had expected. Josh had described him as beautiful, which was true, but she had expected an almost feminine beauty. Billy, despite his youth and his calling, was decidedly masculine, and his beauty was male beauty, the kind that Michelangelo would have wanted to sculpt, the kind that two-dimensional paintings could never quite reproduce.

But that beauty, she felt sure, went no deeper than his flawless skin.

SCENE VIII—CORNWALL
Saturday, July 12th, 4:05 P.M.
The car park at Penhallin harbour

Angela watched from her car, and saw *Lazy Sunday* take on its diving customers and make its way out of the harbour to the dive site. She had almost gone down before they left, then had decided against it.

But that *had* been Elizabeth with Paul in the supermarket car park; she had been sure of it, and now she had confirmed it. And while it might shock any normal mother to see her son with another woman, it shocked her to see Paul with his wife. Elizabeth had never so much as considered the possibility of joining Paul when he went diving.

That in itself hadn't surprised Angela, who, despite being born and brought up by the sea, had no desire to explore it; it seemed to her that the sea was full of things she particularly *didn't* want to look at. Even though she had been married to a diving nut, the idea of spending your leisure time in an environment hostile to human life hadn't appealed to her.

But Elizabeth's sudden appearance in Penhallin did surprise Angela. Why now? Why accompany Paul this weekend? Paul had been coming to Penhallin at the weekends since the beginning of May. It had to be because Elizabeth thought Paul was up to something, and she was hoping to catch him out. There had been a girl in the car with them; Angela didn't know if that meant anything, but she was desperate to find out. She lived in constant dread of one of the boys being disinherited, because that would truly tear the family apart.

If Josh put a foot wrong, her late husband would expect her to invoke the conditions of his will, and she would do it if she had to. But she already felt like a prison wardress, just doing what he had requested of her; she didn't go out of her way to catch her stepson out. And Elizabeth hadn't gone out of her way to catch Paul out either, until now, and that worried Angela, because it might mean that this time she thought she could.

That worry, plus the insatiable curiosity that had turned Angela into a writer, a novelist, an observer of the human condition, and the sheer determination with which she had always, against all the odds, held her family together, was what was making her itch to find out what was going on. It was only by a great effort of will that she had forced herself to stay in the car, and now she wished she had just gone down to the boat.

But the boat was out now, and there was no chance of finding out what was going on until it got back, so she might as well go back to the cottage and get on with her work. And she was having second thoughts about going down there this evening; Josh wouldn't like it, not with all his customers there. She'd pop down tomorrow morning, maybe, before the first diving session. That would be better.

Because then it would be just the family.

SCENE IX—CORNWALL
The following day: Sunday, July 13th, 8:15 A.M.
The deck of *Lazy Sunday*

Elizabeth stifled an early morning yawn as Josh headed the boat out of the little harbour for the shooting lesson that Sandie was so keen to have. Paul was determined to make her watch him every second, see for herself that he barely knew the girl. She was beginning to wonder if this whole thing had been some sort of bluff; it could be that Sandie really was Josh's girlfriend, because there certainly seemed to be something almost tangible between them, and you couldn't fake that. Their conversation was entirely routine, but you could tell when two people were intensely interested in one another, even if they were just sitting and chatting.

That didn't mean that Paul was here for a blameless weekend, of course; it just meant that she had got the wrong girl. She had asked Josh if Sandie was a red herring, if Paul was trying to throw her off the real scent, but he had pretended not to know what she was talking about, of course.

Sandie was wearing the skimpy bikini again, and sat with Josh in the wheelhouse, as she had done almost all the time. Josh anchored the boat, which bobbed gently on the undulating water as he nailed up a makeshift target made out of a wooden box stuffed with an old mattress from the cabin he didn't sleep in.

Paul screwed in the silencer and handed Sandie the revolver, then turned her so she was facing the target, the length of the boat between her and it. "Just take aim, pull back the hammer until it clicks, and press the trigger," he said. "Like you did before."

Sandie aimed; there was a dull report, but the target didn't have a mark on it. She moved much closer, tried again, and missed again. All six bullets missed.

"I wasn't quite brave enough to take the place of the target," Paul said, taking the gun from her and reloading. "But I could have done. Now I'll show you how to do it properly."

Elizabeth watched as he stood behind Sandie and took a long time over placing her hands exactly how they should be on the gun. Closing his hands round hers, he pressed her finger on the trigger, their bodies coming together with the now-controlled kick. Elizabeth glanced at the target; it had a small black hole in it. It happened six times; six muffled shots, six holes. All this Freudian imagery and proximity to a seminaked female was giving Paul a buzz, that much was obvious. And Paul knew that it was obvious. It was meant to be. He reloaded, and looked over at her with a smile as he began all over again.

Paul had been the perfect choice for whatever behind-the-lines job it was that he had done in the army, too secret to be discussed even now. He had no conscience, no qualms about betraying those who trusted him, or about the damage his actions might cause to innocent people. No hesitation in lying, no guilt. A cruel streak that surfaced from time to time, as it was doing now. Look at me, he was saying. Look at me with my fancy woman. You can't prove a thing. All you can do is watch me get turned on by her.

If Paul's father hadn't dangled the prospect of a multi-million-pound payoff, she would have left Paul long ago. After all, she had been denied her conjugal rights for years, and that would be reason enough to divorce him; it would still leave her relatively well-off. But after years and years of continuing to love him, of hoping he would settle down, that he would want her again, she was unwilling to give up now that the love had gone. Proving his adultery would make her very, very rich.

She had met Paul at a Boxing Day party given by his mother, famous for her elegant dinner parties, which combined the best of both the centuries in which the Esterbrooks seemed to live. They had consummated the relationship that very evening, when everyone else was downstairs indulging in more decorous pursuits. But she still didn't know why he had married her, because it had become clear early on that he had no intention of staying faithful to her.

Josh, on the other hand, had come out of prison and had met someone, married her, and, Elizabeth believed, truly loved her. But it hadn't lasted. It would be nice to think that Sandie really was his girlfriend, but any doubts Elizabeth had entertained as to exactly whose girlfriend she was evaporated as she watched Paul show Sandie how to shoot the revolver. He had taught her too, long ago, because he occasionally carried a gun off duty, and he thought anyone with access to a gun should know how to use it; but he hadn't taught her like that.

She had hoped that her unscheduled appearance might throw Paul's well-oiled machinery out of gear, but it hadn't, and she had had enough. There were other ways of catching him out, ways she had regarded as beneath her at one time, but which were rapidly becoming more and more attractive as Paul became less and less so.

Sandie, perhaps not quite so happy with blatant insults as Paul, announced that she had had enough tuition and wanted to see Paul shoot. Paul walked to where she had stood for her first attempt, turned and loosed off six shots in rapid succession, showing off for his girlfriend, who applauded when the bullets peppered the target. But as Josh once again took the wheel to take the boat into harbour, Sandie followed him into the wheelhouse, standing beside him, her arm round his waist, and Paul clearly didn't like that.

He followed her in and started looking in the drawer for something. "Oh, sorry," he said as his bowed head brushed against her. "Was that your thigh?"

Elizabeth decided to see if Angela needed any help at the cottage; she wasn't staying here to be humiliated.

SCENE X—CORNWALL
Sunday, July 13th, 8:30 A.M.
The wheelhouse of *Lazy Sunday*

Paul found the wherewithal to clean the gun, something he always did, and Josh never did. He was glad to have something to do; he

needed an activity to take his mind off Sandie, after his erotic shooting session with her. It had been necessary, both to show Elizabeth
she was wasting her time trying to prove anything, and to remind
Sandie what was what. She was coming on to Josh, of all people;
she'd been doing it all weekend.

"Is it like driving a car?" she asked as Josh got the boat under way
again.

"Sort of."

Paul worked on the gun while Josh, on his way back to the harbour,
slowly negotiated the rocky coastline that they had explored in row-
ing boats as kids.

"Can I have a go sometime?" she asked.

"No," said Josh. "I don't trust women drivers."

Paul, though his opinion of those of the female persuasion was
probably even lower than his brother's, would never have said that.
After almost ten years of office diplomacy, he'd had such blatant sex-
ism wrung out of him. In his army days he wouldn't have dared *not*
be sexist, but you had to adapt. He had to, at any rate. He couldn't
be independent of the rest of the world like Josh; he relied on the rest
of the world too much.

Josh said that he was a slave to convention, and, with prison-cell
psychology put his desire for sexual variety down to the moral recti-
tude that governed the rest of his dealings with the world. It was true
that it was the only area of his life that would not stand up to
scrutiny, and that he was running the risk of losing everything if he
got caught, but the risk was part of it; maybe all of it. Calculated
risk-taking was in their blood; their father had taken risks to get
where he had, and Josh had taken risks all his life, for even flimsier
reasons than Paul's.

Paul made to put the gun away, but Josh guessed what he was up to.

"Leave it loaded," he said without even turning round.

"That's dangerous."

"I want it dangerous. He could be out any day now. I'm vulnerable
on this boat at night."

Paul shook his head. "You played a very stupid part in a pathetic little holdup that went wrong," he reminded him. "Your accomplice was fifty if he was a day. He'll be coming out to his state pension, not to kill you."

"Maybe. Leave it loaded."

Paul left it loaded. He was a year older than Josh, but their childhood together had been spent with Josh giving the instructions and Paul obeying them, sometimes to his cost. A little later he had worked out that Josh was not a good role model. A little later still, that he could always blame Josh for whatever it was he had done, and his father would believe him. He put the gun and silencer back in the drawer. "Doesn't this drawer lock?" he asked.

"What use would a locked drawer be?"

Paul shrugged. The need for risk-taking might be the result of some family gene, but at least his way of satisfying it was less likely to lead to fatalities than his brother's.

He could see the knot of people walking down the harbour, coming for the afternoon session, and began to ache with almost adolescent anticipation, like he always did. He might even have to screw his bitch of a wife again if he wasn't going to get it any other way.

The small crowd of people on the harbour resolved themselves into individuals, and one of them was his mother. That was all he needed. That was all he bloody needed.

SCENE XI—CORNWALL
Sunday, July 13th, 8:55 A.M.
Penhallin harbour

Angela smiled at Elizabeth as she was helped onto the boat. "I thought I saw you at the supermarket yesterday," she said. "What made you finally decide to see what it was all about?"

Elizabeth shrugged. "I'm not sure," she said. "I just thought Cornwall might be nice on a weekend like this. I can't say I'm enjoying myself."

Elizabeth looked a little strained, Angela thought, and she wished that she didn't. But she couldn't remember a time when there hadn't been family tensions, and so far they were at least still all on speaking terms. She saw the girl who had been with Paul and Elizabeth in the car, sitting on her own in the wheelhouse. "Who's that?" she asked. "She came down with you, didn't she?"

"Sandie Townsend. She works for Paul—he says she's Josh's girlfriend."

"Really?" Angela looked more critically at the girl as she sat perched on the cabinet, two strips of material just about preserving her modesty, her long legs crossed. Intelligent face. Neat figure. It would be nice if Josh could find himself a girl.

The divers were coming on board now, and Angela watched them all with the practised eye of a novelist. The show-off, the serious holiday-maker, the earnest hobbyist, the . . . she frowned. The one talking to Josh at the door down to the cabins defeated her. He was very young, and had a quite beautiful face spoiled by a selfish mouth, and an even more beautiful body spoiled by a horrible tattoo of a spider on his left shoulder, as she discovered when he divested himself of all but his swimming trunks and began to pull on his wet suit.

"And who's that?" she asked.

"That's Billy," Paul said, joining them as she asked.

"He's very young to be able to afford this sort of weekend. Never mind all the state-of-the-art diving equipment he's got with him. How old is he?"

"Fifteen, I think."

"So he must still be at school?"

"I doubt if Billy's seen the inside of a classroom since he was ten," said Paul. "He's in business for himself. He's a rent-boy—you know? A prostitute?"

"I know what a rent-boy is," said Angela. "And he earns enough to spend his leisure time like this?"

"He's some sort of friend of Josh's, so he probably doesn't have to pay for anything."

"When you say a 'friend' of Josh's, what exactly do you mean?"

"Well, he was in prison, remember. They get up to all sorts in there."

"And where does Sandie fit into this picture?" asked Elizabeth immediately.

"I think she believes she can turn Josh round."

Angela had no feelings on the matter of anyone's sexuality, as Paul knew, or he wouldn't have been so frank, but she knew Josh, and he needed a woman's influence, not some rent-boy's. If this girl was interested in Josh, perhaps she could give her some help.

"You know," she said to Elizabeth, "I think I'm going to go back to Little Elmley now. There's quite a lot of work to do on the family album—if you're not enjoying yourself, would you like to come back with me? We could have dinner—Paul can bring Josh home." She looked across to where Josh stood deep in conversation with Billy. "Josh?" she called. "Elizabeth and I are going back now to do some work at Little Elmley—Paul will take you and Sandie back. Ask Sandie if she would like to come to dinner."

"I'd like that very much, Mrs. Esterbrook," said the girl. "Thank you."

Good. Angela left the boat, unsure, as she always was when she interfered with Josh's arrangements, if she had done the right thing. He was so perverse, so likely to do the very opposite of what you would expect. Just like his mother.

SCENE XII—BARTONSHIRE
Sunday, July 13th, 7:00 P.M.
The house at Little Elmley

Angela and Elizabeth had spoken about anything and everything on the journey back except family matters. Neither of them had mentioned Paul's belief about Josh, neither of them had mentioned Elizabeth's belief about Sandie. And that was just how Angela liked it. If things weren't endlessly discussed and worried over, they sometimes simply resolved themselves.

That wife of Josh's had given him a considerable knock-back running out on him as she had, and if Josh had made, well, alternative arrangements while he was in prison—which was, after all, during the period when men were supposed to be at their most sexually active—then falling back on them was only to be expected, if he thought that women couldn't be trusted. Of course, his wife might not have left him if he had told her about his past, but then . . . how did you go about that? It must be difficult to tell people you've been in prison for manslaughter.

Perhaps, Angela thought, as she and Elizabeth prepared dinner, she ought just to see if Sandie knew what was what before it happened again. It was worth risking the possibility of serious discussion to see if Elizabeth knew what Josh had told Sandie about himself. "Has Josh told this girl about being in prison?" she asked.

Elizabeth sighed. "Oh, yes," she said. "But you don't honestly believe that she's Josh's—"

"What I believe," said Angela firmly, "is that Josh needs a woman, and Paul already has one. So let's hope that things work out the way they should, shall we?"

Elizabeth sighed again, but the discussion had been averted, and Elizabeth carried on dicing vegetables with perhaps a little more venom than was strictly necessary. This was what Angela liked doing best: preparing food for dinner guests. And she would have preferred not to have help, but someone else had to do the things she found really difficult, like chopping vegetables. For this reason she had trained the young woman she actually employed to do things her way, but she could hardly complain if Elizabeth did them her way. So she didn't complain, but she was relieved when she could tell Elizabeth to go and put her feet up, to have a drink out on the terrace, and she had the kitchen to herself.

When the others arrived back from Cornwall, Paul joined Elizabeth on the terrace, but Josh wanted to show Sandie round before dinner, and whatever status Sandie had had to start with, Angela felt certain that Josh would not be spending this amount of time with someone in whom he had no interest. Besides, you could tell they were entirely wrapped up in one another. Josh wasn't gay; he just needed a little encouragement, and she felt sure that Sandie would provide that.

SCENE XIII—BARTONSHIRE
Sunday, July 13th, 8:10 P.M.
The grounds of Little Elmley

"This place is absolutely huge," Sandie said as Josh gave her a guided tour of the exterior. "I don't think I've seen the same part of the house twice."

"I know. See what bottled gases can do for you?"

Josh liked bringing people in by the front door and out through the kitchen; from the front, it looked like a reasonably large house, but from the rear, you got the full impact of the extensions that his father had had built on anywhere and everywhere, every time he had thought of something else he needed space for.

It had once been the manor house of a very small village, but by the middle of the twentieth century the village had been reduced to a handful of houses, and those had been flooded to create a reservoir. The area still retained the village name of Little Elmley, but this was the only house still extant, so that was the house's name now, incongruous though the adjective was when applied to this rambling house that went on forever, and the acres of land on which it sat.

As they walked round, he gave her the authorized family history. His father had come to Stansfield to oversee the building of the head office of Industrial and Medical Gases across the road from an existing IMG bottling plant. This personal visit to the town had meant that he discovered Little Elmley, just thirty miles away. First, he had bought the house because he could more easily indulge his diving hobby in the reservoir which had been thought necessary to provide backup during the war but which in the end had not been needed. Then, bit by bit, as his father's empire grew, he acquired more and more of the land surrounding the house. A wood here, a meadow there, until he owned it all. Every blade of grass. His final coup had been to buy the reservoir itself.

He had brought his sons up so that they were as much at home underwater as they were on land; Josh and Paul had been into every house in Little Elmley, immersed by water since before they were born, and marine life flourished where once children had played and women had washed and cleaned while their men worked in the woods and fields that surrounded the isolated house.

"You actually own the entire village?"

"Not yet," said Josh. "But I will."

SCENE XIV—BARTONSHIRE
Sunday, July 13th, 8:10 P.M.
The garden at Little Elmley

They walked through a little copse, and Sandie found herself back more or less where she had started, looking across a long mowed and clipped lawn to the terrace where the Esterbrooks were gathered, having their predinner drinks, unaware of her and Josh's proximity.

Josh stopped walking, and drew her under the branches of a weeping willow that trailed down into a small pond. "Paul wants you to learn to dive," he said.

"Does he?" What Paul wanted was of very little interest to Sandie right now.

"I could give you a crash course next weekend," Josh said. "If that would suit you. It would be here, not at the club. We've got a pool."

She frowned. "You're going to give me diving lessons instead of taking your boat out?"

He nodded. "We could do the theory over a couple of evenings during the week. You'll have to complete a medical declaration that says you're fit to dive, and get it signed by your doctor, and then we can do the practical instruction at the weekend."

"But you'll lose money if you don't take the boat out, won't you?"

"That's up to me. Does it suit you?"

Sandie wasn't sure she fancied the idea of swimming underwater. "Why on earth did he tell Elizabeth I could dive?" she asked.

"He'd be explaining you away," he said, and smiled. "And we wouldn't want to make a liar of him, would we?"

She didn't want to learn how to dive. But she wanted to be with Josh. "No," she said, smiling back. "We wouldn't." She leant back on the tree, looking at him. "You don't like him, do you?"

"Not much. Do you?"

She looked through the leafy branches to where Paul sat chatting to his wife and mother, acting the part of the perfect husband, even though they both must know that he wasn't. Lying when people knew you were lying was somehow worse than actually deceiving them, but whether or not she liked him wasn't something to which she had given any thought before today; he had just been there, a stepping-stone to a better life.

He had always been all right up until now; they'd met in seedy city hotels, at invented business meetings, but she hadn't minded that. She hadn't minded anything much; that was why she had been able to get herself the job at IMG. And when he had told her his plans for his weekend in Cornwall, she hadn't even minded that. But his wife taking him up on the mocking invitation that he had clearly offered her every time he went to Josh's boat had brought him out in his true colours, and she had minded that.

First, he had used her to humiliate Elizabeth, then, upon Elizabeth's unexpected departure before the morning session, had bundled her down into Josh's cabin, and stinging slaps had landed on bare skin tender from the sun in a space too confined for her to get out of the way of them. She had been told, when he had finished, that it was for taking too much interest in Josh, had been warned that if she came on to him again she would get a great deal worse. Afterwards, she was locked in the cabin so the angry red marks would fade before anyone saw her. He hadn't let her out until the afternoon divers had boarded, and now he was chatting to his wife and mother as though none of that had happened.

"If you want to know, I think he's a shit," she said.

"I couldn't agree more," said Josh.

"So why do you let him use you like he does?"

Josh smiled. "Shouldn't that be my question?"

"I didn't grow up with all of this. A good job, a good salary, and a company car are what I get out of the arrangement. If I don't like it, I can move on, and I might do just that. What do you get out of it?"

"It never hurts to be owed a favour or two by someone who wants to pass his girlfriend off as your girlfriend." He smiled, and moved closer to her. "And we just agreed we didn't want to make a liar of him, didn't we?"

His hand was moving up under her skirt, pushing down her bikini bottoms, and she caught her breath when he touched her. She had known it would happen sooner or later; she just hadn't expected it to happen in broad daylight with Paul as a possible onlooker. She glanced over her shoulder at the group on the terrace, just a few thin branches between her and them, and looked back at Josh. All anyone had to do was look in their direction, but somehow the imminent possibility of being seen just made what Josh was doing all the more arousing.

"This is crazy," she said.

"But you want to do it. I know you do."

She could feel her face grow a little hot as her excitement grew, her heart beating faster as she pulled down his zip. And it happened, as it had been going to happen ever since that question had appeared in his eyes, happened in as near silence as they could manage, her swift climax leaving her breathless and exhilarated.

She glanced over at the terrace as they got their breath back and rearranged their clothes; no one had seen; no one had heard. She looked back at Josh. "Why did you do that?" she asked.

"Because it was dangerous," he said, smiling at her. "Why did you let me?"

"Because it was exciting."

Josh nodded. "Shall we join the others?" he said.

SCENE XV—BARTONSHIRE
The following weekend: Saturday, July 19th, 8:15 A.M.
The master bedroom

Paul opened his eyes to see Elizabeth putting on her housecoat. Morning. It always took him a few moments to sort out his thoughts when he had been asleep, but that didn't stop Elizabeth immediately beginning a conversation because his eyelids had parted.

"It's past eight," she said. "I take it there's no diving this weekend?"

He blinked a little, then sat up. "No," he said, rubbing his eyes. He'd spent all week looking forward to the weekend, only to have Josh ring him up last night and tell him he wasn't taking the boat out. He was giving Sandie a weekend diving course, he'd said, and Paul was far from happy about that. He had thought he'd made his feelings clear. Still, perhaps he could turn it to some sort of advantage; it did, after all, reinforce his cover story. "He's doing something with Sandie this weekend."

Elizabeth didn't believe him, of course. "So how long have she and Josh been an item?" she asked.

Paul threw back the duvet, and swung his legs out of bed. "I don't know."

"Well—how long has she worked at IMG?"

Paul sighed. "Two months or so," he said.

Josh would be taking Sandie to the reservoir tomorrow, and he had informed his brother that he would pop over there to check up on her progress. There had better *be* some progress, he thought grimly. No sudden colds in the head or any other excuse. If she'd been doing anything with Josh other than learning sub aqua, she'd be very sorry.

"And how long was it before you offered her the job?"

"I can't remember." He got off the bed and went into the bathroom, closing and locking the door.

SCENE XVI—BARTONSHIRE
Saturday, July 19th, 8:25 A.M.
The en suite bathroom

She was doing this on purpose, the bitch, he thought angrily as he relieved his bladder, and sighed aloud when she knocked at the door. "What?" he said, flushing the lavatory.

"I need some stuff that's in there. Why have you locked the door?"

He pulled back the bolt, and she came in as he stepped into the shower and slid the panel over. He could hear her busily picking things up that she had no need for at all; she just wanted to carry on this conversation because she knew it annoyed him.

"Strange that Angela didn't know about her," she said, raising her voice so he could hear her above the shower.

"Well, Josh doesn't exactly confide in her anymore, you know." That was true. Every now and then he had the luxury of telling the truth. Josh used to be great mates with his stepmother, but not anymore. Of course, it was his bloody mother he had to thank for Josh's monopolization of Sandie; she was determined to throw him at the first woman he looked remotely interested in.

"What happened between Josh and Angela?" Elizabeth asked.

At least he'd got her off the subject of Sandie for the moment. "I really don't know," he said. Also the truth. "It was after father died. Perhaps it was just being forced to move back in with her that caused a problem."

"Josh wouldn't blame her for that."

"No," Paul agreed. Josh hadn't blamed her; indeed, he had seemed relatively happy with the idea at the time. It was a bit later on that it happened, whatever it was. "They must have had a row about something, I suppose," he said. "Though they seemed to be getting on all right last week," he added. Of course they were, with Josh squiring Sandie round like some sort of son of the big house, instead of the ne'er-do-well that he was, and Sandie behaving like every mother's dream daughter instead of the tart that she was.

"She's very keen on Sandie, isn't she?"

Jesus. Between them, his mother and his wife were making his life even more difficult than it had to be. Sandie would never have had the chance to discover that she fancied Josh if it hadn't been for Elizabeth's insistence on going to Cornwall with him, because she would barely have spoken to him. And his mother would have minded her own business; it was Elizabeth's presence that had bothered her, not Sandie's.

Then something occurred to him. The precautions that he'd taken had until now been the sort that any good undercover man would. Assume the enemy knows more than you think he does, and act accordingly. But now, as he thought about it, he began to wonder about that pincer movement that had ended up with Sandie's feet literally under Josh's table. Did Elizabeth *really* have someone watching him? Someone who had already told her about Sandie? And had she gone running to his mother? Had they arranged this between them? Why *had* Elizabeth decided to come with him? Why *had* his mother come down to the boat? She never came to the boat. Damn it, his wife and his mother were conspiring against him, and Paul felt a sweep of sheer, impotent rage as Elizabeth's voice reached him again.

"Are you ever coming out of that shower?"

"For Christ's sake!" he roared. "We've got two fucking showers and a whole other fucking bathroom! What's so fucking great about this one?"

"Do you speak to your employees like that?" she asked archly. "Sandie, for instance?"

Yes, he thought, as he heard the door close. He had not only spoken to Sandie like that, he had given her a good hard slapping while he was at it. What he wouldn't give to do that to Elizabeth. He sighed, because he knew what he wouldn't give. Three-quarters of IMG was what he wouldn't give, and that was what it would cost him.

SCENE XVII—BARTONSHIRE
Saturday, July 19th, 8:45 A.M.
The swimming pool at Little Elmley

Josh led the way through the grounds until they were walking along the green glass wall of the covered swimming pool. "He had it put in so that Paul and I could learn what you're just about to learn," he said, pushing open the door. "Angela wanted somewhere a bit safer than the reservoir."

They walked into the damp warmth that was always present despite the cool marble floor. The three high sandstone walls were inset here and there with thick stained glass, the deep, rich colours glowing with reflections from the water, and the pool itself was lit by the morning sunshine that filtered, tinged with green, through the plate glass of the fourth wall.

"Wow."

Josh smiled. "He never did anything by half," he said.

"You never answered my question," she said.

"Which was what?"

"Why does everyone in this family have money but you?"

"You wouldn't believe me if I told you," he said. "Anyway—the deep end is much deeper than a normal pool, so that you can learn how to do all the things you need to know before you do a sheltered-water dive. It had to be as long as it is so that it wasn't a sheer drop, but it's still got a very steep rake, so you have to watch yourself."

"And that's safer than the reservoir?"

"Oh, I'm sure my father thought a good drowning would make men of us. This was his idea of a compromise. He built it where Angela could keep an eye on us from her study."

"Try me," she said.

Josh frowned. "Try you with what?"

"With whatever it is I wouldn't believe about why they're rich and you're not."

"It's all very embarrassing," he said. "My father made one of those ridiculous wills."

"Ridiculous how?"

"The capital and his seventy-five percent share of the business got put in what he called the Esterbrook Family Trust," he began.

"I thought Paul owned the business."

"Not yet. He's the boss. He can hire and fire. He runs it. But he only gets the controlling interest if he stays married to Elizabeth for at least twenty-five years, does not choose to live apart from her, and isn't divorced by her for adultery or cruelty." He grinned. "He can control his temper but not his urges. Hence his complex weekend arrangements, because if she can prove his adultery in court, sixty percent of IMG goes to the Esterbrook Marine Research Fund, and the other fifteen percent goes to Elizabeth. None of it goes to Paul."

"And what about you?"

"I'm not allowed anywhere near the business. Nor any member of my family, should I ever have one. My father thought I had tainted blood or something."

"Tainted with what?"

"Madness," he said with a leer. "He had a very Victorian outlook on everything. My mother wasn't exactly—" He didn't go on with what he was going to say, but gave a short sigh and changed the subject. "Did you get a proper swimming costume like I told you to?"

"Yes, sir."

She removed her blouse and skirt and revealed an eminently sensible swimming costume, and he watched as she let herself into the pool's warm depths, walking down a little way, finding out for herself just how steep an incline the pool had. She regained her composure, and swam to and fro across the pool until he told her to come out. She was a good, strong swimmer, so there was no problem there.

"So your half brother's rich because he's the chairman of IMG," she said as she climbed out of the pool. "What about your stepmother?"

"My stepmother got left the income from the capital, and the right to apply to the Trust for anything she requires over and above her income, providing the Trust regard the request as reasonable. That's how come she bought *Lazy Sunday*. The Trust decided it was reasonable, as long as it was registered to her."

"I take it that your stepmother's reasonable too, or she wouldn't have got it for you."

"Oh, yes. My stepmother's life is a monument to reason. Unlike my mother's, apparently."

"Do you remember much about your mother?"

"Yes." Josh blinked away the tears that still, after over thirty years, would threaten when he spoke of her. "I remember someone who was great fun to be with sometimes and difficult other times." He shrugged. "My father said it was much worse than that. And he believed I take after her." He smiled. "I probably do."

"Did he cut you out of the will altogether?"

"Not quite. I'm on probation, like Paul, but for a lot less, for a lot longer, and with considerably more restrictions." He motioned to the bag that she had brought with her. "Let's see what you bought," he said.

She opened the bag to reveal shocking pink fins, mask, and snorkel. "Don't blame me," she said when he grinned. "It was either that or lime green."

Josh watched as she put on the wet suit, which flattened her breasts and made her look more like a cat than ever. A pink and blue cat.

She looked at him in his traditional black, and shrugged. "This was the nearest I could get to good taste," she said. "What restrictions?"

Josh smiled at her persistence, and rewarded it with the information she wanted. "The judge had recommended fifteen years before parole for my partner in crime, so my father said he was giving me fifteen years to serve on top of my sentence, to reflect the enormity of my deed, which the court had failed to do."

She frowned. "What did he mean?"

"Fifteen years after the date of his death, I'll get what it pleased him to call the family home, but only if I live in the aforesaid family home at the time, and have lived there continuously since the date of his death. If I'm away from the family home for anything other than what he called 'normal breaks of reasonable length and frequency,' or if I indulge in inappropriate behaviour while I'm there, I forfeit any claim on the estate."

He knew the wording by heart. He had pored over that will, trying to find a loophole, but his father had left none.

"I take it indulging in a quick knee-trembler in broad daylight where your stepmother could have seen you is inappropriate behaviour?"

"Highly."

She nodded slowly. "But you only did that *because* of the inappropriate behaviour clause," she said. "Why did he have it in the will in the first place?"

Josh smiled. It had been a long time since anyone had truly understood him and his motives for doing anything. His mother had. "My stepmother has the right of abode until my sentence is up, and the inappropriate behaviour clause was put in so that I couldn't make her life a misery and force her out, either deliberately or because of my inherited madness. My father thought of everything."

"Is she here now?"

"No—she went to Penhallin yesterday, as usual, which surprised me a little."

She smiled at him. "So you can behave as inappropriately as you like?"

"You're here to work," he said. "One day in here, and one day at the reservoir, and I can have you ready for your first open-water dive."

She looked a little sceptical about that. "Two days?" she repeated. "How long did it take you and Paul to learn?"

"We learned very gradually, but this way is perfectly possible. You'll need to get in a lot of practice after that before you can call yourself a novice, even, but you'll have all the basics so you'll be able to practise to your heart's content if you join the diving club." He already felt sure that she would be doing just that.

"When did your father die?"

"Three years ago. I'll be off the leash when I'm forty-eight, if I make it to forty-eight without any mishaps. He didn't cut me out altogether because that might have made contesting it worthwhile. As it stands, I inherit all this, in theory, so contesting it would be a gamble, and I've no money to gamble with. The barrister thought it was possible that the court would simply say that it was up to me to choose whether or not to live at the family home in order to acquire the title to it in due course."

"What did your stepmother think about his will?"

"She said that she would understand entirely if Paul and I did contest it, but that we had to understand that she couldn't support us, because as far as she's concerned, my father's wishes are paramount. Paul wasn't prepared to go ahead, so I'd have been on my own." He smiled. "And that means I'm stuck with it. And stepmother."

"Is it worth being in prison all over again?"

He looked at her for a moment before he answered. "Could be," he said thoughtfully. Now that Sandie had arrived, it really could be. "And it's no hardship sharing a house this size." He stood up. "OK, time to try out your technique. Do you remember what I told you?"

"I think so."

He watched her as she finned her way round the middle of the pool, eventually getting confident enough to move up to the deep end. It was clearly not coming naturally to her, but sooner than he had imagined she would be, she was finning along under the surface of the water, breathing easily through the snorkel. She swam to the steps, cleared the snorkel, and he helped her out.

"Do you think you can jump in at the deep end?" he asked when she had had what he considered a long enough rest, though she was of a different opinion.

She smiled. "I always do," she said.

He fastened the weight belt round her waist. "That's to help you descend," he said. "Your lungs and your wet suit will give you the buoyancy to get back up again. Stand on the edge of the pool."

She didn't like this much, he could tell. She stood on the edge, already holding her breath.

"Don't do that," he said. "Breathe normally just now. Once you're kitted up, hold the mask so you don't lose it when you go in, and don't look down. Keep your legs straight. You'll come back up of your own accord, but if you slowly move your fins backward and forward it'll help you rise."

She looked at him, her eyes wide.

"Don't look so scared," he said. "Put on your mask, take a deep breath through your snorkel, and a big step out."

He watched her descend and then start doing everything he'd told her not to do. She panicked; he jumped in and helped her to the surface, where she pulled off the mask and snorkel, letting them go, and gulped air. Then she swam to the steps, sitting on them, her chest heaving. Josh laughed; she pulled off the fins and threw them at him, first one and then the other, with deadly aim.

He grinned, took a breath, duck-dived back down, and retrieved her various pieces of equipment, but he didn't come back up; he finned under the water, doing as little as possible so that he could stay there as long as possible. When he felt that he really couldn't stay under any longer, he surfaced, and swam over to her.

She sat on the steps, still breathing heavily. "How can you *do* that?" she asked. "It was only because I could see you moving about that I knew you hadn't drowned."

"Practice," he said as his breath returned to normal. "I've been doing it since I was a kid." He gave her back the mask and snorkel. "Before today's out, I'll have you jumping in wearing full diving kit, taking it all off, leaving it on the bottom, surfacing, then going back down and putting it all on again."

She looked appalled, but sheer determination, or pride, or a bit of both, made her get kitted up again, and jump in again. This time she didn't panic, and she surfaced like a veteran. She swam over and sat on the steps. "What happens if you don't make it to forty-eight without contravening the conditions?" she asked when she could speak.

"Paul would get Little Elmley automatically."

"So if he'd seen you and me last Sunday . . ."

"Suddenly, our father's wishes would have been paramount to him too. He'd have had me in court by Monday morning. Not because he has any desire to own Little Elmley, of course. Just because."

She nodded again, her eyes thoughtful. "What happens if your stepmother dies before your time's up?"

He could see the way her mind was working. Exactly as his had when he had heard that will being read, which of course it had been, at the request of the testator, with full Victorian solemnity, to all interested parties. "Paul would get the capital from the Trust on her death anyway, and if she died before I'd completed my sentence, he would get Little Elmley too. And to anticipate your next question, if Paul's already dead, or has disqualified himself from inheriting, anything remaining in the Esterbrook Family Trust would go to the Esterbrook Marine Research Fund automatically on her death. Including Little Elmley."

Sandie frowned. "Why? If your father was prepared to let you have it after fifteen years, why not let you have it if they both die before then?"

"Because he didn't want to give me an incentive for murder, since I am, after all, given to killing people. I told you he'd thought of everything."

"What if Paul dies before he gets to his silver wedding?"

Josh grinned. "You won't catch my father out that way," he said. "The seventy-five percent share in IMG would go to Angela, and if she has predeceased him, it forms part of Paul's estate."

Sandie got to her feet, giving up trying to find loopholes. "What's next?" she said.

He smiled. He doubted very much that she was enjoying any of this, or that she really wanted to do it at all. But she was going to do it, come hell or, appropriately enough, high water. He picked up the aqualung. "This," he said.

SCENE XVIII—CORNWALL
Saturday, July 19th, 11:00 A.M.
Angela's cottage

Angela was supposed to be working; she was sorting through her diaries, marking entries, but she couldn't settle into it; her boys were giving her trouble, as they always had, each in their different ways. She was sitting at her desk, and swivelled round to look out of the open sitting room window, from which she still had a view of the sea.

The cottage was built on the widest part of a slender point of land,

and once she had been able to see the sea both front and back, but the town had been built up since then, and there were buildings between the cottage and the harbour. But at the back, the big old tree and its treehouse still had the grey-green backdrop of the sea. It was more blue-green today; she liked it best on its wild black days. Today it just sat there, docile and uncomplaining, the surface barely rippling. Her husband had liked it like that.

She missed Paul dreadfully. Oh, other people thought that he was strange and stiff and born out of his time, but he had opened her eyes to the world, made her believe in herself. He had had a terrible time with Josephine, but he had never once used that as an excuse. Rather the opposite. He had refused to use it, refused to leave her because of the way she was. Refused to let someone else deal with her, and release him from his vow to keep her in sickness and in health.

But it was that unbending attitude that had caused all the problems; if he hadn't been so strict with the boys, perhaps they wouldn't have found ways of rebelling. If he hadn't been so straitlaced, perhaps the rebellion would have been less dramatic. But he had always thought that punishment and the threat of punishment would keep them under control, despite the evidence to the contrary. His will threatened such severe punishment, should either of them transgress, that it was causing correspondingly severe problems, and would continue to cause them for years and years.

She just wanted the boys to do what their father had asked, and collect what was due to them; they wouldn't do that if one of them was having an affair with his personal assistant, and the other was—well . . . behaving in a way not conducive to staying out of trouble, because that boy was not, in the eyes of the law, a consenting adult. But they were grown men, and they knew the stakes as well as she did. She wouldn't interfere.

Well—no more than was necessary.

SCENE XIX—BARTONSHIRE
Saturday, July 19th, 5:00 P.M.
A public park in Barton

Elizabeth had looked in the yellow pages, and had been startled at the vast number of firms at her disposal.

She didn't know if they worked on Saturdays. She supposed by the nature of their job they worked seven days a week, but their offices might not be open on Saturdays. She had written down a few names and addresses and telephone numbers, and then had gone out. She wasn't going to phone from the house, with Paul quite possibly listening in on an extension.

A private detective. She had once thought that no one could stoop lower than to have someone followed, snooped on. But Paul's behaviour with that girl on the boat had hardened her heart. He was deliberately flaunting his infidelity, hoping to humiliate her into leaving him, and releasing him from his straitjacket. She had thought he would be away this weekend too, which is why she had waited until now before looking for someone.

She had got into the car and driven off, but she hadn't really known where she was going. She had thought she would just go to whoever could see her straightaway. If she made an appointment, she might chicken out, let it all drift again, and she didn't want to do that. Not after the way he'd behaved. Not after the way he'd spoken to her this morning. But all that happened was that she had afternoon tea in the café in the park, then sat on a bench and watched the children play.

She would have liked to have children, but Paul had always wanted to wait, in the days when they still had a relationship, of sorts. She still could have a baby, but Paul wanted nothing to do with her, and she certainly wasn't going to get involved with someone else. There was nothing Paul would like better than to be able to divorce *her* for adultery.

She should have gone through with it, she told herself, as the children's shadows grew long and people started packing up the debris of their picnics and whistling for their dogs. She should have gone through with it. She would. On Monday, when their offices were bound to be open. She would go to . . . she held the list in her hand, closed her eyes, and pointed.

Ian R. Foster, Private Enquiry Agent.

SCENE XX—BARTONSHIRE
Saturday, July 19th, 8:00 P.M.
The Little Elmley grounds and reservoir

Sandie had done it. She would never have believed it, never have put one penny on her chances, when she had been sitting on the steps, throwing her fins at Josh for laughing at her. She was here because she wanted to be with Josh, not because she wanted to do this. But she didn't want to let him down, so she had done it. She had learned how to get in and out, how to move about under the water, how to surface, and bit by bit she accomplished what she now knew was called a ditch and retrieve, just as he had promised she would. She had been scared to death, but she had done it. Then he had shown her lifesaving techniques, a reminder, which she hardly needed, that there were a lot of dangers inherent in swimming about in deep water, and now they were leaving the building.

"It isn't dangerous if you know what you're doing," Josh said.

Sandie smiled. She hadn't the faintest idea what she was doing, or why she was doing it, but she was damn sure it *was* dangerous, whatever it was. Josh wasn't doing all this for Paul's sake.

"Are you tired?"

"Yes." She was very, very tired. There was more theory first thing tomorrow, about the bends, and panicking, and nitrogen narcosis, which seemed to be a risk of temporarily losing your marbles on deep dives. She strongly suspected that she had already lost hers, because after all that, her day-long sheltered diving instruction would begin.

"Now I'll show you where you'll be doing that," he said.

She followed him wearily as he led her past the terrace towards the high hedge. She glanced at the weeping willow, but he didn't; he just strode towards a gate, and they were walking along a wooden jetty, down to a landing stage, where a rubber dinghy sat at the edge of the reservoir.

He helped her in, then rowed out a little way and headed round the curve of the banking. He didn't speak; the sturdy little boat took some handling, but he wasn't bothering with the outboard motor. As the boat rounded the shoreline, Sandie could see a structure rising out of the water, close to the sloping shore. Josh let the boat ride the gently rippling water, and she lit her first cigarette of the day.

"When you do a sheltered-water dive, you'll start off from the shore, walking down the slope to the diving platform, getting used to the water pressure as it comes up to and over your chest. Then you'll let yourself down the pole. But Howard will be with you, so don't worry about that."

"Who's Howard? Won't you be diving with me?"

"No. I'll be on the shore. Howard's an experienced diver, so you'll be fine. Later on, you'll learn how to dive from the boat, out in the middle, where it's really deep, and I'll be diving with you then. Howard will look after the boat."

She nodded. "Are there really houses down there?"

"Yes." He looked at her. "But you won't see them this time round." He looked concerned. "Does the idea of going under there scare you?"

"No." No, it didn't scare her, not now that she knew more or less what to expect. But right now she didn't think she ever wanted to immerse herself in water again, especially if she was going to be diving with someone else altogether. Maybe she would feel better in the morning.

A fish jumped with a tiny plop.

"Are you really going to sit it out here until you're nearly fifty?" she asked.

"What do you think?" he said.

"I think you have other plans."

"What plans? I have no option but to serve my sentence, and hope

they both stay in good health." He grinned, and nodded at her cigarette with mock disapproval. "Neither of them smokes, I'm glad to
say, so there's a chance they'll survive."

Sandie flicked ash into the water. "I presume a three-quarter share
of IMG is worth having?"

"It's worth at least half a billion pounds," said Josh.

Sandie's eyebrows rose. She had known they were rich, but she
hadn't realized how rich. "That explains why he's paranoid about
getting caught," she said.

"It doesn't explain why he does it in the first place, though."

Sandie dropped her cigarette end in the water, where it landed
with a hiss, and Josh rowed back, tied the boat up at the landing
stage, and walked ahead of her up to the house.

SCENE XXI—BARTONSHIRE
Saturday, July 19th, 9:00 P.M.
The house at Little Elmley

He cooked this time; she had produced lunch, which had been pretty
good, if she said so herself, but they ate from the freezer now that he
was in charge. And in Angela's kitchen, as they had at lunchtime.
She had yet to see his part of the house, and her reference that
morning to the business under the willow tree had been the only
time it had been mentioned since it had happened. He had felt like
behaving inappropriately, and she had afforded him the opportunity,
that was all. It hadn't meant anything. That disappointed her, but it
didn't surprise her.

But the business about the will surprised her; it seemed to suggest
that the brothers were more alike than she had thought. Paul would
sit it out until he got his share of the business, using elaborate subterfuge to avoid being caught breaking the terms of the will, but
Josh? She couldn't really believe in Josh's quiet acceptance of his lot,
his preparedness to live for the next twelve years with his stepmother
in order to inherit Little Elmley. It didn't sit well with the reckless-

ness of a fatal armed robbery, with the ownership of a revolver, with the deliberately inappropriate behaviour of last Sunday.

After dinner she lit her second cigarette of the day, picked up her coffee and looked at him. "Why do you hate your stepmother?" she asked.

"I don't," he said. "I get on very well with Angela. A lot better than her son does, whatever impression he likes to give."

Sandie took the tiny opening she was being offered. "Why doesn't *he* get on with her?"

"He's never really got over being uprooted at the age of six. Taken away from his friends, his school, the sea—and brought to live with a man who thought that sparing the rod spoiled the child."

"Literally?"

"To start with it was smacked legs, or a slipper, if you'd been naughty enough to deserve it. Then a cane, when he deemed us old enough. About eleven, I think."

"What did your stepmother think of that?"

"She didn't believe in corporal punishment. But I told you—his word was law, so the cane stayed. Don't misunderstand—it was never excessive, or ritualistic. He just came looking for you, grabbed your collar, whacked you a few times, and then told you why." He grinned. "Well, I came in for a bit more than a few whacks at times—you can tell how successful his method was, can't you?"

"Didn't you resent it too?"

"I was used to it. Practically every time I saw him he had some implement in his hand to beat me with. And when we got too old for that, it was stopped allowances, but by that time, unlike me, Paul was doing well at school, taking his advice about an army career, and becoming the apple of his eye."

She could detect a note of jealousy, still.

"Paul's problems started at some party they were having here. Paul Senior thought Paul Junior had run out on the guests, went up to his room to remonstrate with him, and found him rogering their friends' seventeen-year-old daughter senseless, and so engrossed in the task that he didn't even know he had been seen."

She could believe that. "Was that Elizabeth?"

He nodded. "Threats were issued about cutting him out of the will if he didn't make an honest woman of her, which he duly did. Then he got involved in a scandal, and escaped being cashiered or whatever it is only because Daddy had a word with the right person and the whole thing got hushed up. But Paul had to resign his commission and come to work under him at IMG, and he was told if he ever dishonoured his marriage vows again, and Paul Senior got to hear about it, he'd inherit nothing. And Paul Junior thinks he should never have been married in the first place, so he resents Elizabeth like hell for that, and she doesn't even know why."

She frowned. "But you do," she said. "Does Paul tell you everything?"

"Yep. Always has. I'm never sure if he's boasting or confessing. He's told me all about you."

She raised her eyebrows.

" 'What's twocking?' " he said, mimicking her, his eyes widely innocent.

She smiled.

His face became serious then. "He didn't tell me what he did to you last Sunday, but I heard what was going on. And I heard his threat."

Sandie reflected on that. If Josh knew about that, then he had been putting her in jeopardy quite deliberately with that virtually public quickie; he had engineered it, planned it, meant her to be running a risk. She had passed some sort of test under that willow tree. But he had evened up the stakes by putting his future on the line along with her physical well-being, and that was more like the man she thought he was. Paul had too healthy a regard for his own skin to take totally unnecessary risks; Josh didn't give a toss about his own skin, but he didn't give a toss about anyone else's either.

Josh was dangerous. She liked that.

"Anyway—after going into the army because Daddy wanted him to, and marrying Elizabeth for fear of losing out, then working at IMG, which was the last thing he wanted to do, he finds when the will is read that he *still* has to wait for his inheritance, and Mummy *still* won't make the nasty man stop smacking his legs. So he resents her like hell too."

"But why do you hate her?"

"I don't," he said again, and stood up. "You should go home now. Get a good night's sleep, and be here at eight o'clock tomorrow morning."

He walked with her to the front door; she stopped and turned on her way out. "Is Paul paying you for this?"

"No."

"Then why give up a weekend on the boat?"

He smiled. "Because you're not the only one receiving tuition. I'm teaching my half brother a lesson too."

"How?"

"By depriving him of your services."

Oh. This time the disappointment *was* a surprise, and an unpleasant one. He was using her to get back at Paul for something, just as Paul had used her to get at Elizabeth. Perhaps her assessment of the two brothers had been right after all.

"You needn't have gone to all this trouble and expense," she said. "I'm going to deprive him of my services myself."

"Don't do that," he said. "How can I deprive him of services you're not offering?"

She gasped. "So I'm to be available to him unless it suits you that I'm not?"

"Something like that."

He could at least tell her what Paul had done to him that she was being used in this way. "What are you teaching him a lesson for?" she asked.

"What he did to you."

She stared at him, blinked a little, then smiled. "Do you care what he does to me?"

"Yes," he said.

She left then, though she really didn't want to. Not that she felt she was likely to do anything other than fall into bed and go to sleep, but she would rather have done that with Josh than without him.

She felt a little giddy; one moment she had come to terms with the fact that she meant nothing to Josh, that last Sunday had just been a bit of bravado, and the next he was telling her that what Paul had done mattered to him. She didn't know how he felt, and she wanted to know; she needed to know.

Because whatever was going on in his head, whether or not she mattered to him, Josh mattered to her. He mattered more than anyone she had ever met.

SCENE XXII—BARTONSHIRE
The following day: Sunday, July 20th, 10:15 A.M.
The reservoir

Paul pulled up at the reservoir and watched, shading his eyes from the bright sunshine, as the two divers who were about to go in went through their predive checks, slowly and carefully. Through the open windows of the car he could hear the birds sing, feel the slight, warm breeze that made the day perfect. He should be in Cornwall, not sitting here, he thought, his anger not one whit abated by the fact that one of the divers was indeed Sandie, who stood at the water's edge and leant on her codiver as she put on a pair of bright pink fins.

He waited until they had reached the pole at the far end of the platform and had signaled their intention to descend, before he got out of the car and, his feet crunching on the pebbled banking, walked to where Josh stood. In the quiet of a Sunday morning in Little Elmley, Josh must have heard him coming, but he didn't acknowledge the fact. He continued to watch the water; the ripples set up by the divers caught the light, making the reservoir look like an impressionist painting.

"So what's all this about?" Paul asked.

"Giving Sandie basic diving instruction."

"And she's going on some urgent mission, is she, that she has to do a crash course?"

Josh shook his head. "I don't think she'll be quite ready for putting bombs under bridges," he said. "But she'll be ready for an open-water dive, so no one watching the activities on board *Lazy Sunday* will ever suspect that last Saturday was the first time she'd even seen an aqualung." He looked over at him for the first time. "That was the idea, wasn't it?"

"I didn't mean you to instruct her on my fucking time!"

Josh raised an eyebrow. "An appropriate choice of words," he said.

"You know what I mean! You could have picked any two days. Why the weekend?"

"I hoped to teach you some manners," said Josh. "I heard what was going on last Sunday."

Paul hadn't the faintest idea what he was talking about. "Going on where?" he asked. "When?"

"On my boat. I don't appreciate my guests being assaulted."

Paul's eyes widened. "It's none of your business what I do with her," he said.

"Then don't make it my business. Stay off my boat." He walked away from Paul, down to the shoreline, as the divers surfaced.

Paul went after him, slithering over the pebbles on the steep banking. "Since when have you given a fuck what I do to women?" he asked.

"I don't. But don't do it on my boat, or you can forget your so-called diving weekends in Cornwall."

He meant it. Paul could see his carefully planned and organized weekends slipping away, and he knew when he was beaten. He just didn't know why he was being given the fight in the first place. But he could guess. "All right," he said. "All right. But you keep your hands off her too."

"I don't hit women."

"You know what I mean."

"I'm not interested, Paul. I couldn't afford the going rate, anyway."

"She's interested in you, though."

"You still don't get it, do you?" Josh stepped closer to him and lowered his voice." You told Elizabeth she was my girlfriend. So she was playing my girlfriend—what else did you expect her to do?"

Paul hadn't thought of that. And he certainly hadn't given Sandie a chance to explain. "You mean all that was an act?" he said.

Josh jerked his thumb in her direction. "Look at her. She hates this. But she's doing it, because she doesn't want to lose her job. She's not interested in anything but her good job and her company car, and I can't offer that. Why would she be interested in me?"

Paul watched her as she moved with difficulty through the shallows, then looked back at Josh. "She was pretty bloody convincing," he muttered.

"Today she's a pretty convincing diver—but yesterday she was panicking in the swimming pool. And she was working just as hard last week. You'd have been in a bit of a hole if she *hadn't* been convincing."

He would, but he still didn't see what all the fuss was about. "It was only a bit of a slap," he said. "What's she been telling you?"

"Nothing. I told you—I heard what was happening. And you can do what you like to her anywhere else, but on my boat you mind your manners. And you don't *ever* use me as an excuse again. All right?"

"Fine." Paul turned to go.

"I think you should apologize."

"What?" Paul almost laughed.

"She's talking about walking out on you. I'm trying to save your bacon here, big brother."

"Why?"

Josh smiled. "Because that way you'll owe me."

Paul nodded. That was what this was all about. He didn't like owing Josh anything, but Sandie was an asset that he didn't want to lose, as Josh well knew. She was even an asset in the office, which had come as a pleasant surprise. If she really was talking about leaving, he probably ought to do something.

She was clear of the water, and removing the heavy aqualung, taking off the mask, shaking the water from her short hair like a wet puppy as she walked towards them.

"Howard?" Josh said. "Can you nip up to the club and get a log-book for Sandie? I forgot to bring one."

Howard complied, and Paul smiled at Sandie apologetically. "Look, Sandie," he said. "I'm really sorry about what happened. I couldn't say anything at work, obviously, but I wanted to. I was angry with Elizabeth—I had no right taking it out on you." There. He'd apologized to her. But he'd better try to make amends, he thought. "I want to make up for it," he said. "Buy you a present. What do you want? Jewellery? Perfume? Clothes? Anything—you name it."

"Real shooting lessons," she said.

Paul had seen the way she had looked at the revolver, handled it. He'd seen men like that in the army, and he didn't trust them. Besides, he'd already had to teach Josh how to use the bloody thing in return for making use of his boat, and he hadn't wanted to do that. For all he knew, Josh would use it to kill someone, and not by accident this time. "It's not my gun," he said, looking at Josh, willing him to veto the idea.

Josh smiled. "I've no objection."

Paul sighed. If she got a gleam in her eye just looking at a gun, she was going to get even more excited about using it. But, he reasoned with himself, it was a gun to which she had regular access, and his golden rule was that it was better that she knew how to use it than she didn't. "All right," he said as Howard came back.

Paul walked back to the car a little less at odds with the world. But now he had to go home to Elizabeth, and that wasn't something he was looking forward to.

"This," he heard Howard saying, "is your logbook. You log every dive you . . ."

Sandie was all right, Paul thought. She hadn't made a scene or anything, which was what he had been dreading, with that Howard person hanging round. He turned back and looked at her, a garish splash of colour beside the two traditionalists, smiled, and decided to stay a while and watch her progress. Anything to delay going home.

SCENE XXIII—CORNWALL
Sunday, July 20th, 11:10 A.M.
Angela's cottage

Angela switched off the cassette player as the phone rang, and sighed. She didn't feel it was right to be incommunicado here, so she had to keep the bell on, unlike in her study at Little Elmley. She went out into the hallway and picked it up resignedly.

It was Elizabeth, wanting to know where Josh and Sandie were so that she could invite them to dinner. And her too, of course. As a thank-you for dinner last week. Elizabeth knew she didn't like being interrupted while she was working, but she'd only just thought of it, really, and she would so like them to come to dinner.

Angela accepted the invitation, but told Elizabeth that she was unable to help as to Josh and Sandie's whereabouts. She didn't want Elizabeth to know that they were just at Little Elmley; she had left them so that they could spend the weekend together without her presence inhibiting them, because even in a house that size, new relationships blossomed best without a third party hovering in the wings. And she wasn't about to let anyone else interrupt them either.

And for someone who hadn't wanted to interrupt *her*, Elizabeth had an awful lot to say about nothing. She sounded a little hyper to Angela; or tipsy, even, but it seemed a little early in the day to be drinking. Thankfully, Paul eventually returned from wherever he had been, and this apparently meant that Elizabeth had to hang up, for which Angela could only be grateful. She looked at her watch, and then checked the time of the phone call. Elizabeth had been on the phone for forty-two minutes.

But she hadn't wanted to interrupt her while she was working.

SCENE XXIV—BARTONSHIRE
Sunday, July 20th, 12:05 P.M.
Paul and Elizabeth's house

"Angela's coming to dinner," Elizabeth said.

Paul didn't reply; he just went to the sideboard and poured himself a whisky, then sank down in an armchair with the Sunday paper and began sorting through all the various sections and magazines, looking for the one he wanted.

"Where were you?" She helped herself to another gin and tonic. She had had her first just before she finally decided to phone Angela, and another one while she was on the phone. Or maybe it was two. She didn't care. All she knew was she had had enough of this fiction about Josh and Sandie, but Angela didn't seem to know anything.

"I just popped down to the diving platform," he said, depositing the unwanted portions on the floor beside him.

"But you didn't have your diving gear."

"I wasn't diving." He folded the paper elaborately, taking great care to align the edges.

"Was she there?" Elizabeth took ice from the bucket, but it had mostly melted.

"Who?"

"Sandie Townsend." It was too hot; the breeze that shifted the curtains slightly just seemed to be pushing more hot air into the room.

He jumped up. "Are you going to stop doing this?"

"Doing what?" asked Elizabeth, all wide-eyed innocence. "Getting ice for my drink?"

"Dragging Sandie Townsend's name into every conversation we have!"

"Why wouldn't you want me to talk about Josh's girlfriend?"

"I'm sorry if she didn't see fit to tell you where she intended spending the weekend, but it must be manifestly clear even to you that she isn't with me!"

"How do I know who's been with you? You've been at Little Elmley." Elizabeth put down her drink as a thought occurred to her. "Is that where they are? Little Elmley?" Of course. It was all clear to her now. "That's what it is, isn't it? They've not gone away at all! They're in Little Elmley. Why else would you go there?"

"To get away from you! But there was no one there. So I went to the club."

"You're a liar, Paul. You were afraid that I would turn up again if you went to Penhallin, so you cancelled the whole weekend, and Josh brought her to you. Did you have to reimburse him for doing that?"

"You're talking nonsense, Elizabeth."

"Have you just been screwing her? You have, haven't you?"

"You—" He raised his hand.

"Oh, go on, Paul! You've been dying to do it for years!"

"One day you'll go too far," he said, getting himself under control, lowering his hand again. "Are you drunk?"

Very probably, thought Elizabeth. She had been pouring herself very large gins, and she had been drinking them very quickly. She was very probably drunk. But she wasn't stupid. It was obvious now what was going on. "Oh, it's very neat," she said. "If she's Josh's girlfriend, that keeps Angela off his back and me off yours!"

"I went down to the diving club," he said, his voice quiet. "They said that there were divers at the platform, so I went to pass the time of day with them. So whatever paranoid fantasy you've dreamed up, forget it."

"Paranoid fantasy? Was watching you get horny showing her how to shoot the revolver a paranoid fantasy?"

"I guided her aim. Nothing more. If you want to read something into it . . ."

She picked up her glass and threw it at him; he ducked, and it hit the wall. She didn't even get the satisfaction of smashing it; it bounced off the wall and rolled back towards her, dribbling gin and tonic on the carpet.

"I suggest you go and lie down if you're supposed to be cooking dinner for my mother this evening."

Oh, yes. It wouldn't do to mess up Mummy's dinner. As long as Mummy was happy, nothing else mattered, because Mummy could turn just as nasty as her son if she was crossed. That was where he got his temper from.

Elizabeth stooped and picked up the glass, putting it down on the sideboard again. She took Paul's advice, however, and went up to the bedroom and lay down. The room did seem to be swaying slightly.

They were bastards. All of them. They were all in it together. Josh, Paul, and his bloody mother. She wasn't being deceived at all; she was in on it—she must be if they were at Little Elmley. They were all covering up for Paul in case she got her hands on fifteen percent of their precious family business. They thought if they covered up for him for long enough, then she would just go away and stop being a nuisance, but they were wrong. They were wrong.

She fell asleep then, and woke to a refreshing breeze stirring the curtains as the sun, low in the sky, cast moving shadows on the wall. She had a bit of a headache, but she was all right to make dinner for Paul's mother, so that made everything just fine.

SCENE XXV—BARTONSHIRE
Sunday, July 20th, 8:15 P.M.
Little Elmley

The evening was as warm as the afternoon had been, but after her final dive of the day, her first proper long one, Sandie felt cold. Water lapped gently round the boat as Josh took it into the platform and tied it up, and they walked the short distance to the dive centre to shower and change, calling goodbye to Howard as they left to go back to the boat. Josh headed it off, this time using the outboard motor, back round the curve of the banking, and at last it was chugging towards the landing stage.

They passed the willow tree again, and the sun, low in the sky now, but still warm, lent everything a rosy, romantic hue that Sandie felt was probably unwarranted. Dangerous and exciting it might have been, but there had been nothing romantic about the interlude under the willow tree, and Josh still didn't so much as glance at it as he struck off down a path that she hadn't even seen before.

"Why did you put yourself through the last two days?" he asked.

"It seemed important to you," she said as she followed him round the outside of the house. The sun was dipping below the horizon, and Venus became visible. It *was* romantic, but Josh didn't seem to notice. "How did you get Paul to apologize?"

"It's easy when you know how. Why shooting lessons?"

Because on the boat she had felt powerful with that gun in her hand, and then Paul had wrapped himself round her and made her feel used. He'd taken the power from her, just by taking control of the gun in her hands, and she hadn't been able to stop him. "I want to feel like God," she said.

He smiled. "This part houses my apartment," he said, unlocking the door, letting her in. "I told you that sharing the house is no hardship. Even the ever-vigilant Angela can't see me come and go."

"There you go again. Little digs at your stepmother. All the time." She sat at the kitchen table as he busied himself browning mince and putting the kettle on, and opening a jar of bolognese sauce. "Why do you hate her?"

"Angela and I get on really well. Ask anyone."

"You hate her. And I'm not anyone." Her eyes met his. "Am I?"

Josh looked at her for a long time, then shook his head slowly. "No," he said. "You're not." He turned back to the cooker. "When my mother died," he said, "I cried for days. My father told me to grow up. A little while after that he introduced me to Angela, who was going to marry him, he said. She said she was going to be my new mummy. She had a little boy of her own, so I would have someone to play with. And he was called Paul, just like Daddy. I liked that. He was six, but I could tell him what to do, and he just did it. I liked that too."

Things hadn't changed, thought Sandie. "And you got him into trouble," she said to his back.

"Frequently."

"And he got punished, and resented your father more and more. Is that what you wanted?"

He stopped what he was doing, turned. "Maybe. Don't psychoanalyze me. Just let me tell you, if you really want to know."

"Sorry."

He filled a pot with the boiling water, and went into a cupboard for the spaghetti. "I didn't think much of the haste," he said. "But I liked Angela. I even called her 'Mummy,' like she wanted me to. She wasn't fun like my mother, but she was kind, and life was a lot more tranquil. She gave great birthday parties, and Christmas was like Disneyland. I even stopped being just as much of a handful."

"You?" said Sandie. "A handful?"

He turned and smiled. "From the beginning, people remarked on the likeness between Paul and me, but I thought nothing of it." He resumed his unnecessary attentions to the food. "Then my father adopted him, and he changed his named to Esterbrook, so people stopped remarking on it so much, since they thought we were brothers anyway. But then one day when I was about twelve, and Paul was thirteen, and we were pretty much the same height and build, someone mistook us for twins. And that was when I finally began putting two and two together." He looked over his shoulder at her. "Quick, or what?"

"Quicker than Paul."

"Everyone's quicker than Paul."

True, thought Sandie.

"He confirmed that Paul was indeed my half brother, and said that he had wanted to wait until I was old enough to understand. That my mother had been a very difficult woman, and he had sought refuge with the ultrareasonable Angela in her little cottage by the sea. She had been a welcome respite from my unpredictable and unreasonable mother, and Paul had been a mistake. Why, I wanted to know, had he called him Paul? If he was a mistake, and I wasn't, why didn't he keep his name for me? He said that they had thought that my mother couldn't have babies, but they had been wrong, because I had come along when they had been married for ten years, and less than a year after Paul. He even told me how relieved he was that she hadn't wanted to call me Paul too."

Sandie broke the long silence that followed. "Why does that mean that you hate Angela?"

"Oh, it doesn't. I didn't hate Angela. But I had been kept in the dark for years about what had really happened, about who Paul was. My father, upright guardian of my morals, who took a cane to me if I told a lie, had lied to me, and nothing was the same."

"How did Paul take it?"

"That was the funny thing. He felt better about everything because Paul Senior really was his father. What he'd resented was being disciplined and ordered about by someone that he thought was an interloper, and his really being his father made it all right, apparently. They began to get on pretty well then." He finally left his meal to cook itself, and sat down with her. "And—no psychoanalysis please— that was when I began to get into real trouble."

"I'm not surprised."

"No, well. Maybe I'd have got into trouble anyway. I was always a bit wild. But the things I did got worse and worse. And when I came out of prison, I felt guilty about putting my father and Angela through all that. I tried—I really tried to settle down, to make amends, I suppose. And the ever-reasonable Angela welcomed me back with open arms, unlike my father."

"But he did let you come back."

"I think my reasonable stepmother reasoned with him. But I married as soon as I could to get away from him." He got up and stirred his bolognese, then sat down again and looked at her. "Then he died, and even from the grave he managed to put the kibosh on my life. The will was read to the assembled company, Cheryl found out about the robbery, and she felt like I had when I'd found out about Angela. She had been kept in the dark, and she didn't like it. Besides, we were going to have to move into the family home, and she didn't want to do that either. So she took her sizeable and unconditional lump sum and left."

"How long had you been married?"

"Nearly six years. I was quite glad to move back in with Angela. I didn't want to be entirely on my own, and neither did she. She was devastated by my father's death, so she needed someone round. Eventually she asked me to sort through his private things, because she hadn't the heart to do it. That's when I found a whole bundle of letters from Angela to him."

"And read them."

"Of course. They began when Paul was about three years old, and went on for a couple of years, one every two months or so, addressed to him at work. She would always ask when he was going to tell my mother about her and Paul. Then suddenly she began bombarding him with letters, putting him under real pressure—said if he didn't tell her, she would, all that. And she did. Turned up here out of the blue, with Paul, when my father was at work, told my mother who she was, who Paul was. Then she wrote and told my father what she had done. My mother died three days later."

Sandie frowned. "How did she die?" she asked.

"She took an overdose. But then, she wasn't reasonable, was she? Not like Angela." He stood up and got knives and forks, then served the meal.

They ate the spaghetti bolognese in near silence, partly because they were both so hungry after their long, strenuous day, and partly because Sandie was sure that Josh had more to say, and she didn't want to sidetrack him. When they'd finished, he made coffee, and they went into the sitting room.

"You're right," he said, as he sat down. "I did get Paul into trouble deliberately when we were kids. But he eventually realized that I got into even more trouble, and he could always shift the blame for anything he really had done. No one ever questioned it. He got away with murder, and I was the one whose collar kept getting grabbed. Of course I resented it."

Sandie still didn't speak.

"Then we were sent away to school. Paul became a prefect, and I was expelled, sent to a local comprehensive, got suspended from it. Paul went to Sandhurst, and I went to a young offenders' institution. My father had to choose between Paul's passing-out parade and my court appearance for sentence on the manslaughter charge. He went to the passing-out parade. But Angela came to court, and I loved her for that, I really did. She had missed her own son's passing-out parade for me, and I'd never been anything but trouble to her."

"That was why you tried to make up for it when you came out?"

He nodded. "But then I read those letters, and I found that it was just a guilty conscience that had made her do that. That had made her persuade my father to take me back in when I got out of prison. Because none of it would have happened if it hadn't been for her."

He stood up and opened a cupboard, bringing out two glasses and a bottle of brandy, and spoke to her reflection in the mirror.

"She killed my mother. She knew she wasn't stable. My father had said she wouldn't be able to take it if *he* told her, never mind hearing it from Angela. She knew what it would do to her, finding out like that. She killed my mother, and then she came here and took her place, bringing her bastard son with her, and he'd even stolen my name. And, yes, your psychoanalysis is right, because then he stole my father." He turned to face her. "And I'm damned if I'm going to let them steal any more that's rightfully mine."

"But what can you do?"

"I've been trying to get Paul so deeply in hock to me that he wouldn't dare take me to court whatever I did," he said.

"But you can't do that with Angela, can you?"

"No. All I can do with Angela is amuse myself by seeing how far I can go, and keep her alive." He poured two large brandies, and pushed one across the coffee table towards her, then lifted his own. "Here's to us," he said.

Sandie lifted her glass. "Is there an us?"

"Oh, yes," he said. "I think so. Don't you?"

"Because of a few minutes' inappropriate behaviour?"

He shook his head. "Our relationship is based on something altogether more dangerous and exciting than sex," he said, and smiled. "Isn't it?"

She smiled back, and stood up, touching her glass with his, and they drank.

"You do have other plans, don't you?" she said as they sat down again.

"I didn't," he said. "I had an idea. A crazy idea. It isn't a plan, not yet. But it will be, if I work on it, and you help me."

"But how can I help?" she asked, puzzled.

"You already have, without even knowing it. Since you came, everything just seems to have begun falling into place. You've been sent to me, Sandie. I know you have."

"Sent?" she repeated uncomprehendingly, and then she smiled, her head nodding. It was true. There had been a bond from the moment they had met; she had been drawn to him in a way that she had never been drawn to anyone. He had become more important to her in a single hour than anyone else in the world, and yes, she could believe that she had been sent to him. "Yes," she said. "Yes, I think I must have been."

Josh took a sip of brandy. "So I want to tell you something," he said, "and then I want to ask you something."

For the first time since she'd met him, Sandie could see that he was nervous, could hear it when he spoke.

He took a deep breath. "It's about Billy the rent-boy," he said.

SCENE XXVI—BARTONSHIRE
Sunday, July 20th, 11:00 P.M.
The house at Little Elmley

They had finished their drinks and he had poured two more in the silence that had followed his question. "Well?" he said, when he felt that he had waited as long as he could.

"It would be dangerous."

"You get off on danger. You know you do."

She nodded. "But do you? Look what happened to you last time. Doesn't that worry you?"

"That won't happen this time. Not with you. That was—" He shrugged "—a mistake. You're the one who thinks I'm wasting my life," he continued. "So I'm going to do something about it, like you said I should."

She frowned. "Did I say that?"

"I can read your mind."

She smiled. "Yes, all right. But this? It's—"

"Crazy," he finished for her. "But you quite like crazy too, don't you?" He leant forward. "And you *want* to do it. I know you do."

She thought for a moment, and then he saw the faint flush of excitement on her cheeks, just as he had under the willow tree when he had spoken those words. He had known she would agree then, and he knew she would agree now. She *had* been sent to help him. From where, he wasn't sure, but he doubted very much that it was from heaven.

"Yes," she said.

He sat back, relaxed for the first time since he had walked into the room, and smiled. "I've got a special licence," he said. "We can get married anytime we like."

And when they did, Sandie would become a fully-paid-up member of his gloriously dysfunctional family.

Act II
The Private Detectives

If circumstances lead me, I will find
Where truth is hid, though it were hid indeed
Within the centre.

Hamlet, Act 2, Scene 2

SCENE I—BARTONSHIRE
Monday, July 21st, 10:30 A.M.
The Copes' house

"Can't you get it through your thick head, woman? We're broke! The building society's threatening repossession!" Andy Cope slapped the letter he held in his hand, and wheeled his chair over to where she sat. "Look, if you don't believe me!"

Kathy Cope, her thin face drawn, her fair hair uncombed, was at the desk on which, still in its box, sat the computer that was causing all the trouble. Her husband, red in the face with frustrated rage, was roaring as though she were at the bottom of the garden. He should be careful, she thought; he could have a heart attack like that. He was the right age, the right build. Middle-aged, running to fat, overfond of fried food and beer, and now that he was confined to a wheelchair, he didn't get the kind of exercise he needed to work it off.

"Read it!" He banged the letter down on the desk. "Then file it away in your nice new filing cabinet! Another sheer extravagance!"

"It's not an extravagance," she said. "It's a necessity."

"A necessity?" he bellowed. "You can keep files anywhere! You've not got above a half dozen! You're not Pinkerton's, woman!"

"You have to make a good impression when someone comes," Kathy said. "It looks more professional."

"Desks, filing cabinets, display ads, a bloody computer—for God's sake! What next? Surveillance equipment?"

She already had some surveillance equipment, if Andy did but know it. She hadn't used it yet, not on a job, but she had put two cameras up in the house to see if Andy noticed, and he hadn't. They were tiny little things; one was in the centre of the kitchen clock, and the other was in the picture frame on the wall in the sitting room.

"We're not making anything like enough money for the sort of things you're buying! I'm supposed to look after the business side! How the hell can I do that if you're going to go out and order bloody computers?"

"It's on monthly payments," she said.

"Monthly payments? Is that supposed to make me feel better? We've got bills coming with every post! We can't afford all this, can't you understand? I'm having to do deals about the gas and electricity, and you're buying bloody computers? Christ, I can carry all your so-called clients' details in my head!"

It wasn't her fault they'd had so few clients. She had had to turn a lot of jobs down because one person couldn't handle them. And she had had an offer from an old friend that would solve their problems, but the ground had to be very carefully prepared if their plan was to work, and watching Andy getting apoplectic was part of the spadework. "It's not just for that," she said. "The Internet can make the job easier—"

"The Inter-bloody-net?" he roared. "Have you signed up for that?" He leant over her, one hand on the desk, the other on the back of her chair, his face thrust close to hers. "Have you? Answer me, woman!"

"Yes. It's not that expensive—you just pay a flat rate, and you can log on. You can find things out without having to trail round offices and things. It'll save us money in the long run."

"Find things out!" His voice was contemptuous. "Find things out? Spy, you mean. Check up on people, sneak on them. I should never have let you do this in the first place. It's—it's . . . demeaning. Degrading. If I wasn't in this bloody thing, you wouldn't be doing any of this!"

"It's not like that anymore."

"Oh, don't kid yourself! All you do is sneak up on people, serving writs, collecting debts, ferreting out where people have gone to try to avoid their creditors." He made a sound, a cross between a laugh and a sob. "You'll be getting asked to trace me any day now!"

"If you'd let me stay on in the job we wouldn't be in this mess," said Kathy. "I'd have been able to retire by now. On a good pension. We would have a cushion for when we didn't have much work on. We could make a go of this if we had some more capital, more staff."

Besides, she hadn't been a detective. Joe had been in CID, and that had given him contacts everywhere, which would be invaluable on its own. And he had already put hard cash in as well. He had supplied all the equipment that was giving Andy high blood pressure. It was bought and paid for, though Andy didn't know that. He'd supplied the other stuff too, and with state-of-the-art equipment, the two of them out in the field, and Andy running the business—maybe even learning how to use the Internet—it could be good for all of them.

But both she and Joe knew that Andy would never agree to it unless something forced his hand; it had been Kathy's idea to make Andy believe that she was spending money they hadn't got, so that when she did summon up the courage to suggest that Joe come in, it might be the fabled offer that Andy couldn't refuse.

"When I get another job, you're finished with this lark, lady, so you won't be needing the Internet or anything else." He reversed the chair, giving her space to get out of the little room. "Now, for God's sake, go and get the kettle on."

She sighed, rose and went past him, down the corridor to the kitchen.

"And you can send that bloody computer back where it came from!"

SCENE II—CORNWALL
Monday, July 21st, 2:45 P.M.
A stone-built thatched cottage in Penhallin, converted to office accommodation

A discreet brass plate informed Penhallin that Arthur Henderson undertook private enquiries.

He checked that he could see his reflection in it, before pushing open the solid oak door of the listed building, and smiled at young Sally, who had been a very good appointment. He'd hesitated just a little, because she had a stud in her nose, but she had come across well at the interview, and she was fitting in very nicely. She it was who took the Brasso to the plate, because the cleaners left smears, and he really didn't like that.

Arthur had had to employ a number of people since retiring to Cornwall and setting up his business. He had worked on the principle that the world would beat a pathway to his door, when he had chosen Penhallin; he could have set up in a larger town, but he was aiming for the sort of clientele who would appreciate the calm of Penhallin, who would be prepared to go a little further in order to fare a great deal better. Not for him a poky office in a busy city street, with passersby to see his clients when they came, and wonder what their business was with him. He went to his clients, if they so desired, and if they came to him, they came to an old-world stone-built house, cunningly and sympathetically adapted to its purpose.

Now, he had two young men and one young woman in his employ as operatives, Sally on reception and switchboard, and a secretary who devised tastefully worded leaflets—he refused to call them mail-shots, as she did—which he sent to people living in the appropriate socioeconomic band within a forty mile radius. And it was startling, even to him, how many people had availed themselves of his services, and for what a variety of reasons.

Not that he ever ventured into the field himself these days. That wouldn't be dignified. No, he trained his operatives well, and they did any sleuthing or observation that had to be done, while he sat back and reaped the benefits of his very pleasant, very lucrative retirement.

SCENE III—BARTONSHIRE
Monday, July 21st, 4:10 P.M.
An office above a row of shops in a once-commercial street in Barton

Ian Foster terminated both the long, involved telephone conversation he had been having, and his only current investigation, wiped beads of perspiration from his moustache, and opened the window wider, but it didn't make much difference. In the corner of the room a chipped and dented fan oscillated jerkily, lifting the papers on his desk when it was pointing that way, but otherwise making no discernible difference to the heat. Oh, to be in air-conditioned offices. As it was, he was three stories up in an old, run-down office block in Barton.

Without much hope, he buzzed through to Debbie on the intercom that he had bought secondhand the day he had moved in to the office, when he had had visions of making it big, rather than scraping a hand-to-mouth living. He couldn't really afford Debbie, but she was the wife—estranged for the moment, but he didn't think that would last—of an old friend, and she didn't mind waiting for her pay when times got bad. It was very nearly going-home time, so she might as well do that as hang about until the arbitrary time he had laid down for ending the day's work.

"Anything doing, sweetheart?" he asked in the Bermondsey accent that he tried to hide from clients.

"Yes," she said, trying to keep the excitement out of her voice. "There's a Mrs. Esterbrook with me. She doesn't have an appointment, but I said you might be able to fit her in if she didn't mind waiting."

He felt like Sam Spade when Debbie opened the door and Mrs. Esterbrook came in. A blonde with a pair of pins that could knock a guy's eyes out at fifty paces. He ought to have one of those glass doors with his name written backwards on it. He got to his feet. "Ian Foster," he said, extending his hand. "At your service."

"Elizabeth Esterbrook," she said.

And an accent that could polish diamonds. You didn't buy vowels like that at no state school. "How can I help?" he asked.

"I think my husband's having an affair," she said. "I expect you've heard that before."

He had. Oh, well. No one was out to get her because of the knowledge she possessed. She didn't need him to trace the whereabouts of a mysterious artefact. She wasn't crossing her legs to reveal black fishnet stockings and red suspenders when her skirt rode up, but she was a good-looking blonde, she was wearing what even he could see was some very expensive schmutter, and she was in his office, giving him a job, however routine and boring. God bless her.

"Right," he said, drawing a lined pad towards him. "And . . . I take it you want me to try to get proof of this?"

"If we can agree terms."

He outlined his rates for the job and gave her a rundown on how the expenses situation operated. A little higher than his usual rate, a little more on the mileage rate. She could afford it. "Still interested?" he asked.

"Yes," she said. "Because if you do get proof of his adultery, I will come into a legacy worth over a hundred million pounds."

His mouth fell open. He had fallen asleep, he thought, the heat getting to him. He would wake up to find Debbie telling him that it was morning and he'd slept in the office all night. He rubbed his eyes, but Mrs. Esterbrook was still there; she hadn't turned into a wood pigeon or a camel or his old maths teacher or anything; he might not be dreaming. But why had she come to him?

He asked her. He had had to ask her. He would like to look as though he didn't roll over for no broad, however classy, no amount of money, however astronomical, but he had to ask her.

"Because I don't have that kind of money now," she said. "I have very little money of my own. I pay for most things with my husband's charge card, but I think he might smell a rat if he had to pay for a private investigator, so I'm having to use my own rather limited reserves. This is going to be a long job—it might take years, for all I know. I want your exclusive services every weekend from May to September inclusive for as long as it takes, and in short, Mr. Foster, you're all I can afford."

He didn't mind her frankness. He *was* Sam Spade, he must be. And it got better.

"If you succeed," she said, "I will pay you a bonus of point one percent of the net amount I receive, if and when I receive it. There would be an expensive and doubtless long court battle, but I would win, if your evidence was good enough."

He found out where and when Mrs. Esterbrook suspected her husband of carrying on this affair. She wanted him to go there, watch him. That would be no hardship, but he frowned. "If he works with the girl," he said, "isn't it more likely to be going on there?"

She shook her head. "He wouldn't dare conduct a liaison on the premises," she said. "I doubt very much if they so much as mention it to one another at work. And taking her to mythical conferences was always risky. He uses these diving weekends. I know he does. You see—he stands to lose five times that amount if he's caught, so he makes very certain that he isn't."

Foster looked down at his pad, at the locations she had given him, the names she had given him, the inflated rate that she had agreed, and wished he'd asked for more. Mrs. Esterbrook's notion of limited reserves differed a little from his.

"It won't be easy," she said. "He runs the whole thing like a military operation. You'll have to catch him off guard, and I'm not convinced he ever is off guard. But as long as you stick to the rate we've agreed, and don't go overboard on expenses, I can afford to have you do it for as long as it takes. Will you take the job?"

He nodded. He wanted to reach into the top drawer of the desk, draw out a bottle and pour two slugs of bourbon to seal the deal. But a quick glance into the open drawer revealed several rubber bands, a stapler that hadn't worked for years, about a dozen ballpoint pens that might or might not work, and a funny little black plastic thing with a sort of spring clip that he had found on the floor and had thought must belong to something, so he hadn't thrown it away.

Oh, well. He looked back down at his pad. "I don't know the area," he said. "And there are a lot of places to check out. It might be an idea if I went down there for a day or two during the week, to get the lie of the land, so to speak."

She didn't react at all, and he explained his reasoning.

"That way, you see, I can perhaps work out what strategy to adopt without running the risk of them seeing me. Knowing the terrain, so to speak, will help." He didn't really think that a freebie with no prospect of evidence-gathering would be acceptable, but it had been worth a try.

"Whatever you think is best, Mr. Foster," she said.

A freebie it was, then.

"And maybe," he added, "I should get a camcorder. If you need incontrovertible proof, it's just possible I could get them on video doing something that would count as evidence."

She nodded. "That seems sensible," she said. "Buy whatever you need. But ask me first."

Sam, you're on a roll. "Leave it to me, Mrs. Esterbrook," he said, standing up, shaking her hand again, opening the door for her. "Just leave it all to me."

That afternoon he purchased a camcorder that fitted into the palm of his hand. That night he packed a bag and booked himself in at the Excalibur in Plymouth, the husband's regular hotel, for a few nights, sucking in his breath at the inflated single supplement, but it wasn't his money, so who cared? And once he'd done a bit of recceing and sleuthing there, it would be time for a drive over the Tamar, time to book into the Egon Ronay recommended luxury guest house favoured by the girlfriend, time to walk the mean streets of Penhallin.

It was a dirty job, but someone had to do it.

SCENE IV—CORNWALL
Tuesday, July 22nd, 10:15 A.M.
Penhallin

The Excalibur was a big, busy hotel, with people coming and going at all hours of the day and night, and the perfect place in which to carry on an affair, but Mrs. Esterbrook's own sleuthing seemed to suggest that this Townsend girl didn't stay in the same hotel as Esterbrook. Of course, he had money coming out of his ears, and it would be more than worth it to book her into some other hotel in order to deal with just such an eventuality as his wife accompanying him. Foster imagined that that was what he had done.

After his full English breakfast, he had driven to Penhallin, and The Point, when he eventually located it, turned out to be where you might expect: right on the seafront, an old house built above the rocky coast. He wouldn't fancy being there in a force ten, but today, with the sea doing a good impersonation of the Mediterranean, and the sun beating down from a cloudless sky, it sat smugly on some of the best views in Cornwall, slightly weather-beaten and ragged, like an old alleycat surveying its domain. The rocks over which it was built formed a channel into which the sea rushed, making froth and spray shower upwards, however calm the day. That sea spray cooled the air, and Foster could have happily wandered round here all day, but he had work to do.

He booked himself into The Point from Friday to Sunday; that way he would already be there when Townsend arrived, an established resident, and therefore not suspicious. Watching where *she* went might be more fruitful than watching Esterbrook himself.

He got back into the car, and looked at the neat map Mrs. Esterbrook had drawn of how to get to her mother-in-law's cottage. It turned out to be not all that far from The Point, as the crow flew, but he had to take the car down narrow, cobbled streets, and then out along a windswept coastal road, at the end of which the cottage stood alone. Not much good for trailing purposes. But he drove round, and worked out that if he drove past the turning for the coast road and parked up in one of the larger streets, he could walk along there, and then go down a jetty to the harbour, on the opposite side of the small spit of land from the cottage. From there he could walk along the shore itself, and if he was right, he would find himself at the rear of the cottage.

He tested his theory, and discovered that not only was he right, but that the cottage had a hedge rather than a fence, and the winter winds had made it simplicity itself to slip into the garden in which there was an old, solid tree complete with a treehouse just about roomy enough to conceal a not very large private eye.

He checked that there was no one in the cottage, and cautiously climbed up the ladder, testing each rung before putting his weight on it. One rung was unsafe, but the others were all right, and he arrived at the top, sitting on a thick branch to assess the soundness of the structure itself. It had been built by a craftsman, that much was obvious; he decided that it was worth the risk, and crawled through into the warm, spidery depths. It was happy to take his weight, and that hideout might be worth knowing about at some time in the future, because he could see right into the bedroom from here.

He took out his camcorder and made a test video, playing with the zoom and the focus and making certain that he knew exactly how to operate it, in case he got lucky. Sometimes he did.

His last port of call, so to speak, was *Lazy Sunday*, which sat in the quiet harbour. He hopped on board over another couple of boats. Apart from the glass-sided wheelhouse, there was nothing much to see, or to record, though once again he used the camcorder; all the doors were padlocked, and there was nothing of interest on deck.

"Did you want something?"

Foster turned to the neighbouring boat to see a man of about fifty, with a short white beard, cream slacks which stretched over an ample stomach, and a blue jacket. It didn't have braid on it, but it clearly wished it had.

"Just wondered if there was somewhere I could hire one of these," he said.

"Not like that one," said the man. "It's not for hire. But you can hire outboards along there." He pointed, his eyes still suspicious. "If that's what you're after."

"Yes," said Foster. "I fancy a spot of sea-fishing."

He did fancy a spot of sea-fishing; he had brought his fishing tackle with him, in the hope of a bit of leisure time, and now he could see that hiring a boat was a legitimate expense. If there were any shenanigans on *Lazy Sunday,* he'd be perfectly placed to see them while he was fishing. See them, and record them.

He made arrangements to hire a motorboat, then headed back to Plymouth for lunch at the Excalibur. The sun glinted on the water, a warm breeze ruffled his hair as he drove with the windows down, and he felt a little sorry for Debbie, back in Barton, battling with the fan.

SCENE V—BARTONSHIRE
Tuesday, July 22nd, 1:45 P.M.
The Copes' house

Kathy had taken on a job. It meant being away for the weekend, but it wasn't until next month, and she had plenty of time to think of how to get round Andy, who wouldn't like her being away from home.

But that wasn't the important part. Mrs. Esterbrook was going to book her into a hotel, and Kathy had said she thought it would be better if she was there as part of a couple, that she thought her husband ought to accompany her. *That* was the important part, because she had no intention of taking Andy with her. It didn't have to happen—she hadn't spoken to Joe yet. It depended on Andy, really, and how he reacted to her proposal. If he agreed, then she would take Joe on as a full business partner and nothing else, and go to Plymouth alone. If not . . . well, the die would be cast.

She dried the last of the cutlery and put it in the drawer. There wasn't going to be a right time to broach the subject, but she'd made him a really good lunch, and after he'd just had an enjoyable meal was a better time than most. She took a beer from the fridge and went through into the other room.

"We would get a lot more work if we had someone else working with us," she said, handing him the can. "Some jobs need two people."

He motioned to the sideboard; Kathy went over and took out a glass. He used to drink beer straight from the can, but these days he used a glass, because she had to get it for him, since opening the cupboard door was difficult when you were in a wheelchair.

"I've had an offer," she said. "From Joe Miller."

He stared at her. "Joe Miller?" he repeated. "Joe *Miller?*"

She smiled. "You're not still jealous?" she said. "It was you I married."

"And it was Joe Miller who kept ringing up and writing to you and hanging round outside for months afterwards."

"I let you read the letters, didn't I?" she said. "And all that's ancient history. He married someone else in the end."

"She left him six months ago. He'd be in there like a bloody shot, given half a chance, and so would you, I shouldn't wonder! I'm not exactly keeping you satisfied in that area anymore, am I?"

He could. The doctor had said. He just wouldn't. She didn't know if she would have ever thought of Joe again if things had been different; she would never know. But she did know that life with Andy became almost intolerable at times, and seeing Joe again had given her some hope for the future. One way or the other. It was up to Andy which way.

"He's a good detective, and he's getting early retirement. He'd be putting his lump sum in—don't you see? It would make all the difference. We might even get enough work to start employing other people to do the dirty work, as you call it."

Andy wheeled himself over to her and roared at her, his face an inch from hers. "When I get a job, this nonsense will stop, so don't start making bloody expansion plans. Do you hear me?"

Everyone in the neighbourhood could hear him, probably. But Andy wasn't going to get a job; he knew that, and so did she. He applied for jobs, even went for the odd interview. But he wasn't going to get one, because he didn't want one, not the kind that people in his position got. No qualifications, no education past the age of sixteen, no computer skills, and disabled. She had thought that if she could get him to agree to the partnership with Joe, then he would find that he was doing something useful at last, and she truly believed that he would become again the man she had married, and not the bitter, defeated man he was now. But she wasn't winning the argument.

"And you can forget your ex-bloody-boyfriend! You must think I'm simple! Am I supposed to sit here and watch you carrying on with him? Is that it?"

Despite what he was saying, he knew she would never do that. He was partially right about Joe's motives, of course, but Joe knew the score. If he came in with them, there would be none of that; Joe knew that, and accepted it. "We'd be working together, not carrying on," she said.

"I know what that bastard's after, and you'd not say no, would you?" His eyes narrowed. "Or has he already had what he's after?" he asked, his voice rising even more. "Is that it? Eh? Is that it? Are you and him at it behind my back?"

No thought Kathy. They weren't. But they would be. Starting with a weekend in Devon.

SCENE VI—CORNWALL
Tuesday, July 22nd, 4:15 P.M.
Henderson's office

Arthur Henderson shook his client's hand as he bade her au revoir at the door of his immaculately renovated fisherman's cottage, and smiled as she walked away down Penhallin High Street.

Nice woman, Mrs. Esterbrook.

Act III
The Plots

Let's further think of this;
Weigh what convenience both of time and means
May fit us to our shape; if this should fail,
And that our drift look through our bad
performance,
'Twere better not assay'd: therefore this project
Should have a back or second, that might hold,
If this should blast in proof.

Hamlet, Act 4, Scene 7

SCENE I—CORNWALL
Four weeks later, Saturday, August 23rd, 12:45 P.M.
Aboard *Lazy Sunday*

Josh waved when he saw Sandie on the harbour. She always arrived first; Paul would drop her off in Plymouth and send her the rest of the way by taxi, because that way, he reasoned, it looked as though she was coming to be with Josh, not him. Josh and Sandie had been working hard to establish a relationship that Paul wouldn't question; Sandie was much better at it than he was, striking exactly the right note of friendly disinterest. She had totally convinced Paul, which was just as well, because over the last five weeks, this hour or so before Paul arrived was the only time they had had alone together, and their being allowed that time was proof that he had no idea at all what was happening.

"It's today," Josh said.

Sandie's eyes widened a little, and Josh saw the flush of excitement with which he had grown familiar. "Is it really going to work?" she asked.

"Of course it'll work." He motioned to the side. "Take a look."

She went to the rail and peered over, then looked back. "We're not going to sink, are we?"

Josh shook his head. "It would be below the waterline with a full complement of divers, but they won't be getting on, so we should be all right."

"When did you do it?"

"After this morning's session. I took her somewhere quiet and secluded and abused her. I hope she forgives me."

"Does this mean you still haven't brought the proper targets?"

"No," said Josh, smiling. "It doesn't. They're in the cabin."

They went down, and he showed her the paper targets with numbered rings that they could pin up on their mattress-stuffed box, so that Sandie could find out how good she really was with the revolver. Then they made love where they were, preferring the clutter of a storeroom to what they thought of as Paul's cabin.

Paul arrived as they were decorously eating lunch on deck.

"Josh has got proper targets," Sandie said when she finished eating. "Can we have our contest?"

"No. I don't approve of contests," said Paul.

Sandie was disappointed, and Josh doubted that she would take no for an answer.

"Are you frightened I'll beat you?"

"Of course you wouldn't beat me," he said. "Which is one reason why a contest would be a waste of time."

"You can give me a shot a round or something, to even things up. You said we'd do it when I got good enough."

A motorboat started up, setting up ripples in the calm water as it manoeuvred itself to where it wanted, and *Lazy Sunday* gently bumped her neighbour.

"In a weak moment," said Paul. "I hoped you'd forgotten. Guns aren't playthings."

Oh, Sandie hadn't forgotten, thought Josh. She had been pestering him for the last two weeks to get real targets; she had taken to shooting much more readily than she had taken to diving. It had suited him to wait until now, that was all, because it was obvious even to Paul when Sandie was excited about some prospect; he would put it down to her desire to show off with the revolver, and wouldn't start getting suspicious. It didn't really matter whether Sandie talked him into it or not now; the reason for her excitement had been established.

"I hadn't forgotten," said Sandie. "And I haven't forgotten why you're teaching me in the first place."

"All right," Paul said reluctantly. "But if we do this, no more lessons. We're quits. All right? I'll give you a range advantage. Let's get on with it."

Josh took the boat out and anchored at the usual spot, further along the coast than any of the other little craft, except one. The motorboat that had been getting itself under way while Paul and Sandie were talking had left not long after they had, and its occupant had anchored some way out to sea, safely away from the rocks.

"Who's that?" Paul asked, tapping him on the shoulder and pointing to the little boat. "Do you know him? How come he's always where we are? Have you got binoculars anywhere?"

"No. He's just a fisherman, Paul."

"I'm sure that bitch has put someone on to me," Paul muttered. "I'm bringing binoculars next time. Get a good look at the bastard."

Josh pointed out that even if someone was watching him, they'd see nothing they shouldn't. Paul made certain of that, but he was still paranoid about it, which suited Josh admirably, because that was what had given him the idea in the first place.

The idea that he and Sandie had honed and polished and perfected over the last few weeks.

SCENE II—BARTONSHIRE
Saturday, August 23rd, 2:00 P.M.
Paul and Elizabeth's house

Elizabeth looked at the clock. Paul would be in Penhallin now, she thought. And her detective would be right behind him. In a hire car, a different one each time, so that Paul wouldn't spot that he was being followed.

The surveillance hadn't, of course, produced anything at all, but she hadn't expected it to. Only an interruption to Paul's routine would be likely to make him drop his guard, and it would have to be an interruption that he could not have foreseen.

Foster had suggested that it might not *be* Sandie that Paul was seeing; it seemed that she really was a diver, contrary to what Elizabeth had believed. But she knew it was Sandie, and if Paul didn't ever drop his guard, she might.

It would take a long time, she supposed. A long time, and a lot of patience. But at least she was doing *something*.

SCENE III—CORNWALL
Saturday, August 23rd, 2:10 P.M.
On board a small motorboat

The red dot told Ian Foster that he was recording the scene on the distant boat. He zoomed in, and he could have been on the boat with them as they got ready for their shooting lesson. They'd got a proper target this time, he noticed. He panned back to Townsend and Esterbrook, but they were, as usual, doing nothing at all suspicious, just standing and talking with Esterbrook's brother.

It looked as though they were having some sort of competition. Whatever sort of gun they were always playing with, it was probably illegal, but Foster had no interest in illegal firearms, and he doubted if Mrs. Esterbrook had. He switched off the camcorder with a little sigh of resignation.

Esterbrook's routine was always the same. He dropped Townsend off in Plymouth, checked into his hotel and had lunch. He just dropped his weekend bag off at the hotel; didn't even go up to the room. He always ate lunch alone. Then he'd drive to Penhallin, and if the sea was calm enough, they'd take the boat out and have some shooting practice. Esterbrook and Townsend always stayed up on deck, and the brother was always there too.

He was never evidently alone with anyone, never mind Townsend. He waited, crafty devil, until the other divers came on board for the afternoon session, and then at some point he would disappear below. But all the divers went below at various times, Townsend included; they stowed their stuff down there. Esterbrook, however, tended not to come up again until the boat was back in harbour for the night.

When the Saturday afternoon session was over, they would all go off to various inns and hotels, except the ones who lived locally, and the brother, who stayed on the boat. Esterbrook never turned up at Townsend's hotel, and she never left it once she had gone there. Mrs. Esterbrook had let him employ another investigator for one weekend only to spend the night at the Excalibur, and no one else had visited Esterbrook at his hotel either.

As far as Foster had been able to work out, there were two possibilities, assuming the man *was* up to something. One, that whoever he was seeing was already in his hotel room by the time he went to it, and had nothing to do with the diving sessions, and two, that it was happening on the boat. Mrs. Esterbrook had shelled out for someone to watch her husband's room at the Excalibur for one weekend, and no one at all had turned up at it but Esterbrook himself, so Foster had told Mrs. Esterbrook that it must be happening on the boat.

He had added that he didn't think it was Sandie Townsend he was seeing, but she insisted that it was, so for a couple of weeks he had watched her rather than Esterbrook. He'd followed her taxi from Plymouth, and each time she had gone to the boat, and each time she and Esterbrook's brother had disappeared below. He'd told Mrs. Esterbrook that, but she said it was a bluff, and he mustn't let them pull the wool over his eyes.

When the shorter Sunday afternoon session was over, Esterbrook would drive Townsend back to Bartonshire. He would drop her in Stansfield at her flat, without so much as a peck on the cheek, then drive on to Barton, to the opulent terraced house in the wealthy part of town where he and his wife lived, and in all the time that Foster had been watching him, if it was Townsend he was playing round with, Esterbrook hadn't dropped his guard once. Not once.

SCENE IV—CORNWALL
Saturday, August 23rd, 2:20 P.M.
The deck of *Lazy Sunday*

Josh pinned up a virgin target and walked back to where she stood. "You have to get thirty to beat him," he said.

Sandie's lips were dry. This was very, very important to her. If she could beat Paul at this, it would give her more satisfaction than anything else ever had, except Josh. Paul had used her to humiliate Elizabeth, used her when she'd had a loaded gun in her hand. No one would ever do that again, and certainly not Paul Esterbrook.

She took a deep breath, steadied herself, remembered everything she had been told, took aim, and fired. Good. Again. Another close one. Again. Centre ring. She could feel the excitement mounting as she watched the bullets rip into the target to bury themselves in the mattress, a new one that Josh had bought to replace the bullet-riddled one they'd used to start with. One more. Not so good. She closed her eyes, opened them, steadied herself again. One more. She swore under her breath as it went into the outer ring. A boat wasn't the best place to be doing this; any movement put your aim out. One more, just one more, but it would have to be dead centre. Her last chance. She could do it. She could.

And she did. Josh and Paul both applauded as though they were at a football match, with whoops and hollers and stamps and whistles that rocked the little boat and made her worry about the hole in its side.

"You are *good*," Paul said, taking the gun from her as Josh started up the boat again. "On dry land you'd be a match for anyone."

She smiled. "But it was from the ladies' tee," she said.

"I think you might have beaten me anyway." He lowered his voice. "I gave you an advantage so that I had an excuse if I lost," he said. "But don't tell Josh I said that."

She wanted to share her triumph with Josh, not Paul, but she couldn't, not yet. Paul went into the wheelhouse to clean the gun, and she stayed out on deck, sunning herself, feeling utterly contented. She had beaten Paul Esterbrook, and now she was going to help Josh do the same.

It was an omen.

SCENE V—CORNWALL
Saturday, August 23rd, 2:45 P.M.
On board *Lazy Sunday*, and in Penhallin harbour

Oh, well, Paul thought as he cleaned the gun, at least if she did go on the rampage, she would hit what she was aiming at.

The boat was nosing its way into harbour, and he grew impatient, as always. Waiting for the diving to begin was always the worst part, and Sandie's excitement was infectious. It was the August Bank Holiday; he had a whole extra day this weekend, and he was going to make the most of it.

Josh looked at him and grinned. "Do you ever think of anything else?" he said.

Josh knew him too well. He baited him, as he always had, about anything and everything, but particularly about this, especially since he had started using the boat for his assignations. Josh was still grinning at him as they neared the harbour wall, and Paul could see that the boat's attitude was all wrong. "Look out!" he shouted, but it was too late. His words had been drowned by the grind of wood on stone, and a sickening crunch.

Josh stopped the engine, ran to the side and looked over. "Jesus," he said.

Paul, still in the wheelhouse, couldn't believe what was happening. Didn't want to believe it. Slowly, reluctantly, he walked to where Josh stood, saw the gaping hole, and his temper snapped. "You can negotiate rocks that have wrecked dozens of ships, and you bang into a fucking harbour wall?" he shouted. "Why weren't you looking where you were fucking going, you stupid bastard?"

Sandie had come running over to see what was happening. She looked over the side, and up at Josh. "What was that you once said about women drivers?" she asked.

Josh held his arms wide in a confession. "Sorry," he said. "I should have been looking where I was going." He turned to the people on the harbour, who had run over to see what was happening. "I don't know how I did that," he said. "I'm sorry. She'll have to go in for repair. The weekend's cancelled, I'm afraid."

None of the dismayed people who lined the wall could have been as keenly disappointed as Paul. He helped Josh get their stuff from the cabins, unable to speak. He wanted to hit the stupid bugger, but a brawl would be a little unseemly in Penhallin harbour.

"Sorry," Josh said again.

Paul picked up dive bags and went up the steps, throwing them down, going back for more. He wouldn't put it past his unpredictable brother to have done it on purpose just to frustrate him. He handed the last of the bags up to Josh and joined him on deck.

"I'll refund you for the whole weekend," Josh was saying to each of the paying customers as he handed them their stuff.

He turned to Paul. "I'm honestly sorry," he said, his voice quiet, and reached down for the last two bags. "But I've had a thought."

Paul didn't want to know. His weekend was ruined.

"Angela's in London this weekend."

Oh, no. He wasn't using Little Elmley. Elizabeth thought that was what he'd done last time the boat didn't go out, and he wasn't about to risk really doing it.

"Shopping, dinner, and a show with the girls," said Josh.

Paul failed to see the relevance. He was supposed to be gleaning something from all of this. If Josh didn't speak in bloody riddles it would help.

"Going to the Notting Hill Carnival on Monday."

It was the first Paul had heard of it, but then he didn't enquire after his mother's doings. He had known that she was doing something different from usual this weekend, that was all. He frowned. "I thought she and Elizabeth were working on her book on Sunday," he said. "Something about sorting out the photographs."

Josh shook his head. "She's away all weekend."

"So?"

Josh handed one of the bags to a retired bank manager with what was now sounding like an incantation as he promised to refund the fee, adding that he hoped he would still enjoy the weekend, then turned back to Paul.

"So far as your wife is concerned, you're still on a diving weekend. And the cottage is free."

"The cottage?" Paul frowned.

"Yes. There's no reason why you can't do what you were going to do. Just use the cottage rather than the boat."

Paul's eyes widened as Josh's idea was finally spelled out to him. "Right," he said. "Yes. Look—she should get there first. Have you got your key? Can you let her have it?"

"It's the least I can do," said Josh, then hesitated, uncharacteristically, before he spoke again. "What about your hotel room?" he asked. "Have you got the key to it?"

"Yes, but—"

"There's no sense in letting it go to waste, is there?" said Josh, and glanced over to where Billy stood by his motorbike.

Paul looked across at Billy and back at Josh. "Oh, I don't know, Josh," he said.

"Oh, come on! Who's going to know?"

Against his better judgement, Paul dug in his pocket, gave Josh the key, then walked quickly to his car, watching in his mirror as Josh handed the last bag to its youthful owner and a few words were exchanged. The boy nodded as he mounted the bike and fired the engine. Josh was speaking to Sandie as Paul reversed out of the little space with difficulty.

He glanced out over the bay as he drove, and the fisherman still sat there, patiently waiting for a catch. Josh was right; he probably was being paranoid. He was just a fisherman. But this way, if Elizabeth *did* have someone following him or Sandie, whoever it was would have to back off; there was nowhere to go after his mother's cottage but into the sea, and they would know if someone trailed them there. That meant that once he was there, he could relax.

He had a key to the cottage, as did every member of the family, though it was an unspoken rule that they were only to be used with permission from the owner. He was about to break that rule for a purpose of which his mother would deeply disapprove, and if it occurred to him briefly that he was once again allowing Josh to lead him into temptation, and that he had always got into severe trouble for that in the past, Paul chased the thought away.

SCENE VI—DEVON
Saturday, August 23rd, 6:30 P.M.
A hotel room in Plymouth

"I've got something to tell you," Joe said, and could feel her body stiffen as he spoke the words; they were, after all, never the preamble to anything anyone wanted to hear.

They were lying in a double bed in a curtained room of the Excalibur Hotel. They had had a nice lunch, followed by a nice afternoon, and now he was going to spoil it all, but he did have to tell her.

"I didn't win that money. I got a loan for all that equipment."

"Why?" Kathy sounded startled, as well she might. "Why did you pretend you had spare money if you didn't?"

"I wanted to help you out." He sighed. "And I told the bank manager I would be going into partnership with another ex-police officer who already had an established business. But I won't be, not now."

"But when we set up together, we can pay it off from the business takings. The bank might be prepared to give us a longer term or something."

"That's just it. We can't set up together."

There was a long silence; Joe waited for the questions, but they didn't come, so he ploughed on.

"I was going to pay the loan off when I got my severance pay. But I'm not getting early retirement after all. The job at HQ's going to be full-time. So the bottom line is that I can't work in any sort of detective agency. And you can't afford the loan repayments either, so the stuff will all have to go back. I'll stand any loss—I don't want you to be out of pocket because I was a bloody fool."

She turned towards him. "We might not have to send it back," she said. "I can get a job. With two incomes coming in, we can still pay off the loan, and then when you do retire, we'll have all the equipment we need to set up."

Joe took a metaphorical deep breath. "Maybe we should think about it a bit more before we rush into anything," he said.

"What do you mean?" she asked, her voice sharp.

Joe shrugged. "It's just that . . . well, stealing you back from Andy might have been all right once, but now . . . well. I don't know."

"What's different about now?"

"He's in a wheelchair, Kathy!" Joe got out of bed, pulled on the complimentary bathrobe, and walked to the window, drawing back the heavy curtain to look out at the well-kept grounds of the hotel. That was below the belt, he told himself, and he hadn't really meant it to be. The wheelchair had damn-all to do with it, but it had seemed like a better reason than the truth. That setting up home with Kathy was the last thing he wanted to do. That he wanted Debbie back, not Kathy, and the whole thing had been a dreadful and costly mistake.

The light went on, and he let the curtain fall back, turned to look at Kathy, who was sitting up in bed, angry.

"He was in a wheelchair when we met up again," she said. "He was in a wheelchair when we discussed our options. Leaving him and moving in with you was one of them, if you remember."

"I know. I just don't think I can do it to him," he said. "Andy was my best friend, even if he hasn't spoken to me for twenty years. It doesn't seem right taking advantage of him like this."

"It's you that should have the grudge against *him*," said Kathy. "Not the other way round."

Joe knew that. Andy had stolen his fiancée, and to start with, he had indeed thought that he had a grudge against him. That was why he'd made a nuisance of himself just after Kathy had married Andy, trying to spoil what they had. But Debbie had come along, and he had realized then that he didn't begrudge Andy whatever happiness he had found with Kathy. All that his phone calls and letters had done was to turn Andy against him.

It was when they had checked in as Mr. and Mrs. Cope that he'd begun to realize how wrong he'd been. And then he'd seen Ian Foster, of all people, and had felt a stab of jealousy. Not because there would be anything going on between him and Debbie, but because Ian saw her every day, and Joe didn't.

"It's me you've got the grudge against," she said. "Isn't it? Is this your way of getting back at me?"

"No!" He turned to look at her, and shook his head. "No," he said again.

"Why did you let me make a fool of myself, then?"

He sat down on the bed. "I didn't. You haven't."

She looked at him for a long time, then shook her head. "I said that we couldn't sleep together unless we were serious about it," she said. "And I am serious about it, Joe. That's why I'm here. Why are you here?"

Because he'd fancied a weekend in Devon, and because he'd thought that Kathy could fill the gap in his life. But whatever he had once felt for Kathy, whatever he had imagined had been rekindled by their meeting again, had gone for good; the doubts that had crept in with the signing of the register and bumping into Foster had been confirmed the minute the hotel room door had closed behind them and Kathy had turned the key in the old-fashioned lock. A more honest man than him would have told her that before he spent the afternoon in bed with her. A slightly more honest man than him would tell her that now. He just didn't answer.

"You don't want to take advantage of Andy? That's a laugh. He was right about you. That's exactly what you want to do!"

"Maybe," Joe said. "But I don't think you really want to leave him. You want him back the way he was, that's what you really want." Andy seemed to have changed since his accident, but Kathy had thought that he could be rescued from the self-pity, and Joe had truly wanted to help bring that about. It wasn't going to happen if she left him. "You don't want me," he said. "You want Andy." But it would have been more truthful to say that *he* wanted Andy.

He and Andy had grown up together; they had played in puddles together, climbed trees together, suffered adolescence together. They had shared a flat, gone to football matches, got drunk, helped one another out with money, given one another quiet, uncomplicated moral support when it was needed. It was Andy's friendship that he had truly missed all these years; it was Andy's friendship that he had hoped to buy back with his misguided loan. He had missed Andy, not Kathy, and she would never understand that, not in a million years. He had only really understood it himself this afternoon. He wanted Andy's friendship and Debbie's love, and he didn't really want Kathy at all.

"I'm sorry," she said. "I'm moving too fast, I know I am. But it isn't going to happen tonight. I won't just walk out on him without making sure he's all right." She threw back the sheet. "I'm going to have a bath."

"Do you want me to go?"

"No. I want you to show me how to use the briefcase thing. If you don't have to have it back before tomorrow morning, that is," she added with a smile. "What do you want me to do with the other stuff? And all the office equipment?"

He smiled back. "You can keep it until you've worked out what you're going to do. Maybe you'll think of some way of keeping going."

He had to sell it, try to get as much for it as he could, maybe even get the money back on some of it—most of it hadn't been used. But he didn't want to make things any worse between him and Kathy than they already were; he truly hadn't meant to deceive her, and demanding the return of all that stuff seemed a bit mean. Besides, if she didn't want him to go, his generosity might not go unrewarded, and he had always held the notion that if you couldn't be with the one you loved . . .

She went into the bathroom, and he opened the briefcase, taking out the tiny camera, embedded in a lapel pin. "It's just like the ones you're already using at home," he told her, raising his voice above the sound of running water. "Except it's portable, and the business end is in the briefcase."

"Will you be able to get frames off it for me to send to Mrs. Esterbrook?" she asked. "She won't be able to play the video."

"Yeah, sure," said Joe. There was a frame-grabber in the computer suite at work. But there was something funny about all this. "Did you say this poor bloke's got the room below this one?" he asked.

"Yes. She booked us into this room so it would look like a genuine mistake if he checks up."

"But won't you have to pretend you're room service or something?" he asked. "How can you just walk into his room? He'll have locked the door, won't he?"

"She says not."

Joe frowned. "She *knows* the door's going to be unlocked?" He went to the bathroom door. "It sounds like a setup, Kathy. Blackmail, maybe."

She looked a little worried, then got into the bath. "Well, what if it is?" she said with a touch of defiance. "I'm not doing anything wrong. What she does with the information is her business."

And blackmail was his business, Joe thought. But not for much longer. Not once he'd gone to be a glorified secretary in Barton. A glorified secretary with a wife and two kids who had to be maintained, a loan for office equipment and gadgetry that he couldn't use, and an insatiable desire to keep bookies in the manner to which they had become accustomed.

Oh, what the hell, he thought. Kathy was right. What her client did with the information was her business. But . . . he could make it his, he supposed. He'd be getting his hands on that video before Kathy did, so he'd be very well placed to do just that.

SCENE VII—CORNWALL
The following day, Sunday, August 24th, 9:15 A.M.
Angela's cottage

Paul, almost as interested in his stomach as he was in other pleasures of the flesh, had bought bacon and eggs, having found a twenty-four-hour garage that sold such things at seven o'clock on a Sunday morning. His mother's provisions at the cottage ran to dry goods only, and he had had no intention of missing Sunday breakfast. Now even more wary of being followed, he had kept his eye on the cars behind him, but none of them had followed him out to the cottage.

He was suspicious of every stranger, everyone who seemed to be where he was for no good reason, but whenever he had been able to check up on them, they turned out to be just what they said they were. Like the fisherman who had been hiring the boat for weeks and had first hired it on a Tuesday, when he wasn't even *in* Penhallin.

Paul had decided that he had to try to curb the paranoia, to relax and make up for the morning's unpromising start. Thus it was that he was lying in a delicious state of semiconsciousness, having had Sunday breakfast with Sandie, after which they had retired to the bedroom. She had fallen asleep afterwards; he hadn't, and was just thinking of waking her again when his mood was rudely interrupted by the phone ringing downstairs in the hallway. He waited for it to stop, but it didn't, and he got out of bed and padded downstairs. Whoever was ringing knew that there was someone here, and only one person knew that, so he thought he'd better answer it.

"Paul, it's Josh. Sorry, but your weekend's being cut short. Angela's just rung me."

Paul frowned. "Where are you?"

"Little Elmley."

"Little Elmley?" Paul repeated, then realized what that meant.

"She must know the diving's been cancelled—she'll tell Elizabeth! What the hell am I going to do?"

"Relax," said Josh. "She called me on my mobile. She thought I was still in Penhallin, and I didn't tell her any different. But there's been a change of plan—she's coming back this morning, and she needs a letter she left at the cottage, so she wants you to pick it up and bring it to her. She apologized for making you miss your long weekend."

Paul worked on that. "But if she's going back to Little Elmley this morning, she'll know you're *not* in Penhallin," he said.

"I'll make myself scarce, don't worry."

How could he not worry? This sounded very odd to him. "What is this letter, anyway?" he asked.

"It's from a firm of solicitors—someone's coming specially to pick it up from her, and she wants it by four o'clock this afternoon. Hang on, I'll find the details."

While he was hanging on, Paul began to realize what his interfering mother was doing. No one was coming to pick up any letter. It was a holiday weekend, for God's sake. "Why can't I just fax it to her?" he demanded as soon as Josh came back on.

"She has to sign the original. It's some sort of release clause for a publisher or something."

Oh, sure. This was pure harassment. But he'd have to do what she asked, all the same; his mother was a better ally than an enemy, and as long as he kept in with her, she would do nothing to give him away to Elizabeth. Crossed, there was no telling what she would do.

Josh gave him the details about the letter. "She says it might be in her desk, but to check the drawer in her bedside cabinet first, because she was going over it in bed."

He had to leave a message on his mother's answering machine to let her know he'd found the letter, and that he was on his way. She would be back at about ten o'clock, and she would expect to have heard from him by then. Her and her bloody answering machine.

"What time is it now?" Paul asked.

"Half past nine."

He groaned. "Yes, OK," he said. "Thanks." He'd have to get a move on. He hated rushing. He went back upstairs and nudged Sandie. "We've got to go," he said, getting a grunt in reply. "Get up. Now." Sandie didn't move; he walked to the window and drew back the curtains, letting light flood in through the open sash window, and was transported back thirty years.

"What?" Sandie said, sitting up. "What is it?"

He had almost forgotten the treehouse; his mother had had it made for him when he was four years old, and he had spent hours up there, doing what, he couldn't really remember. Playing. Imagining. Being a pirate, being an Indian scout, being one of Robin Hood's merry men. He wasn't sure now what that had entailed, but he knew it had been fun. He remembered making a bow and arrow, which had never quite worked. He had had sole occupancy of the treehouse until they had moved to Little Elmley and he had acquired a brother.

Then Penhallin had become their holiday cottage, with his mother and father in one small bedroom and him and Josh in the other. Since then his mother had knocked the two rooms together, but this part had been his room, and he had been able to look out at his treehouse. After he'd had to share it with Josh, it had never been quite the same; when Josh played, he was Captain Hook, he was Hawkeye, he *was* Robin Hood, not one of his merry men. The significance of that distinction between them had escaped him until now.

He left the window and sat on the bed, sliding open the drawer. "I've got to find a letter for my mother," he said. "I've got to take it to her." After a few minutes' careful searching through various bits and pieces untidily pushed into the drawer, he discovered it. He stood up. "I'm just going to ring her," he said. "Be up and dressed when I get back."

"Use this." She handed him her mobile.

"I told you not to bring that," he said.

"Are you going to refuse to use it on principle?"

He took it from her, and sat down on the bed, punching the numbers angrily. His bloody mother thought this was clever, he supposed.

SCENE VIII—CORNWALL
Sunday, August 24th, 9:40 A.M.
The treehouse in the garden of Angela's cottage

Paydirt, Sam.

Ian Foster had gradually realized the day before that the boat
wasn't coming out for its afternoon session, and had taken his hired
motorboat back, got into his car, and driven to The Point in the hope
that Townsend would be there and he could, so to speak, pick up the
trail again. She, however, had cancelled her reservation; according to
the receptionist, something had happened to the boat. Foster had
given up, thinking that they would all have headed back eastwards,
but he had stayed at the hotel as planned, rather than drive all the
way back to Barton.

He had made an early start that morning, pulled into a garage to
fill up, and had been about to drive off when Esterbrook's car
had drawn up and Esterbrook had got out and gone into the
shop. This was it, Foster had thought. The change of routine that
Mrs. Esterbrook had said would be needed if he was to catch her
husband at it.

Esterbrook had driven out to his mother's cottage; Foster had
known, as soon as he had seen him take the turnoff, where he was going, and had congratulated himself on his forward planning, even if
it had really been a bit of a scam to get a few days at the coast. He
had arrived at the back garden of the cottage to find the windows
open but still curtained, and had thus been able to slip up the ladder
and into the treehouse unobserved.

Sounds had come floating through that open, curtained window that were unmistakable, and he had duly noted the time
and the nature of the sounds. Since then he had been keeping
an eye, and more importantly an ear, on the curtained house,

because as soon as he heard them moving round in there, he had to get ready to record. They would want to leave things as they found them, and that would presumably mean opening the curtains again. Just catching Paul Esterbrook on video in the cottage with Townsend might not be proof of adultery, but it would be all he'd need to keep Mrs. Esterbrook from giving up on him.

The bedroom curtains had indeed opened, and Foster had reached for the camcorder, his heart beating fast when he saw the subject, as he called him in his reports, stark naked. He had used the slow zoom as Esterbrook had sat on the bed and looked in the drawer for something, focusing first of all on his face, to ensure that there could be no dispute as to his identity, then had pulled back to include his companion.

And as Paul Esterbrook made a phone call, Foster was getting the reward for all that patient watching and following. Esterbrook had slipped up at last.

SCENE IX—BARTONSHIRE
Sunday, August 24th, 9:45 A.M.
The house at Little Elmley

Elizabeth arrived at Little Elmley and let herself in. She was never sure how she had been inveigled into working with Angela like this; naturally, she wasn't paid for it, and once wouldn't have wanted to be, but now she had a private investigator's bills coming in, and she could do with some income. She wasn't really that desirous of doing it at all, but it had somehow evolved into a routine that she didn't know how to break. Now she had even less incentive; Angela Esterbrook was part of what she saw as a conspiracy to defraud her of the shares her father-in-law had meant her to have if his son failed to mend his ways. He had seen Paul for what he was; Angela saw only what she wanted to see, and turned a blind eye to anything she didn't.

But Josh had had some sort of accident with the boat, apparently; Paul might have slipped up this time, with any luck, because his plans depended on what he could foresee. If there was any justice, Foster would have something to report.

She went into the office, switched on the computer and the printer, then glanced at the telephone, where a message was flashing.

SCENE X—BARTONSHIRE
Sunday, August 24th, 3:00 P.M.
On the road from Cornwall to Bartonshire

Sandie had listened to what Paul thought of his mother, listened to his effing and blinding hour after hour, mile after mile, until she felt like jumping out of the car.

"This is just to let me know that she knows what I'm up to," he said, for what Sandie was pretty sure was the fifteenth time. She had started counting after about the fourth or fifth, but she might have missed a few. "She and Elizabeth are in this together, I know they are. Whoever that bitch has got watching me must have lost me when Josh holed the boat, and my darling mother worked out where I'd be."

"But I thought you'd checked out everyone you were worried about?"

"Except the right fucking one," muttered Paul.

Sandie suggested that his mother might simply have his best interests at heart, was trying to make sure Elizabeth *didn't* catch him, but Paul would have none of it. They were in a conspiracy together, and that was all there was to it. And when he'd exhausted that topic, he started complaining that he was late, blaming her because she had detained him after he had made his call to his mother's answering machine.

"There isn't an exact time for driving from Penhallin to Little Elmley," she pointed out. "You can't be late for something that hasn't got a fixed time."

After what seemed like a hundred years, they were coming into home territory; he was still swearing and muttering to himself when he pulled up at her block of flats, and groaned when he saw Josh walking towards the car. "What now?" he said.

Josh grinned. "Relax," he said. "I'm doing you a favour. Angela found out about the boat being holed."

Paul went pale. "How?"

"She has to foot the bills. The guy rang her about something that he wanted to do, and she called me, wanting to know what it was all about. I told her that it happened right after she had rung this morning, and that we would all be coming back as soon as I got things organized. She told me to bring Sandie back with me for dinner, and not to forget her letter."

Paul looked quickly at her again, his eyes narrowing slightly. "See?" he said. "I told you. She's doing this on fucking purpose! She still thinks she can pair you and Josh off."

"Anyway, I assumed you'd be bringing Sandie home, so here I am, to pick her up. You can give me the letter, and no one will be any the wiser."

The color slowly returned to Paul's face. "Thanks," he said. "Thanks, Josh. I owe you one."

Josh smiled. "You owe me several, big brother."

Sandie got out of the car, and watched Paul drive off.

"Well?" said Josh, opening the passenger door of his car. "Are you ready for this?"

Ready for it? She had thought it was never going to happen. But it was happening, and she couldn't be happier, couldn't be more ready. She got into the car and smiled up at Josh as he closed the door and walked round.

He got into the car, and smiled back at her. "You might not thank me for moving you in with Angela," he said.

"It's not Angela I'm moving in with."

SCENE XI—BARTONSHIRE
Sunday, August 24th, 4:00 P.M.
The house at Little Elmley

Angela was still in her office, telling Elizabeth which photographs she wanted to use in the book; she raised a hand in greeting as Josh went in, and carried on marking photographs as she spoke. "You weren't trying to ring me, were you?" she asked.

"No," said Josh. "Why?"

"The answering machine's gone funny."

Josh pulled the phone towards him. "There's a message flashing," he said.

"I know, but it won't play."

Josh fiddled with it, pressed play, fiddled with it some more, and then took it out, inserted a pen and rewound it. "Try recording a new message," he said.

Angela recorded a new message, then Sandie went out to the hallway and rang the number; her call was answered, she left a message, and the machine played it.

"All we needed was a man, obviously," said Elizabeth. "I'd better be going, I suppose, if Paul's home."

Angela shook her head. "How on earth did you manage to hole the boat, Josh? You've been messing about in boats in Penhallin harbour since you were eight years old."

"I wasn't looking where I was going," said Josh, and glanced at Sandie. "I had other things on my mind."

"Oh, well. The man rang because he says it's in need of a complete overhaul, so I suppose it's just as well. You should have been keeping an eye on what needed doing to it, as well as on where you were going, Josh."

"Yes," said Josh. "I know. I'm sorry."

Elizabeth left then, and Josh waited until he heard the front door close. "I really did have my mind on other things," he said. "Sandie and I have some news." He fancied he saw a hint of relief as he told her that he and Sandie were man and wife.

She looked from him to Sandie, smiling, shaking her head. "When?" she asked.

"Last month," said Josh, taking out the marriage certificate. "Proof, since you'll need it for the antifornication clause."

"Josh! I won't have you talking like that."

Angela disapproved of jokes about Paul Sr.'s Victorian outlook. But she would have asked to see it if Josh hadn't volunteered it. He knew that, and so did she. Living in sin would not have been tolerated by his father, and it wouldn't, therefore, have been tolerated by Angela.

"But—" Angela shook her head as she read it. "But why didn't you *tell* anyone?"

Josh sat down. "Because of the will," he said. "Sandie's got a good job, and we're not sure whether she counts as a member of my family or not. Paul might not be able to carry on employing her."

Angela frowned slightly as she thought about that. "It might be all right," she said. "It would depend how the Trust board saw it, I suppose. I think your father really meant . . . well . . . blood relations. Because of . . ." She shook her head rather than finish the sentence. "He had these old-fashioned notions," she said to Sandie.

"Well, we didn't fancy them putting it to the vote, so we thought we'd keep it quiet, and carry on living in separate houses," said Josh. "But . . . well, we'd much rather be together."

Angela nodded vigorously. "Of course you would," she said. Then she jumped up again. "What am I thinking of? This calls for champagne. Come along."

They followed her into her sitting room, champagne was produced, and Angela drank to their health and happiness.

"The thing is," Josh said, "Sandie doesn't want to stop work, because I don't earn enough to keep us both—"

"You mustn't worry about that! I can let you have anything you want—anything you need."

Sandie smiled. "I know you'd be very generous, Mrs. Esterbrook, but—"

"Call me Angela, dear."

"Angela. But—please don't be offended—I really would prefer it if Josh and I were independent, financially."

Angela was not offended. She was a reasonable woman, and reasonable women didn't take offence over things like that, could entirely understand that their stepdaughters-in-law wouldn't want to live off them. Josh took up the conversational baton when Angela had finished being reasonable.

"So what we thought," he said, "was that Sandie would look for another job, one as good as she's got at IMG, hopefully, and when she gets one, then we'll make it public. Once she's no longer on the payroll, there will be no danger of overzealous trustees pulling the plug on Paul."

"Good," Angela said, smiling. "He's always looked out for Paul," she told Sandie, and turned back to him. "Haven't you? It's as though you were the older brother."

He found it hard to believe how self-deluding his stepmother was; despite her intimate knowledge of her so-called family, she genuinely believed that he didn't want to do anything that would put Paul in a difficult position. If she only knew. The more apparently difficult a situation he got Paul into, the deeper in hock Paul would be to him when he apparently extricated Paul from it. And he had just put Paul exactly where he wanted him.

"So far as Paul is concerned, Sandie still lives in her flat in Stansfield," Josh said. "All right?"

"Of course," said his stepmother. "I won't tell a soul anything different until you tell me I can."

Josh smiled. "Good," he said. "I knew you'd understand."

How could she not understand? She was, after all, so very reasonable.

SCENE XII—BARTONSHIRE
Sunday, August 24th, 10:30 P.M.
Joe Miller's house

Kathy dropped him off and handed him the video.

"You won't forget, will you?"

"I won't forget," said Joe. He wasn't likely to forget. She had told him what she had seen in Room 312, and that video was destined to be blackmail material or he was a Dutchman. He could imagine that the guy would be prepared to part with a lot of money to get his hands on it.

He bent and gave her a kiss, feeling a sudden stab of conscience, not something that he had felt too often in his life. He had taken advantage of her yesterday, and he still was taking advantage of her, because last night after dinner she had clearly decided that all he had had was an attack of cold feet.

She obviously believed that everything was going to go ahead as originally planned, and he hadn't tried very hard to disabuse her of the notion. He wished, a little wistfully, as he let himself into his empty house, that he were a better person. But it had been a bloody good weekend. Pity it had ended so abruptly; once Esterbrook had checked out, Kathy had had no reason to stay the extra day.

He went to bed early and alone, unlike last night, and lay awake, thinking. All in all, the weekend had given Joe lots of food for thought; he thought about the financial mess he'd got himself into, about Debbie, about the video he now had in his possession.

He might do a little digging. Find out what sort of money this Esterbrook bloke had and just how good a prospect for blackmail he was.

SCENE XIII—BARTONSHIRE
The following day, Monday, August 25th
Paul and Elizabeth's house

Elizabeth was very anxious to get her private investigator's report of the weekend, because she wanted to know what Paul had been doing while Josh was arranging for the repairs to the boat to be carried out. The break in his routine had to have thrown something off, surely, even though he had come home immediately. He certainly wouldn't have been ready to leave, and that could just mean that this time she would have something on him.

She rang the number and let it ring out for three minutes before she realized that it was, of course, Bank Holiday Monday, and she presumed that even private detectives' secretaries got the day off. Foster would have been working, though, if Josh hadn't holed the boat, so perhaps he would go into the office at some point.

She tried several times throughout the day, every time Paul went far enough away for it to be safe, but got no reply. She was going to have to be patient for one more day.

SCENE XIV—BARTONSHIRE
The following day, Tuesday, August 26th
The house at Little Elmley

"IMG Limited, Trish speaking, how may I help you?"

Josh shook his head a little. Trust Paul to have them say that when they answered the phone. "Good morning, Trish." he said. "You may help me by putting me through to my brother."

"Who's calling, please?"

"Josh Esterbrook. My brother is your boss."

"One moment, I'll see if he's in."

One of the Four Seasons was played into his ear in case he got bored. Poor Vivaldi. If he had thought for one moment of the crass uses to which his music would be put, he would never have written a note.

"Josh?"

"Yes. I thought I'd better ring you in an Elizabeth-free zone. It isn't very good news, I'm afraid. I'm not getting the boat back this weekend. In fact, it's going to be out of commission for a few weeks."

The disappointment was audible.

"Sorry," Josh said. "It seems it wasn't in as good nick as I thought when I got it. It needs a lot of work. It won't be back in business until the twenty-sixth of September." And after several weekends in his wife's company, nothing would keep Paul away from Penhallin when the boat was finally back in service.

"Oh, that's a pity."

Josh grinned. Paul must have someone with him, so he couldn't give vent to his true feelings. "Sorry," he said. "Nothing I can do about it." He had persuaded the boatyard to tell Angela that it was essential maintenance; that way she would foot the bill without asking awkward questions.

"Well, I suppose it can't be helped." Another sigh. "Thanks for letting me know, anyway."

It was fun listening to Paul having to take the news without filling the air with four-letter words. "You're welcome," Josh said, smiling broadly, and hung up.

SCENE XV—BARTONSHIRE
The following day, Wednesday, August 27th
Ian Foster's office

"Where were you yesterday?" Debbie demanded as soon as he walked in.

"Working," said Foster.

"Nursing a hangover, I presume. Couldn't you have rung in?"

Foster went back out and looked at the scratched and scuffed plate clinging by one and a half of its screws to the wall outside. He must do something about that, he thought. "Ian R. Foster, Private Enquiry Agent," he read aloud, then looked back in at Debbie. "*I'm* called Ian R. Foster," he said. "Does that mean I'm the boss?"

"Very funny. Mrs. Esterbrook rang for her report yesterday—she wasn't very pleased when I said you hadn't been in all day."

"I told her I was a one-man band," said Foster, coming in again and closing the door. "She can't expect me to be here all the time."

Debbie pulled a face. "She's practically your only client," she said. "The only one worth being here for, at any rate."

This was entirely true, but that job was almost certainly finished, unless he extended it a little, as he'd been thinking of doing. But he'd had a good win yesterday, and that proved that his luck really was in, so he might try something even more risky. He hadn't quite made up his mind yet what to do. He pulled a face back. "You're getting paid, aren't you?" he said.

"For the moment," she said dryly. "Anyway, I said you'd give her a ring when you came into the office."

"Right." He went into his own office, closed the door, and switched on the fan. The matter of Mrs. Esterbrook's report was a little complicated; he usually gave his notes to Debbie to type up, but he didn't want to do that this time.

He went back into Debbie's office. "I'm just off out again," he said.

"*Have* you got another job on?"

He touched his nose.

"I work for you, in case you hadn't noticed! When you've got any work for me to do."

"Don't worry, sweetheart," he said. "Things will pick up."

"They'd better," Debbie called after him as he went back out. "I've got two kids to feed, and I can't do that on your promises."

He turned back and took a wad of notes from his back pocket, peeling five off. "Here," he said. "A bonus."

Debbie took the money, her eyes widening. "A hundred quid?" she said.

"For holding the fort yesterday and—" He made his mind up about one thing, at least. "—and for telling Mrs. Esterbrook that I'm away sick. Came down with it on Saturday, and wasn't able to let her know. I was unable to fulfil my commitment to her, so to speak."

"You never went to Penhallin?"

"Yes," said Foster. "I did. But I lost him, and I don't want to admit that."

"So where did you get this from?" she asked, holding up the money. "You lost him because you were in the bookie's, is that it?"

"I told you where I got it from. I was working. Earning. Putting food on your table, unlike your estranged husband."

"You had a win on the dogs," she said with near total accuracy, folding the money and stuffing it into her purse. "Unlike my estranged husband."

"Oh, I meant to tell you—I saw him," said Foster. "In Plymouth. Having lunch with Kathy White in the hotel Esterbrook stays at." That would make her sit up and take notice, he thought. It was high time these two were back together, and he couldn't think of a quicker way of bringing that about than by warning Debbie that she had competition.

Debbie stared at him. "Kathy White? The woman he was once engaged to? Are you sure?"

"Of course I'm sure. We all worked together."

"What was he doing in Plymouth?"

"I don't know! I wasn't investigating him, was I?"

"You weren't investigating anybody! You were at some dog track. Was it my wages you were gambling with?"

He winked at her. "I felt lucky," he said. "And I still do. Better times are coming—you mark my words."

"What the hell was he doing in Plymouth with his ex-fiancée?" she asked again, her brow furrowed.

Foster shrugged, and this time, with Debbie thus preoccupied, he escaped. He wanted to do a little bit of checking up before he took the big gamble, if he did take it. How lucky did he feel? How big a gambler was he?

SCENE XVI—BARTONSHIRE
The following day, Thursday, August 28th
The Managing Director's office of Industrial and Medical Gases in Stansfield

"There's a call for you, Mr. Esterbrook," said the telephonist. "The caller wouldn't give you his name, but he said to tell you it was about Sunday morning in Cornwall, and you'd know what that meant."

Paul went a little cold. "Thank you, Trish," he said. "Put him on." Perhaps it was Josh again, messing round.

"Mr. Esterbrook?" The voice was slightly nasal, conjuring in Paul's mind an image of the archetypal secondhand car salesman. It was also a little sinister. And it wasn't Josh.

"Yes," he said guardedly.

"Have you seen your mail this morning, Mr. Esterbrook?"

He craned his neck to look at Sandie, who was making a neat pile of opened letters. She would be answering them, not him. He very rarely had to see any mail these days. "Not yet," he said.

"You should have a package marked private and personal," he said.

A very unpleasant sensation caused Paul's pulse to quicken and his skin to become moist. "What is this?" he said.

"I suggest you open the package first, and then I'll be pleased to explain why I'm ringing."

Blackmail. It had to be. When in doubt, say nowt, as his old drill sergeant used to say. He hung up.

Moments later the phone rang again, and Paul took a breath, picked it up.

"Mr. Esterbrook, it's the gentleman you were just speaking to. He says he thinks you were cut off."

"Put him through," said Paul, and heard the click. "What do you want?" he asked.

"I want you to open the package, that's all. It'll give you some idea of what I'm offering."

The sensation moved to the pit of his stomach. "Hang on," he said, and put down the phone. He sat for a moment, gathering his wits, then walked into Sandie's office, feeling light-headed. "Do . . . do you have a package for me?" he said. "Marked 'Personal'?"

"Yes," she said, and picked up an unopened envelope with a stiffened back, handing it to him.

It was indeed marked private and personal. It had been delivered by courier. The address label was printed. Across the top in red letters were the words PHOTOGRAPHS: DO NOT BEND. "Thank you," he said, and walked, dazed, back into his own office and closed the door.

Unable to get his thumb in between the flap and the envelope, he tried to tear it open, but there was no slack to get hold of. He looked round for something to use as a paper knife. Why didn't he have a paper knife, for God's sake? Picking at the corner with a paper clip finally made enough of a space for him to rip the rest of it open, and the torn packing revealed the photograph, which confirmed his worst fears.

It was a fuzzy video still, by the look of it; it wasn't of itself worth anything, but the blackmailer had clearly got a video of the entire proceedings, and Paul knew what was on it.

He stood quite still for a few minutes, the photograph in his hand, looking out of the open window at the industrial landscape, drabber even than usual on this hot, overcast day, trying to come to terms with what was happening to him. Should he call Sandie in, see what she thought he should do? She thought much more quickly and clearly than he did in a crisis.

Tentatively, he opened the adjoining door again. She was busy with the word processor; she didn't notice him. No, he thought. No. She seemed quite innocent, but for all he knew, she was behind it. You couldn't trust anyone. But that was paranoid, he knew that even as he thought it. It was his own actions that had brought this about; it had had nothing to do with her. All the same, he thought, he'd leave her out of it. Just to be on the safe side. He closed the door again and walked round the desk, pausing to look out of the window.

Traffic moved along the dual carriageway, stopping and starting at the traffic lights, which had recently been deemed necessary, and across the wide road stood the IMG bottling plant, which had been here even longer than the sixties office block in which he stood; in this youthful town, it was practically an ancient monument. An IMG tanker was pulling up in the delivery area as he watched, just as they were pulling into IMG bottling plants all over the United Kingdom. Most of the gases were actually produced by subsidiaries of IMG these days; his father had bought up the suppliers whenever he could, taken a stake in them when he couldn't.

This company was big, and he had worked for it for ten years. He had another seven to go; and then his controlling interest would mean that he could sell, float the company on the stock market, retire from it, do what he liked with it. Whatever was the most attractive option. He would have real, serious money to work with, to play with, to invest in projects that interested him, to do what he wanted to do, not what his father wanted him to do. He looked at the video still that threatened that rosy future, tore it into tiny pieces, stuffed them into his pocket, and picked up the phone again, but the line had gone dead.

He hung up, and five minutes later the phone rang; once more he got the perplexed operator.

"It's the same man again, Mr. Esterbrook. He says—"

"Yes. Put him through."

"I hope you weren't trying to get the call traced. It would be a waste of everybody's time."

No. It hadn't occurred to him to get the call traced. He needed time to think about this. "What do you want?" he demanded.

"I think you can tell from the photograph I've sent you that I am in possession of more—shall we say explicit?—material concerning your activities on Sunday morning. I'm prepared to sell you that material, Mr. Esterbrook. It's yours if you meet the asking price. It is an exclusive offer."

Paul shook his head. "It's a still from a video, right? You can copy videos. I don't call that an exclusive offer."

"Providing you meet the asking price, Mr. Esterbrook, you can rest assured that no one will ever know the material existed. Or find out by any other means what was taking place while the camera was recording. Because if I did that, you would then have no reason not to tell the police about our little transaction. I would be putting my head in the noose, and why would I want to do that?"

Paul could see that it wasn't worth his caller's while to double cross him, but they said that blackmailers never stopped with the first payment. Then again, blackmail was a risky business, with ample scope for being apprehended while picking up the payments, or delivering the merchandise. A onetime hit was obviously the likeliest way to get away with it. Besides, it wasn't the cash he was worried about.

"How much?" he asked.

"Well . . ." he said. "I know what you stand to lose, and how you stand to lose it."

"How do you know?" As if he didn't know how the bastard knew. Elizabeth had employed him, that's how he knew. He could deal with him once he'd flushed him into the open, but he still needed time to think about his strategy.

"Wills are public documents, Mr. Esterbrook."

"How much?"

"A hundred thousand pounds."

"*How* much?"

"Come on! What's that to you? Two months' salary? Three months'?"

Something between the two. Paul knew he would have no trouble raising the money, and suppressing that tape was worth infinitely more to him than that. But he wasn't going to agree to anything when he'd been put on the spot like this. This was a situation for which he hadn't bargained; now, he needed time to look at it with a cooler head. Play for time, Paul, he told himself, play for time.

"I haven't even seen what's on the video yet," he said. "How do I know it's worth that sort of money?"

"You *know* what's on it," he said. "You're starring in it. And the only way you're going to see it is if you buy it, Mr. Esterbrook. I'll leave you to think it over, and I'll ring you at lunchtime."

Paul cancelled two appointments, diverted all his calls to Sandie, and spent the morning thinking it over, as advised. Paying him was probably the wisest course, but the blackmailer would, of course, keep a copy of the tape, with which to come back for more when he ran out of money. He could happily keep the blackmailer supplied with cash for the next seven years, but he really didn't think he could live with that hanging over him as well.

Two words from that telephone conversation had stuck in his head. Rest assured. He hadn't done that for years, and certainly not since his father's will had been read. And he worked out how he really could rest assured. It would take a fair bit of organizing, but it could be done. When Sandie went for lunch, he took the divert instruction off the phone and locked the adjoining door. At half past one, his phone rang.

"Have you thought it over?"

Paul took a breath. "OK," he said. "I can get the money. How do we do this?"

"I thought you'd see the advantages of accepting my offer. We do it in Penhallin, this coming weekend. Go to your usual hotel, and have the cash with you. I'll take it from there."

"I won't be there this weekend," he said. "The boat's out of commission. And I couldn't get that kind of money that quickly anyway—even I can't get a hundred thousand from a hole-in-the-wall machine."

There was a silence.

"All right," said the voice reluctantly. "But you'd better not be messing me about."

An amateur. This was going to work out just fine.

"When will you be in Penhallin next?"

"The last weekend in September." When he fully intended making up for the fallow weekends he was going to have to endure while the boat was being made over. That had seemed like a disaster, but not anymore. Without having to come up with anything clever, he had got the time he needed to work out how he was going to deal with this, and by then it would have been made abundantly clear to the blackmailer just who was calling the shots. In fact, he would start now. "But I have better things to do in Penhallin," he said. "And my time there is limited. We do it on the Friday." He flicked over his calendar. "Friday the twenty-sixth of September. Here. In Bartonshire. Anywhere you like, any time you like."

"All right. I'll be in touch."

SCENE XVII—BARTONSHIRE
The following day, Friday August 29th
The house at Little Elmley

Sandie had been desperate to talk to Josh since yesterday, but he had been in Penhallin dealing with the boat, staying overnight at The Point, and she hadn't wanted to tell him on the phone.

"What's wrong?" he asked as soon as he saw her.

Sandie took a deep breath. "I think Paul's being blackmailed," she said.

Josh stared at her. "Are you sure?" he asked.

"Well, no—I'm not *sure*. But there was an envelope in the mail yesterday morning with photographs in it, and it was marked private. Then he'd only been in his office two minutes when he got a call, and he seemed to hang up on whoever it was. Then he got another, and he came in and asked if he had a package marked private. Then he went into his office and closed the adjoining door, and he never does that unless he's got someone with him, and—"

Josh held up a hand. "Whoa," he said.

"But what are we going to *do*?" she said. "We can't do all that again."

"No," agreed Josh. "Even Paul wouldn't fall for it twice."

"So what are we going to do?"

"What can we do?" Josh smiled. "Nothing, except wait and see."

How could he be so calm? After all that planning, all that work? She had been worried sick all day about telling him. Maybe he hadn't quite grasped the implications. "But Josh," she said. "If he's being blackmailed—"

"I do understand what you're telling me," Josh said, "but I learned in prison that there's no point getting agitated about something you can do nothing about. And it might not be what you think. You might have got the wrong impression."

She might. But she doubted it. "But if I am right, what are we going to do? Oh, Josh, it's not fair!"

He came over and put his arms round her. "If you're right," he said, "then we're stuck with it. So we'll just bide our time and devise a new plan." He kissed her, and smiled. "If he is being blackmailed, he'll tell me all about it sooner or later. He always does."

Sandie couldn't see how that would help. "What good will that do?" she said.

"Everything Paul tells me about his sordid little life makes it easier and easier for me to manipulate him," Josh said. "So don't you worry. If we can't do it this way, we'll find another way."

He held her close, and she wanted him so badly that she wanted to cry. She had never felt like this with anyone before. Never.

"Even if you're right, we'll have other chances," he said.

Oh, she hoped so. She hoped so. She couldn't bear to see Josh lose.

Act IV
The Murders

O proud death
What feast is toward in thine eternal cell,
That thou so many princes at a shot
So bloodily hast struck?
                    Hamlet, Act 5, Scene 2

SCENE I—BARTONSHIRE
Four weeks later, Friday, September 26th, 4:45 P.M.
The house at Little Elmley

Josh popped his head round the patio window in Angela's office. "I'm just off," he said

She frowned. "Off where, dear?"

"To the club for an hour with a pupil and then to Penhallin. I've got the boat back, remember?"

Oh, of course. She'd forgotten. "Is Paul going to join you tomorrow?" she asked.

"Yes, I imagine so. Why?"

Angela sighed. "Because Elizabeth's going to London tomorrow, and she's going to come home to an empty house if he's off with you. And he'll be giving Sandie a lift down, won't he? She'll only start getting suspicious again."

"Not this time," said Josh. "Sandie isn't coming to Penhallin. A group of divers are doing a night dive in the reservoir before they go off to do it for real in the Red Sea. Sandie wants to do it with them."

"Oh, good." Angela smiled. "I've had an idea," she said. "How about if I invite Sandie and Elizabeth for dinner? That way, Elizabeth will see for herself that she's not with Paul. It'll be the next best thing to telling her the truth."

"Why not?" said Josh. "Sandie might not be finished until quite late, though. Anyway—I've got to go. See you on Sunday." And he was gone.

Angela smiled. It was almost like the old days at Little Elmley now that Sandie was here. Not since he was a small boy had she seen Josh so relaxed, so content with life. She really wanted Josh to be happy, and it seemed that at last he was. That was the principal reason that she herself was happier than she had been in years, because she had always felt she owed Josh some of her happiness.

Perhaps, at last, she had repaid her debt.

SCENE II—BARTONSHIRE
Friday, September 26th, 5:20 P.M.
The Managing Director's office at IMG

Sandie put the postdated letters between the leaves of a book for Paul to sign on Monday, and sighed. Josh's boat was seaworthy again, and she wished it wasn't; she had spent the last few weeks at Little Elmley, and it had been wonderful. There was something perfect about her and Josh; nothing could ever spoil it or harm it, not even her having to continue to accommodate his half brother's urges, as Josh called them. But her weekends with Paul were utterly boring, and she wasn't looking forward to this one.

Working with Paul wasn't as boring; she liked the job, and she was good at it, but the boat being out of commission had not made her job any easier. Today had been all right, because he hadn't been in the office, but the last few weeks had been sheer hell, with his temper getting worse and worse, and the air turning bluer by the day. Josh said it was all part of the softening-up process, and that it would be worth it.

The phone rang, making her jump.

"Hello," Josh said.

"Josh—it's dangerous ringing me here. What if Paul had been here? I told you, he never closes the door. He'd know I was talking to you."

"Relax," said Josh. "I asked for him and got put through to you."

"Oh." She smiled. "I'm afraid Mr. Esterbrook is away at a conference today, Mr. Esterbrook, and won't be back in the office until Monday. Would you like to leave a message?"

"Monday would be a bit late. I called to tell him that I'm going to have to be at the club school this weekend, so I won't be taking the boat out after all. I'll have to ring him at home."

Sandie's mouth fell open. "Paul will have six fits!" she said.

"I know."

"Does this mean you're going to carry on depriving him of my services?"

"No, I'm afraid not," said Josh. "But it does mean that you get to go in your own car. You can smoke yourself silly all the way there and all the way back if you want."

Her eyes grew wide and her heart began to beat faster. She could feel her face grow hot. "Josh—is it this weekend?"

"Yes. See you later." And he hung up.

She went to the ladies' room and splashed her face with water, trying to stay calm. Josh said she always showed it when she was excited. She had to think about something else. Anything else. Anything that didn't excite her in the least.

Paul. She'd think about Paul.

SCENE III—BARTONSHIRE
Friday, September 26th, 6:50 P.M.
Paul and Elizabeth's house

"It'll just be you and me and Sandie," said Angela. "She'll be night-diving at the reservoir, so I thought it would be nice if she came up here for a bite to eat. I'm sure you and she will get on—she's a nice girl, Elizabeth. And she's very good for Josh."

Elizabeth shook her head slightly. Angela and Paul were still trying to convince her that Sandie Townsend and Josh were getting it together. It was true that Sandie had been spending a lot of time at Little Elmley, but that was for Paul's convenience, Elizabeth was sure. And Elizabeth was convinced now that Angela was in on it.

"I don't actually know when I'll get back from London," she said. "It might be quite late."

She could hear Paul arriving home from work, and was very thankful that this weekend at least she would be getting a day off from him when she was in London. She wished Josh's boat would get back from the menders, because then Sandie wouldn't be in the safe and secure environment of a house with private grounds; she would be with Paul on Josh's boat, and the surveillance could begin again. She might have to wait a long time for another break in Paul's routine to throw him out of gear, but at least she wouldn't have to suffer his presence during her precious solitary weekends.

"Well, Josh says Sandie will probably be quite late too, so we'll make it a late dinner," said Angela. "Say nine-thirty or ten? Will you be back by then? I can do something that will keep, if you might be later than that."

She might as well go to Angela's hen party as not, she thought; she had no objections to Sandie per se. Indeed, she was counting on Sandie to help her pay this bloody family off, albeit unwittingly.

"Oh, yes, I think I'll be back. That'll be lovely. See you tomorrow night."

She put down the phone and went into the sitting room, where

Paul was getting himself a drink from the refrigerated compartment of their drinks cabinet.

"I'm going to London tomorrow, in case you've forgotten," she said. "And I'm invited to a girls-only dinner at Little Elmley tomorrow night. You'll have to look after yourself."

Paul picked up the remote control for the TV, and it flashed into life with the music that heralded the seven o'clock news. "Makes no difference to me," he said, looking at the screen. "I'll be in Cornwall."

Elizabeth frowned. If Paul was going diving again, then Josh's boat must be back in business. But if Sandie Townsend was going to be at this dinner, she presumably wasn't going on the weekend with them, and she wondered if Paul knew that. "*Sandie* won't be in Cornwall," she said.

It was the tiniest of reactions. A fleeting pause as he opened the can. He carried on immediately, but she had seen it.

"She's doing a night dive at Little Elmley, apparently," Elizabeth went on, ramming home her advantage. "And then coming to dinner with Angela and me. Didn't she tell you?"

"No," said Paul, sitting down. "I haven't been in the office."

Of course, thought Elizabeth, this whole thing could be an even more elaborate ploy to cover up Paul's behaviour. She, after all, had to leave Barton before first light to get to London with at least a chance of getting a decent place in the queue; it was a two-and-a-half-hour drive, and it would take the best part of an hour to get where she was going once she was in London.

As she thought about it, it came on the news; a late silly-season story. The camera panned along the people who were settling in for the night, and she just had to hope that eight o'clock was early enough to join the queue. They were predicting record numbers, and the tickets were limited to two per person.

If she had had more courage, she would have gone up yesterday, and camped out overnight like these people; it would have been no hardship in this weather. But going at all was as much of a stand as she had had the nerve to take in the face of her husband's mocking disparagement and her mother-in-law's baffled indulgence. She just had to hope that she at least got there with a chance; some people, the news said, would arrive to find that they were being advised to go home.

But her early start meant that if Paul and Sandie left immediately after she did, Sandie could spend several hours with him on Josh's boat and still be back by ten for dinner with Angela. The Esterbrook minds were quite devious enough to produce such a plan, and she wondered about this night-diving that Sandie Townsend was supposed to be doing. It might be worth checking into that.

When they had eaten, Paul rose from the table, announced that he was going out and didn't know how long he'd be. Perhaps she had imagined the momentary reaction she had believed she had seen; the Esterbrooks probably didn't need to go to such elaborate lengths to pull the wool over her eyes. He was probably going to Sandie Townsend right now, with his mother's blessing.

All the same, she thought, picking up the phone, if he was going to Penhallin tomorrow—with or without Sandie Townsend—so was her private detective.

SCENE IV—BARTONSHIRE
Friday, September 26th, 9:00 P.M.
A street in Barton

Paul drove angrily and too fast until he was well away from Elizabeth. His desire to beat her senseless had grown to almost irresistible proportions over the last month, and now that she and his bloody mother seemed to be trying to block his escape route as soon as it had opened up again, it had taken all his strength not to wipe the triumphant smile off her face.

He had things to do tonight. It was after nine already, and now he was going to have to take time out to sort out what all this was about, he thought angrily, pulling into a lay-by and squealing to a halt. He dialled Josh's mobile number and got a voice telling him that the phone was busy but that the subscriber knew he was waiting on the line. It didn't make him answer the bloody call, though.

Who was he talking to? Was it Elizabeth? He could never be certain of Josh, and he had had a long time to think about things. Was Josh up to something? Was he deliberately keeping the boat out of commission? Or was it his mother's doing? To keep Sandie from him? Was she still trying to pair Josh off with her? Paul watched the cars and lorries shooting past him while he waited for Josh to get off the bloody phone. After this weekend, he wouldn't need Josh and his bloody boat, so—Josh finally answered, interrupting his mental tirade. "What the fuck's going on?" Paul demanded.

"Good evening, Paul," said Josh smoothly. "I just tried to ring you, but Elizabeth said you'd gone out. You know how hard it is to get Elizabeth off the phone."

Elizabeth. He *had* been talking to Elizabeth. "I *said*, what the—"

"I heard you. What's going on about what?"

"My wife's just informed me that Sandie is having dinner with my mother tomorrow evening," he said.

"Oh, that. No—forget it. Angela obviously invited Elizabeth before she'd spoken to Sandie. Don't worry, Sandie'll tell her she can't make it. I told her Sandie would be doing a night dive at the reservoir, so she suddenly got it into her head to invite her to dinner."

"Why the hell did you tell her that?"

"Angela said Elizabeth would start getting suspicious again, so I thought if they both believed Sandie wasn't going to be in Cornwall, it might take some of the heat off, that's all."

Paul didn't trust Josh when he did him unasked-for favours. He didn't trust Josh at all.

"The thing is, I won't be taking the boat out this weekend after all. I'm at the diving school."

There was a moment while Paul processed that, then he exploded. "Jesus Christ, Josh! What the fuck are you trying to do to me? I thought you were in Penhallin!"

"There was a mix-up over the schedules at the club. Ade's away for the weekend, so I'm having to do his people instead. I've been here all afternoon, I've got a full day tomorrow, and Howard and I have got a group doing night-diving tomorrow evening at the reservoir. So, no boat, I'm afraid."

Paul tried to make sense of it all. If Josh wasn't going to be in Penhallin, then Sandie might as well go to dinner with his mother, because she was no use to him if the boat wasn't going out. He said as much to Josh, every noun and most verbs preceded by the same expletive.

"Just relax, and listen," said Josh.

Paul listened. He did not relax.

"The cottage will be free again. Sandie can go to Penhallin in her own car tomorrow morning. You go at your usual time, go down to the boat in case someone is following you, then just do what you did last time. If you leave the cottage first on Sunday, no one will be able to prove anything. You can tell Elizabeth you stayed overnight when you discovered the mix-up rather than do the journey twice in one day."

"For your information, little brother, the last time I took your advice I ended up being blackmailed. Some bugger got a video of me."

For possibly the first time in his life, Paul had succeeded in rendering his laid-back brother speechless. For at least ten seconds. "Blackmailed?" he said. "What do you mean, blackmailed?"

"Blackmailed as in demanding money with menaces. Don't worry, I'm dealing with it. So there won't *be* anyone following me tomorrow, and I won't need to fart about with the boat or anything else. But since you're not going to be there, I don't see how any of this is going to help."

"But no one knows I'm not taking the boat out," Josh said when he'd finished.

"Oh, no," said Paul. "Only a load of fucking divers."

"Who are all going to be in Egypt by tomorrow afternoon. Elizabeth and Angela will have no reason to think I'm not in Penhallin."

"But you're *not* going to be in Penhallin! You're going to be in Little sodding Elmley!"

"But Elizabeth and Angela aren't going to know that until late on Saturday, are they? I'll say I forgot to tell you I wasn't going. And there *will* be night-diving at the reservoir, if Elizabeth stops by to check. She's not going to know whether one of the divers is Sandie or not. No proof of anything."

When Sandie didn't turn up for this dinner, she'd know. But then, Paul told himself as he calmed down a little, she didn't have to believe it for it to work. It was proof that bitch needed, and Josh was right. There would be no proof that Sandie wasn't diving. But he still didn't understand why Josh had ever said that she was. There was a great big rat here; he could smell it, and he was going to find out exactly where it was.

"Right," he said. "OK. But I'll be picking Sandie up. I want her in my car—I'm not wasting any more bloody time. So if you've told her any different, *un*tell her."

"You're *that* certain no one's going to be following you?"

"I will be. I've got a bit of business to attend to first."

SCENE V—BARTONSHIRE
Friday, September 26th, 9:10 P.M.
On the road from Little Elmley to Stansfield

Josh put away his phone and drove out of the diving club, still trying to make sense of it. They had been certain that Sandie must have misread the signs, that Paul wasn't being blackmailed after all. But she had been right. Paul seemed pretty certain that no one would be following him tomorrow, but Josh didn't see how he could be. What did he mean, he was dealing with it?

Oh, well. He couldn't spend time worrying about that, he thought, as he drove out of Little Elmley and towards Stansfield. He had things to do, not least of which was to issue Sandie with her new orders, which wouldn't please her, because smoking was probably the only thing she wouldn't be doing on the adjectival journey down.

He wondered a little about his half brother's constant use of a word with sexual connotations as an expletive; he thought perhaps that Paul truly did think of nothing else, and during enforced periods of celibacy the word was almost as satisfying to him as the act itself, like a baby with a dummy as a substitute for a breast.

But his half brother's sexual psychology was not something he wished to dwell on. It was useful, but unpleasant. Like sewers.

SCENE VI—BARTONSHIRE
Friday, September 26th, 9:30 P.M.
A supermarket in Stansfield

Kathy Cope pushed her husband round the supermarket while he picked things off the shelves he could reach and told her what to get from the ones he couldn't. It had always been like that, even before the wheelchair. Andy had decided what food they bought. They always came at this time on a Friday night; the aisles were clearer then, and she could hook him up to one of the special trolleys.

She hadn't decided yet what she was going to do. Joe had told her it was all over, if it had ever really started. He wanted his wife back, apparently—and all the stuff he'd bought, unless she could buy it from him. He'd said she could hang on to it until she had decided what to do. She had hoped that jobs might have started coming in, but they hadn't, so she supposed she would have to give up the agency. Whatever she did, she was going to have to talk to Lucy, try to persuade her to take her dad. It wasn't going to be easy, but even if Lucy refused, she wasn't going to stay with Andy. She was going to leave him, get a job. Anything.

At last they were heading up in the lift, back to their old, specially adapted car, which she couldn't drive because she'd never learned how to use her hands rather than her feet. It stood alone in a line of disabled parking spaces, and that was another reason why they came late—the disabled spaces were quite often all taken at peak times, usually by people who had nothing wrong with them.

She got Andy into the driving seat, put the chair in the boot, then got in herself, and he drove home, going on at her about something, but she wasn't listening.

SCENE VII—BARTONSHIRE
Friday, September 26th, 9:55 P.M.
The garage of the Copes' house

Kathy got out of the car and opened the garage door, her heart almost stopping as a figure appeared from the side passage and a gloved hand covered her mouth. She was pushed into the garage, where Andy could see her in the headlights, and she felt something hard and cold against the side of her head.

"This is a gun," said a man's voice. "Don't make any noise, and you won't get hurt." He motioned to Andy to bring the car in.

She couldn't have made any noise even if his hand hadn't been covering her mouth; she felt as if this was a dream, a nightmare, it wasn't happening. Why was it happening? What did he want? The car drove slowly past them, and she saw Andy's horrified face as her assailant tapped on the window with the gun.

Andy wound it down.

"Open the passenger door," the man said, then took her round to the other side of the car. "Now the back one."

Andy complied, and Kathy watched as the gun was levelled at Andy's head.

"Close the garage door."

She pushed the door shut, and the headlights glared into the brick wall, reflecting back into the car; he was in the backseat, the gun still trained on Andy.

"Get in the front."

She got in, the gun now touching the back of her head. "Kill the engine and the lights," he said to Andy. "Undo your seat belt. Wind the window back up, and give me your keys."

Andy did what he was told, and found his voice. "If it's money you want," he said, "my wallet's in—"

"Hold hands," he said. "And count."

"What?" said Andy.

"Hold hands."

Kathy felt Andy's hand come into hers and hold it tightly.

"Now count. One, two, three . . . count. Out loud. Both of you."

They both began to count. Kathy felt self-conscious, of all things. It seemed such a foolish thing to be doing, and she wasn't . . . wasn't entirely . . . sure what came next. Seven. Eight? Had she done them already?

Andy wasn't counting anymore, and she felt very . . . very . . .

SCENE VIII—BARTONSHIRE
The following day, Saturday, September 27th, 4:30 A.M.
Outside Paul and Elizabeth's house

Elizabeth drove away but she didn't go far; she waited just round the corner, where she could see the house in her wing mirror. She wanted to see if Paul left immediately after her. If Paul's time with Sandie was going to be curtailed, she presumed that he would want to get as early a start as possible; if he didn't go now, then he would probably go at his usual time, and she felt that it was safe enough to leave him to Foster, who would arrive at six. She waited for twenty minutes, long enough, she would have thought, for the doubtless desperate Paul to get himself ready, but he didn't appear. Perhaps he really was just going diving, she thought. But then again, perhaps he wasn't. And if he was trying to be clever, perhaps this time he would slip up.

SCENE IX—BARTONSHIRE
Saturday, September 27th, 9:30 A.M.
The house at Little Elmley

Josh rose at eight, and by nine o'clock had breakfasted, showered, and shaved, and thought of nothing but Sandie. She should be halfway there by now, assuming that Paul's urges hadn't held them up too often and for too long.

There was a long day ahead of him; the hot summer had produced a lot of new recruits, and the one-to-one tuition offered by the school meant that the volunteer instructors were kept very busy. He had two beginners' theory classes; one at ten o'clock this morning, and one at seven-thirty this evening, each consisting of just two or three people. In between, he had three recruits all at various stages of training. And when he'd finished the evening theory session, it would be time to go down to the diving platform with the night divers.

He left the car in his garage and walked to the club; it wouldn't do for Angela to spot his car in Little Elmley when it ought to be in Penhallin. At ten o'clock he began his marathon day. All the same, he thought—judging from his half brother's anguished phone call last night—Sandie had an even more arduous day ahead of her than she might have supposed. And hers had almost certainly started already.

SCENE X—CORNWALL
Saturday, September 27th, 12:30 P.M.
Bodmin Moor

Paul had been sorely tempted to use the Range Rover's off-road capabilities as soon as the surrounding countryside afforded him the opportunity, but he hadn't. He had driven straight to where he was going.

Sandie had been waiting for him when he had arrived at her flat, wearing a short cornflower-blue summer dress that he hadn't seen before, a bag over her bare, suntanned shoulder, her big straw hat shading her eyes. Her weekend bag had joined his in the boot, and she had got in and started chatting to him, as she always did. He hadn't said much to her, but her mere presence had aroused him, and there was even a hint of excited anticipation in her eyes, on her face, which he had never really seen before. Perhaps the long separation had been getting to her, too. But he hadn't stopped the car, because he had a particular destination in mind, one which would admirably serve both his purposes.

He had thought about the situation he had found himself in, thought about it long and hard, and yesterday's bombshell about the boat had made it essential that he find out what Josh was up to. Sandie might well be in on it, because Josh was right about her—she was only interested in money. For all he knew, Josh was plotting with Elizabeth against him, with the promise of a payoff, and they could have bought Sandie's cooperation. If they had, he was going to buy it back.

Sandie had brought sandwiches and cold drinks, which they had consumed on the move, and it wasn't until they were in Cornwall that he had put the Range Rover through its paces, driving out onto the moors which he had spent his childhood roaming. It wasn't difficult to take the car further from civilization than Sandie had ever been, and when he stopped in the shade of the towering rock formations that shielded them from even nature's prying eyes, he made up for the last bleak month.

He lay back, eyes closed, opening them as he felt Sandie get off him. He watched as she reached over to the front for her cigarettes, taking one from the packet, then opened the door and got out. She lit the cigarette, throwing the lighter back in through the open driver's door onto the seat, then leant against the car, releasing smoke to drift up into the still cloudless sky. After a few moments he joined her, closing the rear door.

"What's Josh up to?" he asked.

"Josh?"

He smiled. "I'm the first to admit," he said, "that I can't think quickly, not like you and Josh. But I'm not stupid, and I've had a lot of time to think at my own pace."

She frowned. "Think about what?"

"Josh is far too good with boats to ram one into a harbour wall. He's far too good with boats not to know when one is overdue for maintenance. He did that on purpose, and then kept it in dry dock for as long as he could. Do you know why?"

She looked a little wary. "No," she said.

"And why did he tell my mother a totally unnecessary lie about where you'd be this weekend?"

"I don't know," she said. "I didn't know he had."

"Did he think that when he told me he wasn't taking the boat out this weekend, I'd be so desperate after all this time that I'd jump at any suggestion he made?"

Sandie shook her head, her eyes puzzled. "I don't know," she said.

"That's all right, then," said Paul, getting into the car, closing the door. He pulled on his driving gloves and started the engine as she stubbed her cigarette out on the rock and walked round to the passenger side.

"The door's locked," she said through the open window.

"I know. And I'm going to drive away and leave you here unless you tell me what's going on." He looked at her as he fastened his seat belt. "Well?" he said.

"You're not really going to leave me," she said. "I don't even know where we are."

"I do. I grew up here. Josh and I used to walk here every weekend. I know exactly how to get back to civilization, but you don't. And you don't get too many tourists coming this far at the best of times, never mind at this end of the summer, so you probably won't find anyone to ask."

She shook her head slightly. "You wouldn't leave me here," she said.

"I would. And I will. I'll be driving off with—" He looked over his shoulder. "—your shoes, and your shoulder bag, your weekend bag, your cigarettes and lighter. Even your sun hat and your knickers. *Are* you going to tell me what's going on?"

"But I don't *know* what's going on. You *can't* leave me here like this!"

He didn't really think she did know, but this was a fairly certain way of making sure. He drove off, bumping over the moorland, watching her dismay in the rearview mirror. He'd go back for her in half an hour or so, but he had to make absolutely certain first.

"No—wait! Wait!" she shouted, running after the car. "Wait, Paul! I'll tell you!"

She *did* know. She *was* in on it with them. He jammed on the brakes and got out, waiting for her. He would pay her whatever she charged for loyalty, but first he had to know what was going on.

Sandie slowed to walking pace, and arrived reluctantly at the car. She took a breath. "I didn't know he'd done that to the boat on purpose," she said. "I swear, Paul, I didn't."

"But you do know why he isn't taking it out this weekend," he said. "'Has it got something to do with the cottage? Is Elizabeth going to turn up there, or something? Is that why he wanted me to go there?"

"No," she said, her eyes wide, her head shaking. "It's nothing like that!"

"If you know it's nothing like that, then you know what it *is* like. Why didn't he take the boat out this weekend?"

There was a heartbeat before she answered. "Because he thought if we were going to the cottage, you'd want us to arrive separately, in case someone was watching. He thought you'd go down on your own, and—" She swallowed. "—and I wasn't supposed to go at all."

Paul frowned. "Why?"

Her eyes looked briefly, imploringly into his, before closing. "Why do you think?" she whispered, then opened them again, with a look of resignation.

It took him a moment, and then his eyes widened as he realized. It was the one, simple explanation that he hadn't even considered. "You've been screwing Josh," he said.

"Yes. He wanted me to stand you up this morning, but I wouldn't."

He was paying through the nose for services he hadn't been receiving, worrying himself sick about what was going on, and all the time she'd been screwing *Josh*?

"I told him he wasn't worth losing my job over," she said.

SCENE XI—BARTONSHIRE
Saturday, September 27th, 1:10 P.M.
The house at Little Elmley

Angela's plan for making Elizabeth see sense wasn't working out. Sandie had turned down her invitation to dinner; she had said that

Elizabeth made her feel uncomfortable, being so suspicious of her all the time. She was afraid that she might blurt out the truth, just to make her see that her suspicion was unfounded, but Josh had made her swear not to tell anyone, in case she shouldn't be working at IMG.

Elizabeth might just be spiteful enough to use the information against Paul, and Angela had agreed that it wouldn't be wise to have them both to dinner after all. She had always lived by the precept of least said, soonest mended, and had deviated from it only once, with disastrous results.

She had found that working on her autobiography was proving therapeutic now that the narrative had reached that crisis point in her life. The careful sorting out of incidents and the marshalling of facts was putting the whole business into some sort of perspective at last. She even felt that she could face editing the correspondence, to which end she had asked Elizabeth to begin transcribing the letters to the word processor, but of course Elizabeth was in London to get the ticket for her concert, so that was going to have to wait until tomorrow now.

Angela wasn't entirely sure who this group or band or whatever you called them these days was, but she knew that they were some sort of seventies supergroup, and seeing them had been an ambition of Elizabeth's since she was a teenager. So it was nice that she was at last getting the chance to see them, even if it was on her own. Paul should really make more of an effort to share things with Elizabeth, Angela thought, if he didn't want her being so suspicious of him all the time. She might have a word with him about that.

She was about to have her monthly treat; she would be going into Barton to have lunch, then she would go to the beauticians and be pampered. Then she would shop for dinner, and tonight she would cook, and eat, and try to make Elizabeth understand that Sandie was not having an affair with her husband, without letting any cats out of any bags.

SCENE XII—CORNWALL
Saturday, September 27th, 2:30 P.M.
Outside Angela's cottage

They arrived at the cottage just before half past two, two hours later than intended, because of the moorland detour. Sandie didn't move as Paul got out of the car, took their bags from the boot, and unlocked the cottage door, waiting for her to join him.

Gingerly, she dabbed at her mouth with a tissue; it had stopped bleeding at last. His fists had connected so suddenly and so swiftly that she had had no chance to protect herself; now, she reached up and turned the mirror so that she could see the result. The fragile skin round her right eye was already blackening, her cheek was swollen, her jaw bruised. When she had raised her arms to protect herself, a body blow had left her on her knees.

"Is he worth that?" he had said, and had walked away.

Yes, she thought, as she looked at herself, he is. She opened her bag and took out her sunglasses, putting them on to see if she looked any less horrific like that. Not really.

He came back to the open door of the car. "Are you going to get out of the car?" he said. "Or do I have to drag you out?"

She sighed. "I could go to the police," she said. It was difficult to speak; it was the first time she had tried. Her mouth started bleeding again, and she pulled another tissue from the box.

"You do that," said Paul. "You go to the police. I'll be long gone by the time they get here. And do you know something, Sandie? I can say I was anywhere I like when that happened to you, and they'll believe me. So it'll do you no good." He opened the door wider and stood aside.

Still she sat there, for long minutes, while he waited. It was only when he swore at her and reached in, ready to make good his threat of dragging her out, that she gave in. Her bare feet touched hot paving; she pulled her legs back in and found her shoes, and her cigarettes and lighter. Then she walked slowly to the porch and leant against the upright, trying to ignore the ache behind her sunglasses, taking out a cigarette. If it was difficult to talk, it would probably be even more difficult to smoke, but she needed this cigarette as she had needed no other.

He pointed the remote at the car, and its lights flashed on and off. Then he looked at her and sighed loudly. "Do you have to do that?" he said.

"You won't let me smoke in the car, and you won't let me smoke in there, so I'll have one here."

"Fine," he said, taking the packet and the lighter out of her hand. "But it will just be one. I'll be in the bedroom when you've finished."

"And you want me in there with you?" she said. "Like this?"

"It doesn't bother me." He picked up the bags. "And if it bothers you, you should have thought of that before you started screwing Josh." He went in, kicking the door shut behind him.

She had had to tell him about her and Josh, or he would have left her there; she had known what was going to happen when she did. She had vomited after the fourth and final punch, and had heard him getting into the car and driving off. She thought she had been left in that godforsaken place despite her confession, and she had never been so scared in her life. But he had come back; the car door had opened, and she had been told to get in and not to let any blood get on the seats.

She drew smoke deep into her lungs and let it out in a huge sigh of relief. Bruised and bloodied though she was, she was here, and it was a beautiful day, she noticed for the first time. A fresh sea breeze lifted the folds of her bloodstained, soiled dress and soothed her damaged skin a little. The view of the shifting, murmuring sea was marred by a van that had been abandoned at the top of the rocky incline down to the shoreline, but it was still uplifting enough to raise her spirits.

Out of the corner of her good eye she could see Paul moving round downstairs, getting glasses from the sideboard, behaving as though nothing at all had happened, just like last time. He'd said she would get worse if she came on to Josh again, and she had. She wondered what he had meant about being able to say he was anywhere he liked if she told the police, but since she had no intention of going to the police anyway, it hardly mattered. She dropped her cigarette end and ground it out.

And that was when Paul came back out, his face pale, his eyes blazing. "We've got to go straight back," he said, as the car lights blinked again, and he heaved himself into the driving seat, reversing out as he closed the door, letting down the window. "I'll be back for you!" he shouted. "Take care of things in there!" He turned the wheel furiously as his speed took the Range Rover off the confined roadway and towards the rotting, rusting van, missing it by inches as it roared back down the road, signalling the turn for the harbour.

Sandie watched him go, then went into the cottage to take care of things in there, as instructed. It wouldn't do to cross him again.

SCENE XIII—CORNWALL
Saturday, September 27th, 3:10 P.M.
Penhallin harbour

Paul left *Lazy Sunday* and approached a group of people who were walking towards one of the other boats. He was trying to calm down just a little, trying to remember what impression he wanted to give. He would be angry if he'd come all this way to find that Josh hadn't turned up, but he wouldn't be panic-stricken.

"Have you seen anything of Josh Esterbrook?" he asked. "He owns the diving boat."

They shook their heads, called to some other people. No one had seen Josh, not today. Not for a few weeks.

Right, thought Paul. That would do. If anyone was checking up, he'd been asking round for Josh. He got back into the car and headed back to the cottage. She had better have done what he'd told her. He had unpacked some stuff, so she'd better have made certain she packed it all up again. If there was anything at all in that cottage to suggest they'd been there . . . well, a few more bruises wouldn't make any difference, as she'd realized when she had scrambled out of the car.

He shouldn't have lost his temper with her; that had been stupid, but she was on the ground before he'd even thought of the consequences. The state she was in would need explaining, and whatever she said had happened to her, Elizabeth would guess. He'd driven off, intending to leave her there, intending to say he'd been somewhere else, anywhere else. He'd had his driving gloves on; there were no bruises on his fists to give him away.

But someone would have found her wandering about on the moor; his alibi would have been subjected to real scrutiny if he was being accused of abduction and God knows what all. She could have cried rape, even, with all the evidence the police needed to convict him. Whereas, as long as she wasn't actually wandering about the moors when she told it, he could disprove her story, and she wouldn't be believed. So he had gone back for her.

Even with the less congested late-season traffic, there were stops and starts all the way from the harbour, and he cursed and swore at everyone else on the road until he was free of the town and at last driving along the headland. He checked his watch; it was twenty past three, and Sandie was waiting outside the cottage, the bags at her feet, wearing her hat and her sunglasses to disguise the bruises as best she could.

"Is everything out of the cottage?"

"Not quite," she said.

SCENE XIV—BARTONSHIRE
Saturday, September 27th, 7:30 P.M.
On the road to Little Elmley

By half past four, they had got on to the A38; Paul was taking a rather more direct route back than he had taken coming, and by seven o'clock he had left the M5. Now he was on the last lap, swearing at every car he was obliged to overtake, at every give-way sign, at every speed limit, at every opportunity.

Sandie felt very much improved now her weekend with Paul had been brought to its abrupt end, and she was almost used to her aching eye and bruised cheekbone, her throbbing jaw and swollen mouth, her punched ribs. She was dying for a cigarette, but Paul hadn't given them back to her, and he wouldn't have let her smoke anyway. Even so, she had felt better with every mile they had put between themselves and the cottage, and was even rather enjoying Paul's predicament and his reaction to it.

She had had to begin the journey crawling about the car in order to pick up all the bloodstained tissues, and check for any that might be lurking under seats or in glove or map compartments, not to mention any items of underwear that might still be lying round, and that had struck her as funny. But laughing made her lip bleed, and her chauffeur even angrier.

Once on the motorway, she had asked for an explanation of their instant turnround, but even for Paul the expletives had been so abundant as to render the account incoherent. At one point he had seemed to suspect Josh of having had carnal knowledge of Angela, but she assumed, on reflection, that he had merely being employing his usual term of abuse when referring to Josh and had tripped up over the syntax. Mother and brother were very similar words, after all.

The other problem was that the word he used when referring to her sexual relations with Josh and the word he used for emphasis were one and the same; this led to confusing repetition. When she had asked him originally what the problem was, his answer had consisted of the word "you" and the word "Josh," with the same word inserted three times in between.

At last he felt able to ration himself to one four-letter word per sentence or so, and had told her that when he had gone into the living room to get glasses for the red wine he had brought with him, he had found a fax from Josh. That Elizabeth hadn't stayed in London; when she had seen the size of the queue, she had known she had no chance, had come back and had booked herself into Josh's theory class, to let Paul know that she was on to him.

Sandie had said that she couldn't see the problem; Josh would just say he'd forgotten to let Paul know. She had then been treated to a five-minute tirade about her and Josh *being* the problem. If Josh hadn't been trying to make a fool of him, none of this would have happened. It wasn't Elizabeth seeing Josh that mattered; it was her *not* seeing Sandie.

"She's booked in so that she can see the divers, see for herself if you're there! So you're going to be there, and you're going to do this dive, because she's quite likely to go to the dive site to see that you do. Is your gear at the club?"

"Yes. But I might not be fit to dive," Sandie had said.

"I don't care if you fucking drown."

Her nose and her ears were all right, and they were the bits that mattered. She might not drown. She looked at Paul's watch as the car sped along. It was twenty past seven; they were cutting it very fine. The night dive was scheduled for half-past eight. She pointed out that if one of them had had a mobile phone, this wouldn't be happening. It didn't go down too well with Paul.

She had been told that he was going to drop her off on the dual carriageway where she could cross a field down to the reservoir; she would be able to see the landing stage. All she had to do then, according to Paul, was run along the shoreline, and she could reach the club in only a few minutes, whereas the car would take significantly longer. That way, she would arrive in time to assemble with the other divers, and she would do the dive, or else.

Meanwhile, after he'd dropped her off, he would be carrying on to his mother's house, because if he had really gone to the boat and found Josh wasn't there, that was what he would have done, to ask where Josh was. Then he would go to the diving platform, ostensibly so he could ask her, Sandie, if she knew where Josh was. Once she'd done her dive, he would go home and wait for Elizabeth to come back from dinner with his mother, and pretend that he thought she'd been in London all day.

Where, Sandie had asked, had he gone shooting off to when he'd found the fax? The boat. Because if Elizabeth was snooping round at the club, she was quite likely to snoop round at the boat, and his story would be blown if he hadn't been there. Someone, Paul had added, had apparently broken into the boat; the lock on the wheel-house door had been smashed. She might care to let Josh know.

At ten past eight he threw her out, bag and baggage, at the appropriate place on the dual carriageway, and she stood for a moment watching the Range Rover's rear lights shoot off into the distance, before picking up her belongings and beginning her jog to the diving club.

SCENE XV—BARTONSHIRE
Saturday, September 27th, 8:20 P.M.
Little Elmley diving club

Sandie arrived at the club at twenty past, thinking that she could slip into the changing room and put enough gear on to mask the injuries, but the first person she saw was Howard, and the sun hat and glasses were inadequate to the purpose.

"God Almighty," he said. "What happened to you?"

Sandie couldn't believe that she hadn't given a thought to a cover story, but things had happened too fast. "I was mugged," she said. "But you should see the other guys."

"Mugged? Did they get anything?"

"No. I hung onto my bags. That's why I'm in this state."

"What on earth are you doing here? You can't dive like that."

"I'm not going to let a couple of thieving bastards stop me doing what I was going to do," she said. She did hope that this third degree would stop soon. Her mental processes weren't as quick as they might be. "Where's Josh?"

"He's still taking the theory class. Where did it happen?"

"In the multi-storey in Stansfield."

"Did you tell the police?"

"No. What would be the point? I didn't see them well enough to describe them or anything."

She looked anxiously over his shoulder at the room where Josh was taking the theory class, and caught a glimpse of him through the little glass pane in the door. "Can you tell him I'm here when he comes out?" she asked Howard. "I'll be in the changing room."

SCENE XVI—BARTONSHIRE
Saturday, September 27th, 8:45 P.M.
The house at Little Elmley

Angela had arrived back from Barton at five o'clock, and had spent a pleasant afternoon in the garden, doing the little jobs that the part-time man never bothered with. She should have spoken to him about them, but she hadn't, because she really rather liked doing the light work. She used a special tool that she didn't have to grip too tightly, and took her time.

As the light faded, she had come in and spent some time choosing wine to go with the meal; she might be able to tempt Elizabeth with it, and get her into a more relaxed frame of mind. There was no need for her to drive home, after all; Paul wasn't going to be there. She could stay the night. She did hope she had got her ticket; that would, presumably, cheer her up a little.

Angela wished she hadn't actually organized this tête-à-tête; it wasn't what she had intended in the first place, and an evening of unadulterated Elizabeth would not have been her choice. It was what she was going to have, though, and she would make her as welcome as she could.

She was in the hallway, on her way to the dining room with the open bottle of wine, when she heard the car pull up, heard the key being inserted in the lock. She was early, Angela thought. And it didn't really seem right, Elizabeth having to let herself in just as though she was coming to work on the book. This was a social occasion, and she must try to strike the right note from the start. She put down the wine, forestalled the unlocking, and opened the door with a determinedly welcoming smile.

But it wasn't Elizabeth.

SCENE XVII—BARTONSHIRE
Saturday, September 27th, 8:55 P.M.
The reservoir at Little Elmley

Howard was down with the first diver, and Josh stayed on the boat, keeping an anxious eye on Sandie. She shouldn't be doing this dive, he thought, not in the state she was in. But she had very little option about that.

He couldn't take his eyes off the bruises, and he didn't want to look at them. He wanted to hold her, to cry, to go after Paul. And he would do all of these things in time, but for the moment there was nothing he could do except what he had to do, which was make the dive with her.

It was all his fault; he had underestimated Paul, who had worked out that what had happened to the boat had been no accident. Sandie had had to admit that she and he were lovers in order to drag Paul off the scent and get him to the cottage, and she had taken that beating for it. Josh smiled sadly. Sandie thought like lightning; Paul had had no chance against her. Just as she had had no chance against his fists.

In the gloom he could see Paul standing by his car, his recently acquired binoculars trained on the boat. Sandie could go down next, now that he was here. If Josh hadn't already hated his half brother, this violation alone would have given him the motivation to go through with his plan.

SCENE XVIII—BARTONSHIRE
Saturday, September 27th, 9:00 P.M.
Paul and Elizabeth's house

Elizabeth got home at about nine; she had a quick shower and changed out of her jeans and T-shirt, into something more fitting for dinner with her mother-in-law. She was tired after her long day, but she had a date with Angela and she was keeping it.

She was getting ready to leave when Paul came home; he looked pale and angry, and brushed past her in the hallway, going into the sitting room, pouring himself a drink. Elizabeth smiled. Something had upset his plans; what a pity. She went in after him. "What are you doing home?" she asked.

"I got to Penhallin to find that Josh wasn't there," he said. "The boat had been broken into."

"And you drove all the way back again? Why didn't you just stay at the hotel?"

"I wanted to find out what had happened to Josh! But he's taking this night dive that Sandie's doing. He just didn't think of letting me know."

SCENE XIX—BARTONSHIRE
Saturday, September 27th, 9:25 P.M.
Outside the house at Little Elmley

Elizabeth arrived at Little Elmley at twenty-five past nine. She parked the car and wondered, briefly, if she should use her key or ring the bell. She thought perhaps she should ring the bell. Angela was a bit of a stickler for protocol, and Elizabeth was sure that dinner guests shouldn't let themselves in.

It was one of those old-fashioned bells, and always reminded Elizabeth, not inappropriately, of the ones in horror films. She heard it toll deep in the house somewhere, and waited. When nothing had happened for some moments, she reached out her hand to repeat her summons, but withdrew it. Angela could be anywhere in that house. It took about a week to get from some parts of it to the front door.

But after another few moments, she did ring again.

SCENE XX—BARTONSHIRE
Saturday, September 27th, 10:30 P.M.
The reservoir

Josh had taken her to the submerged houses, just in case the torch-light gave away their location to anyone watching, but she hadn't spent any time exploring them; she would have found it hard to see anything with two good eyes, and anyway the diving mask had been too painful to wear, so she had taken it off. The mouthpiece of the aqualung was doing her no good either, but it was less damaging to leave it in than to keep taking it in and out.

Josh had been worried about her doing the dive, but she had been all right. Relieved, though, when he had swum up to her and indicated in the light of his torch that they were going to surface. Then she had sat in an uncomfortable heap as Howard and Josh took turns at minding the boat and going down with the divers.

Sandie wasn't sure Howard had believed her story about being mugged, but it was the most plausible explanation she had been able to come up with in her less than perfect condition, and she hadn't felt that she could explain away a black eye, bruises to both sides of her face, and a cut mouth by anything other than a human agency. It would have had to be a very aggressive door.

The near-euphoria that she had felt on the trip home with Paul, which had made her find the situation almost funny, had left her; that had been the adrenaline pumping, giving her a high. Now she felt very down, and all she wanted was for this ridiculous dive to be over, to be back in the club, to have a shower and change into something that wasn't wet, that didn't smell of sick and hadn't had blood dripped all over it.

Josh surfaced with the final diver; they took off their aqualungs and handed them up to Howard and one of the others, then were hauled aboard. Sandie's ribs ached again just watching the process. Josh came and sat beside her as she dabbed at her mouth with yet another tissue.

"I thought you said you didn't tell the police," said Howard as he guided the boat in.

"I didn't," she said.

"I think someone must have," he said. "Or why else are they here?"

"What?" Sandie looked up and saw the police car that waited on the roadway, lights glaring, and the two police officers who stood by the shore. She looked at Josh.

"Is there a Mr. Josh Esterbrook here?" one of the policemen called as Howard tied the boat up.

Josh stood up and stepped out of the boat. "Yes," he said. "That's me."

Sandie felt very strange when she stood up, and Howard had to help her out. She could hear the police talking in low voices to Josh, then look over at her.

"What's happened to you, love?"

SCENE XXI—BARTONSHIRE
Saturday, September 27th, 11:45 P.M.
The house at Little Elmley

Josh was taken into the dining room via the french window, to find a woman—dark-haired, well-dressed, attractive—in charge. Elizabeth and Paul were already there, sitting at the table, twisting round when he came in. The woman went out to talk to one of the policemen, and Josh sat down a little way away from the other two, his fingers nervously tapping the table.

He was worried about Sandie; she had looked terrible after the dive, and it had been obvious when Howard had helped her out of the boat that she was disoriented and unwell. The police had, of course, asked what had happened to her, and she had stuck to her story about the mugging, but he wasn't sure she could keep it up. The police had called an ambulance and had persuaded Sandie to go for a checkup, promising to bring her back as soon as she had been passed fit. Josh sighed tiredly; Sandie's injuries had made her a suspect, presumably, or she wouldn't be getting a taxi service from the police.

The woman came back in and introduced herself to Josh as

Detective Inspector Hill of Barton CID; she wanted to know where he had been, and he told her, then Josh watched his half brother's display of checked grief with distaste, as he trotted out the story he had had to concoct on his way home with Sandie. He especially liked the part about how worried Paul had been about him when he had found the boat broken into, and the emotional catch in his throat as he got to the end, when he'd found out what had happened to Angela. He got himself under manly control, Josh was pleased to note; his father would have been proud of him. Paul wouldn't cry for days just because his mother had died.

Josh didn't feel anything about Angela's death, and he wasn't going to pretend to. They could make of that what they liked.

Detective Chief Inspector Lloyd—not very tall, dark-complexioned, with a fringe of slightly greying hair round a mainly bald scalp—came in then; Josh had seen him in the kitchen with his stepmother's body as he had arrived in the police car. He would have thought they would have covered it up, but they hadn't.

When Sandie arrived back, Josh took her to one of the small, high-backed upholstered benches that were dotted at intervals round the walls, so he could sit beside her. She looked ill, much worse than she had when he had first seen her at the club, and that had been bad enough. She should never have done that dive.

Paul's simulated shock was no better than his grief, Josh thought, as he looked over at him. Elizabeth, of course, hadn't been anywhere near the club; Josh hadn't thought that she would be. And while poor Sandie trotted out her mugging story yet again, Josh caught Paul's eye and held it until Paul looked away.

Obviously, Elizabeth didn't believe a word of it, but she didn't challenge it openly in front of the police. The Esterbrooks were all playing their cards very close to their chests, thought Josh, and some of them were cheating. It was quite possible that he was the only person who had given them a true account of his movements that day.

Paul thought a burglar must have got in, but Lloyd didn't seem too happy with that explanation, wanting to know why he would have carried a gun if he had expected the house to be empty. Josh knew people who carried guns all the time; he was surprised that Chief Inspector Lloyd didn't.

Another detective came in then—youngish, blond curls, wearing clear plastic gloves. "There's an answering machine in your mother's—" he began.

"Stepmother." It was a simple enough concept, one which even the police ought to be able to grasp, but Josh had had to correct several of them already tonight. This one wanted to know what was on the tape in Angela's answering machine, but Elizabeth told him that the machine wasn't working properly and he wouldn't be able to play the tape. He didn't seem too bothered by that.

DCI Lloyd asked permission to use their first names; all this courtesy was amusing Josh, because once they had checked him out, it would vanish, and he would be treated as he always had been before. And the courtesy was skin deep, obviously, because Sandie looked dreadful, and they had no business questioning her. But she had been given a beating, and his stepmother was dead, and as far as the police were concerned, that couldn't possibly be a coincidence. Oh, they didn't say anything like that, but Josh knew how policemen's minds worked. They probably had him down for both offences already, and they certainly would once they knew his history.

Lloyd was more than a little impressed by the sum of money that would be going immediately to Paul, and if the fact that he, Josh, now stood to gain nothing whatever puzzled him, he was much too well brought up to show it. Josh thought it might be fun to let him see the will for himself. Lloyd moved on then to the odd lack of staff at the weekends in a house this size; he seemed quite unwilling to accept that Angela hadn't wanted staff, though that was one of the few absolute truths he had been told all night.

"She should be in bed, Josh," Elizabeth said when the police left the room.

Josh realized that somewhere along the line Sandie had fallen asleep, her head on his shoulder.

"The police have finished," Elizabeth said. "Take her to bed."

"He's already done that, apparently," said Paul with what he seemed to believe was a shaft of wit. "Just what clause were you protecting me from by not telling me you and Sandie were married, Josh?"

Josh smiled coldly. "It's all in the will, Paul," he said. "Believe me, it is."

"Are you *really* married?" asked Elizabeth.

Sandie opened her eyes with a little groan of pain, and Josh wanted to pick up the nearest heavy object and brain Paul with it, but he didn't. "Yes," he said to Elizabeth. "We're really married."

When the police reappeared, it was to ask Paul to accompany them to the station, and he was led off by the blond policeman, who had now divested himself of his plastic gloves. Josh watched Paul being taken out to a police car, then went round to his own part of the house to get his copy of the will for Chief Inspector Lloyd. When Lloyd and Inspector Hill left, only the people who were sealing off Angela's study and the kitchen, and the uniformed inspector, remained.

"Will you be all right to drive home, Mrs. Esterbrook?" the inspector asked Elizabeth.

Such concern. Nothing to do with the money that was oozing out of the walls, of course, thought Josh. He was sure they treated gasfitters and shop assistants with exactly the same polite concern for their finer feelings. But he had been pleasantly surprised by Lloyd and Hill; they were much more civilized police officers than the ones that he was used to.

"Yes, thank you," said Elizabeth, who had at least spared them all any pretence at deep grief, Josh thought. Just the odd shudder here and there.

SCENE XXII—BARTONSHIRE
Sunday, September 28th, 12:45 A.M.
Outside the house at Little Elmley

Elizabeth got into her car, her mind in a turmoil. She was having to do a complete rethink. Josh and Sandie, *married?* Josh would have to produce the marriage certificate before she would really believe it. Josh wasn't interested in women. She couldn't see why they would want to lie about it, but then, she had never heard so many people tell so many lies in so short a space of time in her life.

For a start, Sandie hadn't been mugged by anyone; Paul had done that to her, and Josh clearly knew he had; he had been glaring at Paul all night, and he had effectively tendered Sandie's resignation. Paul had hit her too, just once, when, early in their marriage, she had ve- toed a sexual suggestion of his and had found out about his violent temper. The next day she had gone straight to Paul's father, and he had put a stop to it, had even made certain that it wouldn't hap- pen after he'd gone, with his divorce clause. Now she occasionally amused herself by trying to goad Paul into doing it again, but Paul wasn't stupid.

Sandie hadn't had the protection of the will; Paul would have no hesitation in taking his anger out on her if she refused to comply with a request. But then, Sandie was with him precisely because she was prepared to do these things, so that particular situation wouldn't have arisen. Then why *had* he done it? Had he found out that she and Josh were married? Was *that* what had made him angry? But if she was still seeing him despite her marriage, what difference would it make to him? *Why* was she still seeing him, anyway? If being Paul's mistress was what she wanted, why on earth had she married Josh? And if she hadn't married him, why would they lie about it?

The questions took her round in a circle, which was broken only when she allowed herself to forget her preconceptions, her rigidly held belief that Sandie and Paul had been having an affair. He had al- ways denied it, naturally, and she had set no store by that denial at all. As perhaps she had been meant to do.

Angela had told her over and over again that it was *Josh* and Sandie who were the couple. She had taken that for, at best, wishful thinking, and at worst, deliberate falsehood. Even though she had seen it for herself on the boat that weekend, and that same evening at dinner, she had simply chosen to overlook it. But she had seen it again tonight; there was a chemistry, a bond, between Josh and Sandie, which was obvious even when they were at opposite sides of the room, and unmistakable when they were together, as they had been when Sandie had fallen into an exhausted sleep in his arms.

And Josh had told her that Sandie was *his* girlfriend, not Paul's, but she had thought that was just the skewed Esterbrook family loyalty. That they had been closing ranks on her, the outsider, so that she couldn't relieve them of some of their millions and cheat Paul of his great prize. She had never seen Josh so much as take a girl to the cinema since his marriage had broken up, and though Paul had said that Billy was just a stop-gap, it had blinded her to what she now had to accept was the truth. Sandie really had turned Josh round, just as Angela had hoped she would.

And, of course, Sandie had been at the house almost every time she had had occasion to go there in the last few weeks, but she had apparently been there at Angela's invitation, which Elizabeth had taken for a desperate attempt to get Josh's life sorted out.

Her private detective had told her it was Josh and Sandie who were the couple, and she had told him he was being misled. And she herself had thought, on that humiliating day on the boat, that Sandie might be a deliberate red herring being drawn across the trail, but she had dismissed that thought after Paul's lewd behaviour with Sandie.

That, of course, had also been a deliberate diversionary tactic. Josh was in on it, and Sandie was part of the conspiracy. And her marriage to Josh meant that her red-herring status was irrevocably compromised; that would certainly make Paul angry enough to do that to her, since it would mess up all his carefully laid strategy.

But it really didn't matter, Elizabeth told herself tiredly. It had been a wrong assumption, that was all. Nothing else had changed.

SCENE XXIII—BARTONSHIRE
Sunday, September 28th, 12:50 A.M.
Stansfield police station

Paul looked at the small tape, encased in a plastic bag, marked TF1, like the lady said. He was in an interview room with Detective Inspector Hill and Detective Sergeant Finch; they were taping the interview. He wasn't under arrest, they had said, but he had been cautioned as though he was, and he didn't really understand why. They had asked him about going to Little Elmley that evening, asked if he'd noticed anything suspicious, anything out of the ordinary. What he had said, what his mother had said. How long he'd been there, when he had got home to Barton, and what he'd done when he got there.

He had fallen asleep, his whisky untouched, not long after Elizabeth had left for dinner with his mother. The day had been too long, too stressful, too difficult and dangerous for him to remain conscious once he had reached a plateau. Risk-taking might be in the Esterbrook blood, he had thought, as he had practically fallen into the armchair, but he liked his risks to be calculated, not thrown at him as today's had been. He had been tired and shell-shocked, and he hadn't been able to summon up the energy to drink the whisky, or the brain power to work out whether or not he really had got away with it.

When he had opened his eyes, he had wondered, briefly, if he had dreamed it all. But he hadn't; it had all really happened, and he had realized that all he could do was wait and see if there was to be a reckoning. He had got up, his body stiff with tension, when the phone had rung, and had answered it to Elizabeth, telling him that his mother was dead.

And now he was here, and they seemed to think he had called his mother from the cottage. He had lied to them, said that he hadn't even been at the cottage. But he certainly *hadn't* made a phone call to his mother from there, and now they had produced this tape from the answering machine. He had no idea what was likely to be on it, but he had a bad feeling about it. Was this the reckoning? Were his chickens coming home to roost? He smiled a little tiredly, a little bitterly. One chicken in particular would cost him dear if it came strolling home.

"A copy has been made of that tape. I am now going to play it to you."

Paul heard his own voice, strained and gruff and unnatural.

"What the fuck are you doing? Are you trying to get me fucking dis-inherited? Jesus! I'm at the cottage, I've got your letter, and I'm on my way back right now."

"Did you leave that message for your mother, Mr. Esterbrook?" she asked.

"Yes," he said. He knew that his face had reddened as he had realized that his mother must have heard all that. He was barely listening to the question. Then he understood what they thought. "But I didn't make it today," he added hurriedly.

"When did you make it?" Finch asked.

"A month ago. The last time we all went to Josh's boat."

Naturally, they wanted the number of his mobile, and he had to say that he hadn't used his own. Naturally, they wanted to know whose phone he had used, and naturally, he wasn't going to tell them. "I can't remember," he said lamely. It occurred to him that Sandie, who could lie with total conviction, would be handling this a lot better than he was.

"You can't *remember?*" It was Finch who had spoken. The aggressiveness and naked disbelief was even more threatening after the mild-mannered Inspector Hill. Paul thought double acts belonged in old films, but here they were, Finch and Hill. Nasty cop and nice cop.

"No," he said, beginning to feel a little more in control now that it had become confrontational. "I can't remember. I'd borrowed one. Everyone I know has a mobile phone."

Inspector Hill smiled. "Well, don't worry about that just now Mr. Esterbrook. You might remember when you've had a chance to get over the shock of your mother's death."

Oh, Jesus. Not so nice cop, maybe. But he couldn't do everything at once. Grief had had to be put on the back burner. He looked down at the tabletop.

"Were you at your mother's cottage today?" she asked again.

It wasn't his mother's cottage anymore, he thought. It would be Josh's now; his mother had made it clear to all of them that Josh wouldn't find himself homeless if he lost his right to occupancy at Little Elmley. He would get *Lazy Sunday* and the cottage.

But he had lost his right of occupancy, and that great barn of a place was going on the market as soon as the lawyers said it could, as far as Paul was concerned; he would take great pleasure in kicking his brother out. He might donate it and its upkeep to some charitable institution; a convalescent home, or a hospice, or something. That would be good for a CBE, maybe. His father had turned down a knighthood, for some reason; he wouldn't.

They still wouldn't believe him about the call. Since it was one of the few true statements he had made since he had got here, you would think they would do him the courtesy of believing it.

DI Hill looked as though she really wanted to believe him but just couldn't bring herself to. "It's a strange call, Mr. Esterbrook," she said. "A little threatening, I would have thought. Would you like to explain it?"

No, he would not. "I didn't make it this afternoon," he repeated.

They seemed to be under the misapprehension that his mother had written a letter to him and left it at the cottage, and DI Hill quoted his apparent greeting to his mother. The word that Paul used almost constantly, without conscious thought, sounded shocking to him when it issued from her mouth, and he could feel himself flush with embarrassment again.

"That seems an odd way to talk to your mother," she said.

He hadn't *been* speaking to his mother. He'd been speaking to Sandie, who had begun making free with his body while he was waiting for his mother's answering machine message to play; he had laid the phone down on his chest as he remonstrated with her, and had realized too late that it had started recording. The phone had picked up every word. Bloody hell, they would have to find that call, of all

222 [· *Jill McGown* ·]

calls. His mother, of course, had never mentioned it, on her famous least-said-soonest-mended principle.

Now the inspector was saying that someone had made a call from the cottage this afternoon, about six hours before he got to Little Elmley. There was something very odd going on here.

She smiled. "Were you at your mother's cottage today?" she asked again.

"No." What the hell was going *on*?

"Do you know who else might have been there?"

Yes, he had a very good idea who else was there, but he wasn't going to tell them, and risk giving Elizabeth ammunition. Paul's brain was numb with all the lies, all the confusion. "No," he said. "But everyone's got keys."

"Does the cottage belong to the Trust too?"

"No. No, it was my mother's. But she thought we all ought to be able to use it."

"All?"

"Josh and me and my wife." And of course, Josh had a wife too now, he remembered, still finding that hard to believe. Why would he marry Sandie, for God's sake? He knew what she was. "I don't know about Sandie," he added. "Look—this is just a coincidence. My mother obviously put in an old tape when the machine went on the blink, whether she has arthritis or not, whether you've found a discarded one or not. I don't know who made the call today, but it wasn't me. I made that call the last time I was in Penhallin." But it didn't make *sense*. He knew it didn't. His mother couldn't have changed the tape.

Finch started in on him then, and she just sat back and let him. Paul didn't have time to answer one question before the next one was asked, all accusing him of lying, and sometimes, yes, he *had* been lying, but sometimes he had been telling the truth, and he didn't know which was which because the questions came so quickly.

But the pieces began to fall into place. He was being set up. He was being set *up*. And the only way he could prove that he hadn't made that call today would give Elizabeth the evidence she needed to divorce him. He could feel his face reddening as he realized that he had walked right into some trap. He was between a rock and a hard place, and it wasn't happening by accident. Josh—it had to be Josh. He had known, known from the moment he'd realized that Josh would never be so stupid as to ram the boat into the harbour wall by mistake, that he was plotting something. But why this? What good would it do him?

And he could prove, as far as the police were concerned, that he had been nowhere near the cottage today, which was something Josh didn't know he could do. He could make them believe a lie, in time. But they wouldn't believe the truth right now, that he had made that call a month ago. Everything he said got him in deeper; it even sounded to him as though he was making it up as he went along, but it was the truth. It was the *truth*. The only person who could prove his story was Josh, and it was Josh who was doing this to him. He might not get out of here at this rate, and if he was a suspect for murder then he couldn't even be certain of his alibi.

He forced himself to think straight. If he had been captured, if he were being tortured by some enemy's secret service, he would be giving his name, rank, and number. There was a drill like that in this situation too.

"I think if you intend to continue questioning me, I would like my solicitor to be present after all," he said.

But she was saying that he was free to go, that she had no more questions, and Paul stood up, dazed. Please God, let this be a dream. Still a dream. He had dreamed everything. Dreamed he had woken from a dream, found it wasn't a dream, but it *was* still a dream. Except that it wasn't.

He left the station and hailed a cab. "Little Elmley," he said, still in a fog of confusion. That was where his car was, and he didn't want to leave it there and have to get it in broad daylight. He hoped he could just sneak in and pick it up without Josh seeing him; Josh was going to be less than pleased by what he'd done to Sandie, in view of the fuss he'd made when all he'd done was slap her round a bit, and in view of the fact that he'd *married* her. Why, for God's sake? And anyway, he didn't want to see either of them until he'd had a chance to think.

Either he had been set up, or the whole thing was a ghastly co-incidence, and he had to work out which, because if Josh was behind this, then there would be more to come. He hadn't gone to all this trouble just to inconvenience him; he must have something worse up his sleeve. But he couldn't see how Josh would gain by any of it; it made no sense at all. So perhaps, perhaps, it was just a coincidence.

SCENE XXIV—BARTONSHIRE
Sunday, September 28th, 2:10 A.M.
Outside the house at Little Elmley

The taxi drove through the grounds of Little Elmley, and Paul stopped it as soon as he got within walking distance of his car. The front of the house, he noted with relief, was in darkness. He paid the taxi driver, waving away the change, and walked slowly, carefully, quietly, on the grass rather than the gravel driveway, to his own car, closing the door as quietly as he could.

There was a slight incline all the way back down to the wood; it was possible that he could put the car in reverse and coast down, not starting the engine until he was far enough away not to produce any sort of confrontation. He found reverse, let off the hand brake, and held his breath while the car's wheels crunched on the driveway, turning in his seat to see by the light of the moon where he was going.

And that was when he realized that he was not alone.

SCENE XXV—BARTONSHIRE
Sunday, September 28th, 6:25 A.M.
The house at Little Elmley

Sandie woke to find Josh looking down at her, and she smiled. Her lip didn't bleed this time, thank goodness. "Make love to me," she said.

He smiled, shook his head. "Not yet," he said.

"You said not until I'd had a good night's sleep, and I've had a good night's sleep."

"It's half past six in the morning," Josh pointed out. "You weren't in bed till past midnight. I don't call that a good night's sleep."

"But it was quality sleep," she said with a smile. "I didn't even hear you come to bed."

"I know. I was worried you might have a concussion or something."

"He didn't hit me *that* hard." She sat up, wincing as her body protested at the movement, trying not to show it. He had hit her quite hard enough to be going on with. But she didn't care, she wanted Josh. She needed him.

She needed the high, after the deep lows of yesterday: bruised and bleeding and being sick in the middle of nowhere, her miserable exhausting dive, sitting in Angela's dining room, with Elizabeth and Josh both glaring at Paul, and Paul pretending to be shocked; lying to the police, worrying that they would realize it was a lie as soon as she had spotted her mistake. Now, she needed Josh to make her feel better.

She kissed him, but he didn't respond, and she pulled back a little. "Does it put you off, me looking like this?" she asked.

"No! Not like that, it doesn't. But I'm afraid I'll hurt you." His fingertip gently touched her lip, and she saw blood on it. "See?" he said. "You're bleeding again."

"Then I won't kiss you." She pushed him down onto his back. "It's only a few bruises," she said.

Thus it was that when the phone rang, neither of them felt inclined to answer it. Or when it rang again. Or even the third time it rang.

SCENE XXVI—BARTONSHIRE
Sunday, September 28th, 7:10 A.M.
Elizabeth's house

Elizabeth had tried every phone in the whole of Little Elmley. Josh's phone, the main phone, Angela's phone. There were extensions everywhere; the place must have sounded as though it was on fire. Then she'd tried them all again, and now she was back to Josh's phone. Where were they, for God's sake? She hung up and tried the other two numbers with little hope of anyone answering.

She had fallen asleep in the chair last night, waking at five o'clock in the morning. She had been going to ring the police to ask why they were still holding Paul, but had thought better of it; if they had still been holding him, she would have been told. She didn't want the police here, asking more questions. She had waited an hour or so before trying to raise an answer from Little Elmley.

She hung up and rang Josh's number again.

SCENE XXVII—BARTONSHIRE
Sunday, September 28th, 7:25 A.M.
Little Elmley

Josh heard the tiny ping that his phone made before it gave its shrill announcement, and picked the receiver up quickly before it wakened Sandie, who had fallen asleep after they had made love, unlike him. He had lain awake, wondering how all this was going to resolve itself.

"Josh Esterbrook."

"Where have you been? Is Paul with you?"

"Well, someone's in bed with me. I'll just check." Josh looked over his shoulder at the sleeping Sandie, picked up a tissue and dabbed at her lip, which had of course started bleeding again. He turned away and addressed the receiver once more. "No," he said. "It's Sandie, I'm glad to say."

"It's not funny! He hasn't come home. I thought he might have gone back to Little Elmley. I think he might be afraid to face me."

"He might be," said Josh. "But if he did come here, he wisely didn't let me see him." He heard the front doorbell echo through the house. Why was everyone in the world so desperate to get him out of bed at this time on a Sunday morning?

"He might be there somewhere," Elizabeth said. "But he won't answer the phone if he is. Will you look for him? And send him back, when you've finished with him."

She was trying to get him to do her a favour, Josh thought as the front doorbell pealed again. She wanted to cross-examine her husband about yesterday, but she wouldn't mind if she got him back in the same state as he'd left Sandie. He heard his own doorbell then, and sighed. "Someone's at the door," he said. "I'll ring you back." He pulled on a pair of jeans and padded barefoot down the hallway, smoothing down his tousled hair as he opened the door to Chief Inspector Lloyd, Detective Inspector Hill, and the blond one.

Josh was invited to go with Lloyd to Penhallin, and was suspicious enough of police tactics to agree, though a trip to Penhallin was not something he really wanted right now. There were some questions about the last visit to Penhallin, and Josh answered them as he made coffee. They wanted to know if Paul had been at the cottage, and Josh confirmed that he had.

"Did you ring him there?" asked the blond one, whose name, Josh had discovered, was Finch. He was a sergeant; he looked a lot younger than the sergeants that Josh had had dealings with in the past.

The kettle began to sing, much to his relief. He needed a coffee before he could feel that his day had begun. He'd be quicker once he'd had his dose of caffeine, he thought, and he needed to be, because he had said yes to Finch's question before he realized that he'd have had to know that Paul was at the cottage in order to do that. Finch was jumping on it, wanting to know why he had rung the cottage, and he had no answer, so he picked up Sandie's coffee and was on his way with it when he thought he might as well find out if they had seen Paul's car.

At first it seemed they hadn't, but Finch's voice reached him as he went down towards the bedroom.

"There's a Range Rover parked in the wood by the road up to the house. I thought it might be an estate worker or something."

Josh carried on, and went into the bedroom. "Coffee," he said softly, bending, kissing her hair. It didn't tousle; it was too short. He put the mug on the bedside table. "Be careful with it. It's hot."

"What's happening?" she murmured.

"The police are here again, and the woman wants to talk to you about this mugging you invented." He sat on the bed. "You don't have to see her if you don't feel up to it," he said. "But she says she's happy to talk to you here. What do you want to do?"

"I'll see her," she said. "I'm fine, really, I am."

"Are you going to tell her the truth?"

"No. I don't want to bring Paul's name into it," she said. "I'll tell her a different story. One that covers my mistake and keeps Paul out of it. The more lies I tell, the more likely they are to work it out for themselves, but it won't have come from me."

Josh nodded. That was probably very sensible. He smiled sadly, patted her hand. "All right, boss," he said.

"And I don't want her in here. Tell her I'll be through in about fifteen minutes."

"Right." He stood up, still feeling angry every time he looked at her. "I might have to go out," he said. "It won't be for long, I promise. I'll be back before you're dressed." He picked up a T-shirt and pulled it on as he went back to the kitchen.

He told them that he wanted a word with Paul, but that was something they seemed anxious to stop him doing; eventually Lloyd suggested that they take him to the car, and he realized that going down with three policemen in tow would be even better, and agreed. And that was how they all came to find Paul, dead in the Range Rover, a revolver lying on the floor, under the dash. But not just any revolver.

His revolver.

SCENE XXVIII—BARTONSHIRE
Sunday, September 28th, 8:00 A.M.
Little Elmley

Josh hadn't come back before she had finished dressing, as he had promised; Josh hadn't come back at all, and Sandie had gone outside, walked slowly round the house and down towards the main gate. Once again Little Elmley was alive with police cars as the now-familiar yellow crime-scene ribbon flapped and snapped in the brisk breeze, and the wood was cordoned off. She met Josh and Chief Inspector Lloyd on their way back to the house. "What's happened?" she asked, seeing the blond policeman driving away. But DI Hill was still there.

"It's Paul," Josh said. "He's dead."

She made to walk past them, but Josh stopped her.

"No," he said, putting his arm round her and turning her in the direction of the house. "Don't go down there. It isn't very nice. There's blood everywhere."

So Paul had got blood on the car seats after all; Sandie took some pleasure in that irony as she walked with Josh and Lloyd back up to the house, trying to keep up with their longer and doubtless less painful strides. The beating and its aftermath, the discomfort of the dive, the constant fear, and, yes, as Josh had warned her, her considerably more pleasant exertions of the morning were all taking their toll now, as her tense muscles tried to tie themselves in knots. But Josh was still worth it. He always would be.

Josh was going with Lloyd to Penhallin, and it was clear that they were not going to be able to talk before he left, so she would have to play the next bit by ear. Paul was dead, but she still had more lies to tell. If she told them now that Paul had assaulted her, suspicion might fall on Josh, and she wasn't going to let that happen.

DI Hill appeared almost as soon as Lloyd and Josh had left for Penhallin, and she felt the familiar rush of adrenaline. She was sure that DI Hill had nailed her lie about the mugging, but she would weather that easily enough now that she'd had a good night's sleep, and Josh, and a shower. The aches and pains seemed to disappear. Josh was right: she got off on danger.

"I take it your husband's told you what's happened?"

Sandie nodded. She was taking her cue from Josh; he wasn't pretending to be any more moved by Paul's death than his stepmother's, and neither would she.

"You worked for Paul, I gather."

"Yes. I was his personal assistant."

"Is that how you met Josh?"

Sandie decided to stick to the official line, the one that Elizabeth had got. "No," she said. "It was the other way round. I met Paul when he came diving with us, and then I went to work for him."

"How did you get on with him?"

"Very well."

The inspector's eyebrows rose a little. "You seem remarkably calm about his death," she said. "For someone who got on with him very well."

"I didn't like him all that much," she said. "But we worked together very well."

Inspector Hill abandoned questions about Paul. "I would like to go over part of your statement concerning the mugging," she said.

"I wasn't mugged," she said apologetically. "I just said that."

"Well, *something* certainly happened to you, Mrs. Esterbrook," she said quietly. "Would you like to tell me what?"

"Do you think you could call me Sandie?" she asked. "I feel like Josh's stepmother when you call me Mrs. Esterbrook."

Inspector Hill smiled. "Certainly," she said. "Will you tell me who did that to you, Sandie?"

Sandie prepared herself before she spoke. "Josh and I got married on an impulse," she said. "I moved in with him, but most of my stuff was still in my flat, and yesterday I spent all day ferrying things from there to here. But on my last trip, my ex-boyfriend was there."

"Your ex-boyfriend," said Inspector Hill, with a look on her face that suggested that this story wasn't going down any better with her than the last one.

But that was all right, thought Sandie. This was going to be one that couldn't be instantly disproved, not like her below-par attempt of yesterday, when all they'd had to do was check where her car was. She took a deep breath and let it out slowly. "My ex-boyfriend," she repeated.

"And he just happened to know you'd be there, did he?"

"No," said Sandie. "He lives there. I left him for Josh, you see— that's why I hadn't been back for my things. But I thought he'd be working late—he usually does on the last Friday of the month, and that's why I waited until yesterday to get my stuff. But at teatime, he was there, and he thought I'd come back to him. I told him Josh and I had got married, and . . ." She moved her shoulders in a shrug. "He lost his temper."

"Where does he work?"

"I'd rather not say."

"Is he still at the flat?"

"No. He just packed up his own things and left. I rang Josh, and he came for me, brought me here. But he had to go to the club, and I wanted to do the night dive, so I went with him."

"Why didn't you tell us this in the first place?"

"I don't want to get Brendan into trouble. He's never done anything like that before. It was my fault—I should have told him about me and Josh."

"What's Brendan's other name?"

"I'd rather not say."

"It's up to you," said Inspector Hill, shaking her head. "But I don't think anyone should get away with that."

"That's why I didn't want to tell you, said Sandie. "Josh wants me to make a complaint. But it's . . . it's just between Brendan and me."

The inspector didn't believe her, but unless and until she had to, Sandie wasn't going to tell anyone the truth about what had happened to her.

SCENE XXIX—BARTONSHIRE
Sunday, September 28th, 9:00 A.M.
Elizabeth's house

Elizabeth was entertaining Detective Sergeant Finch. She much preferred the courtly Chief Inspector Lloyd, but Finch had broken the news to her reasonably gently. She wasn't attempting a portrayal of deep grief; Paul had tried that last night over his mother, and no one had been fooled. She thought that dignified acceptance might be better. For almost half an hour Finch talked in general terms about Paul before he got down to the difficult questions, ill at ease with his task.

He asked her if Paul might have killed himself, and she told him about the will, and why Paul's father had felt it necessary to make the condition that he had about Paul's inheritance. Then he asked if Paul might have killed Angela. Not in so many words, but as good as. She had to tell him about Foster, of course; he seemed startled that she would have stooped to such a level, and she found herself justifying her actions. Watching people, spying on them, would be, she supposed, part of Finch's job; he had no call to criticize her. But she felt the need to explain to this man how her marriage had got to that pitch.

She had tried Foster's number just before Finch had arrived, just in case he was in the office on a Sunday; she didn't suppose he worked regular hours. He hadn't been there, of course, and she had thought, foolishly, that she would have to wait until he was before she could get his report. It hadn't occurred to her that the police could find him on a Sunday, not until now. But they would find out where he lived, go and see him, and then they would see that Paul hadn't killed his mother.

And then she told Finch about the revolver, and that Josh had been in prison for killing a man. He left right after that.

SCENE XXX—CORNWALL
Sunday, September 28th, 2:00 P.M.
Angela's cottage

Lloyd had got people to search the boat, hoping, no doubt, to find a whole cache of weapons, or a secret compartment bulging with packets of white powder. All they'd find down there would be some tea bags. One of them, Detective Sergeant Comstock—bad complexion, slicked-back hair—had come back up to where they stood, looking disappointed. "Whatever was used to break the lock has been thrown in the sea, probably," he had said.

Lloyd had nodded, and they had moved on to his stepmother's cottage, where Comstock went over to the desk, and Josh could feel waves of triumph emanating from where he stood, as he called Lloyd in from the kitchen.

Josh wandered over, saw the burnt and crushed remains of a piece of paper in the wastepaper basket. The scene-of-crime people were eager to get it to a lab. Comstock took the pad from the desk to get it checked out.

They all went upstairs then, Lloyd opened his stepmother's bedroom door, and Josh found himself looking at Billy Rampton's dead body, half dressed, sprawled across the floor. It was then that the enormity of what was happening hit him for the very first time, and it took him some moments to recover himself, during which the people invading his stepmother's privacy swung into action.

"Stay there, please, Mr. Esterbrook," said Lloyd, and went into the room, crouched down by the body, and shook his head. Then he asked if Josh knew him.

Josh told him some of what he knew of Billy. Not all. But he did indicate that he knew him well enough to know he was no loss.

Lloyd seemed to think that was uncalled-for, but then he didn't know Billy, and Josh did. Josh knew him much better than he would ever have chosen to know someone like that, but sometimes life just threw people together. Now, Lloyd was asking him if his position under the will would change if Paul had murdered his mother. He was still being very polite; his manner hadn't changed, not at all, once he'd discovered that Josh had a criminal record, but deep down he was just the same as all the others.

Josh was a suspect.

SCENE XXXI—CORNWALL
Sunday, September 28th, 3:15 P.M.
Penhallin police station

Josh was invited to help the Penhallin police with their enquiries, and it was almost like the old days. He was asked what he knew of Billy, and he still admitted to a lot less than he did know. They didn't seem to think that he'd murdered him, whatever Lloyd thought, but they did think that his revolver had been used, so he had made a statement concerning the revolver, saying that he had kept it for self-defence. As Paul had warned him, the silencer knocked that on the head, and he was told that it was an offence to own even it, never mind the revolver. That he might be charged with possession of a firearm with intent to endanger life.

"You are aware that in view of your criminal record, you are quite likely to receive a prison sentence?" said Comstock.

"You don't need a licence for a firearm that forms part of a ship's equipment," said Josh, his face entirely serious. "It's one of the exemptions."

Comstock looked a little fazed, and Josh smiled.

"Do you think this is funny?" demanded Comstock.

That was more like it. That was what Josh was used to. "Yes," he said.

"You wouldn't be granted a licence, therefore the exemption wouldn't apply in your case. And you kept the gun in an unlocked drawer, according to your statement. Plus, it's almost certainly been used in the commission of a murder. Plus, you've got a silencer for it. They'll throw the book at you, Esterbrook."

"Sure about that?" asked Josh.

In the end they decided to send details of the firearms offence to the CPS, being unable to decide whether Josh's boat counted as a ship, and if a handgun in a drawer counted as part of that ship's equipment, even if his boat *was* a ship for purpose of law, or if that drawer being unlocked constituted an offence in itself, and whether any or all of that applied to the separate offence of owning a silencer. Not to mention whether any exemption would apply to him in the first place, in view of his criminal conviction. And since all handguns had been outlawed anyway, it seemed more than likely, they said, that he would be charged.

Josh had smiled. He knew that. He was just winding them up, because it was fun. "Am I free to go now?" he asked.

"Yes, I suppose so," said Comstock.

Josh found a quiet spot and rang Sandie, told her what had happened and when he expected to be home. He terminated the call as Comstock came to escort him off the premises, and grinned at him. "Just phoning my wife," he said. "Do I need a licence for that?"

"You won't think it's so funny if you go back inside," said Comstock as he saw him back to the car where Lloyd waited, impatient to get back.

No, probably not. But he had survived it before, and he could survive it again, especially if Sandie were waiting for him on the outside.

SCENE XXXII—BARTONSHIRE
Sunday, September 28th, 9:00 P.M.
Little Elmley

It was dark by the time they got back to Little Elmley, but Lloyd, instead of telling the driver to take him back to Stansfield, got out of the car. "I'd like another word with your wife," he said.

Sandie was in the sitting room, and jumped up as Josh opened the door, only to see Lloyd coming in behind him. She sat down again, and Lloyd sat opposite her.

"Josh rang and told me what you found at Angela's cottage," she said. "That's awful."

"Yes," said Lloyd. "But that's not exactly why I'm here, Mrs. Ester-brook. You had a word with Inspector Hill this morning, I believe."

She nodded. "Call me Sandie," she said.

"I'm afraid DI Hill doesn't think much more of ex-boyfriends with no surname and no fixed abode than I did of two phantom mug-gers." He suddenly sounded infinitely more Welsh than he had in Penhallin, thought Josh. "Apparently, no one in your block of flats re-members seeing any man living at your address."

So that was what she'd told them this time round, Josh thought with a smile. She would stick to it for as long as she could, he knew. He wasn't convinced that it mattered as much as she thought it did, and the chief inspector's next statement made her reticence redundant.

"We saw you at about eleven o'clock last night," he said. "And be-lieve me, we see a lot of bruises in our line of work. Yours had been inflicted much earlier than you told us. I would say you got those in-juries at about lunchtime yesterday, and Elizabeth Esterbrook has accused her husband of causing them. Is she right?"

Sandie looked at Josh in dismay. Paul's violent temper and Eliza-beth's intimate knowledge of him was going to force her hand whether she liked it or not. It might as well all come out now, Josh thought, and he gave her a little nod.

"Yes," she said.

Lloyd nodded. "What exactly was your job with Mr. Esterbrook?" he asked.

"I was his P.A., officially. But really, I was a decoy."

Lloyd nodded; he didn't seem surprised, or ask for an explanation. But Sandie gave him one anyway.

"He was sure Elizabeth was having him watched, and he employed me to stand in the spotlight, to be a sort of visible target," she said. "That way, anyone watching would be busy keeping an eye on me, and not notice what was really happening."

"Which was?"

"He was seeing Billy Rampton."

Lloyd looked at Josh. "You knew, did you, that Sandie was em-ployed in this way?"

"Yes," said Josh. "That's how I met her." He grinned, genuinely amused by the memory of that day. "Paul brought Elizabeth and Sandie to the boat, making it so abundantly clear to Elizabeth that Sandie was *my* girlfriend that she would be bound to believe the opposite." He smiled at Lloyd's slightly baffled expression. "You have to understand that the Esterbrook mind is a very devious and cunning thing," he said. "The more Paul made it look as though it was his relationship with Sandie that he was trying to cover up, the less likely it became that Elizabeth or anyone she employed to watch him would realize what was really happening. Insisting that she was my girlfriend was part of the deception. But his fiction became reality."

"How did this subterfuge operate?" Lloyd asked Sandie.

She took a breath. "When the Saturday afternoon diving began, Paul would go below. Everyone goes down there at one time or another—we use the other cabin for our gear. Billy and I always went down together. When no one else was round, he'd go to Paul, and I'd hang about in the other cabin. If anyone asked where Billy was, Josh would say he was diving, without mentioning who with."

"I'm the only one who knows exactly who's in the water at any time, so that was easy," said Josh.

Sandie carried on. "When Billy was ready to leave, he'd bang on the wall, and I'd knock back once the coast was clear. He'd change into his diving gear, and no one was any the wiser. As long as the three of us were together, Paul was safe."

Lloyd looked like someone playing some sort of parlour game to which everyone knew the rules but him. "And how did this result in your being assaulted?"

"My job was to accompany Paul on his weekends on the boat," Sandie said. "That's what he paid me to do. But Josh didn't really want me to go on doing it, so . . ." She shrugged. "He put the boat out of commission for a few weeks."

Lloyd's eyes flicked over to Josh. "You holed it on purpose?"

"Yes," said Josh. "Then I persuaded the boatyard to say it needed a complete overhaul. It was supposed to be back in business at the weekend, but I had to be at the diving club, so I told Paul he'd have to use the cottage if he wanted his weekend fix."

Sandie continued. "Paul had been getting more and more paranoid—seeing conspiracies everywhere. First, it was his mother and Elizabeth who were plotting against him, then on Saturday he'd decided that it was me and Josh, because he'd realized that Josh had holed the boat deliberately. I had to tell him why Josh had really done it." She pointed to her eye. "This was the result. He paid me to work for him, not screw Josh, that's what he said."

Josh felt the anger, just as strongly as ever. Paul was dead, and it made no difference. That bastard hadn't been content with knocking her about; he had scared her half to death after he'd done it, driving off and leaving her there. Josh had let her down; he had misjudged Paul, mishandled the situation.

"Where did the assault take place?"

He could feel Sandie's discomfort at having to talk about it at all. "On Bodmin Moor, I suppose," she said. "He made a long detour. I don't know where we were—it was deserted and creepy."

He took her somewhere quiet and secluded, and abused her. That was what Josh had told Sandie he'd done to the boat, and he had actually felt guilt when he had done that to *Lazy Sunday*. What had Paul felt after he'd done it to Sandie? Anything?

"That was why I had to tell him," Sandie said. "He was going to leave me there if I didn't. He did leave me there after he'd hit me." She reached across Josh for cigarettes. Those moments on the moor still made her feel sick, he knew, and he knew she didn't want to think about it, far less talk about it. "But he came back. If he'd done that to me anywhere else, I'd have told him to get lost. But I had to get back in the car and go with him."

"And he was going to the cottage to meet Billy Rampton?"

"Yes."

"How often did he use the cottage?"

"He didn't, not really. He only used it twice. The Bank Holiday weekend, and yesterday."

"Were you there the first time he used the cottage?"

"Yes. It was when Josh holed the boat. Paul sent me off to the cottage, in case someone was watching *me*, because that way I'd lead them away from what was really happening. And Josh gave Billy Paul's hotel key. Billy went to the hotel, and Paul joined him there a little later."

"How did he end up at the cottage?" asked Lloyd.

"Something made Paul edgy about the hotel—he had never used his hotel room before. Just the boat."

"Did anything specific happen to make him edgy?"

Sandie shrugged. "I'm not sure. Billy's a liar, so you can't place much store by what he says, but he told me that someone had walked in on them by mistake, and after that Paul had told him to get dressed and go to the cottage. All I know for certain is that Billy arrived at the cottage at half past seven on Sunday morning, and Paul came a little while later with breakfast for everyone, and said he wasn't staying at the hotel, because it wasn't safe."

"And did Paul make a phone call while he was there?"

"I think he rang his mother. He was with Billy most of the time, so I don't really know."

"And yesterday," said Lloyd. "Did Paul pick Billy up, or what?"

"Billy was already there when we got there. I didn't realize that until I went inside."

Sandie told him about her being outside having a cigarette, when Paul had come out, agitated. That he'd driven off, saying he would be back for her, and she had gone in to tidy up anything he'd disturbed, to repack what he'd unpacked, and that was when she realized that Billy was there. She told him to go, but Billy refused to leave without being paid; he wouldn't even get dressed. She had no money, because her bag was still in the car, so she waited for Paul, and when he came back, she told him that Billy was still inside. Paul went into the cottage for a few moments, and when he came out, told her that he was letting Billy stay there rather than go all the way back to Plymouth, and then they'd driven back.

"Did that surprise you?"

"Everything was happening so quickly, I didn't really think about it, but yes. I mean, I wouldn't have thought he'd have let Billy stay there. But I didn't see his motorbike, so maybe it really was difficult for him to get back. To be honest, I wasn't all that interested in Billy. I just wanted to get home."

"I'm sure you did. Did Paul explain what had gone wrong?"

"After a bit," said Sandie, and recounted her ride home with Paul, leaving out the expletives, Josh noticed, with a smile. She'd made him laugh when she told him, but Lloyd was getting the serious version.

Lloyd asked her if she had seen the fax, and she said she hadn't. He asked Josh if he had sent a fax, and Josh said no, that he hadn't had the faintest idea what Sandie was talking about when she had arrived at the diving club.

"She thought Elizabeth was there, but she wasn't, and she hadn't been there," he said. "But Paul was," he added grimly. "Making sure Sandie did her dive as instructed." He sighed. "And the rest you know. When we finished the dive, your people were waiting for me."

Lloyd's blue eyes rested on Josh's for a moment, before turning back to Sandie. "You said that Paul took deliberately over-elaborate precautions where you were concerned, Sandie. Making it obvious that he didn't want to be seen alone with you."

Sandie nodded.

"And yet he picked you up on Saturday morning even though you weren't even supposed to be going to Penhallin. That was hardly in keeping with the secret rendezvous image. Why would he do that?"

"I asked him that," said Josh. "I thought he'd want Sandie to go down under her own steam. But he said he was being blackmailed. Or, rather, than he *had* been being blackmailed. Someone had got a video of him somehow. He said he was taking care of it, whatever that meant. And that no one would be following him."

Lloyd's eyebrows rose. "When did you have that conversation?" he asked.

"Friday night. And he said that he'd pick Sandie up in his car."

"If no one was following him," said Lloyd, almost to himself, "then he didn't really *need* a decoy, did he?"

Josh stiffened.

"But I presume," he went on, glancing over at Sandie, "that he just wanted to get you on your own so he could get the truth out of you about why Josh had holed the boat."

"I suppose you're right," Sandie said. "I never thought about it at the time."

"Why didn't you tell us all this in the first place?" Lloyd asked as he rose to leave.

"With Paul sitting there?" said Sandie. "You're joking."

"After Paul ceased to be a threat to you. Why didn't you tell Inspector Hill this morning?"

Sandie looked at Josh, then back at Lloyd, and told the absolute truth for the very first time. "I thought you'd think Josh had killed him," she said.

Lloyd smiled, nodded a little. "Well, thank you for telling us the truth now," he said.

Josh and Sandie laughed about that, after he'd gone.

Act V
The
Investigation

See you now;
Your bait of falsehood takes this carp of truth;
And thus do we of wisdom and of reach,
With windlasses and with assays of bias,
By indirections find directions out . . .

                           Hamlet, Act 2, Scene 1

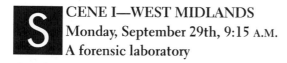

SCENE I—WEST MIDLANDS
Monday, September 29th, 9:15 A.M.
A forensic laboratory

Judy was at the police forensic laboratory, which had been built, to the Bartonshire Constabulary's lasting gratitude, outside Birmingham, just fifty miles from Stansfield, with the M6 practically door-to-door. It took her just over an hour in good weather, provided she didn't have Lloyd in the car. The top sheet of the pad found at Angela Esterbrook's cottage was to be submitted to an ESDA test, and with luck they would find out what she had written in the letter that she had left for her son to find.

She was in time to see it being done, and she watched, fascinated as she always was by the process, as the bed on which the paper lay under its clear plastic sheet was tipped up, the toner was sprinkled over the surface, and the writing became visible. She got the same thrill as she had as a child when she had learned that lemon juice worked as invisible ink.

Most of it showed up; some parts had failed, but the words could be pieced together. Angela Esterbrook's spacing was a little eccentric, making it sometimes difficult to tell if words had been in the spaces or not. But for the most part it was fairly unequivocal. It had been written angrily; the impressions were deep, and the handwriting not only legible, but, Judy imagined, recognizable.

Paul, it began, baldly. *I know what's been going on. You've been very good at deceiving me and everyone else, including your wife presumably, but you couldn't hope to get away with it forever. How dare you think you can use this cottage as some sort of sleazy love nest? How could you take advantage of me*—a space—*like that? If you don't want the world to know all about the*—a space that might have contained another word or words, but there were no evident marks—*little boy that you keep secret, come home immediately and give me a good reason why I shouldn't tell the police. Don't think I wouldn't do it. Don't ignore this letter.*

It was signed *Angela.*

" 'Angela,' " said Judy, frowning. "That seems an odd way to sign it."

"I suppose she could hardly put, 'Love, Mum,' " said the girl.

Judy smiled. "But Paul Esterbrook called her 'Mother' whenever he referred to her," she said. "She could have put that. It's formal enough. It's her stepson who calls her Angela."

"Are you going to send it to a handwriting expert?"

"I don't know if they can do much with recovered imprints."

"But if you think it might not be genuine . . ."

She'd have to see what Lloyd thought. It could certainly be what had brought Paul out of the cottage so suddenly, what had caused him to murder the two people who knew what he had been doing at his mother's cottage. But not Sandie Esterbrook, who also knew. He had had ample opportunity; why was she exempt from his apparent killing spree?

"Thank you," she said absently, and drove back to Stansfield not sure whether the ESDA test had wrapped up this investigation or presented another puzzle. There was something about that letter that bothered her. Nothing specific. Just the odd spacing, and the signature, and the luck with which all these pointers to Paul Esterbrook's guilt were falling in their laps. Sometimes murders needed no investigation, particularly domestics. But these murders could have presented considerably more difficulty than they had, and she just didn't like it.

SCENE II—BARTONSHIRE
Monday, September 29th, 10:30 A.M.
Judy's office, Stansfield police station

When Judy got back, Lloyd came in with yet another of the clues that he already felt were just too numerous. The scene-of-crime people had, as he had instructed, gone through everything in Angela Esterbrook's study at Little Elmley, and had found a concealed drawer in the antique bureau, in which she had clearly kept things that she hadn't wanted lying round for everyone to see. A bundle of love letters from her husband, written in the late fifties, an early, unfinished attempt at a novel, and the clue, the report from the Cope Detective Agency. Lloyd sat on the edge of her desk and read Angela Esterbrook's letter to Paul while Judy read the report:

At six-thirty a.m. on Sunday the 24th of August, I opened the door of Room 312 of the above mentioned hotel. There were two male people in the room. One, in his late thirties, about six feet tall, with dark wavy hair, dressed in an open bathrobe, was sitting on the edge of the single bed. The other, in his teens, about five feet six inches tall, with dyed blond hair and a tattoo of a spider on his left shoulder, was naked, and was performing a sexual act on the older man.

As per your instructions, I indicated to the occupants that I had inadvertently gone to the wrong floor, apologized, and left. A covert video, lasting only a few seconds, was made, but I regret that this was of very poor quality, and will be of no use to you. I enclose the printout of the only frame recoverable, and have not of course charged you for this. I hope the still photograph will suffice for your purposes.

"The hotel room was registered to Paul Esterbrook," said Lloyd. "The report was still in its envelope, and date-stamped Friday the twenty-ninth of August—but the video-frame wasn't with it."

Judy had questions. Why would Paul remove the visual evidence but leave the report? Why had his mother had a private detective checking up on him in the first place? Why on earth did she want a video? And what exactly had happened to it that it was of no use?

Lloyd, as ever, had different questions, ones that homed in on the little puzzles thrown up by the report. "How do you suppose Kathy Cope was able to take a covert video, however poor the quality?" he asked. "How could a little business like that have that sort of equipment? And why didn't we find it in the house?"

"Maybe she hired it," said Judy.

"With more of this money that she didn't have?" said Lloyd. "But I think it answers one little puzzle. It explains why a zillionaire would use Kathy Cope."

Judy frowned. "Does it?" she said.

"Tom established that the Copes had Room 412, directly above Esterbrook's," said Lloyd. "It seems to me that Mrs. Esterbrook knew the room number well in advance, and made certain Mrs. Cope booked the same room on a different floor so it would look like an honest mistake if Esterbrook checked up. And Kathy was able simply to walk in on them, so the door must have been unlocked, *and* they were conveniently *in flagrante* when she did." He shrugged slightly. "It looks as though someone arranged for that to happen at the appointed time."

"Billy?" said Judy.

"Billy. And he, presumably, told Mrs. Esterbrook that Paul had taken him to her cottage after that interruption to the proceedings, and that really got her blood boiling, so she left that letter for him to find the next time he tried that."

Judy wasn't happy with that letter.

"And it explains why she would use Kathy, because a more experienced private detective would have guessed that Mrs. Esterbrook was in league with whoever was in the room, and might have turned the job down. But Kathy wouldn't question it. She'd just go blundering in."

Judy stared at him. "You're saying his own mother colluded with a rent-boy to set him up?" she said.

Lloyd shrugged. "As I said, families are funny things. And this one is funnier than most, you have to concede." He pushed his chair back and rocked gently on the back legs. "And I don't know that she was setting him up, as such," he said. "The letter suggests she was just trying to scare Paul out of his way of life . . . after all, if his wife caught him, he'd lose everything."

"She got someone to video him for his own *good*?" said Judy.

Lloyd grinned, and let the chair fall forward. "Or—perhaps more importantly—a part of the business would leave the family if Elizabeth found out, and the family seems to have been very important to Angela Esterbrook, from what I hear."

"It seems Kathy sold the video to Esterbrook rather than send it to her client," Judy said, aware that she might be given an argument. "He said someone had got a video of him. And that he was dealing with it. He told Josh that the night the Copes died."

"But Kathy wouldn't blackmail anyone," said Lloyd, then backtracked. "Well, not of her own volition, anyway. She could get talked into it, I expect."

"By her husband, do you think?"

Lloyd shook his head. "From what I've heard about Andy Cope, he found the whole idea of spying on people unacceptable. I can't see him turning blackmailer."

But Kathy Cope had brand-new office equipment that she had paid for somehow, and that letter left little room for doubt, thought Judy—a faulty video, with just one frame that was of any use. And Lloyd's belief that they had been murdered surely clinched it.

"If they did blackmail him, and Esterbrook found out they'd sent a frame from it to Angela despite that," she said, "he might well have murdered them."

"Perhaps. Keep working on the little puzzles," Lloyd said, and looked at his watch. "Tom should be with Elizabeth Esterbrook's enquiry agent right about now, so that might help. In view of the Copes' report, I've told him to have a word with Mrs. Esterbrook while he's in Barton—try to find out what she knew about her husband's homosexual activities."

Tom? He seemed a very brave choice for something that required sensitive handling. Judy smiled. "Was that wise?" she said as she picked up the phone, thinking of a little puzzle that might not take too long to solve.

Lloyd grinned. "You're the one who said he needed to learn a bit of diplomacy."

"Yes, but he hasn't yet, not really." She held up a hand as her call was answered. "Excalibur Hotel, Plymouth," she said, listening to the recorded number, taking a note of it.

"I think this family can take Tom without cracking under the strain," said Lloyd. "He'll be all right, and he gets results. We've still got to prove that Paul Esterbrook did these murders, however helpful he's been about leaving us clues. Even Sandie's statement doesn't really do that—it just places him at the scene. And that's all that Foster's will do, I imagine."

"You're still not exactly happy with any of this, are you?" Judy asked.

"No," he said. "But I believe Sandie Esterbrook was telling the truth."

"Even the bit about being a decoy?"

Lloyd shrugged. "Paul Esterbrook stood to lose an enormous fortune," he said. "And the Esterbrook mind *is* a devious and cunning thing, as Josh said. Read the will—Paul Esterbrook *père* covered every conceivable eventuality."

"Except this one," said Judy.

"Yes. Which is one of the reasons that I'm not happy with it."

"Sandie Esterbrook needn't be lying," said Judy. "I think there's something funny about that letter. Why would she sign it 'Angela'?" Her eyebrows rose as a thought occurred to her. "It might have been written to her husband," she said. "The little boy she's talking about could be Paul himself. It could be an old letter, lying round because she's writing her autobiography." A terrible thought occurred to her then. "You don't think Paul just made a ghastly mistake, do you?" she asked.

Lloyd thought about that, then shook his head. "No," he said. "She's threatening him with the police over it. It might be a bit galling to be the mother of an unacknowledged son, but it's not against the law to have an illegitimate child." He smiled. "Besides, no one would be taken in by a letter that would have to be at least thirty years old, however slow on the uptake. I think it was written to Paul Junior, all right. I'm just not convinced that Angela wrote it."

"But what about the fax? Do you think he made that up?"

"No," said Lloyd, illogically. "I don't. Can you get someone on to that? Check out all the faxes available to other members of the family for a start, see if a fax was sent from one of their numbers to that number anytime in the last week. And ask the lab if the burned paper could be the remains of a fax."

"Right," said Judy, and turned her attention to her call. "Oh, good morning," she said when the hotel answered with commendable speed. "This is Detective Inspector Judy Hill, Stansfield CID, Barton-shire. I'm making enquiries about a couple who stayed with you over the twenty-third and twenty-fourth of August—Cope, Room 412. You're welcome to ring me back if you want to check my credentials, but I don't think you'll need to. I would just like you to check and see if Mr. Cope had any special requirements. Did he need wheelchair access?"

The girl didn't think it necessary to make sure that Judy was who she said she was. Judy could hear her checking back, then the phone being picked up.

"No," she said. "Nothing like that. And we would have to know, because people in wheelchairs have to use the service lift."

"You don't happen to remember what Mr. Cope looked like, do you?"

"No, I'm sorry. It was very busy then. It was the Bank Holiday."

"Of course. Thank you," said Judy, and hung up, glancing at Lloyd. "I thought the fourth floor was a bit unlikely for a wheelchair-bound guest," she said, and smiled. "I think we might have found the other man the neighbours heard the row about, the provider of surveillance equipment, and our blackmailer, all rolled into one."

"Yes, I rather think we have," said Lloyd. "That makes much more sense. Some boyfriend of Kathy's who talked her into blackmail—that I can believe." He pushed himself off her desk and went to the door. "We're going to have to find out who he is as well as everything else," he said with a sigh. "In the meantime, I'm going to the Copes' postmortem, which I believe will provide some answers, rather than conveniently useful clues."

SCENE III—BARTONSHIRE
Monday, September 29th, 11:00 A.M.
Ian Foster's office

"DS Finch, Stansfield CID."

The street door, sandwiched between a kebab house and a bookie, buzzed, and Tom pushed it open, going up two flights of a narrow staircase to find the business premises of Ian R. Foster, Private Enquiry Agent.

He opened it to find an office the size of Elizabeth Esterbrook's front porch, its walls lined with sagging shelving piled high with telephone directories, yearbooks, old copies of *Who's Who*, everything and anything that a jobbing enquiry agent might want to have to hand. A small L-shaped desk held a well-used word processor, a printer, photocopier, fax machine, and an electric kettle, leaving barely enough room for the woman who was wedged in behind it.

"I rang earlier," said Tom. "Mr. Foster is expecting me."

"Just go through," she said.

Tom pushed open another door into a very slightly larger office. Behind the desk sat, presumably, Ian R. Foster, Private Enquiry Agent, small, shabbily dapper, with a dark moustache. He looked suspicious; Tom had not said why he wanted to see him.

"What can I do for you, Sergeant Finch?"

"I'm told you were observing the husband of a Mrs. Elizabeth Esterbrook at the weekend," said Tom. "I'd like to know what he did."

Foster looked horrified. "I'm sorry, Sergeant," he said. "But I couldn't possibly discuss that without my client's permission. You should have said when you rang. I would have told you it was impossible."

"It's your client who wants you to tell me."

"Well, I can't just take your word for that, can I? I would be failing in my duty to my client. I am not, of course, confirming that I have a client of that name."

Tom picked up the phone on the desk and dumped it down in front of him. "Yes, you have," he said. "Ring her."

Ian R. Foster called the client he wouldn't confirm that he had, told her Tom was there, asked if he could divulge the contents of her report, and hung up. "She seems very anxious that I tell you what's in it," he said. "I can't imagine why. What's it got to do with the police?"

Tom smiled without humour. "I couldn't possibly discuss that without my Chief Inspector's permission," he said. "Just tell me what Esterbrook did on Saturday."

Foster sighed, and reached into his pocket for a small loose-leaf notebook, turning back a few pages. "Saturday, the twenty-seventh of September. I arrived at subject's residence at six A.M., but subject did not leave until seven-thirty."

"What time did he normally leave?"

"Half past six. He usually went to Stansfield and picked up his secretary or whatever she is, but he didn't do that this time." Foster carried on. "Subject drove, with one stop at a motorway service area, to Plymouth, where he stopped at the Excalibur Hotel. He ate lunch alone, and left the Excalibur at 1420 hours, arriving in Penhallin harbour at 1510 hours. He left his vehicle and boarded the boat *Lazy Sunday*, which appeared to me to be deserted. While aboard the boat he spent some moments examining the wheelhouse doors—"

"Examining them?"

"—opening and closing them several times. I was unable to ascertain the reason for his interest in—"

"Did he go into the wheelhouse?"

Foster frowned. "No."

"OK, carry on."

"He then left the boat and spoke to a number of other boat owners before returning to his vehicle and driving back to Plymouth, where he went into the Excalibur Hotel and picked up his weekend case. He then drove back to Bartonshire without stopping."

This was going to put the proverbial among the whatsit, thought Tom. So much for Sandie Esterbrook's story about Paul taking her out to Bodmin Moor and duffing her up. Lloyd had believed her; he wouldn't like it when he knew he'd been fooled.

"Subject drove to Little Elmley—" Foster looked up. "That's a private estate belonging to the family," he said.

"I know. What happened there?"

Foster consulted his notebook once more. "I allowed the subject to go out of sight before driving in after him, and drove as close to the house as I could without detection before taking my own vehicle off the road, into the woods. I walked the rest of the way until I could see the subject at the front door of the house, talking to his mother."

"You know Mrs. Esterbrook?"

"By sight," said Foster. "We don't exactly move in the same circles. But I've been following this geezer for weeks, and you get to know the family, so to speak."

Do you ever, thought Tom. But not for long; they had a nasty habit of being shot to death. Funny, that Foster didn't seem to know that there had been ructions at Little Elmley. "Did you see any other members of the family there?" he asked.

"No."

"Anyone else at all?"

He looked uncomfortable. "No. Why?"

"Never mind. You saw him talking to his mother. Did he go into the house?"

He addressed his notebook. "No," he said. "When the subject left his mother at the door, I returned to my vehicle—"

Tom had had enough of subjects and vehicles. "Forget the note-book," he said. "Just tell me in plain English."

Foster put down the notebook a little reluctantly, and shrugged. "I gave him time to get clear, went after him, caught up with him just as he turned down to the reservoir. I took a walk down, and there were people doing a dive, so I just hung about with the ones on the shore. Esterbrook spoke to a couple of people, then watched the divers with binoculars for a few minutes. Then he got back in his car, went home, and I was off watch, so to speak."

Tom grinned. "I hope your bladder was as strong as his," he said. "No stops at all on the way back?"

"What?" Foster looked puzzled. "Oh, no. No stops. It was a bit difficult, but I managed."

"You must miss having backup," said Tom. "Not so easy going private, is it?"

Foster smiled. "Very good," he said. "How did you know?"

"The notebook. I kept expecting you to ask permission to consult it. How long were you in the job for?"

"Too long."

Tom grinned. "Can you let me have a copy of your notes?"

"Yeah, sure." Foster removed the appropriate pages and went out to his secretary's office. "Can you copy them for me, sweetheart?" he said.

"Where were you yesterday?" asked Tom, following him through as his secretary arranged the small sheets on the platen.

"What?" Foster looked suspicious again, then shrugged. "I was at a Sunday race meeting," he said. "I had the day off, because Esterbrook went back early. Is that all right?"

"Got back late, did you? Just fell into bed?"

Foster frowned. "Are you having *me* followed, or what?"

Tom smiled. "You didn't catch up on the local news, did you?"

"No. Should I have?" He took out the photocopy. "It's on the house," he said sardonically as he handed it to Tom.

"Thank you." Tom folded it, put it in his inside pocket. "Two people have been shot dead at Little Elmley," he said. "One of them might have been shot while you were in the grounds." He made for the door while the gobsmacked Ian R. Foster was at a loss for words. "You might have to give evidence, so it's a case of don't leave town, so to speak, Mr. Foster," he said, grinning at him, and left.

Well, well, well, thought Tom, as he rattled down the stairs and out. Not like Lloyd to let himself be taken in, but he had been, good and proper. He wondered how much, if any, of Sandie Esterbrook's story was true, and which order he should do things in.

Sandie Esterbrook would have to be taken in for questioning, but she didn't know that anyone was on to her, so that could wait until he'd spoken to Elizabeth Esterbrook. Some of what Sandie had told Lloyd had come from Elizabeth Esterbrook in the first place; the suggestion that Paul had given her the beating, for instance. Perhaps she too had to be approached with caution.

He drove out of Barton's run-down, somewhat seedy, once-busy shopping area, superseded by the big indoor complex, and out to its wealthy suburbs.

SCENE IV—BARTONSHIRE
Monday, September 29th, 11:50 A.M.
Elizabeth's house

Tom climbed the imposing steps up to Elizabeth Esterbrook's cream-painted pillared front door, with its brass lion's head door knocker.

"Sergeant Finch—please, come in." She shivered slightly. "My goodness, it's getting quite autumnal, isn't it?"

Finch agreed that it was, and went in. The house always made him feel as though he should have dressed for the occasion; a woman was polishing the hall floor with a machine, and he was shown into what he just knew had to be the morning room.

"Well?" she said. "Did Foster's report clear Paul?"

"It certainly agrees substantially with what he told us on Saturday night," said Tom.

"So someone else killed that boy, and Angela. And then killed Paul and made it look as though he'd shot himself."

"It's a possibility. And I'm sorry, but it does mean that I have more questions."

She sat down, motioning to him to do the same.

The chair looked a bit spindly, but it seemed prepared to take his weight. "When I was here before," he said, "you told me that you thought Sandie Esterbrook had been used by your husband as a sort of decoy." That was another suggestion that had come from Elizabeth Esterbrook and been confirmed by Sandie Esterbrook, he thought, suspicious as ever. But since the lies that Sandie had told had been uncovered by Mrs. Esterbrook's private eye, collusion between the two women seemed unlikely.

It took Tom a moment to work out how to phrase it, but eventually he asked if it had occurred to her that Paul might have been using Sandie to cover up a homosexual affair.

"You're talking about Billy," she said, her eyes wide. "Aren't you? The boy who was killed in Angela's cottage."

Tom didn't reply.

"It was Josh who was seeing that boy, not Paul! Why on earth would you think it was Paul? Who told you that?"

"No one told us. It was a description we were given, that's all."

She looked relieved. "Then I don't know who your informant is, Sergeant, but I think he was describing Josh." She gave a short sigh. "I know that must make things look bad for Josh," she said. "It was his gun, wasn't it, that you found with Paul?"

"I'm afraid I can't tell you that."

"Josh told me it was. But Paul said, didn't he, that Josh's boat had been broken into? It wouldn't surprise me if that boy took the gun in the first place. He probably knew it was there. I—well, ever since I knew that boy had been killed too, I wondered if it might not have been a robbery gone wrong, as Paul suggested."

Tom was happy to listen to anyone's theory about this business.

"Paul said that boy wasn't really any good, and I wondered if he and one of his friends had intended burgling Little Elmley but had a falling out. And whoever it was went there, found Angela, killed her, and thought Paul had seen him."

There was far too much money sloshing about via Esterbrook's will to believe in a burglary, Tom thought, but a falling out among thieves was interesting, and Elizabeth Esterbrook's theory might contain enough truth to get some answers, if he put it to his suspect. But he ought to get to the bottom of who exactly it was Billy had been seeing, and he thought it best to accept what Mrs. Esterbrook had said at face value.

"Did you know Josh was gay?" he asked.

"Well, no, not until I found out about Billy. I was a bit surprised. But Paul thought he must have got into the habit in prison."

"Did you ever meet Billy?"

"In a manner of speaking. I wasn't introduced or anything, but I went with Paul to Josh's boat one weekend, and Billy was there. Josh took him off into a corner as soon as he came on board. The next day, Angela saw them with one another, and she was worried about it, I can tell you that. She got Josh and Sandie together that very evening."

Tom thought about that, and the visual evidence that had gone missing from the Copes' report. The description given could just as easily apply to Josh as to Paul. Josh had said he'd come back to Bartonshire when the boat had been holed, and Paul had stayed over; it would be nice to know if that was true, at least. Tom cleared his throat, not sure how Mrs. Esterbrook would feel about this invasion of her privacy.

"Your private investigator's reports," he said. "I'd like to see them, if that would be all right."

"Yes, of course," she said. "They're in the study."

SCENE V—BARTONSHIRE
Monday, September 29th, 12:20 P.M.
The study

Elizabeth decided that she rather liked Sergeant Finch, as he followed her into the study that Paul had had kitted out and then had never used. That was why she had kept Foster's reports in there. She unlocked the bottom drawer of the desk and drew out the reports, handing them to him, inviting him to take a seat.

The contrast between the curly blond hair, which made him look almost angelic, and the tough, suspicious approach that offset his looks had put her off a bit to start with, but he was trying so hard to be diplomatic that it made her smile, even though having to admit that she had done this was no fun at all.

"I don't know that they'll be much help," she said as Sergeant Finch glanced through them. "They certainly weren't much help to me."

"I had hoped they might help with a previous time that interests us," he said. "The Bank Holiday weekend, when there was an accident to the boat. But that one seems to be missing."

"I don't have a report about that weekend," she said. "The man had flu or something."

"Oh, well, it doesn't really matter. But I understand that Josh came home and that your husband stayed over?"

She frowned. "No, they both came home," she said. "On the Sunday, just after it happened."

"But the boat was holed on the Saturday, wasn't it?"

"No, the Sunday."

He looked puzzled. "Are you certain about that?" he asked.

"Yes. Angela rang and told me. So I'd know to expect Paul home. And I was at Little Elmley when Josh and Sandie came back. When I got back here, Paul was here. So they all returned at the same time."

He stood up. "'You've been very helpful, Mrs. Esterbrook. Thank you for your time, and—I'm sorry. You know. If all these questions are a bit upsetting."

She smiled. "You have your job to do," she said as she escorted him to the front door. "And I'm relieved that you know now that Paul had nothing to do with it. Just get it sorted out, please."

"We will," he promised, and turned to go, then turned back. "You don't happen to know Sandie's maiden name, do you?" he asked. "It's not important, but it might help—"

"Townsend."

"Thank you," he said, and left.

She stood at the window and watched him get into his car and drive off. At least the enquiry was pointing in the right direction now, she thought. Any direction suited her, as long as it was away from Paul.

SCENE VI—BARTONSHIRE
Monday, September 29th, 1:15 P.M.
The house at Little Elmley

Josh opened the door as Finch approached. "Sergeant Finch," he said, smiling a welcome as though Finch was his dearest friend. "Do come in."

Finch stood on the doorstep, despite the invitation. "Is your wife here, Mr. Esterbrook?" he asked.

"She isn't, I'm afraid. She's at work. I didn't think she should go in, but she's having to sort a lot of things out at IMG in view of Paul's death."

Finch nodded. "Right," he said. "Would you excuse me a moment? I'll be right back." He went back to his car and sat in the front seat, using his mobile phone. After a moment he returned. "I'm quite glad your wife's not here," he said. "Because I would like an answer to the question I asked you yesterday morning."

Josh knew exactly which question he had failed to answer, but he frowned as though having difficulty dredging it up. "Which question was that?" he asked, going back into the house.

Finch closed the door and followed him into the sitting room. "Why, if you thought your brother was at the Excalibur Hotel, you rang him at your mother's cottage. Have you had time to think of an answer yet?"

Josh heard the tone of voice that he had grown used to in his youth. Finch clearly had no time for the sort of courtesy displayed unfailingly, so far, by his boss, and Josh once again said nothing.

"Was it because you were using his hotel room?"

Josh's eyes widened. They had got on to that already? They were better than he thought. "No," he said. "What makes you think that?"

Finch didn't answer. "When exactly did you have this accident with the boat?" he asked.

"On the Saturday of the Bank Holiday weekend. Just before the afternoon session."

"Not Sunday?"

Ah. Josh could see that this required a little explanation. "You've been talking to Elizabeth," he said. "No, not Sunday. But that's what we told her. And Angela."

"Why?"

"Well, as you already know, assuming you speak to one another when you all get back to the nick, Paul was . . . shall we say entertaining? . . . Billy at Angela's cottage."

He explained that in order to preserve Paul's good name and his inheritance, it had been necessary to mislead his stepmother and Elizabeth, and he explained how he had accomplished that. "But it happened on the Saturday—if you need corroboration of that, I can supply you with the names and addresses of several disappointed divers."

"I don't think we'll need them," Finch said. "I'm sure it did happen on the Saturday. But on the Sunday, you say your stepmother rang you about this letter. Where did she ring you?"

"Here. But she didn't know that. She rang my mobile because she thought I was in Penhallin, and I didn't tell her I wasn't, because we were all supposed to be having a jolly diving weekend. I knew that Paul had gone to the cottage with Billy, so I rang him there and told him."

"How did you know?"

Josh smiled. "Sandie," he said. "She rang me to tell me Billy had turned up at the cottage. So I knew where to find Paul, didn't I? But then Angela found out about the boat, which presented a problem. I told her it had happened *after* she rang the first time, and that we were all on our way home. Then I went to Sandie's flat to keep out of the way, and came back here at about four o'clock with Sandie, as though we had just arrived from Penhallin."

"But you're saying that you were actually here for Saturday night and Sunday morning? Can anyone verify that?"

Whoops. Verify was a very emotive word. Josh smiled. "No. Do I need someone to verify it?"

Finch sat back too, and looked at him. "It depends," he said. "You see, Paul told his wife that it's you who had the relationship with Billy Rampton."

Josh knew Paul had told her that; Paul had told him he had, as he had always told him everything. He smiled broadly. "Old habits die hard. When in trouble, blame Josh."

Finch nodded. "But he wasn't in trouble, was he? Not then."

"When?"

"The weekend that Paul's wife joined him on your boat. She met Billy Rampton, and Paul told her he was your boyfriend. She had no reason to think that he had anything to do with her husband—he was off in a quiet corner with you. Paul wasn't in trouble. So why would he say it?"

"Billy was there. Elizabeth was there. That would spell trouble in Paul's book. I was off in a quiet corner with Billy in order to let him know the situation."

"And when your mother came on board? Were you off in a quiet corner with him then, too?"

"Stepmother," said Josh. "I don't know. He was a diver—I speak to the divers, obviously. I have to tell them about the conditions, about where we're diving, about all sorts of things. I might have been talking to him." He smiled. "I'm talking to you, Sergeant Finch," he said. "But I'm not having a sexual relationship with you."

Finch looked unimpressed, thanked him, and left.

SCENE VII—BARTONSHIRE
Monday, September 29th, 3:00 P.M.
Interview Room One at Stansfield police station

Sandie had told her colleagues the mugging story, in preference to the Brendan story, and decidedly in preference to the truth. But she had told the police the truth, so she wasn't sure why policemen had turned up at IMG and asked her to accompany them to the police station to answer questions concerning the murder of William Rampton, but they had, and she was in an interview room with Sergeant Finch and Inspector Hill.

"This interview is being taped," Finch said, and then cautioned her.

Sandie lit a cigarette, half expecting to be told not to, but Inspector Hill just reached behind her, got a foil ashtray off the windowsill and handed it to her.

"Paul Esterbrook didn't go anywhere near his mother's cottage on Saturday," Finch said. "He didn't go anywhere near you."

Sandie stared at him, and took the unlit cigarette from her mouth. "He did," she said, shaking her head slightly. She had told them the truth. Some of it, at any rate. She didn't understand. What did he mean, Paul hadn't been anywhere near her?

"We know that story is no more true than the first two you told us," said Inspector Hill.

"But it *is*," said Sandie, bewildered. She wished it wasn't; she was happier lying. You could manipulate people when you were lying, play on their weaknesses and their prejudices and their expectations, tell them what they wanted to hear. The truth was just the truth, and what else could you say?

"Paul Esterbrook drove alone to Penhallin. He stopped for an hour in Plymouth on the way, then went to his brother's boat, turned round and came back again."

"No!" Sandie said. "That's not *true*. It happened exactly like I said."

"Do you want to know what I think?" Finch said. "I think you and Billy planned a burglary."

Sandie's mouth fell open. "You think what?" she said.

"Oh, don't look so shocked. You were in a fair bit of trouble with the police when you were younger, weren't you? It's all here." He tapped a sheet in front of him. "We checked you out."

She had known they'd get on to that sooner or later. "Yes, I was," she said. "Maybe that's why Josh and I clicked the way we did."

Finch looked down at her list of convictions. "You shoplifted, among other things, before you became respectable," he said, and looked up at her. "You were a thief."

She nodded and lit her cigarette.

"You knew there were a lot of things worth stealing at Little Elmley, and you knew that your job was going to be finished once Paul found out about you and Josh. You'd have no money when that happened. But you didn't think you could talk Josh into stealing from his stepmother, so you went behind his back. You got his gun, or you got Billy to steal it for you, and you and he were going to burgle Little Elmley. But Billy wanted things done his way, maybe, or wanted more of the loot than you were prepared to give him—in any event, you had a row. And he beat you up. So you got the gun, and you blew him away."

Sandie didn't deny it. She just listened, smiling a little.

"Then you got back to Little Elmley, and you went to the house. You thought you could get in and out undetected, but Angela Esterbrook disturbed you, and so you shot her too, because the last thing you wanted was for Josh to find out what you had done. But Paul saw you leaving. That was why he said he thought it was a burglar. He was protecting you, Sandie."

Paul? Sandie almost laughed.

"But you knew he'd seen you, so he had to go too. Then you made up this story about him once he was dead, because he couldn't deny it."

Sandie smiled, and looked at Inspector Hill. "Is he for real?" she asked.

Inspector Hill smiled back. "Not quite," she said. "But it's one explanation. Not one that we're too happy with. Are you saying it didn't happen like that?"

Sandie caught her lip and shook her head, still smiling. "Angela Esterbrook would have given me anything I asked for," she said. "She offered me money—I had no need to steal from her. I wouldn't cross the road to speak to Billy Rampton, far less plot a burglary with him. And if I had been going to burgle Little Elmley, why would I choose a weekend when Angela was there? I could do it any time, without anyone's help, without Josh's knowledge, and without the need for a gun. Besides, I was diving in Little Elmley reservoir when Angela was shot. And Paul Esterbrook never protected anyone but himself in his life."

"All right," the inspector said, a warning note in her voice. "But we have an independent witness who has confirmed that Paul Esterbrook went exactly where he said he went, did what he said he did. He did not pick you up, he did not take you to Cornwall, he did not assault you. Who did? *Was* it Billy Rampton?"

An independent witness? What on earth was the woman talking about? For a moment there was a sort of baffled standoff as she stared uncomprehendingly at Inspector Hill, and Inspector Hill's brown eyes looked back at her with total certainty. Then Sandie remembered what Paul had said to her.

"Of course," she said, nodding, feeling better now that she knew she wasn't going mad. "Paul *told* me he could be anywhere he liked when I got beaten up, and the police would believe him." She smiled, shaking her head in grudging admiration of Paul's precautions. "And you do," she said. "You do believe him."

"Paul Esterbrook is dead," said Finch angrily. "He isn't saying anything for us to believe or disbelieve. Someone else is. So do yourself a favour and tell us who you were with and what you were doing on Saturday, and stop messing us about!"

Sandie looked at the angry and frustrated Finch, and the cool, imperturbable Hill, and stubbed her cigarette out in the ashtray. "I've already told you," she said.

"Then you leave us no option," said Inspector Hill. "Alexandra Esterbrook, I am arresting you on suspicion of the murder of William Rampton in Penhallin, Cornwall, on Saturday the twenty-seventh of September. You do not have to say anything . . ."

Sandie wasn't listening. How had Paul managed to do what he'd said he'd do? He was dead, for God's sake.

"You have the right to have someone notified of your arrest."

"Josh Esterbrook," she said. "Barton 258763." She looked at Inspector Hill. "You wouldn't be doing this to Elizabeth Esterbrook," she said. "But I didn't go to Benenden or Roedean or wherever it is she went to school. It was different when you thought I had, wasn't it?"

"The only thing that's changed is that we know you've lied to us."

Sandie didn't know how Paul had done it, but he had been right; no point in telling the police, he had said, and even after he was dead, his precautions were working, his security measures were still in place.

But not for long. Which was just as well, because the cells, she discovered, *were* a nonsmoking environment.

SCENE VIII—BARTONSHIRE
Monday, September 29th, 5:25 P.M.
Lloyd's office in Stansfield police station

Lloyd was not in a good mood. He looked up when Judy knocked and came in.

"I hear you've arrested Sandie Esterbrook," he said. "Why?"

"I have reasonable grounds for suspicion," said Judy, looking offended.

Lloyd sighed. No point in taking it out on Judy. "I know you have," he said. "I've seen Foster's report. She had me fooled, I admit it. But you don't really think she'll disappear if you let her go, do you?"

"No, but she's told us this story, and Penhallin wants to talk to her, obviously. She's the best suspect they've got. They'd be a bit miffed if she *did* disappear."

Lloyd picked up a pen, doodled on a pad. "And you want to hang on to her, because you're afraid that she'll end up like Paul Esterbrook if you let her go," he said. "Isn't that really why she's a guest of this establishment?"

Judy sat down. "Yes," she said. "It was bad enough when I thought he'd killed himself, but now I think I let him go just so someone could murder him. I'm not letting that happen twice. Someone's already had a go at her, and if it wasn't Paul, then maybe it *was* her husband. Maybe she's afraid to tell us the truth."

Lloyd smiled, still working on the shiny top hat he was drawing. It was the only thing he could draw, but he did do top hats very nicely. All the shading, and the highlights. "I don't think she's that easily intimidated," he said.

"Maybe not, but she's obviously involved in some way. She's telling this story to cover up for someone. Who else?"

Lloyd's ballpoint smudged his top hat, and he scribbled through it. It was better with a pencil, anyway. He let the pen drop, roll over the blotter.

"The lab said they'd have to do an analysis of the burnt paper to find out whether or not it could have been a fax," said Judy. "Compare it with the paper in the fax, and the paper on the pad. I told them to go ahead, but I suppose that's a waste of time now, since the whole story is nonsense."

"Probably. Let it stand, though."

"How did the Copes' postmortem go?" Judy asked, a touch apprehensively.

Lloyd smiled tiredly, because Judy already knew that it hadn't gone well; if it had, he'd have been talking about that, not giving her a hard time about Sandie Esterbrook. "Freddie came up with nothing," he said.

Judy made a sympathetic sound. "Nothing at all?" she said.

"Nothing at all."

Freddie had found no trace of drugs or intoxicants in either body; there were no blows to the head, no internal injuries, no signs that either of them had been in any way restrained or had put up a fight. "They died of carbon monoxide poisoning and nothing else, Lloyd," he had said. "Both of them. They were alive when the car filled with gas. There is nothing whatever to suggest that either of them was in any way rendered unconscious or unable to leave the car."

Lloyd had pointed out the flaw in that. "Cope couldn't leave the car," he said. "Not without his wheelchair."

"Yes, he could," Freddie had said. "He was a big, strong man. He could have thrown himself out, pulled himself free. And besides," he had added, with infinite, maddening logic, reminding Lloyd of Judy, "he could have turned off the engine."

Forensics, who had been working for two solid days, had not produced anything he could go on at all. Only the Copes' fingerprints had been found on or in the car, only Andy Cope's on the car keys, the gear lever, and the steering wheel, only Kathy Cope's on the vacuum-cleaner hose and the vacuum cleaner itself. Rubber glove prints had been found on the last two items, but, given the nature of household tasks, that was hardly unusual. The pattern matched that of the rubber gloves found under Kathy Cope's sink, and there was no evidence to suggest that anyone other than Kathy Cope had ever worn them. Indeed, there were minute bloodstains from a minor cut found inside the thumb of one glove, which matched Kathy Cope's blood type, and which had been caused some considerable time prior to Friday night, so they were undoubtedly her rubber gloves. Even Lloyd drew the line at DNA testing to prove it absolutely.

The hose had been attached to the exhaust with insulating tape from which they had been unable to get prints, but that meant nothing; its rough, matt surface had always been a very unlikely source. Kathy's prints had been found on the big garage door, in exactly the position they would have been had she reached up and pushed it shut from the inside.

It wasn't impossible to imagine someone achieving that effect; Kathy could have been forced to close the garage door herself, she would use the Hoover all the time, and wearing her rubber gloves would do the rest. But how could you achieve the actual murder without drugging your victims, or making them drunk, or otherwise rendering them insensible? Even if they had been held at gunpoint, it made no sense. If the gunman had been outside the car, they would have been in possession of as lethal an instrument as he was; if he had been inside, he would have died with them.

And in the desperation of knowing they were going to die, the gun would have made no difference; they would have tried anything. But they had made no attempt to leave the car, and there was nothing to suggest that the doors had been held shut from the outside; no glue on the windows, nothing jamming the mechanism, nothing that anyone could find to prevent them ventilating the car at least. And, as Freddie had said, nothing to stop Andy Cope simply switching off the engine.

But someone had murdered them, all the same; Lloyd was absolutely convinced of that, and his investigation wasn't going to stop here. He wasn't sure where he could possibly take it, but he would think of something, because he wasn't having someone going round thinking they could bump people off willy-nilly.

"I've been summoned to the presence," he said to Judy, getting up, flexing his back. "I'll give you three guesses what about."

SCENE IX—BARTONSHIRE
Monday, September 29th, 5:35 P.M.
The Superintendent's office

Lloyd went up the flight of stairs slowly, still trying to think of something really convincing to say, but all he had was a soul-feeling, and that wouldn't cut any ice at all with Case.

"Come!"

Lloyd went in. "You wanted me, sir?"

"What's this about needing more time to complete your enquiries into the Copes' suicide?"

"I think you'll find I didn't use the word 'suicide,' " said Lloyd.

"*I'm* using it. The pathologist is using it. Forensics are using it. So you're using it. Subject closed."

"The thing is—" Lloyd began.

"The enquiry is *closed*, Lloyd." Case's hand strayed to the cigarette packet on his desk, then he sat back, his hands clasped behind the head of thick grey hair that Lloyd secretly envied. "Do you know how much your obsession with the Cope business has cost us already?" he demanded.

"It isn't an obsession. It's—"

"A hunch. Well, I'm sorry, but they committed suicide, and your hunch is not going to cost us one pennypiece more than it already has. The only reason I'm not nailing you to the wall is that the Esterbrook shootings did make murder a reasonable supposition in the end. You were lucky. So don't push it, Lloyd. Forget the Copes and concentrate on the real murders we've got on our hands."

"Are you quite happy to accept that the Copes' suicide was coincidental to the 'real' murders?" he asked.

"Coincidental? No. This murder has got something to do with Esterbrook's liking for young boys, I'm not denying that. But the Copes were peripheral to it—they happened to be asked to investigate him, that's all. And they were up to their ears in debt, so Kathy Cope blackmailed Esterbrook at the behest of her boyfriend. Isn't that what DI Hill thinks too?"

"Yes," said Lloyd. "And blackmailing someone and then double-crossing him is quite a good way of getting yourself murdered."

Case stopped trying to look relaxed, and took a cigarette from the packet on his desk. "Now you want to pin it on a dead man?" he said, speaking and lighting his cigarette at the same time. "She blued the money on office equipment she didn't need, her husband eventually found out how she got that money, and that was the last straw. They'd sunk as low as you can go, and they did themselves in. It's as simple as that."

"The night before everyone else started getting themselves shot dead?" said Lloyd incredulously, ungrammatically. As simple as that. It *wasn't* as simple as that. It wasn't simple at all.

"There is no way in the world that they were murdered, Lloyd!" Case shouted, his finger jabbing down on the unequivocal reports. "They committed suicide."

"Just like that? Went out shopping, came home and killed themselves?"

"They could have been in that car for hours before they actually decided to do it! We don't *know* what went on, but we do know they committed suicide in the end whether you like it or not."

"They locked all the car doors. Why didn't they lock both the garage doors? Why just the big one?"

"Who cares?" Case laid the cigarette down in the ashtray.

"I do. Someone might have locked the main door, but had to leave by the little one *after* putting Cope's keys back in the ignition. Give me till the end of the week before you close the enquiry."

"What for?"

"To try to get to the bottom of the blackmail business. To find out who this other man is that Kathy was with at the hotel. If he's a blackmailer, we have to find him. Maybe he can shed some light on why they would have killed themselves."

Case shook his head. Smoke spiralled up from the half-smoked cigarette and hung in a cloud over his desk, moving in a shaft of setting sunlight. "No," he said, picking it up again. "We've had no complaint of blackmail. We don't have to find him. We don't need to know why they killed themselves."

Lloyd knew that, but it had been worth a try. He looked at his senior officer through the haze, and decided to go for it. Detective Superintendent Case, confirmed bachelor that he was, lived alone, and it was just possible that his weakest argument would succeed where his strongest had failed.

"Where do you keep your baked beans, sir?" he asked.

Case narrowed his eyes at him. "I don't trust you when you remember to call me sir," he said. "But if you really want to know, I keep them on the second top shelf of the right-hand cupboard above the worktop. Happy?"

"Nowhere else? You don't keep some in that cupboard and some in another?"

"No," said Case, drawing out the word with exaggerated patience. "Do you?"

"No," said Lloyd. "And neither did Kathy Cope. Until Friday night. And she didn't keep her tea bags where they were found, or her eggs in the fridge, but that's where they were. Someone else put her shopping away. Someone who had no idea where anything was kept. It wasn't her husband—he never got out of the car."

There was a long silence after he had spoken; Lloyd didn't move, didn't make a sound.

Case ground out his cigarette and sighed, a deep, theatrical sigh, shaking his head at his own folly. "The end of the week," he groaned.

SCENE X—BARTONSHIRE
The following day, Tuesday, September 30th, 8:30 A.M.
The house at Little Elmley

Josh had gone straight to Stansfield police station as soon as they had rung him last night; they had let Sandie know that he was there, but they hadn't let him see her. He had told various people what he thought of them, but none of the principal players had been in evidence, so it had been a waste of time. And staying there wouldn't have helped; Sandie knew he was with her anyway, wherever he was, wherever she was.

They had said she had been arrested on suspicion of murdering Billy Rampton, but they hadn't, of course, told him how they had come to that conclusion. If it was just because she had been there, why hadn't Lloyd arrested her on Saturday night? It had to be something more than that, and he didn't know what. Things had been taken out of his hands, and he didn't like that.

They said she hadn't asked for a solicitor, but he thought he ought to get hold of one for her. He wasn't sure whether to get one here or in Penhallin, because they had said they might be taking her there. He washed, shaved, drank some coffee, then headed for Stansfield police station to find out what was happening.

SCENE XI—BARTONSHIRE
Tuesday, September 30th, 9:05 A.M.
Stansfield police station

Judy had been at work for half an hour when Penhallin faxed through a statement made to them early that morning by one Arthur Henderson, yet another private investigator who had become involved in this business.

"Why do private eyes keep coming out of the woodwork?" Lloyd demanded when she went in to tell him.

"Well," said Judy, "Elizabeth Esterbrook was pretty well bound to employ one sooner or later, and Angela wanted things done that only private investigators can do, so perhaps it isn't so odd. It's what he has to tell us that's really interesting."

Arthur Henderson was the sort of private investigator that Lloyd accepted Mrs. Esterbrook might more readily employ; Judy had rung Penhallin to check on him, and had discovered that he had had an impeccable thirty years with the Devon and Cornwall police, and ran a thriving agency staffed by handpicked operatives whose credentials were equally impeccable. He clearly wouldn't have touched the Plymouth job, smacking as it did of collusion and setup, so Angela had had to go elsewhere for that.

She had employed Mr. Henderson twice, according to his handwritten, lengthy statement; the first time had been on the twenty-second of July, when she had asked him to investigate a youth she was thinking of employing; he had been entirely unsuitable, and Mr. Henderson had told her that. She had been very grateful to him, and when she had begun to suspect that someone had been using her cottage on the weekends when she wasn't in residence, she had come to him again, three weeks ago. She had wanted a discreet watch kept on her cottage, and a full report of anyone seen using it.

His operatives had concealed themselves in an apparently abandoned vehicle, a favourite ploy of Mr. Henderson's, apparently, and they had maintained a twenty-four-hour surveillance from eight o'clock on Friday morning until they had aborted it on the Sunday, for obvious reasons. Mr. Henderson would not normally reveal a client's business to anyone, but in view of what had occurred on the Sunday, when his operatives saw a body being removed from the cottage by police, he had given the matter deep thought and had in the end decided that it was only right to let the police know what his operatives had seen the previous day.

And since he now understood from the newspapers that the deceased was the boy whom he had investigated for Mrs. Esterbrook, and that his death was being linked to two others at Mrs. Esterbrook's Bartonshire address, he had not sent her a copy of the report, and would not, unless and until he was given the go-ahead by the police.

The report, also faxed through, confirmed every word that Sandie Esterbrook had told them, and the timed and dated photographs, scanned and sent by the Internet in preference to the less desirable fax in order that there should be no doubt about the identities of the people photographed, established that Paul Esterbrook's dramatic exit had been minutes after the call to Little Elmley.

Tom had been most anxious to be the one to speak to Foster, and Judy was happy to let him do that. Foster needed someone with no time for diplomacy to point out the error of his ways.

Lloyd put the report down. "I don't think you can keep her in protective custody any longer," he said.

"It doesn't look as though it's necessary," said Judy. "I doubt if she's in any danger. I think Paul must have carried out the other shootings and then shot himself, don't you?"

But she could see from the look on Lloyd's face that despite Arthur Henderson's indisputable evidence, he didn't think that. "It could still be a setup," he said. "That video-frame Kathy Cope sent to Mrs. Esterbrook is missing, and that has to mean something."

"He'd arranged an alibi, Lloyd," Judy pointed out.

He nodded. "But he told Sandie about it, didn't he? Before anyone had been shot, before he'd seen this letter supposedly from his mother. The alibi might just be coincidental."

It might.

SCENE XII—BARTONSHIRE
Tuesday, September 30th, 9:30 A.M.
The courtyard at Stansfield police station

Sandie had been given breakfast, some exercise in the yard, and allowed, while she was outside, to smoke. These three things had served to put her in a better mood. Being told that she was free to go put her in something approaching a good mood. Finding Josh waiting for her had meant that by the time she saw DI Hill approaching, she had lost the desire to call her names. The woman had only been doing her job, and she had been up against Paul Esterbrook's military-style security; he had told Sandie he would make her look like a liar, and he had.

"I am really very sorry," Inspector Hill said as she took them out, and glanced at Josh. "The apology is for both of you. You must have been very worried, Mr. Esterbrook."

"Why did you think I was lying?" Sandie asked.

DI Hill looked a little uncomfortable. "We had received information which we believed was sound, but which turned out not to be," she said.

"What sort of information?" Josh asked.

"I'm sorry," she said. "I can't tell you. I can only apologize."

Josh looked angry. "Information that you thought was more reliable than my wife's?" he said, unlocking the car.

"No," said the inspector. "Just more objective."

Sandie smiled. "Your independent witness wasn't so independent after all, then?" she said as she got into the car.

"Apparently not," said Inspector Hill.

Josh got in and put his arms round her, held her close. "What happened?" he asked. "Why did they arrest you?"

"I don't know," she said indistinctly, and disengaged herself from him. "I only know what she just told you."

Josh smiled. "At least they've let you go," he said. "But I can guess why. We're going to have to talk about that."

She nodded. "Take me home, Josh. I want a shower before we discuss anything. I'm sure I smell of that place."

He reversed out of the little car park. "No, you don't," he said. "You smell just fine to me."

SCENE XIII—BARTONSHIRE
Tuesday, September 30th, 10:00 A.M.
Ian Foster's office

"I'm sorry," said Foster's secretary. "I just don't know where he is. He left right after you did yesterday, and I haven't seen him since. Why are you looking for him, anyway?"

Tom sighed. This was his second visit of the morning. He had been to Foster's house, which still had the For Sale sign and was just as empty as it had been on Sunday. He leant over the desk. "He gave me duff information," he said. "And I hope you're not doing the same thing." She looked totally unimpressed, and Tom stood up straight again. He could usually alarm people quite effectively.

"My ex is with your lot," she said. "He does all that macho stuff too. It might work with the villains, but it doesn't work with me."

Tom ran a hand over his hair, then checked it. Lloyd did that when he was frustrated, and he was bald. "Do you really not know where Foster is?" he asked.

"Really. It's not that unusual. He often doesn't come in for days."

Tom frowned. "Well, do you know where I'd be likely to find him?"

She smiled. "A dog track, a race track. Did you try the bookie's downstairs?"

Yes, he had. They hadn't seen him. Tom sat down. "Look, er . . ."

"Debbie," she said.

"Look, Debbie," he said. "That report that you photocopied for me—have you still got Foster's original notes?"

"No," she said, looking puzzled. "That was funny, that. I said did he want me to type up the report for the client, and he said no, and just tore them up. Mind you, he didn't half go pale when you said about the shootings, so maybe he just doesn't want her business anymore."

"Yeah," said Tom thoughtfully. "What did he say after I'd gone?"

"Nothing much. He just tore up the report and went into his office again. Then he came out, said he didn't know when he'd be back, and that was the last I saw of him." Her mouth opened. "Oh, my God, you don't think he's dead too, do you?"

"No," said Tom grimly. "I don't. If he shows up, tell him I want to see him."

SCENE XIV—BARTONSHIRE
Tuesday, September 30th, 10:20 A.M.
Judy's office at Stansfield police station

"I'm not surprised," Judy said, when Tom told her that Foster had gone underground. "But the DCI wants us to keep on with the enquiry into this story that Paul told Sandie Esterbrook, just in case he really did get a fax from someone. How's the check going?"

"We've moved on to libraries now," said Tom. "Anywhere that's got a public fax in Bartonshire's being checked out. Not all of them are checkable, though."

"Do your best—oh, and Tom. Don't forget Penhallin public library. If there really was a fax, it could have been sent any time last week, and sat there waiting for Paul to find it."

"Right, guv." God, he thought, as he left her office. All this for a fax that didn't exist.

SCENE XV—BARTONSHIRE
Tuesday, September 30th, 11:00 A.M.
Elizabeth's house

Elizabeth sat down. "What exactly do you mean, worthless?" she asked.

Chief Inspector Lloyd looked at her a little sadly. "Your husband had colluded with Ian Foster," he said. "His report means nothing."

Paul had colluded with her private detective. She should have known. She should have realized that she was wasting her time trying to catch him out. He had always been several steps ahead of her, and would have remained several steps ahead of her until their silver wedding. And even from beyond the grave he was going to cheat her out of the enormous wealth that his death should have brought her.

"Does this mean Paul is a suspect again?"

"I'm afraid so."

Elizabeth shook her head. "He took such elaborate precautions not to be caught out in adultery," she said. "And all they've done for him is to brand him a murderer."

SCENE XVI—BARTONSHIRE
Tuesday, September 30th, 5:00 P.M.
Lloyd's office, Stansfield police station

By the end of the second full day of his investigation into the happenings of the weekend, Lloyd had been summoned to Case's office once more. But first he was having a team talk. He needed Judy and Tom on his side if he was going to get to the bottom of this.

They had amassed a great deal of evidence, and it all pointed one way, at Paul Esterbrook. But now there were *far* too many clues for Lloyd's liking, and he felt that overwhelming though it seemed, the evidence was a touch on the inconclusive side.

The postmortem on Angela Esterbrook had revealed that she had died from the effects of three bullet wounds to the head; the first bullet had almost certainly killed her, the other two were unnecessary. She had been shot in the first instance through the head at close range, probably by someone standing outside on the terrace. The items found on the worktop suggested that she had been standing there when she was shot. The next two bullets had been fired point-blank, after she was dead, perhaps to make certain, perhaps to mutilate the body.

Paul Esterbrook had died instantly from one bullet in the right temple. It was a contact wound, and was consistent with suicide. He had been wearing driving gloves when he was found, and the right-hand glove had had powder burns on it.

The postmortem on Billy Rampton, carried out in Plymouth, had revealed that he'd died instantly from one bullet that had passed between the eyes and out the back of his head. He had been shot by someone standing on the landing while he stood in the bedroom, from a distance of about six feet. The accuracy of the shooting could have been accidental, but suggested someone with a good aim.

That was inconclusive, according to Lloyd. Paul was a good shot, but so, according to her husband, was Sandie Esterbrook. And Lloyd had been skip-reading Angela's diaries, back from the most recent, in the hope of finding a past reference to Josh's sexual preferences, and according to an entry in one of them, Elizabeth Esterbrook had also at one time had the benefit of Paul's tuition, and was "quite a good shot with a revolver," according to what he'd told his mother. The accuracy of the shooting meant nothing, in Lloyd's opinion.

The bullets that had been recovered had been shot from Josh Esterbrook's revolver; it had had no prints on it, but guns rarely yielded prints anyway, so that didn't mean much. The silencer found in the Range Rover's glove compartment and the cartridges still in the chambers of the revolver had had Paul Esterbrook's fingerprints on them. The cartridges had been matched to the recovered bullets.

Josh Esterbrook had offered an explanation for his half brother's prints being on the silencer and the cartridges; Paul always cleaned the gun after it had been used, and he, Josh, had insisted that Paul leave it loaded. They had used the silencer when Paul had given

Sandie shooting lessons, and he had always put it on and taken it off. The prints on the weapon could, therefore, just about be said to be inconclusive, but they certainly didn't preclude Paul having broken into the boat and taken it, so Lloyd wasn't very hopeful of arguing his case on that.

The examination of the boat had definitely proved inconclusive; prints had been found in the wheelhouse belonging to all members of the Esterbrook family except Angela Esterbrook, and Billy Rampton's prints had been found in both the cabins, but not in the wheelhouse. Paul's prints were, however, on the wheelhouse doors, and on the lock of the wheelhouse, and the only other set of prints were those of the man who had brought the boat back to Penhallin harbour.

The examination of the cottage had produced Paul Esterbrook's prints on the front door handle, the back door, and on the sideboard. Billy's prints had been found on the banister, on the bedroom door handle, and in the treehouse, along with a set of less recent unidentified prints. There had been no prints on either of the phones. Billy's motorbike wasn't found at the cottage, and seemed to have gone missing. That was, Lloyd thought, another little puzzle, but possibly one for Penhallin police rather than Stansfield. And he couldn't see that it helped to clear Paul Esterbrook.

Paul Esterbrook had been found still to have Sandie Esterbrook's cigarette packet and throwaway lighter in his pocket, and partial prints of his were on both of them. Since there were no matches in the cottage, it had to be assumed that he had used Sandie's lighter to burn the letter. But thanks to Arthur Henderson's operatives, they knew that Paul had taken her cigarettes and lighter from her, so his prints would be on them anyway; that wasn't entirely conclusive.

Lloyd was a little puzzled about that lack of matches; Angela Esterbrook hadn't been a smoker, and didn't carry matches or a lighter as a matter of course. What had she used to light those emergency candles? A little puzzle with a bit more potential, he felt, though he was hard pressed to see how it would help.

A check on Billy's mobile revealed no call to Little Elmley on the Sunday of the August Bank Holiday. A check on every fax machine available to Josh, Sandie, or Elizabeth Esterbrook was ongoing, and had so far revealed no fax to Penhallin. Lloyd had had Foster's fax number checked out too, since he and Paul Esterbrook were obviously in league with one another, and this whole thing could have been some devious scheme of Paul's that had gone hideously wrong, but there was nothing.

Elizabeth Esterbrook denied ever having said to anyone at all that she was going to the diving club, and had been issued with a ticket for her concert overprinted with the date and time of issue: 1746 hours on Saturday.

And Paul Esterbrook had arranged an alibi with Foster, who had disappeared off the face of the earth. Lloyd tried to see how that could be regarded as inconclusive, with little success.

Judy agreed that Paul Esterbrook had been very generous with clues for someone whose army days had been spent avoiding detection and capture, but his brother Josh had said that Paul had not been a quick thinker, had needed to plan ahead, and when Lloyd had talked to Elizabeth Esterbrook, she had said much the same thing, despite her insistence that her husband had not done any of the things of which he was suspected.

Tom thought that Paul Esterbrook *had* planned ahead as far as he was able, and there was a great deal to be said for that point of view. That he had traced the Copes from the hotel registration, discovered that they were private detectives, and knew that Billy had to have set him up. Only the letter from his mother had been unexpected; up until then, Esterbrook had believed that the Copes had been working for his wife. His initial reaction, with his notoriously short fuse, had been to ring her up and abuse her, but then he had realized that she had to die too if he was to be safe, and she had to die before his wife went to dinner there, in case she told her. His arrangement with Foster meant that he could do all this in the knowledge that an apparently unbiased alibi would, in due course, be produced.

"And he thought up the fax on the spur of the moment?" said Lloyd. "To give himself a reason for turning round and going straight back? All that business about Sandie having to do the night dive, exactly how she should accomplish arriving there before Elizabeth, all to stop Sandie asking questions? Thinking on his feet is precisely what everyone says he couldn't do."

"But he might not have had to, guv," said Tom. "He had to get Sandie away from the cottage if he was going to blow Billy away, hadn't he? So he might have thought up a reason for the quick exit before he ever took her there, before he found the letter from his mother."

"And managed to forget that there was an incriminating message on his mother's answering machine?"

"He said she got a lot of calls—I think he would assume that she'd played it, and it would have got recorded over. It was only because the machine was faulty that his message was still there."

Lloyd looked at them both. "Do you think I'm wrong?" he asked. "Being unhappy with Paul Esterbrook as the answer?"

"Not necessarily," said Judy. "I'm sure there's more to this than meets the eye. I just don't know if we can prove it."

"But we've not finished looking yet, have we?" said Tom.

Lloyd smiled. He had his team backing him even though their answers owed more to loyalty than to truth; Tom would beat every bush he came across until something flew out for Lloyd to shoot at, and Judy would eventually start sniffing the air, and home in on whatever Lloyd had, usually unknowingly, bagged. But they all had to be pointing in the right direction before that could happen, and they needed time to be able to work out which direction that was.

He knew he had a battle on his hands to get that time, as he once again went up to account for himself to Superintendent Case.

SCENE XVII—BARTONSHIRE
Tuesday, September 30th, 5:55 P.M.
The Superintendent's office

Lloyd listened for twenty minutes while Case chewed him out about his profligate use of manpower and resources. Case didn't know that he was having the burned paper analyzed, thank God. He'd have stopped it.

"No more, Lloyd," he said. "This enquiry's over."

"At least let me get that letter checked out by a handwriting expert."

"I don't see the point." Case sat back in his swivel chair, swivelling.

"Why would Angela Esterbrook spend money having twenty-four-hour surveillance on her cottage if she was already so certain that Paul was using it that she left a letter there for him?"

"I don't know, and I don't care. Perhaps something happened in between when she hired Henderson and when he actually began work that *made* her certain. She had money coming out of her ears, Lloyd. She probably forgot to cancel him, like you or I might forget to cancel the papers."

Lloyd shook his head. "I don't think you can dismiss it like that. If Paul Esterbrook is held to have murdered his mother, Josh Esterbrook could possibly stand to gain under the will."

"And if he did gain under the will? How much are we talking about?"

"I don't know," said Lloyd. "How much *are* entire villages with en suite reservoirs worth?"

"They're not worth anything unless someone wants to buy them," said Case.

"He regards that place as his birthright." That sounded like a motive to Lloyd, and it did make Case look a little less sceptical, but he still shook his head.

"I fail to see how Josh Esterbrook *could* have carried out these murders," he said. "He was hundreds of miles away when Rampton died, and diving with a whole lot of other people when his mother died. And if he didn't kill them, then he didn't kill his brother."

Lloyd conceded that those facts were hard to get over, but there was undoubtedly something rotten in the state of Little Elmley, and he wasn't going to let it go.

"Josh Esterbrook told us he got that gun because his partner in crime would be out of prison any day. He's dead. He's been dead for five years."

Case shrugged. "He didn't necessarily know that," he said.

"If you were in fear of your life, isn't his release date something you would try to find out?" asked Lloyd. "Don't tell me he hasn't got contacts. And Sandie Esterbrook's been learning how to shoot that revolver," he said. "*She* wasn't hundreds of miles away when Billy was shot. But she could have been six feet away—she's good enough. She was alone in the cottage with him."

"And how do you know that she can handle a gun? Because her husband told you she could. And that she was alone in the cottage with him? Because *she* told you, for God's sake! Long before Mr. Henderson's report turned up. And she was diving *with* her husband when Mrs. Esterbrook died. Paul Esterbrook, on the other hand, was at the cottage with Billy, and at Little Elmley with his mother, when they both just happened to get shot dead. He had arranged an alibi with this Foster character! What more do you need?"

"But the alibi could have been for his wife, not for us."

"And why did he go and see his mother? Because he was worried about his brother? Do me a favour. They hated one another's guts."

It had sounded less than convincing to Lloyd as well, but then, it had been a lie whatever way you looked at it. Either he'd lied to the police because he'd murdered his mother, or he'd lied to his mother because he was covering his infidelity. He said as much to Case.

"Covering his infidelity, as you so prissily put it, *with Billy*," Case said.

"Perhaps," said Lloyd.

Case sat back, his arms folded across what was becoming an ever bulkier frame. "*Perhaps?*" he repeated.

"We've only got Sandie Esterbrook's word for it that Paul Ester-brook even knew Billy was *at* the cottage."

"Billy was found in the bedroom, half in and half out of his clothes, and the items found in his jacket pocket strongly suggest that he was there with the intention of having sex with someone," said Case.

"But we've only got Sandie Esterbrook's word for it that Billy was expecting to see *Paul* Esterbrook."

Case closed his eyes for a moment. "Hang on," he said. "Let me get this straight. You're suggesting that we've got the wrong end of the stick altogether? That Paul was expecting to spend the weekend with Sandie, and that Billy thought he'd be meeting *Josh* Esterbrook?"

Lloyd had never, ever tried a theory out on Case. He usually reserved them strictly for Judy. Sometimes, at a pinch, Freddie. In dire emergency, Tom Finch. Never Case. But he'd only just thought of this one. "It's a possibility," he said.

"Josh and Sandie Esterbrook are married."

"Paul was married too. That doesn't mean anything."

"But he hadn't been near his wife for ten years. Josh Esterbrook is newly married."

"Why?" said Lloyd.

"Why?" repeated Case, puzzled, then nodded extravagantly. "Oh, right, I've got it," he said. "They got married to put us off the scent, right? So we wouldn't realize that it's *Josh* that's the queer."

Not quite how Lloyd would have put it, but in essence what he was considering as a working hypothesis. "Elizabeth Esterbrook still maintains that it was Josh who was having the relationship with Billy Rampton, not Paul," he said. "What if she's right?"

Case was shaking his head. "She just doesn't *want* to believe it, Lloyd. That's all."

"I'd like to get counsel's opinion," Lloyd said.

"Counsel's opinion on what? Your daft theory?"

"The will. I'd like to see how strong a claim Josh Esterbrook will have if we close this enquiry as it stands."

"Not on your life. Do you know how much an hour barristers charge, for God's sake? Paul Esterbrook murdered Billy and then he murdered his mother, and there isn't anything we can do about that, since he very decently shot himself as well. We issue a statement that no one else is being sought, and stop spending money on this business!"

"And why *did* he kill himself after going to all that trouble?"

"He flipped, Lloyd. He killed the boy, he killed his mother, and once we set Judy Hill on to him, he knew it was all over. I think I'd have shot myself too."

Lloyd ignored the jibe about Judy. Case liked to rattle his cage about their relationship, and he had learned to keep his mouth shut. Soon, she would be based in headquarters, and they would openly be a couple, living together, if he could ever get her to that stage. Case would have no ammunition then. Lloyd was only surprised that he hadn't yet noticed Judy's thickening waistline. "What about this letter that his mother wanted him to collect for her?" he tried. "His brother confirms his story about that. So he could have made that call a month previously, as he said he did, and *if* he did, then he was set up, and that tape was left for us to find."

They had had the tape fingerprinted; Elizabeth Esterbrook's prints had been found, naturally, because she had put the tape in for Angela in the first place, but no one else's prints were on it at all, as Case was quick to point out.

"And once again, it's Josh Esterbrook who told you about the letter, so where does that leave your daft theory that he's masterminding all this? And we are unable to confirm Paul Esterbrook's story about making the call a month previously because of his convenient inability to remember whose mobile phone he was using at the time!"

"We know it wasn't Billy Rampton's," muttered Lloyd.

"That's because he didn't *make* the call a month ago from a mobile phone! He made it on Saturday from the cottage phone. Why would he use a mobile, for God's sake? There are two perfectly good phones at the cottage. He said that to account for the fact that no call was made from the cottage to Little Elmley a month ago. There was no call from a mobile phone. Give up, Lloyd!"

Lloyd blew out his cheeks. He was getting too old for this, but he would not give up. "Why would he insist he'd made that call on a *Sunday?*"

"He'd have said he made it on a Sunday because he was as devious as all hell, and he wanted you to start thinking exactly what you are thinking."

Lloyd gathered himself for his final assault. "But if he did all that because of Kathy Cope's report, doesn't the fact that the visual evidence was removed but the report was still there strike you as a little odd? Why didn't he take the report itself?"

"He didn't have anything to do with that. I don't suppose his mother wanted to keep a picture of her son in that pos—" Case smiled. "—situation," he amended.

Lloyd threw his hands in the air. "But she wanted an entire video of it in the first place, according to the report."

"A few seconds, Lloyd, not a Hollywood production. She felt she needed concrete proof. To be certain that her son really was doing what she suspected he was doing, before she took any action. The still confirmed it to her satisfaction, and she threw it away. The report was in a concealed drawer—he just didn't know where to look for it."

"Of course he'd know where to look for it!" said Lloyd. "I grew up with one of these old bureaus. I could open every secret compartment and hidden drawer by the time I was five! And so could Josh and Paul Esterbrook, I'm sure."

For once, his illustration from his childhood was true; he really had grown up with a bureau like that. And that was a little puzzle that he hadn't even mentioned to Judy yet. His mother had also kept keepsakes in those not-so-hidden drawers; keepsakes were pleasant things. Angela's had been old love letters and her first try at a novel. It seemed odd to Lloyd that she would put something in with them as unpleasant to her as Kathy Cope's report must have been. But he didn't have time to speculate on that, not right now. "I believe the visual evidence was removed because it wasn't Paul Esterbrook who was with Billy Rampton," he said.

288 [· *Jill McGown* ·]

"Oh, yes it was, Lloyd. And Billy Rampton colluded with Angela Esterbrook to trap him. That's why Paul Esterbrook shot Billy, and it's why he shot his mother, and when he realized he could never get away with it, he shot himself." Case stood up, took his jacket from the back of the chair. "Penhallin police are happy to accept that. I'm happy to accept that. So if you want more work done on this, you can pay for your experts yourself, because I'm not authorizing the work. And I'll close the enquiry anyway, so it will be a waste of time."

Yes, thought Lloyd, as Case shrugged on his jacket and cleared his desk. That was what he thought he would say. So he hit Case with his statistic, the one he'd been saving up.

"Five people knew for a fact which of the Esterbrook brothers was in that hotel bedroom with Billy," he said, and illustrated with his fingers, sticking each one up in turn, starting with the little finger of his left hand. "Billy himself, Angela Esterbrook, Kathy Cope, Paul Esterbrook, and Josh Esterbrook." His left hand had the fingers spread wide. "And four of them are dead." He closed his hand, holding the solitary thumb eloquently in the air.

Case looked at the thumb for a long time, then closed his eyes. "I don't believe I'm saying this," he said. "All right, Lloyd, you can have your counsel's opinion and your handwriting expert. What's another couple of thousand on top of what you've already spent? But it's the same deal as the Copes. The end of the week."

"The end of the week," said Lloyd.

The end of the *week*?

SCENE XVIII—NORFOLK
The following day, Wednesday, October 1st, 9:30 A.M.
The home of Letitia Markham

"Sergeant Finch, it just isn't something that you can *do* in twenty-four hours," she said, spreading her arms wide in a huge gesture of hopelessness.

Tom had been chosen to approach the dark and dramatic Lettie, as Lloyd called her, Professor Markham, as he respectfully called her, about the recovered letter from Angela Esterbrook. His boyish charm, Lloyd had said, would bowl Lettie over. So far, it wasn't working terribly well.

"It's not even the original letter!" she said. "Impressions—what am I supposed to tell you about them?" She tossed back her long hair, still suspiciously black despite her sixty-odd summers. "Except that she must have been very angry when she wrote it," she said. "And deep impressions help."

Tom felt a little surge of triumph. He had tried the Judy method. Don't say anything, and if they speak next, they're cracking, she said. She had spoken at length about how she couldn't possibly do it, but she *was* cracking.

"I know, Professor," he said. "But my boss reckoned I'd be able to sweet-talk you into doing it all the same. I don't know where he got that idea from."

She smiled. "I can see through you, Sergeant Finch. Even so, you might be able to sweet-talk me into many things, but not pronouncing on this letter within twenty-four hours." She picked it up, perused it. "Have you any idea how much work is involved?"

"Well—to be honest," said Tom, "I don't. I don't even know how you begin to go about it."

She looked up. "Are you interested?" she said.

"Oh, yes. I think it's fascinating." It was true; he liked things that had to be worried at and pored over and worked at. It gave you something to get your teeth into.

"Well," she said. "Let's take the signature, 'Angela.' Now, people never sign their name the same way twice. Therefore, if this 'Angela' were to match up exactly to another example of her signature, that would in fact suggest . . ."

Tom listened, and watched, and congratulated himself, as he was given instruction on handwriting comparison.

". . . and then you do it all again for the bottom of each letter," she said. "And then you plot the spaces, and the slant of the letters, and the boldness of the downstrokes and—well, that's just some of it. It's very painstaking work. It takes hours, and the report takes even longer. I have a great many other calls on my time, young man."

"Chief Inspector Lloyd thinks that someone is going to get away with murdering five people."

Her dark eyes grew wide. "*Five* people?" she repeated. "That seems like four more than the average murderer allows himself. Why haven't I read about it in the papers?"

"Well, because three of them are believed to be suicide, and the two murders happened in two different counties, neither of them this one. It's never got beyond the local news."

She looked at the letter again. "What exactly is he trying to discover about this document?"

"We need to know if it's genuine or not, and who it was really written to," said Tom, diving into his briefcase. "I've brought lots of examples of Mrs. Esterbrook's writing that are known to be genuine," he said. "Her diaries, and a shopping list. She had arthritis, so the recent examples are fairly short, like the shopping list. She didn't keep a handwritten diary anymore, but we've brought the most recent one. And as many examples as we could get of her signature, including the most recent, which was a postcard to her daughter-in-law, also signed just 'Angela,' like that letter." He put them on the table. "And we would like to be sure that the name 'Paul' is in the same writing as the rest, even if the body of the letter's genuine," he said. "Could it originally have been written to someone called Josh?"

"Mm," she said, and held the letter at a slight angle.

"There are lots of examples of the name 'Paul' in the diaries for comparison purposes," added Tom. "Her husband's name was Paul."

She now had the letter, and the comparison samples. Tom held his breath while she looked at the work she already had, and the work that he had given her.

"I can't possibly give you a definitive answer. I couldn't, with all the time in the world, not with a recovered document. And in twenty-four hours . . . well."

"No," said Tom, inwardly turning somersaults, whooping, punching the air. "Of course not. And we're not expecting anything like that, Professor Markham, just—well, just your best guess, really."

SCENE XIX—BARTONSHIRE
Wednesday, October 1st, 10:30 A.M.
Barristers' chambers in Barton

It was when Lloyd had asked her to take Paul Esterbrook Sr.'s will to James Harper that Judy realized just how strongly he believed in Paul Esterbrook Jr.'s innocence of these murders. Because it was with James Harper—Hotshot Harper, as she had disparagingly once called him—thirty-something, handsome, successful, and charming, that she had come as close as she ever had, as close as she ever would, she hoped, to being unfaithful to Lloyd. And Lloyd knew that.

"You want me to do what?" Harper's grey eyes, as ever, were amused.

She smiled. "I need to know what chance Josh Esterbrook stands of successfully claiming title to Little Elmley, if Paul Esterbrook is deemed to have murdered his mother. You must know someone who could do that."

"In twenty-four hours?"

"Sooner would be preferable," she said.

He looked a little dubious. "Are you in some sort of trouble?" he asked. "Is that why you've come directly to me?"

"No. This is entirely aboveboard, authorized by my Superintendent. It's just very, very urgent. There was no time to go through the usual channels. And since I had a friend at court, you might say . . ."

"Does your Superintendent have the faintest idea how much people in this chambers cost?" He took the bulky will from her and flicked through its pages, absently brushing his fair hair from his forehead with his hand. Then he looked up at her and smiled. "This is a joke right?"

"No joke."

"You want someone to advise you, by this time tomorrow, on what he believes would be the outcome of a court hearing that could last months—years, even?"

"Yes."

His face grew serious. "It can't be done, Judy. Truly."

"Why not?"

He waved a hand round his office, at the law books in their glass cases. "Whoever did it would need to work through practically all of them before he could begin to give you a reasoned opinion."

"Well, of course, that would be impossible," Judy said. "But you see court cases all the time that are grinding on forever, and everyone knows what the result's going to be. All I want your expert to do is second-guess the judge. Give it his best shot."

"How, without going through it in detail?"

"We don't *want* a barrister's opinion, really," she said. "We want to know what Josh Esterbrook's opinion would have been, given that he had a long time to study it. We just think a barrister will be able to home in on the bits that matter more quickly than any of us can. Would Josh Esterbrook believe he stood a good enough chance to murder for it? That's all we need to know."

The twinkle was back in his eye. "In twenty-four hours," he said. "Even your suspect had three years to think about it." He looked at the will again, then set it down and looked up at her. "All right," he said. "I'll give it to a friend of mine who will give it *her* best shot, I promise, because she'll enjoy the challenge. I happen to know she's got the evening free, which, since you are a detective, you will readily realize means that now so have I. Perhaps I can turn that to advantage."

Judy smiled.

"Dinner?" He paused, shook his head. "A couple of glasses of Bolly in a wine bar?" He rested his chin on his hand. "A cappuccino in a coffeehouse? A mug of tea at a mobile café?" He looked at her enquiringly, shaking his head, and sighed. "Then I might not be able to persuade Heather to do it after all," he said. "My powers of persuasion seem to be on the wane."

"I'm sure you'll manage," said Judy. "And I doubt that she would think much of you swanning off to glamorous mobile cafés with other women while she was working, anyway, so I'm saving you from yourself."

"Thank you."

She turned to go. She got as far as opening the door.

"Oh, and Judy?"

She turned, eyebrows raised.

"When's it due?"

She went slightly pink. "You—"

"Now, now. Language is not permitted in chambers. I might have pretended not to notice if you'd been nicer to me." He smiled. "Congratulations. Are you finally going to marry the poor man?"

"Probably."

"You should." He grinned. "I know, I know," he said, lifting his hands. "When you want my opinion, you'll ask for it."

SCENE XX—BARTONSHIRE
Wednesday, October 1st, 11:00 A.M.
On the road from Barton to Stansfield

Judy drove back, rather glad—perhaps for the first time—that she was pregnant, and therefore not exactly fling material, because attractive though she found James Harper, she loved Lloyd and had loved him for twenty years, and had no desire to rock any boats. She was going to have his baby because of that love, and would, in all probability, jump off a cliff for him if for some reason he needed her to, but she had fought shy of marriage. The baby had changed things, and her new job meant that their relationship could be put on an official footing at last. Marriage was on the agenda, as Hotshot had pointed out. That scared her a little. Her new job scared her. The baby scared her.

So she put all of that to the back of her mind as she pulled up at the traffic lights that greeted cars coming into Stansfield from Barton, put there to help the IMG traffic keep moving at the shift

294 [· Jill McGown ·]

changes, and unnecessary at all other times. Since she was here, she thought, she might as well see if Sandie Esterbrook was at work; she wanted to talk to her about something that she might not feel like discussing in front of her husband.

SCENE XXI—BARTONSHIRE
Wednesday, October 1st, 11:10 A.M.
IMG's offices

IMG's head office was functional sixties, square and many-storeyed by Stansfield's low-rise standards; the entrance hall, however, was the epitome of eighties conspicuous consumerism, celebrating the decade in which Paul Esterbrook Sr. had become a serious player. And in amongst the original artwork, the cedar panelling, the hessian wallpaper, the linoleum-and-leather-covered reception desk that swept round one corner, the indoor trees and plants, was a display case of bottled gases; big cylinders, little cylinders, cylinders with multiple attachments, showing the full range of gases and containers offered by IMG, bringing the whole thing down to earth again. Judy smiled at this irritating necessity to display their wares.

"Have you come to arrest me again?" Sandie Esterbrook nodded to the chair in front of the desk. "Take a seat," she said.

"I want to ask you some questions. You don't have to answer them."

She smiled. "But it may harm my defense if I don't?" she said.

"No," said Judy. "Nothing like that. I'd just like to know how you met Paul Esterbrook."

Sandie Esterbrook looked at her, still smiling slightly. "Sergeant Finch thinks I gave up being a prostitute," she said. "But I didn't. I just polished up the image, and moved upmarket, which keeps you out of the magistrates' courts. I still wasn't respectable, though. I was a call girl."

She had polished up the image to considerable effect, Judy thought. She hadn't quite put Sandie in the Roedean bracket, but then Sandie hadn't chosen to place herself there; Judy was sure she could carry off Roedean if she wanted. She came across as something not unlike Judy herself; the product of middle-class, comfortable parents who had paid for her education at a middle-class, comfortable day school, having sadly despaired of state education by the late sixties, in Judy's father's case. But Sandie Esterbrook was the product of a deprived background that she had run away from, and her own quick intelligence.

"Brendan—" She ducked her head in a brief apology. "—who *isn't* my ex-boyfriend, but my ex-pimp, ran a very high-class operation in Barton, and he had boys on his books too. Paul Esterbrook was a client." She picked up her cigarettes, offered Judy one.

Judy took it, and listened as Sandie told her how Brendan had asked her if she would be prepared to act as decoy for Paul Esterbrook in various hotels, with various boys, attracting attention away from them and to herself in case someone was watching him, and she had agreed. How, when Paul had wanted her to accompany him on weekends to Cornwall, Brendan had said no, because he didn't like his girls being that far away from his seat of operations. Besides, Paul wasn't using one of his boys; he had made alternative arrangements in Plymouth, and Brendan, naturally, hadn't liked that. Paul had offered Sandie a deal, and she had taken it, moved to Stansfield in order not to be too close to the irritated Brendan, and had become Paul Esterbrook's personal assistant.

"Did he *know* he was being watched?"

"No. He didn't really believe he was, not to start with. He just did everything on that assumption, because that way he couldn't be caught if and when she did put someone on to him."

"Can I ask you about Saturday?" said Judy. "You told DCI Lloyd that Billy was already there when you got there."

She nodded.

"Would Paul have given Billy a key?"

"No. Billy was probably waiting at the back. You can get into the garden from the shore. I expect Paul let him in when I was still outside."

Billy had been hiding in the treehouse, according to the finger-prints they had found. Paul must have told him to do that, and that didn't seem to accord with his stated belief, according to Josh, that he wasn't going to be watched that weekend. Judy asked Sandie Esterbrook about that.

"But he was convinced Josh was up to something," she said. "He was sure it had something to do with the cottage, so he probably did tell Billy to keep out of sight."

That seemed reasonable to Judy, but Lloyd thought Billy had been hiding from Paul, that Paul didn't even know he was there. And there was one thing bothering Judy about Sandie's story. "When you did go into the cottage, what exactly did you do?" she asked.

"I told Chief Inspector Lloyd everything I could remember," she said.

"Something you might have forgotten when you were telling him. Go through what you did for me."

"I put away the glasses that Paul had taken out," she said. "I checked the fax machine in case he'd left the fax on it, but he hadn't. Josh hadn't sent a fax, of course, so that was hardly surprising."

"So you were over by the desk?"

"Yes."

"You didn't notice anything then?" Judy gave up trying not to prompt her. "A smell of burning, perhaps?"

"No," she said. "Nothing. Josh said that something had been burned in the wastepaper bin, but I didn't notice it."

Paul could have burned whatever it was when he went back in, but why get Sandie to tidy everything up and then leave burned paper for Angela to find? Perhaps Lloyd was right; perhaps he had been set up, and hadn't murdered Billy at all.

If Sandie was part of that setup, she would surely have said that she *had* smelt burning, that she *had* noticed the contents of the wastebin? But since Henderson's men had kept surveillance on the cottage until Billy's body was found, and had seen no one else go near it, Billy's murderer did seem to be a toss-up between Sandie and Paul.

Though of course, Judy thought, it could be approached from the rear, and no one had been watching the back.

SCENE XXII—BARTONSHIRE
Wednesday, October 1st, 12:00 noon
Elizabeth's house

It was Chief Inspector Lloyd again. Elizabeth felt quite disappointed that they seemed to have stopped sending Sergeant Finch, but at least Lloyd was a senior officer, and might be able to tell her more.

"What's happening?" she said.

"Our enquiries are proceeding, Mrs. Esterbrook."

"That's officialese. What's really happening? It's dreadful—everyone thinks Paul did those awful things, and he's not alive to defend himself!"

Her distress was real enough; she didn't actually care that people thought that Paul had murdered that boy and his own mother, but she did care that the police seemed to think it. She sighed. "Last Friday, I was convinced that Paul was seeing Sandie, that all that business about the night dive was a lie. By Saturday, I was convinced that she was just a red herring. And now you're telling me it was this Billy person Paul was involved with, and I don't know what to think."

"It does accord with your belief that Sandie was a red herring," said Lloyd.

"I know, I know," she sighed. And, if truth be told, Elizabeth didn't find it too difficult to believe; Paul's sexual tastes had always been inexplicable as far as she was concerned. They might have included someone like Billy. But Josh was the one who hadn't looked at a woman for three years, not Paul. "All I can do is beg you, Mr. Lloyd, not to take an Esterbrook's word for anything."

"I can only assure you, Mrs. Esterbrook, that we are exploring every avenue." He smiled apologetically. "More officialese, I know, but true nonetheless."

That was easy enough to say, but they didn't have her incentive.

Paul's shares in IMG would form part of his estate providing his name was cleared. She would be immensely wealthy. And if ever anyone deserved to be, she did, after putting up with that bloody family all these years. But if they continued to believe what they seemed to believe, she would be a great deal worse off, not better off.

"You do know," she said, "that if Paul is held responsible for his mother's murder, the entire Esterbrook Family Trust holdings will go to some marine exploration project? My God, they'll be able to raise Atlantis with that sort of cash."

Lloyd smiled. "As I said, our enquiries are proceeding."

"Is that what you're here to tell me?"

"No," he said. "I'm here to ask you something. At your mother-in-law's house on Saturday evening, you told my sergeant that the answering machine had failed to work properly before. Do you by any chance remember when that was?"

"Yes," said Elizabeth. "It was the Sunday of the Bank Holiday weekend, because Angela had been visiting friends in London on Saturday, and you can't get a train back from St. Pancras to Barton after nine o'clock on a Saturday, so she stayed over. And I only had to work on the Sunday, which is why I remember when it was."

Lloyd smiled. "You didn't get Bank Holiday weekends off, then?"

"Volunteers never do," said Elizabeth, with an answering smile. "I went over to Little Elmley and found the answering machine blinking, but it wouldn't play."

"What time was that, Mrs. Esterbrook?"

"It would be about quarter to ten, I suppose."

He nodded, and thought for a moment. "Was Josh at Little Elmley that morning?" he asked. "You said he fixed the answering machine."

"No. He was in Penhallin," Elizabeth said. "It was the day the boat holed."

Lloyd shook his head. "No," he said. "We've established that the boat was holed on the Saturday. I'm afraid you were misled by your husband."

She nodded. Finch had clearly been puzzled when she had said it had happened on the Sunday; she had realized then that she had probably been misled. She shrugged. "As I said—you can't take an Esterbrook's word for anything. Josh always looked out for Paul. Covered up for him, told lies for him. I couldn't compete with both of them."

"So when did Josh fix the machine?"

"When he came home."

"Could you then listen to the message that had been left on it?"

"No. It doesn't work like that. It thinks you've heard it. So it just gets recorded over when it takes another message."

"And did it, to your knowledge, take any more messages?"

"Yes," said Elizabeth. "Because we tested it." She frowned. "Why are you asking about that?"

"It might be important." Lloyd smiled again. "Well, thank you very much, Mrs. Esterbrook. You've been most helpful."

SCENE XXIII—BARTONSHIRE
Wednesday, October 1st, 12:30 P.M.
IMG's office

"You said you wouldn't cross the street to talk to Billy," Inspector Hill said. "Why?"

Sandie shook her head slightly. She had met Billy the same day as she had met Josh; her reactions to the two couldn't haven't been more different. And in neither case had she found any reason to alter her first impression.

"He was into everything," she said. "Drugs, porn, you name it, Billy had a hand in it. He once boasted to me about having supplied the victim for a snuff movie. He was a liar, as I told Chief Inspector Lloyd, so he probably didn't, but it wouldn't be because of his scruples."

"You said you didn't like Paul much, come to that."

She smiled. "No, I didn't," she said. "But if it hadn't been for him,

I wouldn't have met Josh. I'll always be truly grateful to him for that." And that was the truth.

Inspector Hill left then, and Sandie watched the Clio pull out onto the main road and go briskly off, back to the police station, no doubt. Almost everything she had told the inspector had been the truth, but not quite all, and she was confident that Inspector Hill had believed her when she had lied, just as she had refused to believe her when she had told the truth.

But then, lying was so much easier.

SCENE XXIV—BARTONSHIRE
Wednesday, October 1st, 1:10 P.M.
The house at Little Elmley

Angela Esterbrook's study was no longer sealed now that the SOCOs had finished with it, but Lloyd had been given grudging permission by the housekeeper to go in, and was now being given willing assistance by the girl who had helped Mrs. Esterbrook in the kitchen. She expressed her sadness at her previous employer's passing, but again it was with detachment. Angela Esterbrook hadn't really inspired affection, Lloyd found himself thinking. That was a bit sad.

"It was Mrs. Esterbrook got me interested in cooking—she wouldn't have anything out of a packet. And she did the cooking—she wouldn't hear of getting a cook. But she would let me have a go, because she liked teaching me. Everything had to be fresh—even when it was just lunch for herself. But she couldn't chop vegetables or grate cheese or anything like that."

"Did she often eat alone?"

"No. Josh has his own kitchen and all that, but he was usually here for lunch and dinner. And his girlfriend, lately. Well—his wife. I didn't know they were married."

Angela hadn't told anyone that Josh and Sandie were married, presumably, not even someone she worked with every day.

"I thought she was here a lot, but I didn't know she lived here.

They never said she'd moved in, and they didn't say they were married. That's a bit weird."

It was, as she said, a bit weird, but even the cleaners hadn't known, as Lloyd had found out by a similar line of questioning. Josh's rooms had remained resolutely male; young Mrs. Esterbrook's wardrobe had presumably been housed in one of the many guest rooms. Weird seemed to be situation normal for the Esterbrooks. He was beginning to feel that with a family to whom subterfuge, plot, and counterplot was apparently second nature, he might be on a hiding to nothing, but he wasn't beaten yet.

"Right," he said, when he'd recorded a message on a brand-new tape on Angela's machine. "I'd like you to go into the hallway, ring this number, and leave a message on the machine. Then I'll call you back and give you further instructions."

"What'll I say?"

" 'Mary had a little lamb' is a popular choice."

Half an hour later he had established to his own satisfaction that there was nothing wrong with the answering machine, elderly though it was. But if you removed the tape before playing the message, or after saving it, then the light continued to blink. Putting in a different tape then produced exactly the situation Tom Finch had found on Saturday night. A tape that would neither play nor record, with the message light blinking. Lloyd became more than ever convinced that the tape Tom found had been planted.

"Thanks," he said as he left the office. "You've been a great help." He paused on his way to the front door. "You couldn't tell me how to walk to the diving club from here, could you?" he asked.

"Sure. Come through to the kitchen."

He followed her along the corridor into the kitchen, where Angela Esterbrook's body had lain the first time he visited this house.

The girl opened the door. "Do you see the willow tree?" she said. "If you walk past it, you'll come to a wooden gate. The path takes you to a jetty. Go down there to the edge of the water, and then follow the shoreline round to the left. You'll see the diving platform first, and the club's just at the top of the slope."

SCENE XXV—BARTONSHIRE
Wednesday, October 1st, 2:15 P.M.
The reservoir and diving club at Little Elmley

Admirable directions, Lloyd thought, as he found himself at the landing stage. He wasn't starting from the dual carriageway as Sandie Esterbrook claimed she had, but he could see where she would have had to leave the road and scramble down to the water's edge. He would add two minutes to his journey time. He wanted to see if you really could get from there to the club in under ten minutes as she said she had.

Twelve minutes later he was walking up the stony slope towards the club. Plus the two minutes he first thought of, and his journey time came to fourteen minutes. Could that time have had five minutes shaved off it by someone half his age, running rather than walking, and spurred on by sheer necessity? Yes, he thought, it probably could. He had no reason to doubt her on that score. He went into the club, finding himself in a small reception area with a notice board and two shop-window models wearing diving gear.

He had been trying to work out how the Copes were murdered, in the hope that in that way he might be able to prove who had murdered them. And now he was looking at equipment designed to keep you alive in a hostile environment, and that set him thinking.

"Can I help you?" said a voice.

An aqualung? No. It was far too bulky. You couldn't wear it, not without attracting attention to yourself. And you certainly couldn't get into a car, especially not a Ford Fiesta, wearing one of them. And carrying it about with you would hardly be practical.

"You might prefer snorkelling," the man said. "That's what you learn first, anyway."

A snorkel? That seemed more portable. He looked at the two kinds of snorkel the man was pointing out to him, and tried to work out any way in which a tall, well-built man could position himself in the backseat of a Ford Fiesta in such a way that he could hold people at gunpoint and breathe air with the snorkel through a slightly open window at the same time. There wasn't one, he decided, since they were designed to lie flat against the side of the head. His face would be squashed up against the glass. And anyway, his victims would have laughed themselves to death before the fumes had had time to take hold.

The big objection was that no one would just sit there, even if their assailant did have a gun, knowing they were going to die. His mother used to say of unpleasant choices that she would sooner be shot than poisoned, and he imagined that, given the literal choice, most people would. They would have tried to get out; Andy Cope would indeed have switched off the engine. They would have done *something*, and their assailant would have had to shoot them, or let them go, because people simply didn't die to order. He was glad he hadn't shared that nonstarter of a theory with anyone else.

"But you can hire equipment," the man said. "You don't have to buy it all before you even know if you want to do it." He smiled, held out his hand. "Howard," he said. "I'm one of the instructors here. Are you interested in learning to dive?"

"Er . . . no thanks," said Lloyd. "I'm actually here to talk to Josh Esterbrook. DCI Lloyd, Stansfield CID." He showed Howard his card.

"Oh, right!" Howard laughed. "Sorry. He's with a pupil in the pool. Just go through."

"I think Josh's wife mentioned that you were involved in this night dive on Saturday?" said Lloyd.

"Josh's wife?" he said.

"Sandie."

Howard looked startled. "Are they married now?" he said. "I had no idea. You'd think he'd have said. They're a funny lot, the Esterbrooks. Paul's wife rang here the night before that dive, wanting to know if Sandie really was doing it. You'd think she'd just have asked Josh, since he was taking it."

You would, thought Lloyd. But not if you were trying to catch his brother, because Josh watched out for his brother.

"Anyway, she shouldn't have done it, but she insisted."

"I had no idea the reservoir was so close to the Esterbrook house," said Lloyd, absently picking up a booklet on sub aqua, leafing through it.

"Oh, yes. It used to be the manor house in Little Elmley, generations ago. The only reason it didn't get flooded with the rest of the village was because it was built at the top of the incline—it was empty for years before old man Esterbrook bought it. Anyway, Sandie thought it would be romantic to see the village at night. Josh and I told her she'd see a lot more in daylight, but you know women."

Lloyd knew women. "How many people were doing that particular dive? To the submerged houses?"

"Just her and Josh. We give individual instruction, so it's usually just two people at a time." He smiled again. "Have I not got you interested yet?"

"I'm afraid not," said Lloyd.

"Well, keep the booklet. Just in case."

Lloyd would not only keep it, he would read it. It might give him some valuable information. "How long did their dive last?"

"Half an hour or so. And that was half an hour too long for Sandie, if you ask me. Josh should have put his foot down."

Lloyd smiled. "As you say," he said. "No accounting for women." He put the booklet in his pocket. "Thanks," he said, patting it. "I just go through here, do I?"

SCENE XXVI—BARTONSHIRE
Wednesday, October 1st, 2:45 P.M.
The diving club pool

"There you go," said Josh as his pupil surfaced and blew water from his snorkel. "You keep this up, and you won't believe the sort of things you'll see when you start swimming in warm waters."

"For twenty seconds at a time," said the man, with a grin.

"You'll get better at that, too. The more you do it, the longer you'll be able to stay under, the deeper you'll be able to go."

"How long can you manage?"

Josh remembered Sandie saying that if she hadn't been able to see him swimming, she would have thought he had drowned. That had probably been his best ever; he had wanted so much to impress her. "I think my record's about three minutes," he said. "But one and a half, two minutes would be average."

"You're joking!"

"Mr. Esterbrook?"

Josh turned to see Chief Inspector Lloyd. "Come for a lesson, have you?" he asked.

"I'm afraid not," said Lloyd. "I'd just like to ask you a few questions."

Josh left his pupil and mentally braced himself.

"You told my sergeant that on the Bank Holiday weekend, when you holed the boat, you came back to Little Elmley, and you were at the house on Sunday morning when you got the call from your mother about this letter, is that right?"

"Yes," said Josh. He suspected Lloyd didn't believe him, but that didn't bother him. He had spent his life being disbelieved. Sometimes he was even telling the truth.

"Did anyone see you at Little Elmley on Sunday morning?"

"I doubt it. I got back very late on Saturday night, and as you know, we have no staff there at weekends." Josh smiled. "Your sergeant wants to know if anyone can verify that I was there that morning; now you want witnesses. What's this all about?"

Lloyd smiled back. "We're exploring every avenue, as I told your sister-in-law."

Josh watched him as he left, walking down towards the diving platform. He'd walked here, had he? Perhaps he really was exploring every avenue. But would any of these avenues lead him anywhere? That was the question.

SCENE XXVII—BARTONSHIRE
The following day, Thursday, October 2nd, 9:10 A.M.
Stansfield police station

Lloyd could *hear* Freddie grinning as soon as he mentioned the Copes. "What theory did you have this time, Lloyd?" he asked.

"It occurred to me that my chief suspect is an expert diver. He can hold his breath for two minutes on average. Does that help? Would they be woozy enough not to be able to help themselves after two minutes? After all, they might not have reached desperation level before the stuff impaired their judgement."

Freddie laughed. "No, sorry, Lloyd," he said. "Not with that low a concentration of carbon monoxide. They'd practically have to be swigging it straight from the bottle for that to work."

Oh, well, thought Lloyd. It was worth a try. "Thanks, Freddie," he said with a sigh. "I think that might just be my last throw of the—" His eyes widened. "—bottle," he said.

Bottle. He suddenly saw, in his mind's eye, the display, the one Judy had told him about, in the middle of IMG's opulent entrance hall, spoiling its decor. Bottled gases just aren't sexy, she said. *Bottled* gases. He sat back and nodded slowly. Of course, of course. Swigging it straight from the bottle was precisely what they had done.

"Your last throw of the bottle? Lloyd? Are you there? You haven't passed out on me, have you?"

"No," said Lloyd. "I haven't. But how long would the Copes have taken to pass out if we were talking about pure carbon monoxide?"

"Seconds," said Freddie, his voice losing the bantering tone and growing interested. "Less than a minute. They'd have got a fatal dose before they knew what had hit them. A couple of breaths might be all it would take."

"How does this sound, Freddie? A man with a gun, and a small cylinder of pure carbon monoxide, readily available from the family emporium. Odourless, colourless, tasteless, and portable. He's in the car with them, but he's holding his breath, and they're not. They simply don't know what's happening—they think they're being robbed or something, until it's too late. Then, as soon as they go under, he gets out, fixes up the vacuum-cleaner hose, and they die of inhaling exhaust fumes."

There was a silence. "If it *was* murder, then it sounds as though you've cracked how it was done, but you're not much better off," he said. "Yes, it could have been done like that, but your man covered his tracks too well for you to prove it. And it's still a toss-up, isn't it? Between Paul and Josh Esterbrook?"

Yes. It was still a toss-up. And proving it, even if he traced the carbon monoxide back to IMG, would be virtually impossible. He would try, though. And somehow it still made Lloyd feel better, because now all his little puzzles about the Copes had been answered. They knew how Kathy had come by her new office equipment, knew almost certainly how she had had access to sophisticated surveillance devices, and they knew why Mrs. Esterbrook had gone to her, rather than someone more reputable. And he had been right about why the small garage door had had to be left unlocked, and why Kathy's tins of beans had been put away in the wrong place, because the Copes had indeed been murdered, and now they knew how the murder had been achieved.

But they didn't yet know *why* they had been murdered. Because she had been blackmailing Paul Esterbrook? Or because she could identify Josh Esterbrook as the man in the hotel room with Billy? The missing video-frame suggested the latter, but Case could obviously be right; Angela Esterbrook might simply have destroyed it once it had served its purpose. Either way, the murderer had got the wrong man when he murdered Andy Cope, and if Kathy's boyfriend could be found, they might find out exactly who it was that Kathy Cope saw when she walked into Room 312. But their enquiries into who Kathy's boyfriend was had so far proved fruitless.

He had no sooner hung up than the phone rang again and he answered it to Lettie Markham.

"I'm sending my report to you by courier, but the bottom line is that I believe that letter is genuine."

Lloyd sighed. He had had hopes of that letter, but if Lettie thought it was genuine, then perhaps things really were just the way they seemed. Angela Esterbrook had written that letter, and had signed her death warrant.

"It's far from definitive, as I warned your sergeant it would be," she said. "And, of course, the subject's arthritis meant that some differences were to be expected. That seems just to have resulted in a tendency to write more carefully, more the way she used to write as a girl—taking more time about it. There are some spacing queries, but I'm reasonably happy that it wasn't written by anyone other than Angela Esterbrook, and that it was written to someone called Paul—I don't think the name's been interfered with."

"Ah, well," said Lloyd.

"I've gone into quite a bit more detail in the report, but that's the gist of it. A very much qualified thumbs up, because without the time and without the original, I can't give you any more than that."

"Thanks, Lettie," he said. "I owe you a very good meal in a very good restaurant, even it this isn't the answer I wanted."

It didn't therefore surprise Lloyd when Judy came in to show him Hotshot's friend Heather's pronouncement on the will—transported to Stansfield police station through the good offices of a fellow barrister appearing at the magistrates' court—that it was equally inconclusive.

It was Heather's opinion, with a small *o* because she wouldn't dream of regarding it as a professional brief in view of the ridiculously short time she had had to study the problem, that in cases where a situation existed that had been unforeseen by the testator, the spirit of the wishes of the testator carried the day if that could be gleaned from those situations that *had* been foreseen.

In this case, the testator had foreseen the possibility of Angela Esterbrook predeceasing Paul Esterbrook in circumstances in which Paul Esterbrook had already disqualified himself from inheriting and Josh Esterbrook had not completed his period of qualification, and in that event, Josh was not to inherit anything; the entire Little Elmley estate was to be sold, and the proceeds invested in the Esterbrook Marine Research Trust. The fact that murder rather than divorce would be what disqualified Paul Esterbrook in the circumstance outlined could be regarded as incidental, and the testator's wishes would prevail.

But, Heather went on—in true lawyer style—the original stipulation could be seen as constituting a specific deterrent to Josh Esterbrook were he thinking of removing his stepmother by foul means in order to hasten his inheritance, since the basis for all the restrictions and stipulations concerning Josh Esterbrook's inheritance appeared to be his criminal conviction for manslaughter, and his father's belief that he might become mentally unstable, as his mother had before him. Therefore, since, in the circumstance outlined, he would be innocent of such a deed, a court might well decide in his favour.

The layman's reading of it, which she understood was the point of view in which they were most interested, would have led Josh Esterbrook to the conclusion that in the event of his half brother being deemed to have murdered his stepmother, he stood as good a chance of winning as of losing, and he wouldn't be far wrong.

He put down the hastily written note and shrugged. He had homed in on a suspect and had been trying to make the evidence fit his conclusion; it wasn't going to do that, so he might as well accept it.

"I'm pretty sure that Paul *was* seeing Billy," Judy said. "I believe what Sandie told me, and Paul's prints were on the back door handle—that does suggest that he let Billy in."

Judy's pretty sure was good enough for Lloyd. "OK," he said. "I give in. Josh had only half a motive, which isn't enough. Paul Esterbrook killed Billy, and his mother, and himself." He smiled. "And the Copes," he added, and told her how clever he had been.

His phone rang again, and he picked it up, half expecting it to be Case thanking God that he'd come to his senses at last.

"It's Morris here, re the Rampton/Esterbrook murders? DI Hill asked us to check whether the remains found in the wastepaper basket in the Esterbrook cottage was paper from the fax machine or the pad on the desk, and the answer is that it came from neither."

Par for the course, thought Lloyd. Inconclusive evidence was all they were going to get. "Thanks anyway," he said. "She must just have used the pad to lean on, I suppose."

"Well," said Morris, "she might have, but she must have over-ordered her typing paper to one hell of an extent, because our analysis shows that the ashes are composed of materials that haven't been in use in mass paper production since the 1960s. Also, there's a very good chance, going on weight, that it was foolscap paper. I think you're looking at a letter that's near as dammit forty years old."

"I said it was written to her husband!" was Judy's instant and triumphant response when Lloyd told her.

He smiled. She didn't do that, as a rule. He did, whenever he was proved right. But she had indeed said that. "But if it was written to Paul Senior," he said, "why is she threatening him with the police? Where's the copy?" He picked things up from his untidy desk, looking under them, unearthing it. "Ah, here it is." He read it again, and frowned. "And what do you think she means about his having deceived her and everyone else, including his wife?" He handed it to Judy. "And why is she telling him to 'come home' if he was living with his first wife?"

Judy took the letter. "She seems to think he lives with her," she said, frowning. "He couldn't have lived in two places at once." And then she nodded, smiled to herself. "Of course," she said. "He *did* live in two places at once." She looked up. "The funny spaces. I *knew* there was something odd about them."

"What? You're being a gundog, and I don't know what you're pointing at."

"Not the solution of the murders, I'm afraid," she said. "If I'm right, it's a very old crime indeed. It's not against the law to have an illegitimate child, but it is to have an illegitimate *wife*."

"Bigamy?"

"I think you'll have to go even further back with Angela's diaries to be certain, but that space? The one between 'all about the' and 'little boy'? I think that sentence originally read 'all about the *wife and* little boy you keep secret.' And that other one, the one between 'me' and 'that,' where she says 'how could you take advantage of me like that?' I bet that was 'me *and Paul*' or words to that effect." She sat back and smiled at him. "I think Angela had just found out, and was threatening to blow the whistle."

Of course, thought Lloyd, reading the letter again with that thought in mind, wondering how he could possibly not have worked it out already. But where did it leave them and their rather more serious and considerably more current crimes, which now seemed as far from a solution as they had been to start with?

Well, for one thing, it proved that Paul Esterbrook *had* been set up, because Judy might have been right about the addressee, but Paul hadn't made a ghastly mistake, as she had thought, because that letter hadn't just been lying round. It had been indented on a pad.

"Someone traced it on to the pad," he said. "Someone went over it with a stylus or whatever, leaving out the words that didn't quite fit Paul's situation, and producing indentations which would indeed resemble Angela Esterbrook's handwriting when she was younger."

Judy nodded slowly. "And then they burned the original," she said. "Paul didn't read that letter at all." She frowned again. "We were *meant* to find the imprints, to think that was what had made him leave in such a hurry. But something made him leave—maybe he really did get a fax."

"Are we still checking that?"

"Yes. They've moved on to public libraries now."

"We have to know if Josh had access to Angela's letters," Lloyd said. "And if he had, I want him and his wife brought in. Elizabeth Esterbrook will know."

He stared into the middle distance, trying to work out what exactly had been done to Paul Esterbrook, and why. The evidence, as Judy had pointed out, did suggest that Paul was indeed the one who had been seeing Billy, and now they knew that someone had used that relationship to frame him for Billy's murder, and the murder of his own mother.

The only person who could benefit from that was Josh Esterbrook, however touch-and-go the likelihood of success, because Elizabeth would be infinitely worse off if her husband was deemed to have murdered his mother. His estate would be limited to that which he owned himself, and that was really very little, less than a man in his position would normally own. The Esterbrook Family Trust owned their house, IMG owned their cars. He had apparently killed himself, so quite possibly no insurance pay-out. And no huge inheritance, because it would have been gained by the murder of his mother.

"I'll get someone on to Angela's early diaries," said Judy, frowning slightly. "Before I speak to Elizabeth Esterbrook. I want to be sure of my facts."

"The letter's a fake," said Lloyd slowly, "so the message on the answering machine was probably just what Paul said it was. An old message. And someone used it to frame him. That tape was planted for us to find after circumstances had been created to make it seem incriminating." But the tape itself was of no use to them; it didn't even have glove prints on it, never mind Josh Esterbrook's fingerprints, so they weren't going to get him that way.

But it did solve the Copes' murder, after a fashion. Paul Esterbrook had indeed been with Billy in the hotel room, and he had dealt with his blackmailers, just as he had told his brother he had. It was just that Lloyd couldn't prove it.

SCENE XXVIII—BARTONSHIRE
Thursday, October 2nd, 10:45 A.M.
Ian Foster's office

"Sergeant Finch," said Foster, looking less than happy to see him.

"Mr. Foster," said Tom, closing the adjoining door in the face of the hovering, terminally curious secretary. He was going to enjoy this. "Have you been avoiding me, by any chance?"

"No, no—nothing like that. Just a bit of business, that's all. Debbie said when I got in this morning that you'd been trying to get hold of me, so I rang you. Now, I wouldn't have done that if I'd been avoiding you, would I?"

Tom opened the envelope he was carrying and drew out the photographs, laying them on the desk in front of Foster. "Do you recognize either of the people in these photographs?" he asked.

"Yes," Foster said in a small voice. "The man is Paul Esterbrook. The woman—" He looked up at Tom. "What happened to her?" He said. "Someone's given her a going-over."

"The woman," said Tom. "Go on, Mr. Foster. Don't play for time."

"The woman is called Sandie Townsend."

"Do you recognize where they are?"

Foster licked his lips. "It looks like Mrs. Esterbrook's mother-in-law's weekend cottage," he said.

"Very good," said Tom. "You did actually go to Penhallin at least once, then? Now," he said, leaning over the desk and pointing to the first picture. "These photographs come with the date and time printed on the frame. Can you read what it says, Mr. Foster?"

"Yes."

"Out loud," said Tom.

Foster sighed, and read the date and time aloud.

Tom sat down in front of him. "That's Saturday's date," he said. "So how come you gave me an account of Paul Esterbrook's movements on Saturday which entirely contradicts that evidence, and entirely corroborates his?"

Foster licked his lips again. "I didn't know I was giving him an alibi for murder, I swear I didn't. Because that's what it was, wasn't it? He killed that kid in Cornwall. And his own mother. Can you credit that?"

Tom looked at him, nodding. "That's what it looks like," he said. "And then it seems he topped himself when it all went pear-shaped." He smiled. "So you're all we've got, Foster."

Foster went pale. "I knew nothing about it!" he said.

Tom leant menacingly over the desk. "You and Esterbrook cooked this up between you, but you're the one who'll stand trial for murder."

Foster shrank back. "Hey, now, wait a minute. It had nothing to do with me!"

They now knew that Paul Esterbrook had almost certainly not murdered Billy or his mother, but Foster didn't know that, and Tom was enjoying scaring him half to death.

"It wasn't like that!" Foster said. "Look—I was following the man, right? Every weekend. She said it might last months, years even. Every weekend during the summer months, May to September inclusive. It was a steady income, nice work. It suited me. But for five weeks I tried every way I could to catch the bastard at it, all the same. I worked hard, whatever you think. I bought a camcorder, and I went everywhere he was likely to go, working out how to get the best pictures—I can show you the practice videos, if you don't believe me. I was working on it, honest, I was."

Tom's expression didn't change.

"Then, one weekend, I lost him. His brother had an accident with the boat, and I was stuck out in the channel, fishing, waiting for the boat to come out again, and it never did. But I found him the next morning by accident, and he must have thought he'd shaken me off, because he wasn't so careful that time, and I got a video of him at it. From this brilliant vantage point—there's a treehouse in the garden. It overlooks the bedroom, and he opened the curtains. It was brilliant."

The unidentified fingerprints in the treehouse. Tom wondered if any of Paul Esterbrook's doings with Billy *hadn't* been recorded on tape. But he had thought that Esterbrook and Foster had had some cosy arrangement from the off, and that wasn't quite how it was.

"I was going to tell his wife, honest, I was. She'd said I was on a percentage if I came up with the goods, and that would be worth a hundred thousand. But it could take years for her to get the money even if she did have the proof, because he'd fight it. You know how long challenged wills take, and how much they cost. My percentage would be worthless all the time the case was going on. Whereas he stood to lose everything, and he'd got lots of money now, not sometime never. I reckoned he might be just as generous if I told him what I had on him."

Foster had blackmailed him. *Foster* had, not the Copes. Tom wasn't sure where that left Lloyd's theory on their murder. If it was a murder.

"He agreed to do the business last Friday," Foster went on. "I reckoned the old park at Malworth was best, because there's never anyone there after midnight. Told him to get there at midnight, leave the money where I said, and he'd find the video. I got there earlier than I told him, so I could leave the tape and see him leave the money, make sure he was alone and all that. But he'd got there even earlier than that, and jumped me. And he didn't bring a hundred thousand with him."

Someone should have told Foster that his victim had been in the SAS or whatever it was, thought Tom, suddenly visited by a vision of Paul Esterbrook in camouflage, with a blacked-up face and twigs in his helmet, leaping onto the hapless Ian R. Foster, Private Enquiry Agent. He smiled, shook his head.

"He brought *two* hundred thousand."

Tom's smile vanished. "He what?"

"Said it was mine in return for carrying on working for his wife, only when I sent my reports in they would say what he *wanted* them to say. He'd ring me up on the Sunday night each weekend he was there, and tell me what to put. That way, I could put my feet up at the weekend, he said, and he could stop looking over his shoulder."

"And you agreed," said Tom.

"The alternative was that he cut my throat with the knife he was holding to it at the time. So yes. I agreed. What would you have done?"

Tom thought that he might have agreed, in those circumstances. They weren't circumstances in which he was ever likely to find himself, however.

"The weekend just gone was the first time she employed me again. I couldn't hang about in Barton in case Debbie or someone saw me, so I went to London, had a bloody good time on Esterbrook's money. When I got home on Sunday night, there was a message on my answering machine, telling me everything I told you. I jotted it down in my notebook, and brought it in with me as usual, so Debbie didn't know it was any different from the way it had been before. I didn't know what had gone down at his mother's place, I swear I didn't. But I'd have had to do what he'd said anyway—he'd have killed me if I hadn't."

"You still blackmailed him," said Tom. "Whatever he chose to do about it."

"Ah," said Foster. "But Esterbrook's dead. You can't do me for it."

"His wife's not dead," said Tom. "You were defrauding her."

"No," said Foster. "I wasn't. All the reports I sent her were kosher. I never sent her this report, did I? And I never sent her anything at all the weekend I caught him at it. Told her I'd come down with a bug, didn't charge her or anything. You can check."

Tom already knew that was true. He sat back. "Where's the money now?" he asked.

"Ah, that would be telling."

Tom nodded. "You've spent the last two days running round opening bank accounts, and taking a spot of legal advice, haven't you, Mr. Foster?"

Foster smiled. "The way I look at it is, it's my money. He gave me it, fair and square, so to speak."

"Fair and square? He was telling you to defraud his wife, and you were demanding money, with menaces!"

"I wasn't as menacing as him, mate, I can tell you that!"

Tom wasn't at all sure that Foster *wasn't* entitled to keep the money. He was hard pressed to think of any criminal offence with which he could be charged. And quite frankly, he didn't care. It was a drop in the ocean compared to the sort of money that these murders were all about. "Where's the video?" he said.

"I gave it to him, didn't I? Seeing as he asked so nicely."

Tom closed his eyes briefly. "Where's the video?" he asked again, and leant forward. "The copy you kept, just in case."

Foster looked mutinous. "At home," he said.

"Then let's go, Mr. Foster. And when we've seen the video, and I've taken it as evidence, you can accompany me to the station and make a statement while I decide what to charge you with."

SCENE XXIX—BARTONSHIRE
Thursday, October 2nd, 11:15 A.M.
Ian Foster's house

Home was still up for sale, Tom noticed as he pulled up outside. Presumably Ian R. Foster was looking for something a little more up-market. He wondered how long a chancer like Foster could hang on to two hundred thousand, and smiled. Maybe the bookie would give him odds.

Foster produced the video, and his television flickered into life. Tom saw Paul Esterbrook turn away from the bedroom window, then a close-up of his face as he sat on the bed. He took a mobile phone from his companion, and the camera pulled back.

Tom's eyes widened. "That's Sandie Esterbrook!" he said.

"Townsend," said Foster.

"Esterbrook," said Tom absently. "But never mind that. What matters is that she isn't Billy Rampton."

"Who's Billy Rampton?" asked Foster.

SCENE XXX—BARTONSHIRE
Thursday, October 2nd, 11.30 A.M.
Elizabeth's house

"Yes," said Elizabeth. "Angela told me, just before I began helping her with her autobiography. That was why Paul Senior refused a knighthood, in case it all came out, and embarrassed the Queen, or something."

It was good, being able to gossip about this at last. She had been sworn to secrecy by Angela. "Paul was three years old before she found out. He called himself Laurence—she was Mrs. Paul Laurence for five years until, of all things, she's sitting in her little cottage in Penhallin and finds herself reading about Mr. and Mrs. Paul Esterbrook and their son Josh at Henley or Wimbledon or somewhere, in the society pages of a Sunday paper, complete with photograph."

Detective Inspector Hill had come this time; Elizabeth had barely noticed her on Saturday night, what with one thing and another. She was very elegant, very calm and assured, not at all like Sergeant Finch. It was nice, having another woman to talk to that wasn't Angela bloody Esterbrook or Sandie, who seemed to be welded to Josh, even when he wasn't there.

"How did he manage to keep them both in the dark so long?"

Elizabeth poured coffee for each of them before answering the inspector's question. "There were a lot of miles between them," she said, handing the inspector hers. "More than there are now, with motorways to get you there fast. They got married in the fifties, remember. And Paul Laurence was considerably less wealthy than Paul Esterbrook," she added as she sat down. "Mrs. Laurence didn't have a car, and couldn't hop on a train whenever she felt like it. And she was a single parent, to all intents and purposes; she wasn't free to go where she pleased."

"So she was stuck there on her own with a toddler?"

"Most of the time." Elizabeth shook her head. "Mr. and Mrs. Laurence lived in that little two-up, two-down cottage with no money to speak of, while Mr. and Mrs. Esterbrook lived at Little Elmley surrounded by nannies and maids and goodness knows what else. Angela believed when Paul was away from home that he was out selling IMG's wares, and Josephine thought that he was off to high-level conferences."

"And he was shuttling backwards and forwards between Bartonshire and Cornwall? Being two different people?"

"Yes. But apparently he was becoming increasingly worried about leaving Josephine with Josh in order to spend time with Angela, because Josh was a handful even at two, and the nannies kept walking out. Josephine was, well, as mad as a hatter, as far as I can gather. So he was away from Angela for longer and longer periods, and Angela was worried about how hard he was having to work in order to make ends meet—she was besotted by him, and she remained so, even after he died."

"Despite what he did to her? Deceiving her, keeping her short of money?"

"She excused it. He had such a terrible time with Josephine, he just wanted a simple life in a simple cottage—" She smiled. "One is tempted to say with a simple woman, but there you are. Do you know, she never told Paul that she and his father were bigamously married? Made me promise not to tell him. That was why she was having trouble facing that part of the book. Because she would have to tell Paul."

Inspector Hill put down her coffee. "Do you have access to Angela's correspondence from that period?" she asked.

"Yes—I've got it all. Except the premarital—if you can call it that when you're talking about a bigamous marriage—love letters. She kept them in what she called her not-for-publication drawer. And for the first three years of the quote unquote marriage, I've only got letters from Paul to her, of course, because she thought he was on the road when he wasn't with her, and she couldn't write to him. Then after it all blew up, Paul made proper provision for her and Paul Junior, but he stopped dividing his time between his wives, and stayed with Josephine. He visited Angela about once a month or so, but Paul didn't know he was his father until he was about thirteen."

"Oh," said Inspector Hill. "That can't have done him any good."

"It didn't do anyone any good. I think it was worse for Josh, really. Anyway, that carried on for about two years, until Paul was five or so, and she wrote to him at IMG during that period. Do you know, she'd thought he just *worked* for IMG until then? She had no idea he owned it."

"And she forgave all that?"

"Yes. And at first things were all right, but Paul had promised to tell Josephine and sort everything out, and of course he didn't, so in the end every letter was a demand that he tell Josephine about her and Paul. That went on for nearly a year, until eventually she turned up at Little Elmley complete with Paul Junior, and introduced herself. Josephine killed herself, Paul Senior married Angela for real, and they became a family. Not one you'd want to meet up a dark alley, but a family all the same." She smiled briefly. "And if that sounds bitter, Inspector, it is."

Inspector Hill picked up her coffee again. "They do seem to be a little on the devious side," she said.

"You don't know—believe me, you can have no idea. They're all like it! Angela wasn't devious, not being an Esterbrook, but she was dangerous. If you crossed her, you knew all about it, just like Paul Senior did. I was seventeen years old when I married into this family, and now it looks as though I'm going to come out of it with nothing at all. And I've earned a slice of their fortune. Believe me, I've earned it."

"Well," said the inspector, "I didn't just come for a gossip, interesting though it is. You should write the biography anyway," she added.

Elizabeth thought she might think about that. She might *have* to write the biography if she had no income from anywhere else. It would be poetic justice at least if she could profit in some way from the Esterbrooks.

"Who else had access to the letters?"

"Well, Josh actually found all the ones from Angela to Paul. Angela didn't know Paul had kept them, until Josh was clearing out his things after he'd died. Josh was sworn to secrecy about the bigamy too, but that was when she decided to write her autobiography, because she had the entire correspondence and all the diaries. That was when I became involved—she gave them to me to put into the word processor so she could edit them."

"Did you see one written immediately after she had found that she was bigamously married?" asked the inspector.

"No," said Elizabeth, shaking her head. "I didn't know there was one."

"Did you have access to her diaries?"

"Only up to just before she found out about Paul being already married. Then she told me what had happened next, but she didn't let me see her diary. She had written very bitter, very private things in it, she said. She was having to steel herself to deal with that part. And to tell Paul Junior, of course." She shrugged, feeling for the first time a tinge of compassion for her stepmother and her husband. She was glad Angela had never had to tell Paul, even glad, in a way, that Paul had never had to find out.

"We've checked her diaries," said the inspector, "and found the one where she discovered the bigamy. One of the things she wrote in it was that she had written to Paul Senior under his own name at IMG, telling him that she had found out what he'd done. When you were going through them to transcribe them on to the word processor, did she say that one of the letters was missing?"

"No, but she didn't reread them. She was going to, but she found it difficult, and she was killed before she could."

SCENE XXXI—BARTONSHIRE
Thursday, October 2nd, 1:10 P.M.
Interview Room One at Stansfield police station

They had taken them away separately; Josh's car had driven off first, with him sitting beside Sergeant Finch. She had Inspector Hill.

She was taken into the interview room, which had a TV in it. That seemed a little odd. Then Inspector Hill came in, and once again Sandie was cautioned, asked if she wanted a solicitor.

"No," she said. "I don't think so."

"This is a video taken by a private investigator from outside the cottage of Mrs. Angela Esterbrook at the Headland, Penhallin," said Inspector Hill. "I would like you to watch a few moments of it."

Sandie frowned, watched, and saw what all the fuss was about, as the camera moved back, and saw herself hand Paul her mobile phone, and then take her decoy duties just a little more seriously than most decoys would.

"I think you are a very clever, very plausible liar, Sandie," the inspector said, stopping the tape. "You told us two stories that you knew we wouldn't believe, so that we would believe you when you told us the one about being a decoy. And it worked. We did believe it. But your story's come unstuck, and now you are going to have work very, very hard if you want me to believe another word you say."

Sandie shook her head. She wasn't disagreeing with Inspector Hill's assessment of her; she was indeed a very clever, very plausible liar. She would put herself in the premier league of liars when she was on form, which she usually was. She just couldn't believe that her lie had been discovered like this. A pure accident. No one could have known that Paul would open the curtains when he did.

But life was like that sometimes.

SCENE XXXII—BARTONSHIRE
Thursday, October 2nd, 1:15 P.M.
Interview Room Two at Stansfield police station

Josh wondered what was happening with Sandie, and what had happened that had got the police so excited. They had been arrested on different charges; Sandie on suspicion of murdering Billy, again; he on suspicion of murdering Angela and Paul.

Sergeant Finch and Chief Inspector Lloyd finally finished the preliminaries, and presumably he would find out why he was here.

"Where were you at six-thirty in the morning of Sunday the twenty-fourth of August, Mr. Esterbrook?" asked Lloyd.

Josh smiled, as he realized why he was there. "I've told you both several times. I was at Little Elmley. I had driven home the night before, after I'd holed the boat."

Lloyd leant forward a little. "Would it surprise you to learn, Mr. Esterbrook, that a report from a firm called the Cope Detective Agency was found in the bureau in your stepmother's study?"

No, that wouldn't surprise him in the least. Josh didn't speak.

"Mrs. Cope, posing as a guest who had inadvertently got out of the lift at the wrong floor, walked into Room 312 of the Excalibur Hotel in Plymouth, and videoed what she saw. A boy, whom we now know to be Billy Rampton, and an older man."

Lloyd was trying to be clever. He was pretending that they had the video, which of course they did not. Josh still didn't speak.

"The video was apparently unusable, with the exception of one frame," Lloyd went on. "Mrs. Cope had that printed out, but it was no longer with the report when we found it. And, sadly, Mr. and Mrs. Cope apparently committed suicide in the garage of their home, so they could be of no assistance to us."

Josh nodded. "I read about that," he said. Lloyd had thrown in the towel pretty quickly, he thought; he hadn't really tried.

"What you won't have read about, Mr. Esterbrook, is that Kathy Cope wasn't *with* her husband at the hotel. She and her companion registered as Mr. and Mrs. Cope, but she was with another man. Who isn't dead. A lucky break for us, I think you'll agree."

Crafty. He hadn't thrown in the towel at all. Josh smiled. A lucky break indeed.

"I think, Mr. Esterbrook, that you set your brother up, made it look as though *he* was the man in that report, that *he* was having a relationship with Billy Rampton, and that *he* had shot and killed not only Billy, but his own mother, and himself. I think you murdered Mr. and Mrs. Cope in order that they should not be able to identify *you* as the man who was with Billy in the hotel room."

"Is that why you got married?" Finch asked. "So we wouldn't realize that *you* were Billy's client?"

Josh stared at him. It hadn't occurred to him for one minute that anyone would think that their marriage had been purely a ploy. "You think it's a marriage of *convenience*?" he said. "Sandie and I got married because we wanted to live together, and under my father's ludicrous will we had to get married in order to do that. But we knew we were meant for one another—I don't care how corny that sounds, it's true. I told her all about myself, and she was prepared to live with what I'd done."

Finch looked sceptical, but Lloyd, he thought, believed him. It was much more important to Josh that they believe him about that than about anything else at all. Sandie was his life, and always would be.

SCENE XXXIII—BARTONSHIRE
Thursday, October 2nd, 1:30 P.M.
Interview Room One at Stansfield police station

Judy had swallowed every word Sandie Esterbrook had told her, and that hurt her professional pride. She couldn't tell when this girl was lying, and she had never felt quite so at sea with an interviewee in her life. "How about the truth, Sandie?" she said.

Sandie smiled. "I was a call girl, as I told you, but Paul was *my* client. He arranged our meetings through Brendan at first, and then employed me direct, just as I said. All that was true."

"And it was Josh who was seeing Billy," said Judy." "Not Paul." Lloyd's theory, the one that Case had thrown out as soon as Lloyd had uttered it, the one she had told him that he had had no business airing without running it by her first, was right. Lloyd's little puzzle of the missing video-frame had been solved. "Did you marry him to put us off the scent?"

"Oh, no. We got married because we love one another."

"Didn't it bother you?" asked Judy. "Josh having had a relationship with another man?"

Sandie smiled. "Josh and I just clicked, like I said. We knew—the minute we met, we knew."

Judy had felt like that about Lloyd. Not with quite as disastrous consequences. A couple of broken marriages. No murders.

"He told me all about himself," Sandie said. "I didn't need to tell him what my background was—Paul had already done that. We decided to forget the past, and look to the future. And that was when we decided to get Josh his freedom—we sorted out exactly what we were going to do over the next few weeks. It meant we couldn't make the marriage public, and we both had to carry on exactly as before, or Paul would get suspicious."

Judy looked at her notes, and at Sandie Esterbrook, and tried to make sense of what she was being told. "*How* were you going to get Josh what you call his freedom?"

"Before I answer that, can I ask you a question?"

It was an unusual request, but Judy couldn't see why not.

"Am I right in thinking that after you arrested me the first time, you let me go because you got evidence which proved that I *was* at the cottage with Paul, just as I'd told Chief Inspector Lloyd?"

Judy's eyebrows rose slightly. "Yes," she said. "What do you know about that?"

"Everything. I employed the Arthur Henderson agency to be there." She shrugged. "You're going to find out sooner or later, so I might as well tell you it was me before the *Penhallin Gazette* prints a photograph of Angela. She was their most famous resident, after all, even if no one had heard of her. And Arthur Henderson would be on the phone to Penhallin police station immediately."

Judy felt that all her tricks of the trade were deserting her, as she allowed her surprise and puzzlement at that statement to show on her face. Usually, she could remain entirely expressionless whatever the interviewee was telling her. She had no idea for the moment why Sandie Esterbrook had employed Henderson, but she presumed she would be told. In the meantime, she tried to sound less clueless than she felt. "Did you tell Henderson you were Angela?" she asked, drawing her notebook towards her. Tape or no tape, this she had to note down.

"No, but I didn't tell him I wasn't. And I open the mail at Little Elmley. We were both Mrs. A. Esterbrook, you see, so someone had to open the mail, sort out whose was whose, and I haven't got arthritis. I would get his report, whoever he addressed it to." Sandie stubbed out her cigarette. "That was why we married when we did," she said. "So I could do just that. But it isn't *why* we got married."

Judy nodded, but the bafflement must have been showing.

"I don't expect you to understand what we did," Sandie said. "But Josh feels very cheated. Not just by the will, but by everything that's happened to him. The will just made matters much worse."

Judy presumed that this leap back from Saturday to Josh's father's will would make sense eventually; she didn't speak.

"I don't know if you've read it, but his father virtually put him in prison again. Josh was born at Little Elmley. He grew up there. But if he was going to inherit it, he had to behave in a certain way, defer to Angela all the time. He had to live there, he had to obey her rules. He even had to show Angela our marriage certificate before I could move in there, because of what it says in the will about his conditions of residence. That's another reason we got married. We wanted to live together, and Josh had to live at Little Elmley."

"Why didn't he contest the will?" Judy asked. "The courts take quite a dim view these days of that sort of thing."

"His stepmother and his half brother refused to back him, and he wasn't sure he would win, because of what he'd done. He thought that they might think his father had every right to make him sit it out if he wanted to inherit. He only did that holdup because of the way he—" She shook her head. "It's too long a story," she said. "But he couldn't afford to take the chance of contesting the will."

"So he chose to live with his stepmother in order to inherit?" said Judy, determined not to start feeling sorry for Josh Esterbrook. "No one forced him to do that."

"Perhaps not. But he's an Esterbrook too, and they don't give up on what they believe to be theirs by right. The other two watched him like hawks, waiting for him to put a foot wrong. Angela did it because she felt a duty to his father, and Paul did it because he wanted to get one over on Josh." She lit another cigarette. "Josh just wanted to be free. So . . ."

This was the part Judy had been waiting for. People's motivation was something she had long ago given up trying to fathom. Sandie didn't seem at all likely to be confessing to murder, but she was confessing to something. Or she would, once she got round to it.

"Paul was right to be suspicious when he drove me onto Bodmin Moor," she said, lifting her chin. "Josh and I *were* plotting against him. And telling Paul that we were lovers might have been a bit painful, but at least it got him back on the road to the cottage, which was where I wanted him to be. He so nearly guessed what we were up to," she said, shaking her head. "But I got him there." She gave a short sigh, almost a sour little laugh. "Much good it did me," she said.

"What were you plotting to do, exactly?"

"Well, first, I got Henderson to investigate Billy, so I could check that he was thorough, and honest, and all the rest, since Josh knew the sort of thing Billy got up to, and we would know if Henderson's operatives, as he calls them, had really dug for the information. We wanted the evidence to be rock-solid, because we were going to have proof that Paul had spent the weekend with me in that cottage. Times, observations, photographic evidence, the lot."

"You were going to blackmail him?"

"Do a deal with him. Josh and I would leave Little Elmley, and Josh would eventually be disinherited—Angela would see to that. Paul would fall heir to it, and then he'd immediately transfer it back to Josh, or else Elizabeth would get all the evidence she needed. It would have taken a long time, but at least Josh would have been free while he was waiting."

Judy supposed Paul Esterbrook had been something of a sitting duck for blackmailers; he had been going to come into more than enough money to keep several of the species in comparative luxury, and he had felt compelled to risk losing it all.

"Did holing the boat have something to do with all of this?" she asked.

Sandie nodded. "Josh wanted to get the boat out of commission for a while, then make Paul think the weekends were beginning again, only to have a change of plan at the last minute. That way Paul would be more than amenable to his suggestion that he use the cottage, because a month of celibacy to Paul would be like a year to anyone else."

The devious and cunning Esterbrook mind, Judy thought. She was glad she hadn't married into the family, but she had a feeling that Sandie could hold her own with them rather better than Elizabeth had.

"And it was a sort of trial run. We had to be sure that Paul would be prepared to use his mother's cottage in an emergency. And he did, so we went for it. It was quite difficult to arrange, but it seemed simple enough to carry out. As it turned out, it wasn't, because first

328 [· *Jill McGown* ·]

he'd beaten me up, and then when we did get there he came running out and said we weren't staying, so Henderson's men weren't going to get anything at all. We hadn't even been in the cottage together, because I stayed outside and had a cigarette until I stopped shaking." She smiled. "Josh says it was meant, that we weren't cut out to be blackmailers. Fate arranged it so I could prove I wasn't a liar."

"But you are, of course, a liar," said Judy, writing as she spoke. "Because Billy Rampton wasn't involved with Paul Esterbrook." She looked up from her notes. "Why did you say that he was at the cottage with Paul on Saturday? What was all that business about him refusing to leave, if it wasn't to implicate Paul in his murder?"

Sandie tapped ash from her cigarette into the foil ashtray, then rolled the tip round, deciding whether or not to answer. Judy expected her to call for her solicitor, but she didn't.

"When Josh and Chief Inspector Lloyd found Billy dead, and Chief Inspector Lloyd was asking about him, Josh realized that he thought Billy had been involved with *Paul.*"

"And?"

"And then he asked Josh if it would make any difference to his expectations under the will if Paul had killed Angela. Obviously, he meant over what he thought was his relationship with Billy. Josh didn't know whether it made a difference or not—he hadn't thought about it. But he thought about it then. I mean, Angela and Paul were dead, and that meant he didn't get anything at all. But Billy was dead too, and if people thought Paul had killed Angela over him, he wasn't going to be round to tell them any different. Josh thought he might get Little Elmley after all. And so . . ." She shrugged. "He didn't correct Chief Inspector Lloyd's impression."

Lloyd would be annoyed if he had inadvertently put the idea into Josh Esterbrook's head, Judy thought. But it was a long way from there to the decoy story, to the disappearing photograph. She might not be able to sense when Sandie Esterbrook was lying, but she could find holes in stories if they were there to be found. "And who gave you the idea of saying you were just a decoy?" she asked.

"Elizabeth, mainly."

Judy frowned. "Elizabeth?"

"Oh, not on purpose. But Josh rang me from Penhallin, said Billy was dead and that the police thought that Paul had been involved with him. That we could still salvage something, maybe, but I'd have to think of a good reason why I was at the cottage, if we were going to try it. I had several hours to think of a good reason before they got back to Little Elmley. And eventually I remembered Josh telling me that Elizabeth had asked him if I was just a red herring, if Paul was really seeing someone else and just wanted her to believe it was me. I realized that it could have looked like that. So that's what I said." She stubbed out her second cigarette. "And I had to say Billy was there, obviously. But I knew that Henderson's photographs wouldn't show any sign of him, so I said he refused to leave, so as to account for that."

"And how do you account for Billy being killed there?"

"I can't."

All right. Judy decided to leave that topic and move on to the phone call. She started the tape again, and they watched Paul Esterbrook punch out a number on Sandie's mobile phone. She frowned. The call on Saturday had been made from the bedroom phone, according to Lloyd. But there wasn't a phone in the bedroom—that was why Paul was using Sandie's mobile. She made a note of that, then paused the tape.

"Do you remember that call Paul Esterbrook is making?" she asked.

"Yes. It was to his mother. Chief Inspector Lloyd asked about that—I was a bit evasive. I'm sorry. He was leaving a message on her machine to say that he'd found her letter."

Judy glanced at the screen, allowed the action to continue for just long enough, then switched the tape off. "And can you tell me *why* you're doing what you're doing in that video?" she asked.

Sandie smiled suddenly, widely. "Self-preservation," she said. "He was in a foul mood because his mother had interrupted his long weekend, and I can assure you that six hours in a car with Paul Esterbrook in a foul mood is no fun at all. I was hoping I could get him into a better one before we left. But he just blamed me for keeping him late, so it probably made matters worse in the long run." She smiled again. "And Penhallin to Stansfield is a *very* long run," she said.

"Can you remember what he said to his mother?" asked Judy.

"He just said that he'd found the letter and was on his way back, or something like that."

"He didn't swear at her?"

"No!" Sandie grinned again. "Paul wouldn't swear at his mother," she said. "He had to keep on her good side. Everyone had to. She had a wicked temper. Like Paul. He used his fists, but she was vindictive."

As her visit to her bigamous husband's legitimate wife proved, thought Judy. Sandie seemed to be telling the truth, but she couldn't be sure. She tried hard to get in touch with the instinctive feel that she almost always had when she was interviewing, but she couldn't. "Did he swear at *you*?" she asked.

Sandie thought, shaking her head. "I don't think so," she said. "Well—what I mean is that he swore like a trooper all the time if things weren't going his way. He might have sworn while he was talking to me, but I don't know if you'd call that swearing *at* me, exactly. He wasn't calling me names, or anything. Not like when he did this." She gestured to her face, at the now fading bruises. "He was a bit cross because I'd done it when he was on the phone," she said. "He probably did swear. I stopped noticing it. You do, after a while."

Judy tried to catch her with a sudden change of subject. "And what about the still from the other video?" she asked. "The one that should have been with the Cope Detective Agency's report?" She deliberately spoke as though Sandie knew all about that report, in the hope of trapping her in an error, but once again her technique failed her, because there was no puzzled look, no claim not to know what she was talking about, no unprepared lie that she could latch on to. Just the opposite.

"Oh, that," said Sandie. "I destroyed it."

"*You* destroyed it?" Judy sighed, as she realized. "Of course," she said. "You opened the mail." She frowned. "And what did you do with the report?"

"Gave it to Angela. Why not? It didn't matter to me. And if she'd been expecting a report that didn't come, she would soon get a copy of it. I told her I'd destroyed the photograph."

"Why?"

"I didn't think she would like it."

"And what did she do when she read the report?"

"At first she wasn't going to do anything, but then she realized that it had happened after we'd got married, and made Josh promise to love, honour, and cherish me and give up people like Billy. Said she was putting the report in her not-for-publication drawer, but if he did anything to shame the name Esterbrook again, she would include it in her autobiography, to show what lengths she had to go to in order to keep her family together." She smiled, shaking her head. "She was a bitch of the first water," she added.

Judy didn't know when this girl was lying, but the fact was that she *had* lied, and the truth had only come out when she was faced with evidence that she couldn't explain away. "Paul Esterbrook was set up," she said. "Someone left faked evidence to suggest that he was having a homosexual affair with Billy Rampton, and planted the tape of Paul's message to his mother to make it look as though it had been left the day she died. You and Josh compounded that lie, and I see no reason to believe that you didn't perpetrate it."

Sandie Esterbrook was shaking her head vehemently all the time she was speaking. "You don't think *we* murdered them," she said. "You can't."

"I don't know, Sandie. I only know that you have lied and lied and lied throughout this investigation."

"Look, I know we shouldn't have misled you, but all we were doing was trying to stop Josh being cheated out of Little Elmley! And I *haven't* lied and lied and lied," she said. "One lie, that's all, really. I told you I was a decoy. One lie. We didn't kill anyone! Why would we? You can't blackmail a dead man!"

SCENE XXXIV—BARTONSHIRE
Thursday, October 2nd, 3:50 P.M.
Lloyd's office

Judy had ordered tea for Sandie, and gone to Lloyd's office to find Lloyd and Tom already there, Lloyd looking smugger than ever, Tom looking perplexed.

"Well?" Lloyd said. "Didn't I tell you it was that way round all along? Didn't I say that Billy thought he was meeting Josh, and Paul thought he was spending the weekend with Sandie? Didn't I?"

Judy agreed that he had indeed said that, and they compared notes; Josh Esterbrook hadn't said much, but he hadn't denied any of it. And Sandie's more enlightening interview meant that Lloyd's remaining little puzzle, not voiced until now, was answered, because the keepsake drawer *wasn't* a keepsake drawer, but the not-for-publication drawer of which Elizabeth had spoken, and had contained Paul Sr.'s love letters, Angela Esterbrook's unfinished first novel, and the Copes' report that she had kept in order to keep Josh in line.

"But Sandie pointed out to me that you can't blackmail a dead man," said Judy, "and I can't help but agree with her that it would have been a fairly foolish move. Not only couldn't they blackmail him, but Josh's chances of getting Little Elmley were reduced by fifty percent. Paul would certainly have capitulated to the blackmail."

"But the blackmail plot hadn't worked, remember."

Judy had forgotten that. She picked up her notebook and started leafing through it. There were a lot of question marks. "But why would they kill Billy?" she asked. "And would you hire detectives to watch you if you were going to murder someone?"

Lloyd sighed. "Maybe," he said. "If I were an Esterbrook. What do you think, Tom?"

Tom didn't speak, lost in his own thoughts.

"Tom?" Lloyd looked at Judy and shrugged. "I couldn't shut him up five minutes ago," he said. "It's like having a parrot. Talks nineteen to the dozen when you're on your own with him, and won't say a word when the visitors come."

"Guv," Tom said slowly, quite unaware that he had been the topic of conversation, "you know you said that the tape we found on Saturday night was planted, and that's why it wouldn't play?"

"Yes," said Lloyd.

"And that the last time that happened was the day Paul Esterbrook actually made that call, the Sunday of the Bank Holiday?"

"Yes," said Lloyd.

"Well—someone must have switched the tape then too, mustn't they? As soon as they heard it. Otherwise Mrs. Esterbrook would have played it when she got home, and that would have been that. It would have got recorded over when the next call came in."

"Yes," said Lloyd.

"Well—that wasn't Josh Esterbrook, was it, guv? He was in Plymouth at half-six in the morning, and that call was made at half past nine. Even if he left right after Kathy Cope saw him, he'd only be halfway home by then. And Sandie was with Paul Esterbrook the whole time, so it wasn't her either."

Judy and Lloyd looked at one another.

"But that only leaves Elizabeth Esterbrook," said Judy. "And that doesn't make sense."

"It's her prints we found on the tape," said Tom.

"Her prints were bound to be on it," Judy argued. "She put the tape in for Angela in the first place."

"Yeah, but we didn't find anyone else's, did we?"

Lloyd snapped his fingers. "How did I miss that?" he said, his eyes widening.

Judy frowned. "Miss what?"

"We *should* have found someone else's—we should have found Josh Esterbrook's. Elizabeth Esterbrook said that when she got there on the Sunday morning, she found a message flashing, but she couldn't make it play. That Josh got the phone working again that afternoon by taking the tape out and rewinding it manually. So we *should* have found his prints on that tape, but we didn't, because it *wasn't* the tape that he had rewound. Elizabeth Esterbrook had already switched them."

Tom frowned a little.

"She heard that message from her husband to his mother," said Lloyd. "And realized what was going on while he was making it, thought she might be able to use it in some way to prove his adultery. She took the cassette out and put another one in—that's why the machine wasn't working when Angela came home, and why Josh had to fix it. And Josh's fingerprints aren't on the one with Paul's message on it, because he never touched that tape at all." Lloyd tipped his chair back as he warmed to his theme. "Then she worked out that she could do even more with the tape than just use it as evidence of her husband's adultery. She could use it in conjunction with that letter of Angela's to make it look as though her husband had murdered his mother."

Tom looked a touch baffled.

"Oh, I don't believe I missed that!" Lloyd said, letting his chair fall forward. "I was so convinced that Josh Esterbrook was at the bottom of this that I ignored anything that didn't fit my theory. I didn't even check her alibi! Anyone could have got that ticket for her—she wasn't anywhere near London on Saturday. She was too busy murdering people."

Tom shook his head. "I don't get it, guv," he said. "Why would she frame Paul for the murder of his mother? She loses everything that way."

"No," said Lloyd. "Don't you see? She didn't frame Paul—she framed *Josh*." He sat back, his chair balanced on its hind legs once more. "She framed Josh by making it look as though *he* had framed Paul. Josh had no motive at all for murdering Angela and Paul— under the terms of his father's will, if either one of them died before his time was up, he would get nothing. So if Paul and his mother had merely both been murdered, we would have looked very hard at Elizabeth, who would get everything."

"But Josh *did* have a motive for framing Paul for the murder of his mother," said Tom thoughtfully. "Because that way he stood a chance of getting Little Elmley."

"Which Sandie Esterbrook says is very important to him," said Judy.

Lloyd nodded. "So she made it look as though Paul had murdered his mother and killed himself, but she used Josh's gun, and told us of its existence. She made it clear to us that Josh had had access to that tape. She used a letter that Josh had found in the first place, and she used Josh's relationship with Billy, by deliberately making it look on the face of it as though it was *Paul* who had been seeing Billy, when of course it wasn't, as she kept telling us. And all those clues pointing to Paul's guilt—it looked like a setup because it was *meant* to look like a setup, producing just enough doubt to make us dig a bit deeper. And we fell for it. Once we knew the letter was a fake, and the tape had been planted, and that it was *Josh* who was Billy's client, we homed in on Josh and Sandie, and overlooked Elizabeth entirely, even though she *was* going to get everything."

"She was taking a bit of a chance, wasn't she?" said Tom. "You had to fight to keep the case open. She was lucky the whole thing wasn't put to bed on Monday, with Paul as the guilty party."

Lloyd shook his head. "She didn't think she was taking any chance at all. She thought she would be able to produce, as she did, a private investigator's report that cleared Paul of murder, and as long as she could do that, she would collect. What she didn't know was that Paul had her private eye in his pocket, and that his report would be useless. That's the only reason it nearly failed." He smiled. "And you're the only reason it *has* failed," he said.

There were a number of things that irritated Judy about Lloyd, but that was one of the very many pluses. Unlike some senior officers, he gave credit where it was due, and didn't grudge it.

"Can we prove it, guv?" asked Tom.

"Tomorrow is another day," said Lloyd. "We might get the proof we need, if we can trace where that fax came from. In the meantime, someone had better tell Mr. and Mrs. Esterbrook that they're free to go."

Epilogue
The Ending

There's a divinity that shapes our ends,
Rough-hew them how we will.
                    Hamlet Act 5, Scene 2

SCENE I—BARTONSHIRE
The following day, Friday, October 3rd, 9:15 A.M.
Lloyd's office in Stansfield police station

The vital piece of evidence had slotted into place almost as soon as Tom had arrived at work. A fax had been sent from Penhallin public library to Angela Esterbrook's number at two-thirty P.M. on Saturday the twenty-seventh of September.

And at two-thirty last Saturday, Josh Esterbrook had been teaching people how to dive in Little Elmley, and Sandie Esterbrook had been sitting outside Angela Esterbrook's cottage in Paul Esterbrook's Range Rover, examining the damage he'd done to her face. Elizabeth Esterbrook was the only person who *could* have sent that fax.

Now he and DI Hill were presenting the evidence to Lloyd, who nodded and pushed his chair back, rocking gently, worrying Tom, as he always did. Judy opened her notebook, leafing through it as Lloyd spoke.

"She had everything she needed to set the whole thing up," he said. "The letter, and that message from Paul to his mother. All she had to do was contact Billy, then bide her time and wait for the opportunity to present itself. She found out when she rang Howard on the Friday night that Josh was taking that night dive and the boat wouldn't be available. She knew Paul would use the cottage, as he had obviously done before, the day he really left that message. Unfortunately—or fortunately, depending how you look at it—she was supposed to be going to London, so she got someone else to get her ticket for the concert and went to Penhallin instead, got hold of Billy in Plymouth on the way, and arranged for him to go to the cottage and wait for her there, in the treehouse, where he wouldn't be seen." He stopped rocking. "I wonder what Billy thought he was there for?" he asked.

"He was half out of his clothes, guv," said Tom. "And he had no objection to female clients. He probably just thought he was making a few quid with a lonely woman whose husband had been cheating on her for years. Knew she was getting her own back somehow, but didn't know quite what part she had in mind for him."

Lloyd nodded, and resumed rocking, continuing his account of Elizabeth Esterbrook's movements. "She went to Josh's boat, broke in and took the gun, then went to the library and sent a fax, ostensibly from Josh, telling Paul that he had to go back straightaway if he didn't want to be found out. Then she walked along the shore to the back of the cottage, let herself in while Paul was reading the fax, slipped upstairs and rang Angela Esterbrook's number so that it would look as though Paul had called. She stayed out of sight in the bathroom or wherever and waited until Paul and Sandie had left, then let Billy in, killed him, left the pad for us to find, and burned the letter."

Tom nodded. That was why Sandie hadn't noticed a smell of burning, he thought. Because nothing had been burned before she left the cottage.

"Then she drove back home, changed for dinner, went to Little Elmley, shot Angela, put the tape with her husband's message on it in the answering machine, and phoned the police. We arrived, listened to the message, took Paul Esterbrook in for questioning, and left. She knew the tape by itself wouldn't be enough for us to hang on to him, so all she had to do was wait in his Range Rover until he turned up to collect it, and shoot him too. We would jump to the conclusion that Paul had been seeing Billy, had murdered him and his mother when it looked as though he'd been found out, then killed himself when he couldn't face what he had done."

"Then she told me about Josh's gun, and that it was Josh who had been seeing Billy," said Tom. "And about how worried her mother-in-law had been about it. So we started looking for evidence of that."

"But she didn't know that her mother-in-law had been so worried about it that she'd set the Copes on to Josh, for which he should be truly grateful," said Lloyd. "The idiot played right into her hands by lying about that." He sighed. "And having made sure we knew about Josh and Billy, she then produced her private investigator's report, which she believed would be a truthful account of what her husband had really been doing that day. And she knew that whatever else he had been doing, he certainly hadn't been murdering his mother."

Tom couldn't believe it. He had been working like a dog all week, and all the evidence they needed had been right under their noses all along. "I can't believe we've had this whole thing arse about tip," he said.

Judy smiled. "Or, to put it another way, we were looking at things from the wrong angle?"

God. They'd be sending him to finishing school next. It was all right for them; Lloyd was fifty and bald and Welsh and indisputably male. She was good-looking and well-spoken, but she was female, so that was all right. He had blond curly hair and blue eyes and he really had sung in the choir at school, and despite having a wife and two children, he knew that he looked as though he still did. It was only his working-class background that gave him any obvious street-cred at all. That, and the fact that he could more than hold his own in a fight. And he could hold his own with his DI as well, so she could give over trying to polish him up.

"Yeah, right, guv," he said. "But we didn't even think about her, did we? And we knew she could handle a gun, and that she knew where she could get one—damn it all, she told *us* about it!. We knew she had been working on her mother-in-law's correspondence. We knew she'd had access to that message from her husband."

"It was because I was convinced it was Josh Esterbrook," said Lloyd.

"Well, her motive was a little obscure," said Judy.

Shares worth over half a billion quid was what Tom *called* a motive. And her plan had been worthy of one of the Esterbrooks themselves. Judy looked at him a little oddly when he said that, then went back to her notebook.

"I suppose anyone married to a devious and cunning Esterbrook for eighteen years is bound to pick up a wrinkle or two," said Lloyd, getting up. "I'd better let the Super in on this, now that we have some evidence at last."

Judy twisted round as he went. "Hang on a minute," she said, but he had already gone.

"Do you want me to catch him, guv?"

"No," she said, shaking her head. "I think I must be wrong."

But she kept looking through her notebook all the same, Tom noted.

SCENE II—BARTONSHIRE
Friday, October 3rd, 10:00 A.M.
The Superintendent's office

"Does this mean I can finally put the Copes to bed? Presumably they did just commit suicide."

Lloyd hadn't thought about that. "Er . . . no," he said. "No, I don't think so."

Case fell back in his chair, his hands over his face. He parted his fingers and looked at Lloyd. "Tell me if I go wrong," he said. "I'm just a simple copper. Kathy Cope walked in on Josh Esterbrook and Billy, and his stepmother told him that she knew what he'd been up to, made him promise to give all that sort of stuff up or she would tell the world about it in her autobiography. He had no reason to kill the Copes for that, Lloyd."

"He was trying to make us believe that it was his brother who had been with Billy," said Lloyd. "Kathy Cope could have given the lie to that."

"And why was he trying to do that?" said Case. "Because some clever-dick copper put the idea into his head! *After* the Copes were dead."

Oh, yes. That was true. "All the same," said Lloyd, not the most telling phrase he had ever come up with, but now he was not at all sure quite what was what. He was as certain as ever that the Copes had been murdered, but Paul hadn't killed them; he hadn't known anything about them, had no reason in the world to kill them. Neither, as Case had just pointed out, had Josh. And neither had Elizabeth Esterbrook, even if she had had the means, which she didn't. She couldn't hold her breath for minutes on end, not like Josh. She didn't have ready access to IMG's industrial gases, not like Paul. But he wasn't giving up on Kathy, not yet. "It's not close of play yet, sir," he said. "We've all day to go before the final over."

"Suit yourself," said Case with a sigh. "When did you ever not?"

SCENE III—BARTONSHIRE
Friday, October 3rd, 10:30 A.M.
Lloyd's office

Lloyd went back down to his office, a deep frown furrowing his brow. He still wouldn't accept that Kathy had killed herself, and yet there seemed no earthly reason for anyone else to have done it. He sat down and picked up the files, the witness statements, the results of the various tests, as though rereading them would make them resolve themselves into a solution that left no puzzles, no pieces of the jigsaw unaccounted for.

And that was when Judy knocked and came in. "Lloyd, have you got a minute?" she said.

Lloyd looked up, saw his gundog pointing, and smiled broadly. "All the time in the world," he said. "How can I help?"

"You can answer me something," she said. "Something I can't make sense of. I thought I must be wrong, because I don't see how he could have done it. Well, not that, but all the other stuff. Well, she could have helped him, but not on Saturday night. Still—I'm not wrong."

"I don't expect you are wrong," said Lloyd. "You rarely are when you become incoherent." This time, even Judy wasn't sure what she was pointing at, but she was pointing, and that was good enough for him. "What's the problem?" he asked.

"The Copes," said Judy, sitting down.

"They're my problem too. I don't see why they had to die."

"I think I do," said Judy. "But I have to go through it bit by bit before I can make sense of it."

Lloyd tipped his chair back. "Shoot," he said.

"If Angela Esterbrook employed them to catch *Josh*, why were they booked into the room directly above Paul Esterbrook's in the hotel?"

Lloyd thought about that. "Well," he said, "Josh knew he was going to hole the boat that weekend, and that he was going to suggest that Paul use the cottage. And he usually stayed on the boat, didn't he? Billy could have known that he and Josh would be using Paul's hotel room if Paul wasn't using it, and he would have happily told Angela Esterbrook that, once she waved enough money at him."

"But the rooms had to have been booked together, in advance, right?"

"Obviously. It was a holiday weekend."

"So how would Billy know the room number?"

Lloyd thought about that too. It was a simple enough question, but it didn't have a simple answer. There was no reason in the world for Billy to know the room number; no reason, even if he knew himself, for Josh to tell him until they were actually going to use it. Lloyd rocked back and forth, but it didn't help. "He wouldn't," he said.

"So who *would* know Paul Esterbrook's room number in advance?" asked Judy.

"Paul Esterbrook himself," said Lloyd. "But he couldn't have put the Copes on to Josh—for one thing, that report was sent to Mrs. Esterbrook at Little Elmley, and for another, he didn't know Josh was going to hole the boat and produce the situation in the first place."

"Agreed. So who would know the room number, *and* that Josh was going to hole the boat?"

Lloyd shook his head. "Certainly not Angela Esterbrook," he said.

"How about Alexandra Esterbrook?"

"Sandie?" said Lloyd.

"Sandie. Who freely told us that she opened the Cope Detective Agency's report when it arrived. But she didn't show it to Angela Esterbrook, because Angela had nothing to do with it—she never knew it existed."

"Sandie?" said Lloyd again. He couldn't see why she would.

"Sandie. Who else knew about Josh's plan for the boat? Who but Paul's personal assistant would book his hotel rooms for him? Sandie Esterbrook's the only person who *could* have employed Kathy Cope, who could have got her into the right hotel room *and* primed Billy to do what he did."

Lloyd frowned. "But why would Sandie want to connive with Billy to set Josh up?"

Judy smiled. "She didn't set Josh *up*, Lloyd—she was arranging his alibi. The Cope's report was going to prove that Josh couldn't have been switching the tapes at Little Elmley at half past nine that morning, because he was with Billy in Plymouth at half past six. But he wasn't with Billy. He was at Little Elmley." She tapped her notebook. "It was when Tom said the plan was worthy of an Esterbrook that I began to realize," she said. "It was worthy of an Esterbrook because it was an Esterbrook who devised it. And it's even more devious than you think."

Lloyd stopped rocking and frowned.

"You were right, Lloyd. All along. It was Josh Esterbrook who masterminded this whole thing. But he wasn't Billy's boyfriend—he wasn't with Billy at all. Not ever, and certainly not on the Sunday of

346 [· *Jill McGown* ·]

the Bank Holiday weekend. He *was* at Little Elmley. He could—and
did—switch the tapes."

Lloyd's frown grew deeper. "But that tape was used to make us
think Paul had rung his mother with that message the day she died,"
he said. "So whoever switched them had to send the fax to Paul,
and make that call from the cottage last Saturday. Sandie couldn't
have done it—she was outside the cottage, having a cigarette. Josh
couldn't have done it, because he wasn't there—he was giving diving
tuition at Little Elmley. So if Elizabeth Esterbrook didn't send the
fax and make the call, who did?"

"Billy," said Judy.

Lloyd's eyes widened.

"Billy was in Josh's pay all along. He knew he was helping to set up
Paul Esterbrook, I'm sure—perhaps even knew he was setting him up
for murder. What he didn't know was that he was going to be the
corpse." She smiled grimly. "Billy sent the fax. Then left his bike and
ran along the shoreline to the rear of Angela's cottage, and hid in the
treehouse for about thirty seconds."

"Then what?" said Lloyd.

"Then Paul Esterbrook let him in, like I said."

Lloyd stared at her. "You're saying that Paul was involved with *both*
Billy and Sandie?"

"Yes. But Paul told Elizabeth that it was *Josh* who was involved
with Billy, and she believed that, told us. Josh knew she would, once
Billy had been found murdered, and he used that to incriminate her.
Because once we found out about Paul and *Sandie*, we'd start believing it too, and as long as we believed that it was Josh who was with
Billy, that would mean that only Elizabeth Esterbrook had had the
opportunity to switch the tapes."

"Do we have any proof of this?"

"No, but we have evidence. Go back to the Sunday of the Bank
Holiday weekend, and just accept, for the moment, that it was Paul
who was with Billy."

"OK," said Lloyd.

"At half past six that morning, Billy was with Paul, in his hotel room," she said. "Who made certain Billy would be with him there, rather than on the boat, as usual?"

"Josh," said Lloyd. "By holing the boat, and making Paul's usual arrangements fall through."

"Who have we just worked out must have employed Kathy Cope to walk in on him?"

"Sandie," said Lloyd, nodding slowly.

"Who made certain Kathy could gain access to the hotel room, and that she saw something worth seeing?"

"Billy."

"Then later on, at half past nine, Paul was with Sandie, and he made that call to his mother's answering machine. Who told him about this letter his mother wanted?"

"Josh," said Lloyd, watching with a smile as she ticked off notes in her book.

"Who told him that he had to leave a message for his mother about that letter?"

"Josh."

"Who offered her mobile phone for him to make the call?"

"Sandie," said Lloyd obediently.

"And who was at Little Elmley, waiting for that call?"

"Josh?"

"Josh. Elizabeth didn't get there until fifteen minutes after that call was made, and she found the machine exactly as she says she did, with the message light flashing, but unable to be played. She didn't switch the tapes, Lloyd. *Josh* did."

Lloyd nodded slowly.

"And then Paul brings the letter back, but he doesn't take it to his mother, does he? Oh, no. Because Josh turns up and takes it from him, with some other cock-and-bull story. He told Tom that himself. And why? Not to help his brother out, as he said, but because Angela Esterbrook knew nothing about it, so Paul had to be waylaid before he gave it to her. There never was a phone call from Angela, there never was a letter from Angela's solicitors—that letter was planted there by Josh and Sandie. And Paul's message to his mother's answering machine was no accident—no one overheard it, devised a plan round it. This plan was devised round the original letter from Angela to Paul Senior about his bigamy, and the circumstances were produced to fit it, *including* the phone call, and Sandie's ministrations during it."

"You're saying Sandie did that on purpose?" said Lloyd. "To make Paul sound as though he were overwrought?"

"Yes."

"But she couldn't know he would say what he did!"

"They didn't need him to say what he did. They knew he'd be angry with her if she did that, and he would sound angry. That was all they wanted." She glanced up from her notebook. "And it worked. In fact," she said slowly. "I think it worked better than they meant it to."

Lloyd watched, fascinated by seeing the process in action for once, as she leafed through her notebook. Usually by the time he was presented with her logical deductions they had already been made, but this time she was arriving at them as she spoke.

"Because," Judy said, "we took Paul in for questioning, didn't we? And he told us that he had made that call from a mobile phone. But we weren't supposed to know that until after we had found out about Sandie being with Paul at the cottage. And *she* was supposed to tell us."

"Why?"

"Because that way they would be *telling* us that the tape was a fake, apparently in all innocence. And we had to know that the tape was planted before their plan could work. But in the event, we checked Billy's mobile, and when we didn't find anything, we just assumed Paul had been lying. And there was nothing they could do about it."

Lloyd frowned. "But we only found out about Paul and Sandie because Paul Esterbrook happened to open the curtains while Foster was videoing him," he said. "Josh Esterbrook didn't know anything about that, and even if he had, he couldn't have made Paul open the curtains when he did."

"No, Josh didn't know about that at all. That was a stroke of luck, as far as he was concerned."

"Then how were we supposed to get on to it?"

"Think about it, Lloyd. Why did they employ Henderson?"

"To blackmail Paul, according to them."

"Why do it that way? Why not have someone walk in on them, like Kathy Cope? That would be much stronger evidence."

It would. Lloyd nodded. "Then why *did* they employ Henderson?" he asked.

"I think," said Judy, "that if Paul Esterbrook hadn't beaten up Sandie, that would have been the first we knew about her having been at the cottage that day. We would have gone to the cottage, found Billy, and seen a prima facie case for saying that Paul had been there with Billy, had murdered him, then his mother, then killed himself. Sandie wouldn't have come into the reckoning at all. But then we would get Henderson's surveillance reports. Sandie made sure that we would—that's why she picked someone with a spotless reputation, and got him to check out Billy first. That way, they knew he'd give the police what he'd got as soon as he found out that it was Billy who had been murdered. And we would have found out that Sandie had been there with Paul on Saturday, that she had lied to us about her whereabouts that day. And we'd start believing what Elizabeth believed. That Josh was Billy's client. That Paul had been set up."

"They *wanted* us to suspect them?"

"Oh, yes. As it was, Paul did beat her up, and Elizabeth guessed that he had. So Sandie came up with this decoy story, which was never believable, because it wasn't meant to be. But they hadn't reckoned on Foster having an arrangement with Paul which made us think that she was lying about the whole thing, that she had never been at the cottage at all. So Henderson's evidence, instead of implicating her, *cleared* her of suspicion. Which wasn't what they wanted at all. They wanted us to start checking up on Sandie. They wanted us to find the call to Little Elmley on *her* mobile. Then she would tell us what she did tell us. That they had wanted to blackmail him, that holing the boat and getting him to go to the cottage had been a dummy run for that. And—most importantly—that he had left a message for his mother about a letter, and had been swearing, not at his mother, but because of what she was doing while he was trying to make a phone call, which was why he seemed to be under something of a strain. Open. Truthful. Nothing to hide. Why would they tell us all that if *they* had planted the tape?"

"So that when we realized," said Lloyd slowly, "thanks to the Copes, and Henderson, that apparently neither Josh nor Sandie could have switched the tapes, and we knew for a fact that neither of them could have made that call, or sent the fax, we would begin to think, as we did, that Elizabeth had overheard that message, and used it to incriminate not her husband, but Josh. That Josh and Sandie were innocent victims."

Judy nodded. "If we hadn't got there ourselves, you can be certain that one of them would have prompted us. And we would think that she had framed Josh in order to inherit the entire Esterbrook Trust. But it's the other way round, Lloyd. Josh framed her. And I might not be able to prove it, but we might have some evidence, of sorts."

Lloyd smiled. "What?" he asked.

"That call to Little Elmley on Saturday was made from the phone in the bedroom. I've seen Foster's video, and there *isn't* a phone in the bedroom—that's *why* Paul used Sandie's mobile. They took the phone out so that he would. So that she was ideally placed to do what she did."

As usual, it was inconclusive, thought Lloyd. "There might not have *been* a phone in the bedroom a month ago," he said. "Angela could have put one in since then."

"She could," said Judy. "But come and have a look."

SCENE IV—BARTONSHIRE
Friday, October 3rd, 11:30 A.M.
The IT Room at Stansfield police station

Lloyd went and had a look, and watched as Esterbrook sat on the bed, and looked in the bedside cabinet drawer. The bedside cabinet which did not have on it the radio-alarm-telephone that had subsequently been there. The camera began to draw back, and Judy paused the tape. "There," she said. "Look. That's a telephone socket on the wall, isn't it?"

Lloyd nodded. "But it's still inconclusive," he said as Tom came into the room. "She might have had the socket put in *because* she was getting a phone for the bedroom."

"I didn't think you'd want to watch mucky videos, guvs," Tom said as he called up a file on the computer.

"But it's possible that the phone *was* there before," said Judy, "and I'd really like to know if it was. I wish there was one person we could trust to tell us the truth."

"There is," said Tom. "Ian R. Foster, Enquiry Agent. He gave himself a crash course on making videos by doing shots of all the places he might have reason to video Paul Esterbrook. He says he's still got them."

Judy turned to look at him. "Tom," she said, heading for the door with Lloyd in pursuit, "I could kiss you. I want you to get on to Penhallin police—ask if they've found Billy's motorbike yet. If they haven't, tell them to try Penhallin public library."

Of course, thought Lloyd. He had to leave his bike somewhere other than the cottage, so that Henderson's men didn't see it. For Josh Esterbrook's great plan to work, it had to look as though Billy had never had anything to do with Paul Esterbrook. The police had to believe, along with Elizabeth, that Josh was the one having the relationship with Billy.

"That's why the Copes had to die," said Judy as they walked to the car. "Because they would have told us that it *wasn't* Josh who was with Billy that morning, and his alibi would have been blown. But Sandie Esterbrook murdered Billy, and Josh Esterbrook murdered his stepmother and Paul, I know they did. I don't have the faintest idea *how* Josh Esterbrook murdered his stepmother, which is why I thought I must be wrong. But he did. Somehow."

"Oh, I know how Josh did it," said Lloyd. "It's another thing we can't prove, but I know how, all the same." He deliberately didn't tell her; he liked irritating Judy.

SCENE V—BARTONSHIRE
Friday, October 3rd, 12:10 P.M.
Ian Foster's house

The office was closed; a TO LET sign was stuck up in the window. The girl in the bookie's said that Foster had told her he was packing in private investigation. But they ran Ian R. Foster to earth at his house.

"Hello, Lloyd," he said.

Ian Foster was someone else that Lloyd hadn't seen for twenty years. Though some years younger than Lloyd, Foster had been the experienced officer to whom he had been attached in his probationer days, and the first bent police officer he had known. Fortunately, he hadn't known many. Foster was surrounded by packing cases, and carried on filling the last of these as Lloyd and Judy followed him into the sitting room.

"Moving out?" Lloyd said.

"They didn't make you a DCI for nothing, did they?" said Foster with a grin. "I'm moving to a better part of town, since you ask."

Crime didn't pay? That was a laugh. "My sergeant tells me that you took a video of Angela Esterbrook's cottage in Penhallin before the one that made you rich," Lloyd said. "We want to see it."

Foster waved a hand at the packing cases. "No can do," he said. "It'll be at the bottom of one of these."

"Find it."

"I can't. I'll look it out as soon as I get to—"

Lloyd stepped towards him. "Find it," he said. "Or I'm sure I can think of something to charge you with, even if Sergeant Finch was unable to come up with anything."

Foster started attacking one of the packing cases, and ten minutes later Lloyd and Judy were looking at a video of Angela Esterbrook's bedroom, sans Paul and Sandie, but plus a radio-alarm-telephone. A tiny bit of evidence, but it all counted.

They were letting themselves out when Debbie Miller came up the path. "Lloyd!" she said. "It's been ages since I've seen you."

Lloyd smiled. "How are you, Debbie?" he asked.

"Not too bad at all," she said.

Lloyd had known that Debbie worked for Foster, and knew that she and Joe had split up a few months ago, but he hadn't thought that she would be silly enough to hitch her wagon to Foster's tarnished star. "Are you and Ian . . . ?" he said, with a nod of his head back into the sitting room, where Foster was packing everything away again.

"No, nothing like that," she said with a laugh. "I'm just helping him move, that's all."

Good. Foster might be a bit of a villain, but he wasn't at all an unpleasant man; in fact, Lloyd had always rather liked him. He had always been generous with his time and his advice and, whenever he had any, even his money, so Debbie could have fallen for him. But, like Debbie's husband, he was a gambler, and unlike Debbie's husband, he had become dishonest in order to feed his habit; Lloyd was glad that Debbie had resisted his charms.

"I'm glad I've run into you," she said. "When you get back to Stansfield, you can tell Joe I don't appreciate him swanning off to Plymouth with an old flame as soon as my back's turned."

Lloyd smiled. "I won't be seeing him," he said. "He's back at HQ now."

"He's in Barton again?"

"Yes. And if I know Joe, he'll be pining for you, whatever he's been—" He stared at her. "Where did you say he'd swanned off to?"

"Plymouth. Ian saw him there with Kathy White, of all people. Do you remember her? What's she like? She's only a name to me. He used to be engaged to her."

Lloyd didn't have time to explain that she had no reason now to worry about Kathy White; he and Judy were out of Foster's house and on their way to Barton HQ before Debbie had had time to close the door.

SCENE VI—BARTONSHIRE
Friday, October 3rd, 1:00 P.M.
Bartonshire Constabulary headquarters in Barton

Joe was startled to see them, and a little reticent about his dalliance in Plymouth with Kathy Cope. In fact, he wasn't at all sure what they were talking about, wasn't even that certain that he had ever been in Plymouth, with or without Kathy Cope.

"Joe," said Judy, with her nanny voice on. "There are lots of interview rooms here—we can do this officially, if you'd rather."

"Whoa, whoa, hold your horses," said Joe. "All right, I was in Plymouth with Kathy. So what?"

"You were helping her out on a job she'd got from a Mrs. Esterbrook," said Judy.

Joe smiled. "Look," he said. "I wasn't moonlighting, if that's what you think. I wasn't getting paid for it or anything."

"That makes no difference, and you know it."

"No, look—it's not the way it seems."

They listened as Joe explained his involvement with Kathy, his intention to take early retirement and join the Copes in their business venture, Kathy's plan to make Andy more open to this suggestion, and the utter failure of that plan. She had bought office equipment, and surveillance equipment, and Joe had footed the bill.

"So I'm still in hock to the bank, and I haven't had the heart to get any of the stuff back," he said. "I went to see her daughter, but I couldn't make myself mention it."

"So where is this surveillance equipment?" said Lloyd.

"Up in her loft," said Joe. "She couldn't let Andy see it, because he'd know she hadn't got that sort of stuff without advice, and he'd know where the advice had come from. She wanted to choose her moment before she told him about me. But she chose the wrong one anyway."

"Her instructions from Mrs. Esterbrook were that she was to surprise the occupants of Room 312 of the Excalibur," said Judy. "Did you see them?"

"No," said Joe. "I never clapped eyes on them, except on the video."

Lloyd shook his head. What Joe Miller might or might not have seen on a video wasn't evidence. And the video had been no good; he would have thrown it away. That one usable frame might have made all the difference.

"That whole thing was very iffy," Joe went on. "I told her that I thought the bloke was being set up, but you know Kathy, Lloyd—it wasn't her problem what this Mrs. Esterbrook was going to do with the evidence, all that."

That sounded like Kathy, Lloyd thought.

"She wanted me to grab some frames from the video for her to send to her client, so I knew I'd get my hands on it before she did, and I never had much intention of letting her have it back. I did a bit of asking round, to see if Esterbrook was worth blackmailing, and found out he was loaded. I wasn't letting Kathy walk into that kind of setup. So I rang her and said the video was useless. Grabbed a frame where the bloke was masked by the kid, and sent her that. No one could use it to blackmail anyone."

The video *wasn't* useless? Lloyd crossed his fingers as Judy asked her next question, and luck, possibly for the first time in this whole investigation, was on their side. The answer was yes. He still had it. He'd kept it in case Kathy cottoned on to what he'd done, and demanded its return. He'd never thrown it away. In fact . . . he reached into a drawer.

"This is it," he said.

Lloyd looked at it, and then at Joe. For a long time. "You weren't thinking of—" He hesitated to use the actual word. "—making use of it yourself, were you?" he asked. "If times got very hard?"

"No!" said Joe, eyes innocently wide. "As if."

"As if," said Lloyd. Oh, well. It really was useless now, from the blackmailing point of view, and Joe would probably have found that stuck in his throat just as much as asking Kathy's daughter for the equipment had. He would give him the benefit of the doubt.

Especially as five minutes later they were watching as the camera moved unsteadily out of a lift, along a corridor, and the door of Room 312 was pushed open, to reveal Billy, exactly as Kathy had described him, turning quickly towards the doorway, and a shocked and angry Paul Esterbrook getting to his feet as the air turned blue with mouthed, silent expletives. The camera backed out, the door closed, and Joe switched off the tape.

"Any good?" he said.

Lloyd nodded, and looked at Judy. Good enough for them to feel that they could overlook Joe's foray into private investigation, and his possible thoughts on blackmail. And he could safely leave Judy to put the fear of God into Joe about both of these things, he thought. She was going to be his boss, after all; she would want to have the reins firmly in her own hands. But that would have to wait, because meanwhile they had work to do.

Once again Debbie almost collided with them in the doorway, still trying to attach her visitor's pass to her blouse. "You've not arrested him, then?" she said, throwing a less than loving look at her husband.

"No," said Joe, smiling. "They've not arrested me."

Debbie gave up, and stuffed her visitor's pass in her skirt pocket. "You just get into trouble when I'm not round," she said. "And the kids miss you. I'll come back if you want me to, but on my terms."

"Good," said Joe, not one whit bothered about the public nature of this brisk, cross, perfunctory reconciliation. "But you might not want to come back. I've got myself in hock for about four thousand quid."

"What sort of bet was that, for God's sake?"

"A losing one."

"Well," she said, "Ian was a bit luckier, it seems, and he's given me a golden handshake. I'm prepared to pay off your debt if you're prepared to have your salary paid into my account."

Joe looked astonished. "How much did he give you, for God's sake?" he asked.

"Ten percent."

"Ten percent of what?"

"Never you mind. Is it a deal?"

"Yes," said Joe, still a little bewildered. "It's a deal."

Lloyd smiled. "Well," he said, "touching though this romantic reunion is, I'm afraid we have to go now."

They had almost made it to the lift when Joe caught them up. "Lloyd?" he said, his voice low so that his wife wouldn't hear what he had to say. "I—I feel bad about Kathy. I don't want the office equipment back now, and it's worth a bob or two. Her daughter could sell it—help defray the funeral expenses and all that. And the surveillance stuff's up in the loft, like I said. She can get a good price for it."

"Why *is* it in the loft?" said Judy.

"Well, it's difficult to hide a security video recorder and monitor anywhere else. Kathy had a couple of covert security cameras up in the house."

"Why?"

"Oh, at first it was just to see if they worked, and to see whether Andy spotted them." he said. "He never did. They're practically invisible. But until she had a professional use for them, she kept a tape running in case she got burgled or something. Said she'd feel a bit of an idiot if anything happened and they weren't operational."

"So where *are* these cameras, if they're practically invisible?" asked Lloyd. "It would help Kathy's daughter if she knew."

"One's in her office, and the other's in the kitchen clock."

Lloyd blinked at him. "The kitchen clock?"

"Yeah. You can put them anywhere—they're tiny little—" He shook his head when he realized why Lloyd had asked. "Oh, no, sorry—it won't have anything on it that'll help you about the so-called suicide. The tapes run themselves back and start again if no one changes them. Anything the camera picked up last Friday night will have been recorded over half a dozen times."

Par for the course, thought Lloyd as they got into the lift. The rub of the green had not been with them in this enquiry.

SCENE VII—BARTONSHIRE
Friday, October 3rd, 2:00 P.M.
The Superintendent's office, Stansfield police station

Back in Stansfield, Tom told them that Billy's motorbike had indeed been found in the tiny car park of the Penhallin library; naturally enough, the local police had not seen any need to inform Stansfield of that. They had been a little surprised that Billy knew where the library was, that was all.

The Esterbrook mind was even more cunning and even more devious than Lloyd could possibly have imagined, as he told Case before launching into the story that Judy had finally pieced together. Case listened, nodding now and then, but frowning throughout. He was still frowning when Lloyd had finished.

"Let me see if I've got this straight," he said. "Josh Esterbrook wanted to do away with his half brother and his stepmother, right?"

"Almost right," said Lloyd. "He wanted to do away with his stepmother and his half brother. In that order. That was very important."

"And he wanted us to believe that his sister-in-law had done it."

Lloyd nodded.

"So first, he made it look as though Paul had murdered Billy and his mother and then committed suicide, but in such a way as to make it seem a bit too convenient. A letter burned beyond resurrection just happens to have been imprinted on a pad, Mrs. Esterbrook just happens to have a report from a private detective about Billy's activities in Paul's hotel room, an incriminating message is found on Mrs. Esterbrook's answering machine, and so on." He ducked his head by way of apology. "Too many clues, like you said. Why did he do that?"

"Because," said Lloyd patiently, "that was the only way that we would think of suspecting *him*. Framing Paul for his mother's murder was the only way that gave him a financial motive."

"And why did he want us to suspect him?"

"Because that way, we would start listening seriously to Elizabeth when she kept insisting that it was *Josh* who was having a relationship with Billy. The visual evidence that should have been with the Copes' report was missing, and once we found out about Sandie and Paul, and that the letter and tape were fakes, we would think that *Josh* was the man with Billy that morning, and had destroyed the video-still to stop us finding out."

"Whereas he destroyed it to stop us finding out that it was *Paul* who was with Billy." Case scratched his head. "Why did they ask for visual evidence in the first place, then? Why not just a written report?"

"He couldn't trust to luck," said Lloyd. "He killed the Copes to make certain they couldn't tell us who was really with Billy, but he killed them *when* he did so that there was no chance that we would overlook the connection. They died the night before the murders at Little Elmley, and their copy of the report to Mrs. Esterbrook had been removed from their files, so naturally we would be looking for that report once she was found murdered. When we located it, we would discover that the photographic evidence had gone, and once everything else started falling into place, we would be certain that it was Josh who had been with Billy. And he wouldn't deny that, but he would deny trying to frame Paul for murder. We wouldn't believe him until we realized that he had an alibi."

"Because that frame-up relied on someone switching tapes at Little Elmley at a time that Josh Esterbrook couldn't have done it, if he *had* been with Billy," said Case. "Right. I've got that too. So then, finally, we start suspecting Elizabeth Esterbrook of having set *Josh* up."

Lloyd nodded. "He knew she was going to be away all last Saturday, with no one to corroborate her story about where she had been. He knew she would tell us about the gun, that she would tell us that it was he, Josh, who was Billy's client. He knew she could shoot, knew that she had had access to Angela's letters, and apparent access to the tape with Paul's message on it. He arranged things so that once we had his alibi, it would look as though she had set *him* up by making it look as though he had set *Paul* up for murder," he said. "A sort of treble bluff."

Case lit a cigarette. "So instead of just murdering them and framing her for it, he went all round the houses. Why?"

"Because he knew that a frame-up can always be detected. It might *not* be, of course—police officers have a habit of going for the obvious—"

"Yes, yes, all right," said Case.

"—but not always. And once you suspect a setup, it's usually very easy to prove, so Josh Esterbrook would never have risked doing that. But having once found a setup, and proved it, then discovered that my prime suspect couldn't have done it, but the major beneficiary of an enormous fortune could have set *him* up, even I didn't go looking for a third setup. You need Judy Hill for that. Fortunately, for the moment, we've got her."

"So nothing we've been looking at in this case has been real?"

"Nothing. Everything was manufactured by Josh and Sandie Esterbrook. Angela Esterbrook didn't employ the Copes any more than she employed Henderson, Elizabeth Esterbrook never even *saw* the tape with Paul's message on it once the message had been received, and Paul's message to Angela was about a solicitors' letter that existed only because Josh Esterbrook brought it into being—Angela never asked Paul to bring her any letter. The *real* letter—the one they traced onto a pad and then burned, the one from Angela to Paul Senior—was what made Josh dream up this whole fantastic plot, and he's the only person still alive who has ever clapped eyes on it. It took him three years to plan it, and it very nearly worked."

"So what went wrong?"

"Oh, lots of things went wrong," said Lloyd. "But they rode them—unlike Paul, they can both think on their feet. What really did for them was that Kathy Cope had a minor fling with an old flame." He smiled a little sadly. "She was looking for an escape route, just like she always did."

"But why did he do it?" said Case. "For a fifty-fifty chance of getting Little Elmley? A white elephant? He killed five people for the possibility of getting something a few years earlier than he was going to get it anyway? He couldn't get anything else—his father's will doesn't allow for him getting anything else. Not if his stepmother and his half brother are both dead."

Lloyd smiled. "That's why the order in which he killed them mattered. His *father's* will doesn't allow for him getting anything else. But if this had worked, it wouldn't have been his father's will that counted anymore. It would have been *Paul's* will. Because Angela Esterbrook predeceased Paul, the entire Esterbrook Family Trust forms part of the Paul Esterbrook estate, and the bulk of that goes to his wife."

"And if she had been guilty of his murder, she wouldn't inherit," said Case.

"Quite. The estate, everything that came to Paul under his father's will and which *would* have gone to Elizabeth—the whole half-billion pound package—would then have gone to his next of kin."

"Josh Esterbrook," said Case, his brow clearing at last.

SCENE VIII—BARTONSHIRE
Friday, October 3rd, 3:00 P.M.
Interview Room One

Sandie was listening to the caution for the third time, smiling a little. She had said it was dangerous. She had said it was crazy. But then, as Josh had pointed out, she liked dangerous and crazy.

That night at Little Elmley, after her exhaustive and exhausting weekend diving course, he had asked her two questions. One, if she would be prepared to kill Billy Rampton if it helped him get what was due to him: the entire Esterbrook fortune. He was entitled to it, and he needed help to get it. *Her* help. And two, if she would marry him.

She had said yes. Of course she had. She had been sent to help him, and killing Billy Rampton was a positive lure. And she had needed no incentive to marry Josh.

"Tell me about the setup with you and Paul Esterbrook," said Inspector Hill. "The truth, this time, if that's possible."

Oh, the truth was possible. "Paul liked variety," Sandie said. "Sometimes he wanted Billy, sometimes me, sometimes both of us. Sometimes he just wanted to watch Billy and me." She smiled at the inspector. "It was my job," she said. "I found Billy loathsome and I didn't like Paul, but it's what I was paid to do, and I did it. I didn't mind what he wanted me to do, which is why he poached me away from Brendan, gave me that job. It was much safer than using different girls."

Then he had used her to humiliate his wife, slapped her for coming on to Josh. That had been a very big mistake. But a much bigger one had been introducing her to Josh in the first place, because she and Josh together were unstoppable.

"Billy wasn't at the cottage on the Bank Holiday weekend, was he?"

"No," said Sandie. "Paul sent him home after they had been interrupted. But I had to say he was there when Chief Inspector Lloyd asked me, because Josh doesn't know that my contract with Paul was sexual—he really believes I was just a decoy. Is he going to have to find out?" she asked anxiously. Inspector Hill knew, of course, that she was lying, but that didn't matter.

"Don't waste your talent, Sandie," she said. "Save it for the jury."

Sandie smiled, and stopped wasting her talent. Her answer was on the tape; that was what mattered. The real reason for that lie was Josh's slip in saying he had rung the cottage; Josh had known she was there alone with Paul, and she had worked out that if they did get rumbled, as they had been, it would have been obvious that Josh knew exactly what was what between her and Paul *unless* she said that Billy was there. And what Josh did or didn't know was going to be very important, as the inspector would find out.

Inspector Hill turned a page in her notebook. "But Saturday really was a threesome?"

Paul had thought it was going to be, thought Sandie. He had wanted to make up for his month with Elizabeth in style. "Yes," she said. "He told Billy to wait for us at the cottage."

And Josh had told him to watch for Paul's car, send the fax and then run to the cottage, and hide in the treehouse. That way Henderson's men wouldn't see him, and the police would think that Paul had never had anything to do with Billy.

It had very nearly worked. Paul had made things a little tricky, taking away her cigarettes and lighter like that; he had always been going to end up with her lighter, but he had actually taken it from her, and that had pinpointed it as hers, with Henderson's men photographing everything. The police were never meant to know that it was hers; it was just a throwaway lighter—it could have been anyone's. Josh had removed the big box of matches that Angela kept at the cottage; the lighter in Paul's pocket, something he would not normally have carried, was going to be a clue to the fact that he had been set up, but that hadn't worked quite as planned.

"Are you going to come up with another perfectly rational explanation for all the lies you've told? Have you thought of some excellent reason for pretending it was Josh who was in the hotel room with Billy that morning, other than that it gave him an alibi for when the tapes were switched?"

"I never said it was Josh who was in the hotel room with Billy," said Sandie.

The inspector looked a little nonplussed as she flicked back a page or two, but she moved on. "And have you got a really clever story to explain away hiring Arthur Henderson's agency to watch the cottage, other than to mislead us, and give you an alibi for when the call to Little Elmley was made?"

"We were going to blackmail Paul," said Sandie. "I told you. But it didn't work, because Henderson's men never even saw Billy, and I was never in the cottage with Paul."

The inspector smiled. "And perhaps you're going to convince me that shooting Billy Rampton between the eyes was some form of self-defence?"

Oh, no, thought Sandie. It hadn't been self-defence. She smiled again. Billy had laughed, when he'd seen her, with her black eye and her swollen jaw and her split lip. Laughed, as he pulled on his clothes, said it couldn't have happened to a nicer person. Shooting Billy between the eyes hadn't been self-defence; it had been sheer, naked aggression. It had been exquisitely enjoyable. And she *had* felt like God.

Then she had closed the bedroom door, gone downstairs, emptied the already burned and crushed letter into the wastebin, left the pad, packed the gun in her weekend bag, and left the cottage, closing the door, automatically locking it. When Paul had come back, she had told him that she had been unable to find her cigarettes and lighter. He had sworn at her, gone back in, found them, after a few minutes' searching, where she had left them for him to find, and had come back out again. And Arthur Henderson's operatives had taken photographs of it all. If the worse came to the worst, which it had, there would be reasonable doubt as to who had done what to Billy.

"No rejoinder?" said Inspector Hill. "So what *are* you going to say about that, Sandie?"

"Nothing," she said. "I'm not going to say anything. I'm going to let you prove I murdered Billy Rampton." She smiled again. "If you can."

SCENE IX—BARTONSHIRE
Friday, October 3rd, 4:00 P.M.
Interview Room Two

Josh sat back and watched as Lloyd did what he now recognized as his thing. He would wander round the room, standing on tiptoe to look out of the window, reading anything he could lay his hands on, sometimes not apparently taking any notice at all of what was being said, while Sergeant Finch fired questions at Josh that he wasn't answering, so it was all a bit of a waste of time.

Three years ago he had found those letters from Angela. The one in which she told his father about her visit to Little Elmley had been the last one; it had made him want to avenge his mother's death, stop these people getting their hands on his father's money. The one that had set him thinking about how that might be achieved had been the first.

He had seen how it could be adapted to read as though it had been written to his half brother rather than his father. Of course the original wouldn't fool anyone, not even Paul; it was quite evidently thirty years old. But a tracing of it—a tracing of it on to a pad . . . that might work. And if the police found the ashes of a letter, and impressions on a pad, they might check out those impressions. With a little judicious pruning here and there, it could look as though Angela was threatening him with exposure, and that Paul had murdered his mother, and then committed suicide. Easy enough to get the police to check the pad out if they were too stupid or too lazy or just too busy to think of it themselves.

But that was jettisoned because it wasn't good enough—at best, he would only get Little Elmley if Paul had murdered his mother. He wanted something that would get him everything, and the only thing that would do that would be if Angela was already dead, and Elizabeth murdered Paul. At first, that had seemed impossible.

A more complex plot had evolved when Billy had arrived on the scene, involving Billy's demise, but there were lots of reasons why it wouldn't work. Complex plots had a way of unravelling before the gaze of the police. They had a much harder time with murders that took place on the spur of the moment than they did with plots and plans. They would see through a setup; they would be suspicious of this handily imprinted letter. They had all sorts of equipment these days; they might test the ashes. If he burned anything other than the real letter, then any writing on it could be proved to be a forgery. If he burned the real letter, they might be able to analyze the remains, find out that it was written a long time ago. It was too risky.

And that was when his crazy idea had begun to evolve. Give them a setup to unravel, but make it look like Elizabeth's setup. Elizabeth couldn't frame her husband for the murder of his mother, because that way she would get nothing, but she could frame Josh for it, because that way she would get everything. But then, Josh had no motive for murder; his father had seen to that. So she would hardly do that. Unless . . .

Josh had gone back, then, to his very first thought. Little Elmley might not be enough motive for *him*, but it would be enough to make a frame-up by Elizabeth believable. The problem was that he needed help to carry it out, and where could you get that sort of help? Billy was easy. All you had to do was pay him, and Billy would do anything. But if Billy's own murder was part of it, that had to be carried out by a third person, and while three could keep a secret if two of them were dead, Josh couldn't risk killing two accomplices. Billy had to be dispatched by someone in whom Josh had infinite trust, and no such person existed. So the crazy idea remained just that.

Until Sandie. From the moment she had found his revolver, picked it up with that gleam in her eye, he had known she was the one who was going to help him. And she had done it right in front of Elizabeth, slotting into place the very first building block of his plan by letting Elizabeth see the gun. That was when he knew she had been sent; that was when the plan was completed. Not detailed, not worked out, not fine-tuned. He and Sandie had done that between them, and she had thought of all sorts of little touches.

The phone call was her idea; she had printed out the spurious solicitors' letter on the computer at work. And she had thought of how to make Paul's message sound truly anguished. He smiled as he thought of that. He had sat in Little Elmley and listened to Paul's agonized voice, his cursing and swearing, and he couldn't believe it when Paul actually mentioned his inheritance. Though that had turned out to be almost as much of a drawback as a blessing.

Then he had removed the tape with a pair of tweezers, popped it in a polythene bag, wound on a brand-new tape a few inches, and left it on the machine. When Elizabeth had arrived, its light would have been blinking, a message apparently recorded on the tape, but one that she would have been unable to play. That evening, he had rewound the tape, got Angela to record a message, got Sandie to test it, and that was that. He had the incriminating tape, complete with Elizabeth's fingerprints. The lack of his own—which he would have pointed out to the police, if he'd had to—would make it seem that *she* must have removed the tape.

For a while he and Sandie had thought that the Copes were blackmailing Paul, and would send them nothing. But their report had duly arrived, and Josh had nearly had kittens when he found out that Paul was still being blackmailed—especially when he said he was dealing with it. He had had visions of them *both* turning up to murder the Copes.

"All right, Mr. Esterbrook," Lloyd said, coming over and sitting on the edge of the table. "Since you don't want to talk to us, I'll talk to you. I'll tell you, shall I, how you carried out these murders? And you can stop me if I go wrong anywhere."

Josh sat back, relaxed and smiling.

"First of all, you murdered the Copes."

Correct. And, of course, if the Copes died the night before Angela did, the police would want to know what work they had done for her, and they would find the report in her not-for-publication drawer of the bureau, where Josh had left it after he shot her, minus the visual evidence. Elizabeth's conviction that it was Josh who was gay would do the rest.

Lloyd had worked out exactly how he'd murdered the Copes; he had even sent someone to IMG, looking for paperwork on a cylinder of carbon monoxide, and had found a chit, written by Sandie and signed by Paul, for just such an item, needed for demonstration purposes at some fictitious conference. Of course, that wouldn't do him any good, because he had no proof at all of the use to which it had been put, or whether the chit had been initiated by Sandie or Paul. But it had been good work, Josh had to give him that.

The plan had been that Sandie and Paul would go to Penhallin in separate cars; she would arrive at the cottage first, and Billy would watch for Paul's car entering Penhallin, then bomb off to the library on his bike, send the fax, then run along the shore to be in position for Paul to let him into the cottage; Sandie would detain Paul long enough to let him get there, in the way that Paul could always be detained. Then she would go out for a cigarette, Paul would go to the back door to let Billy in, and Billy would go straight upstairs before Paul saw the fax, and would have time to press last number redial, which was all he had to do to register a call to Angela's number.

That had worked too, despite Paul's insistence that they use his

car, and the many problems poor Sandie had had on her way to Penhallin. In some ways, she had told Josh, the beating had helped; she
had simply refused to leave the car, which had given Billy the vital
minutes he needed to get there.

"Sandie waited outside, having a cigarette," said Lloyd. "Paul went
inside, let Billy in, and while Billy was upstairs phoning Little Elmley,
Paul was downstairs finding the fax, which told him exactly what to
do. He'd be in too much of a panic to notice where the fax had come
from. And he'd always done what you'd told him; you'd always covered for him, got him out of trouble before. What he didn't know
was that you very often created the trouble in the first place, just like
this time. You sent him off to the boat, and Sandie went in and killed
Billy."

Billy's body had come as a real shock to Josh; he had realized for
the first time what he had asked Sandie to do for him, the trust that
she had placed in him when she had agreed to do it. Up until then he
had just been deeply grateful that he could trust her; he hadn't realized that trust had to operate both ways.

Paul having given Sandie that beating had made things difficult,
of course, and his suspicion that he was somehow being manipulated
by Josh had even furnished him with a reason for taking Sandie with
him despite his belief that he was not being followed; Lloyd had suggested that reason himself, accepted the whole thing, instead of
querying it, as they had wanted him to.

Lloyd carried on. "Then Sandie went back to Little Elmley with
Paul, being dropped at the point where she could scramble down to
the edge of the reservoir and run to the club to join the night dive,
leaving the gun at the landing stage on her way. She had been beaten
up—you must have found it hard, Mr. Esterbrook, to let her dive in
that condition, but you had to, didn't you?"

Yes, that had hurt.

"Not because Paul would give her another beating if she didn't—
you would never have allowed that to happen—but because it was
during that dive that you were going to murder your stepmother."

Oh, very good. He'd worked that out too. Josh didn't know what had finally done for their plan, but something had, because Lloyd wasn't groping in the dark. He knew what they had done.

"You took Sandie to the submerged houses, and you left her there. These houses are very close to the Esterbrook house—you swam underwater to the landing stage, got out, took off your scuba gear, and picked up the gun, complete with silencer. You walked up to the house, and you stood at the open door of the kitchen and shot your stepmother dead."

Lloyd suggested that the extra shots had been intended to mutilate her, but they hadn't; he just wanted to be certain she was dead. He wasn't a natural with a gun, not like Sandie. Lloyd had even checked with Howard how much air had been in his aqualung when he had surfaced from the dive, but Josh didn't overlook details like that. He'd only had the cylinder half full when he went in, because he would only be in the water for a few minutes, and at nothing like Sandie's depth.

"Then you walked along the terrace, and went into Mrs. Esterbrook's study. You left the Copes' report in the bureau, and you removed the tape from the answering machine and replaced it with the one containing Paul's message, the one with Elizabeth Esterbrook's fingerprints on it. I imagine the one you removed is at the bottom of the reservoir, because then you went back to the landing stage, left the gun where you had found it, put your diving gear back on, rejoined Sandie, and surfaced."

That tape had very nearly stopped the whole thing in its tracks. The police had heard it at the house, somehow, and Paul's mention of his inheritance had meant that they had to take him away for questioning. Josh had wanted to dispose of Paul before he spoke to the police.

"And your brother's car was still at Little Elmley," said Lloyd. "All you had to do was go and get the gun once everyone had gone, and wait. Wait for him to return to his car to pick it up. And when he did, you shot him dead too."

Yes. And Josh had taken some pleasure in nearly blowing his head off. Paul had said, once he knew he was going to die, that he wouldn't get away with it, and he had been right, for once in his life. Josh wasn't sure how they had been found out, but they had. He hadn't known whether or not Elizabeth really did have someone following Paul; they had done everything on the assumption that she had. But no one had bargained for Paul having done a deal with the guy; that apparently arranged alibi had almost scuppered the whole thing, and made the police go with the obvious solution before the investigation had got to the stage where they *could* prompt them. Later on, that would have been easy enough, had it been necessary. Josh would have mentioned the bigamy, and the angry letter he had found from Angela to Paul . . .

But they had got on to that themselves, and had duly started suspecting him. The problem was that they hadn't quite got round to accusing him of being Billy's boyfriend, because the scenario he and Sandie had intended presenting hadn't materialized, thanks to Paul's boorish behaviour, and they believed Sandie's story about being a decoy. It had looked then as though it wasn't going to go beyond suspicion into actual accusation; looked as though their plot had failed, and all the backup plots in the world weren't going to save it. Paul was going to be held responsible for all the murders.

Then they had their stroke of luck. Elizabeth's detective had a video of Paul and Sandie at the cottage, and they were back on course; the police at last believed that it was Josh, and not Paul, who had been in the hotel room with Billy, and finally got round to arresting them. Then he and Sandie had just had to wait until they worked out that he could not have switched the tapes after Paul had left his incriminating message.

Because only Elizabeth could have done that. Only Elizabeth's prints were on the tape. Only Elizabeth could have sent that fax. Only Elizabeth had no real alibi. Only Elizabeth had a real, solid motive. He and Sandie had timed this whole thing round two trips to London; Angela's, at the Bank Holiday, and Elizabeth's, last Saturday. Nothing over which they had any control had been left to chance, and it had worked. They had been released. So why were they back here?

"And you're wondering how come you're not on the brink of inheriting everything in your brother's will," said Lloyd. "Well, I did tell you, Mr. Esterbrook, that Kathy Cope's gentleman friend was still alive and kicking. And this," he said, producing a video in a plastic bag, "is the video, which is, I assure you, far from poor quality, and proof that it was Paul Esterbrook who was with Billy Rampton in the hotel room, not you."

Finch cleared his throat. "Chief Inspector Lloyd is showing the suspect exhibit JH1, a video recovered from . . ."

Josh had never claimed that he had been in the hotel room with Billy. Indeed, he had denied it every time they had asked him about it. Told them that he was at Little Elmley. It wasn't his fault that they hadn't believed him.

"I believe you murdered your stepmother and your half brother, Mr. Esterbrook," Lloyd went on when Finch had finished. "You murdered them in order to inherit the Esterbrook Family Trust in its entirety. But I can assure you, whatever the outcome of our investigation, you will inherit nothing."

Josh didn't much mind, as long as Paul and Angela hadn't got it. That was what he couldn't have borne. Now that suspicion had been lifted from Paul, Elizabeth would get the lot, but that was all right. He had no animosity towards Elizabeth; he didn't mind if she did well out of it.

But if they couldn't prove that he and Sandie had murdered all these people, and he doubted very much that they could, then he would be free. Even if he went to prison over having an illegal gun, he would still be free, freer than he had been for the last three years. And when he'd done his time, he would come out to *Lazy Sunday* and the cottage in Penhallin and Sandie. He would be very happy indeed with just that. Little Elmley wasn't all that important to him, and he couldn't care less about the money. It was the principle of the thing. So Josh said just two words, when he and Sandie were charged with the murders of Billy Rampton, and Paul and Angela Esterbrook.

"Prove it."

SCENE X—BARTONSHIRE
Friday, October 3rd, 5:00 P.M.
Elizabeth's house

Sergeant Finch had been to see Elizabeth again; he had told her that they were charging Josh and Sandie with the murders of that boy and Angela and Paul. But, Sergeant Finch had said, he had to warn her that the case was largely circumstantial, and of such complexity that there was a real possibility that the CPS would feel unable to proceed with the prosecution on the grounds that there was insufficient evidence.

Elizabeth would infinitely prefer that the strange and murderous unit that Josh and Sandie had become was taken out of circulation, but she doubted that they would murder again. They had had an objective, and it had failed; she imagined that would be that. At least there was now no question mark hovering over Paul, and the Esterbrooks would at last repay their debt to her.

And in truth, it was Josh and Sandie that she had to thank for that.

SCENE XI—BARTONSHIRE
Friday, October 3rd, 5:50 P.M.
Lloyd's office, Stansfield police station

Judy could see Lloyd through the glass panel in his door, still working. She knocked and went in. "It's going home time," she said.

"*Folie à deux*, they call it," said Lloyd. "Two people who together commit a crime that neither would have committed singly. They think one's madness rubs off on the other."

"Do you think Josh *is* mad? Like his mother?"

"Not by the legal definition," he said. "He knows right from wrong." He put down his pen. "When the wind is southerly, he knows a hawk from a handsaw," he said, and smiled. "There was, you might say, method in his madness."

Judy nodded. "They're from *Hamlet*, right?"

"Right. But Josh Esterbrook's Ophelia joined forces with him when she went mad too—and had the foresight to use an aqualung, rather than drown. So he got the job done without all the shilly-shallying. But we can't prove it." He ran a tired hand over the wisps of hair that still persisted in growing on his scalp. "I don't think we have any tangible evidence at all, Judy. And I don't think we're going to get any."

"We've got the lies they told!"

"What lies?" He looked up at her. "Listen to the tapes. Find one provable lie she told you under caution."

Judy thought about it. Sandie had admitted to lying when she had said she was just a decoy, but that hadn't been said under caution, and was hardly proof that she had murdered anyone. It had been prompted, according to what *was* said under caution, by a desire not to admit to having had sexual relations with Paul Esterbrook, in view of her recent marriage. Judy had told her to save it for the jury, and the jury would believe it, especially when they heard it from Sandie Esterbrook. They had no proof that Josh knew what was going on between Sandie and Paul—the jury would accept that she had had to lie about that. And Judy wasn't sure that Josh Esterbrook had told any lies at all.

For the most part, they had been playing the role of people who had been set up themselves; they had told the truth. They had told them how Paul's prints had got on the gun, that he really *had* made that call a month previously—even told them that Paul Esterbrook *had* been with Billy in the hotel room. As Judy went through her notes, she couldn't find a single one to indicate that either of them had ever said anything different, and that was the point on which the whole case, such as it was, rested.

"I'm just drafting the statement on the Copes' deaths," Lloyd said. " 'No one else is being sought in connection with the incident' isn't too difficult a sentence, but my hand won't write it. It keeps drawing top hats instead."

Judy sat down. "I somehow don't think you're going to get a confession," she said.

"No." He sighed. "It's just so galling to think that a camera in Kathy's kitchen clock watched Josh Esterbrook come in, a gun in one hand and a cylinder of carbon monoxide supplied by his wife in the other, watched him put Kathy's tins of beans in the wrong place, pull on her rubber gloves, take out her Hoover, cut off its hose." He shook his head. "It was all there."

The light was fading; autumn had truly arrived. Lloyd reached out and switched on his desk lamp, but nothing happened. "Someone forgot to put a shilling in the meter," he said. "Remind me to put in an application in triplicate for a new bulb, will you? I always forget until it gets dark—" He stared at her.

Judy frowned. "What's the matter?" she said. "Have I come out in spots or something?"

"No," he said, smiling triumphantly, tearing up his top hats, picking up the phone, dialling Case's extension. "Sir?" he said. "I think we get an extra half hour's play since there is reasonable expectation of a result this evening." He grinned. "I'm drafting a new statement on the Copes' death, or I will be, as soon as I've been back to the Copes' house. 'A man and woman have been arrested in connection with the incident and will appear before Stansfield magistrates tomorrow'—how does that sound?"

Judy was looking through her notes, trying in vain to find whatever it was that she must have missed.

"Oh, yes, sir, I'm sure. I'll be back with the evidence before stumps are drawn, you have my word."

Judy closed her notebook as he hung up, beaming at her.

"You won't find it in there," he said.

"What won't I find in here?"

"Their electricity was cut off, Judy." He was as excited about that as she had ever seen him. "The Copes' electricity was cut off at ten o'clock last Saturday morning—the tape *hasn't* run itself back. It's *all still there!*"

There was a moment when they just looked at one another, and then Lloyd thumped the desk. "We've got them!" he shouted. "We've *got* them!"

The tape was retrieved, and proved to have almost exactly what Lloyd had described on it, including a quite beautiful shot of the cylinder of carbon monoxide, complete with the IMG logo. The Esterbrooks were charged with the murder of Katherine and Andrew Cope, and it was the end of the week, at last.

Judy and Lloyd walked out to the car park; she reached her car first, thinking about the counsel's opinion she had been given free of charge. Hotshot was right; she should marry Lloyd. And if that seemed like a commitment too far, she should at least meet him halfway. She opened the door, then turned to Lloyd as he made to go towards his own car. "Assuming you don't find another murder tomorrow morning," she said, "I think we should go house hunting. Don't you?"

He nodded, and walked off. She was a little puzzled, a little disappointed, by his lack of enthusiasm, but put it down to weariness. Then she saw his fist punch the air, heard a triumphant, whispered "Yes!" and knew that she had been taken in by his acting skills.

Again.

About the Author

A native of Argyll, Scotland, JILL MCGOWN has lived in Corby, England, since she was ten. She wrote her first novel, A *Perfect Match*, in 1983. Among those that have followed are *Gone to Her Death*, *Murder at the Old Vicarage, Murder . . . Now and Then, The Murders of Mrs. Austin and Mrs. Beale, The Other Woman, A Shred of Evidence, Verdict Unsafe,* and *Picture of Innocence. Plots and Errors* is her tenth Lloyd and Hill mystery.